A Sense of ENTITLEMENT

Scott Crowley

iUniverse, Inc.
New York Bloomington

A Sense of Entitlement

Copyright © 2010 by Scott Crowley

All rights reserved. No part of this book may be used or reproduced by any means, graphic, electronic, or mechanical, including photocopying, recording, taping or by any information storage retrieval system without the written permission of the publisher except in the case of brief quotations embodied in critical articles and reviews.

This is a work of fiction. All of the characters, names, incidents, organizations, and dialogue in this novel are either the products of the author's imagination or are used fictitiously.

iUniverse books may be ordered through booksellers or by contacting:

iUniverse
1663 Liberty Drive
Bloomington, IN 47403
www.iuniverse.com
1-800-Authors (1-800-288-4677)

Because of the dynamic nature of the Internet, any Web addresses or links contained in this book may have changed since publication and may no longer be valid. The views expressed in this work are solely those of the author and do not necessarily reflect the views of the publisher, and the publisher hereby disclaims any responsibility for them.

ISBN: 978-1-4502-4608-8 (sc)
ISBN: 978-1-4502-4610-1 (dj)
ISBN: 978-1-4502-4609-5 (ebook)

Printed in the United States of America

iUniverse rev. date: 09/27/2010

Dedication

I dedicate this sometimes-dark novel to the ultimate light in my life, my daughters, Sydney and Morgan and my son, Colin. You humble me when I am arrogant and inspire me when I am insecure. I adore your innocence and hope you will always remember the simple, cherished love of a proud father.

Acknowledgements

To my infinitely patient wife, Sharon Crowley and friend, Kathie Leech, thank you for the invaluable editorial help. A special thanks to Debbie Catalano, who read through countless revisions without complaint and never stopped encouraging me. To my parents, I am forever grateful to you for exposing me to the wonders of the written word.

Chapter 1

Logan International Airport

THE UNPLEASANT ODOR OF wet carpet and saturated plaster escaped under the polished wood door of the First Class Lounge at Logan International Airport in Boston. A well-dressed older gentleman in a tailored sport coat ignored the stacks of cleaning products partially blocking the door and tried to push it open. He was politely, but firmly stopped by a smiling airline employee.

"Sir, I'm sorry but the First Class Lounge is closed. A water pipe burst last night and the room was flooded. I'm sorry for the inconvenience. Do you have enough time to visit the First Class Lounge in the next terminal?"

"I don't have enough time and I don't feel like walking that far." His response was terse, but not overly disagreeable. He was annoyed and needed a drink to calm his nerves. He hated flying under normal conditions; the journey he was about to embark on could not be categorized as typical.

"Is there anything else I can…"

"How about the Business Class Lounge?"

"Again, I'm sorry but the Business Class lounge shares a wall with the First Class Lounge and it was also damaged. They both need to be completely renovated."

"Wonderful. And please, stop the apologies. I get it."

"I am sor…" He stopped himself from further humiliation; he was accustomed to dealing with condescending passengers who thought he was their personal servant.

"So what do I do now?" The old man asked, his blank gaze confusing the airline employee. It seemed obvious he should take a seat with the coach passengers nearby.

"The general waiting area is directly in front of you. It's a bit crowded today. The thunderstorms have caused delays all day. Many of these folks are waiting to fly to Orlando, in fact they have been waiting for hours. That's why you see so many kids around. I don't envy their parents."

"Orlando! I thought this was the goddamn International Terminal."

"It is sir…but the airport allows discount carriers to operate a few small gates, and many of their flights are domestic to popular locations, like Disney."

"Its proper name is Walt Disney World. Not Disney." He sighed and pulled his carryon bag to the nearest seat. He didn't say thank you or goodbye, he was gone in a blur of anger and superiority. The thought of mingling with tourists waiting for a discount flight to the land of Mickey Mouse sickened him.

The unimaginative décor of the common waiting area mirrored his dark mood. It was sterile and cramped, with a dullness reminiscent of Cold War chic, utilitarian without imagination. After searching for the best hiding place, he sat with a painful groan, trying to remain anonymous by keeping his head down and attitude disagreeable. He was noticed immediately by a smart couple whose bored gaze quickly turned to stunned recognition. They alerted their neighbors with comical discretion, subtle they were not.

After the initial uproar subsided, an uncomfortable silence descended upon the large room, only punctuated by the high-pitched shouts of the raucous children, who in their beautiful ignorance were unimpressed by the old man who looked like their Grandfather.

He scowled and kept to himself, feeling little compassion for the stressful situation thrust upon his fellow travelers. It fit comfortably with their tedious lives of consumption and distraction.

As the day grew long and the fierce thunder clouds roared in final desperation, sapped of their exhaustible energy, an equally dynamic and oppressive force of excited human expectation emerged in its unsettled wake. It pushed many closer to the old man, drawn to his electric orbit like a planet to its sun. His obvious contempt and sour expression never changed until a young girl engaged him in conversation.

"Are you going to Disney, too?" The unperturbed girl wearing a faded Orlando shirt and a bright smile asked innocently. Her mother gently grabbed her arm and tried to pull her away from the intimidating man.

"What did you say?" His distracted manner was gruff, but not rude. He hadn't even noticed her only a few inches from his neatly pressed pants.

"Are you going to Disney? Like me."

"Honey, why don't you sit down next to me?" Her concerned mother tried to intervene.

"No…I'm going to Europe."

"Oh…is that near Disney?"

"No…it's far away." The corners of the old man's mouth gave a hint of looseness, perhaps a small grin. The tension in his boney shoulders slackened.

"Oh. This is my third trip to Disney," she stated proudly.

"Already! How old are you?" He feigned surprise.

"She's five," her perspiring father blurted from across the row. He looked like he was about to faint. He wiped the pooling sweat from his balding hairline with the palm of his hand.

"Yup, I'm five. You look like Walt Disney. I saw a picture of him in my book."

The cantankerous man burst out laughing, startling those around him with his humanness.

"You know, I met Walt Disney…a few times actually. Sadly, it was many, many years before you were born."

The listeners gasped in astonishment at the thought.

"I had a nice dinner with him in 1964. He would have loved to see your smiling face. He lived for children and their families enjoying his creations." He was moved by her dimples and quirky smile. It reminded him of his favorite granddaughter when she was that age.

"What part of Europe are you going?" The mother of the young girl asked bravely.

"Portugal." He bristled; the suddenness of the personal question annoyed him.

"Oh…how exotic. I've never been."

"Yes. I suppose so," he remarked with little enthusiasm.

"Have you been to Portugal before?" She felt like she needed to keep the strained conversation going, hoping to end their moment together on a pleasurable note.

"Many times."

"Did you really meet Walt Disney?" Her daughter asked as she played with a group of Disney figures.

"Yes…we got along very well." He smiled through the lie, the pain of the truth simmered below the surface. It was well known in their circle of friends that Walt Disney thought he was a pretentious snob. It was then, and remained a sharp personal blow to his large ego that a man of unquestioned genius could see through him with such clarity.

"I hope I can meet him. I think he still lives at the Magic Kingdom. In

Cinderella's Castle I think." There was an awkward pause as her parents thought about telling her the truth, but in the end silence was the best solution.

The old man looked around at the eager faces vying for his attention and felt more appreciative, his jaundiced lens modified by the child's sincerity and naïveté. He smiled and nodded at those closest to him, generally feeling better about the unexpected circumstance that brought them together. He felt a surge of goodwill. He was their benevolent king, and they, his worthy subjects. He noticed how the room tilted towards him, their reverence was intoxicating.

"These people are my friends," he tried to rationale the dramatic change of perception. "I don't have to worry about their loyalty, they might not even hear about my deed. They understand intimately the hard road from ordinary to extraordinary, the desperate struggle to have your voice heard among the white noise of a cluttered world. They are and humble and good! Nothing will change their minds about me or my legacy."

"Flight 225 to Orlando will now be boarding at Gate 24…"

The crackling speaker sent the crowd into a frenzy of nervous activity. Children were corralled with rough precision by the adults who moved quickly to secure all of their scattered belongings. Excited voices filled the air, the wait was over and soon they would be off on their magical vacation. In a millisecond he was just another old man, sitting alone and already in their past. They politely nodded goodbye and moved towards the gathering crowd at the desk, fearing they might be left off the overbooked flight.

Twenty minutes later the waiting area was empty and silent, debris of all sorts littered the imitation leather chairs. Only the church remained after the worshippers vanished in a burst of exuberant pleasure-seeking.

The pitiful icon got a troubling glimpse of the near future, crystallized in such a brutal way he felt tears stream down the crags of his weathered face. The tears followed the crooked valleys of his aged face, a sad reminder of all those hot summers days he spent strutting across his private beach, sucking on imported cigarettes and baking under the blazing sun. The excess had left his body worn and diseased, he wore the death mask of the elite.

He wiped his cheek and felt tired, mentally drained by the shallowness of the bourgeois who abandoned him in his hour of crisis. He grabbed his stylish writing bag and extracted a single sheet of paper with ten typed names numbered and evenly spaced. He caressed the edges of the paper, he marveled at the crispness and quality; so many times in his life a sheet of paper was his only true companion. His long, yellowed nails perused the short list of names, stopping and starting with careful consideration at each candidate, many had handwritten notes to help him remember the particulars of the ten finalists. He tapped one name with rhythmic contemplation before tilting his head back and staring at the grotesque fluorescent light above his head. The whiteness blinded him into a coma like trance.

He felt a perverse sense of absolute power picking number seven on the list, it was a deliberate move to shock and anger the other finalists. It would cause quite a stir with the well-connected families that a relative unknown, who did not attend an Ivy League school, would steal such a coveted internship. He knew number seven was all wrong for the summer position, but that wasn't really what he needed him for.

In one graceful motion he unscrewed the top from his thousand dollar fountain pen and placed the gold tip next to number seven.

"Lucky number seven," he mumbled and laughed in a high-pitched tone that can only be described as unattractive and shrill.

His spotted hands shook as he etched a perfect check mark next to the young man's name. The blue mark shimmered and then dried with unconcerned permanence, unaware of its staggering importance. He slammed his bag shut in a show of personal resolve and finality.

"He will never get the chance to thank me for the life I have given him. I will become his disgraced creator to be scorned in public and venerated in private, unable to receive my proper tribute for the unquantifiable gift of relevance."

He crossed his arms and took a deep breath before making one final request to a God he did not believe in. "Please Lord spare my family and let this plane crash."

Chapter 2

One Year Later

— *Martha's Vineyard, Cape Cod, Massachusetts*

Among the many celebrity homes on the small island off the Massachusetts coast, one stood alone. A colossal English Tudor dominates the relatively more modest summer dwellings of its neighbors. The home is part of a large compound that included a private beach with an exquisite view of the open ocean. It is both an architectural jewel and aesthetic eyesore. It lacks the simple elegance of the other million dollar homes that dots the exclusive beach. The home is a better fit for a mainland community like Brookline or Newton; on the tiny island, it is an arrogant statement of wealth and stature.

The arching driveway of the English Tudor is especially busy this humid Monday morning. Late model BMW's, gleaming Mercedes and an army of beastly SUV's speed in and out the circuitous driveway. The hurried occupants of these symbols of wealth all wear the same dour, reflective expressions of grief.

Inside the imposing mansion visitors speak in hushed tones and shuffle aimlessly from room to room. Some are casually dressed in golf shirts and khakis; others look like they just stepped out of their office in Boston.

Upstairs in the most lavish of all the bedrooms, the seventy-eight-year old owner of the house fights for his life. He is dutifully surrounded by family, their tear streaked faces flinching with every auditory convulsions of pain from the distressed patient. His short and painful bout with lung cancer was nearing its final stage. Three years before, he weighed a robust 200 pounds, today he is barely half that. One dose of chemotherapy had cost him his stylish gray hair. He twists in the bed but stops himself from pushing the plunger on his morphine drip. He wants to be somewhat lucid during his last moments. His chest heaves and he tries desperately to catch his breath. His right lung partially collapsed during the night. He wears an oxygen mask all the time these days. His labored breathing and coughing sends most fleeing from the room after only a few minutes. It is more than they can handle.

It is difficult to describe the last hours of a person's life, especially if he is afflicted with the most dehumanizing and painful disease of them all. Witnesses to the last stage of the disease may find it hard to explain, but impossible to forget. The hollow gaze of the afflicted, the skeletal remains of a once healthy body, the excruciating streaks of endless pain challenges even the most faithful. No drug can totally relieve the suffering; it drives many to insanity before it ruthlessly tears life away. Death is a welcome end.

The expansive hallway outside the master suite is filled with transient visitors. Most who came out could not talk for a long time.

"Can you believe this Bob?" One shaken visitor asks his companion.

"Yes… I can, he smoked like a fucking fiend. What did you expect?" He said this last remark with clear bitterness. He tossed his own pack of cigarettes into the trash.

"How long do you think?"

"Who the hell knows, Mark? Does it matter? He's already dead anyway. That is not a living human in that room."

"I know," Mark answered. The pair drifted off, shaking their heads and glumly nodding to other mourners.

The hallways and the descending floors are filled with dignitaries and celebrities of every sort and stature. A slew of well-known writers, a Nobel Prize winner, two Pulitzer Prize winners and two Academy Award winners, the list went on and on…

Who is this man? What kind of man would garner so much attention and adulation? Why is the press camped out on the exquisitely groomed lawn? Why do helicopters circle incessantly? Why does everybody look so sad? The gloom seemed to penetrate the very heart of the estate. Even the dogs are quiet; they seem to understand what is happening to the American Tolstoy.

Among the throngs of the powerful, there is a young man who seemed out of place and lost. He stands alone, avoiding eye contact with all who tried to converse. A few mourners notice his discomfort and offer consolation. He just nods and keeps his eyes glued to the floor. He clenches his fists and chastises himself for acting like a teenager at his first funeral. He isn't a child; he is a twenty-year-old Boston University student.

"Hello. Terrible isn't it?" An amiable looking middle-aged man approaches the young man.

"Yes, sir, it is," he mumbles, immediately recognizing the speaker as Carlton Smithfield. Smithfield is a well-respected novelist who flourished under the tutelage of the dying man.

"My name is Carlton---"

"Yes sir. I know who you are." Drew tries to smile, but it is awkward and nervous so he stops.

"What is your name?" Carlton asks with a calming smile. He had noticed him standing alone and felt bad.

"My name is Drew Engle, sir."

"Stop calling me sir, you're making me feel old. Drew… hmmm that's a nice name. So many silly names these days it's refreshing to hear a nice one."

"I like it, sir… I mean Mr. Smithfield."

"Call me Carlton, please."

"Okay, Carlton."

"So how do you know him?" Smithfield asks with a pained expression, he is clearly struggling with the impending death of his mentor.

"I really don't know him all that well…Carlton. I'm a summer intern. I've been here for two months. I'm supposed to leave in a couple of weeks. I'm an English major at Boston University."

"I bet this is not the summer you expected," Carlton Smithfield sighs.

"No, it's been very tough. He was okay at the beginning of the summer. He wasn't really okay, but he was functional at least."

"I guess you'll have something to tell your kids though. This is turning into quite a spectacle," Smithfield glances around the room scornfully.

"He's well liked I guess." Drew observes innocently.

"Respected, yes, impossible not to, but liked, I don't know if all of these people have genuine fondness for the old bird. He can be a bit cantankerous and impatient." Smithfield rubs his face.

"I understand he's not the easiest to get along with, but his accomplishments, his talent sets him apart…"

"That's why I said respected. He's the greatest I've ever known; he is the inspiration for everything I've accomplished in my comparatively modest career. He's the man; he is very important to American Literature. Forget Hemingway, forget them all. He is THE writer of this century. Don't let some dopey professor in your Lit class tell you differently."

"They don't, usually they echo your sentiments."

"Good I'm glad to hear it."

"Sir…Carlton, were you very close?"

"Yes. I've known him for thirty years. He helped me early on; he took me under his wing so to speak. I wrote *Dragon Queen* under this roof. I had a small bedroom down in the basement with a few other budding authors. He liked *Dragon Queen* and went to bat for me with his publisher. Of course they couldn't say no to him. So here we are decades later and nothing has really changed." Smithfield sighs and looks away. He was thinking about those long days in the bowels of the intimidating home.

The old man was very hard on young writers, especially the ones he believed possessed the raw qualities needed to survive the vicious world of American popular fiction. His paternal care was a blend of charity, self-gratification and a healthy dose of envy. The professional jealously was something Carlton found unfathomable. It gnawed at him for years. Why would one of the most accomplished, critically acclaimed writers of his era worry about the work of mere mortals? His young protégés worshipped him, his critical views and constructive criticism were considered gospel. He was an insatiable, devouring shark swimming with privileged minnows; seldom challenged or questioned.

Carlton was among his most devoted followers; he refrained from questioning his master regardless of the absurdity of the advice. As Smithfield thought about his own experiences he wondered if the young man he was talking to was one of the master's new protégés. He didn't think so though; he had stopped personally working with interns a few years before.

"How did he look today?" Drew Engle asked with more confidence. He felt at ease with Smithfield. He felt Carlton was genuinely interested in him.

"What Drew?" Smithfield snapped out of his dream.

"How did he look today?"

"He looked horrible, the worst condition I've ever seen anybody. He's not alive, Drew, that's not living." He gulped the last of his drink and asked Drew when he saw him last.

"A week ago. I've been in limbo. I'm not sure if I should stay or leave. My internship does not end for a few weeks and I can still help out."

Smithfield smiled. "Answering his business line and taking messages, right?"

"Yes, that's about it. I sometimes open his mail and put it in order for him to read."

"Some introduction to the literary world." He laughed and tried to remember what it was like to be twenty years old.

"Well it helps just to be around…"

"Come on kid, you don't have to polish it up for me. I know it sucks;

you thought you were going to get to pick the brain of a master. Instead you opened his junk mail and watched him die."

"It's a little disappointing." Drew confessed.

"You think! I'm going up to see him…do you want to come?"

"I don't think they'll let me up."

"Sure they will. You're with me," Smithfield said.

"Okay." Drew felt his hands start to tremble as he thought about seeing the legend in such a gruesome state. He followed Carlton Smithfield up the long and intimidating staircase. The curious gaze of other famous artists was on him. Politicians with power he could not imagine glanced at him condescendingly before noticing his companion.

"Carlton, how are you?"

"Fine, Mike, how is he?" Carlton asked his friend who was watching the door.

"Worse than yesterday. He can hardly breathe. Although they gave him some other kind of medication a few hours ago and he seems to be doing a little better. At least he can smile without spitting up blood," Mike exclaimed bitterly. He was also a former intern who shared a room with Carlton.

"How long?"

"Hard to tell, Carlton, he could last another week."

"God I hope not," Carlton said under his breath so only Mike could hear it. He nodded in the affirmative and opened the door.

Carlton moved into the room like he had been there many times before. Drew slid into the room, hugging the wall and not moving. Drew couldn't really see the patient's face. He was sinking low, numerous tubes and wires led from the lump in the large bed. The soft sounds of unsympathetic machines could be heard in the silent room. Machines designed to keep you alive, but not to sustain the dead. A nurse made notations in her notebook. She glanced nervously at the constant flow of important visitors. She was intimidated by the enormity of the situation.

Carlton maneuvered past a cart of medical supplies and stood by the bed. His eyes glistened at the sight.

"Sheldon," Carlton bent over and whispered.

In a raspy, barely audible voice Sheldon asked him how his breakfast was.

"It was okay. I don't really have much of an appetite. How are you feeling? You were asleep when I came in earlier."

"I'm dying, Carlton. How do you think?…" A hacking cough interrupted him. When it subsided, he continued. "How do you think I feel?" He still had some fire left in him. Carlton smiled and grabbed his bony hand for comfort. He angrily glanced at the tubes and machines that kept his friend in this state of inhuman suffering. They should stop feeding him, he thought, what was the use of nourishment when such a fiendish disease prepared for its final charge. Cancer kicks your ass until the end; it never gives you a moment's respite, mocking the very human hope for a dignified exit.

Drew strained to hear the rest of the brief conversation. On his right side Janet Rossi dabbed her eyes and pretended to be miserable. She was the hot actress of moment, recently thrust into the limelight after a starring role in a mindless summer blockbuster. She followed her decent performance with a critically acclaimed independent film and her fifteen minutes of fame began.

Drew thought it was strange she was there, she couldn't have known Sheldon Harrison for long; she was a struggling actress only 12 months earlier. Sheldon liked to surround himself with the hottest pop celebrity of the moment. It was the superficial side of Harrison, the side that always bothered Carlton.

"Drew, boy, come over here." Smithfield got Drew's attention and waved him over. He froze; his feet would not move. His throat was dry, everybody in the room was staring at him curiously. A few whispered, one or two shrugged as if to say, "I don't know who he is."

"Drew…come over here," Smithfield demanded, smiling all the time. Drew moved swiftly to the side of the bed. He wished he hadn't, he gasped at the condition of Sheldon Harrison.

"Hello, sir," Drew managed to mumble.

"This is Drew Engle. He's a summer intern." Carlton tried to help.

"I know who he is!" Harrison snapped furiously.

"Okay Shelly," Smithfield smiled and stepped back.

"I picked him out you know. He's lucky number seven." The oxygen mask and constant phlegm in his throat made him hard to understand. The pair stepped closer.

"You did sir?" Drew was surprised. He didn't think such an important man would worry about such a mundane task as choosing a lowly intern. Drew was ignorant of the fall-out surrounding his appointment or exclusivity of the lengthy selection process.

"I always… {cough}…I always do. You wrote… {cough}…a nice essay on Korolev." He clutched the blanket as a wave of pain swept through his body. He held his breath until it passed. His face was instantly bathed in perspiration. The nurse rushed over and wiped the sweat away. He pressed her hand thankfully.

"Carlton… {cough}…do you know who Korolev was?"

Smithfield thought for a moment and then shrugged unknowingly.

"Do you remember Werner Von Braun?"

"Of course, the German rocket scientist who designed the moon rockets."

"Korolev was his Russian counterpart. Young Mr. Engle wrote a nice essay on the Russian rocket man."

"I would like to read it," Smithfield said with genuine interest.

"Why did you pick such an odd topic for your essay? Most of your peers don't even know we went to the moon," Harrison laughed and then went into a coughing fit.

"Sir I've always been interested in the space race. It was just a natural topic to write about."

"That's nice to hear." Harrison turned his head and dozed off for a few seconds before waking with a start.

"Shelly, we'll leave you alone for a little while."

"No...not yet," he whispered.

"Okay."

"You know, if I could do it all over again, I would do it like JD did. Hide and not give a shit. Or like that kid who wrote *Ian Baxter*, one novel and then disappear. A moment of brilliance then nothing! What a way to do it."

"Shelly, you're getting worked up."

"So what, is it going to kill me? I am already dead. You know it, I can see it in your eyes. I wish I could get out of this room one more time. Trapped like a Goddamn condemned man. I just don't know what time the gallows will swing."

"Don't talk like that," Smithfield responded softly.

"I am trapped, Drew. I hope you never have this done to you."

"I'm sorry, Mr. Harrison."

"Thanks Drew, I know you are. You have honest eyes. You're uncorrupted by money and power. Half of these folks hanging around here don't really care if I live or die."

"Come on, Shelly. That's not true." Harrison softly chastised him.

"It's true and you, above all, know it! As long as they can say they were here at the end, that's all that really matters. That's the hard part about all this, Drew; they will all go on with their lives in a few days. How many do you think will cancel their vacations next month? None! It's just strange to think about how many of them have made plans that don't include me, including my own family. I can't even think beyond tonight. Carlton, I expect you to throw yourself off the rocks into the ocean when I die," Harrison said with a painful laugh, managing a crooked smile.

"Sure, I'll take one for you old friend."

"You are loyal and talented. I don't deserve your friendship."

"Please…"

"I don't! Drew, I want you to come back tomorrow afternoon. I want to talk to you. I too tired today. I'm so damn tired. Carlton, bring him back tomorrow, please don't forget. I need to see him again. I need to see him again, do you understand? Please bring him back." Harrison was nearly sobbing with grief as turned away them.

"Okay, Shelly. I'll bring him." Smithfield escorted Drew from the room.

Chapter 3
Charlotte Emerson

THE GRANDDAUGHTER OF THE dying literary icon lived in a million dollar, three-bedroom townhouse on Boston's exclusive Beacon Street. The twenty-four year old expected nothing less than the opulent luxury that Sheldon Harrison's wealth permitted. Charlotte Emerson lived comfortably off the spoils of her grandfather's apparent genius.

Tall and slender like a model, yet not attractive in the conventional sense, Charlotte possessed clear blue eyes that dazzled but were devoid of any warmth. Her long, thin nose looked correct for her narrow face, but that was only a recent development. Minor plastic surgery transformed her wide nose to a sensuous point, an ugly duckling into a beautiful swan with a quick slice. She was by all reasonable standards, charming and sexy, but not as naturally pleasing as she desired. After all, the granddaughter of the great Sheldon Harrison should be a ravenous beauty!

Any disappointment she might have felt over her minor shortcomings was overshadowed by her superb education at Brown University and postgraduate work at Yale. She possessed unshakable confidence in her abilities and made sure her associates revered her superiority.

Charlotte sighed and sat on her window seat to watch the action on the street below. Her less affluent neighbors were boorishly fighting over a parking space on the narrow and crowded street. She laughed to herself and thought about her two private spots in a nearby garage and the fact she had only one car. Pity never crossed her mind; it was unnatural for her to think of the inconveniences of others. They were ordinary people whose lives would make little impact on the world they inhabited. Their existence barely made a ripple in her neighborhood. Her neighbors were hardly middle class; they were predominately urban professionals of varied wealth. The confined streets were lined with BMWs, Mercedes, Sport Utility Vehicles, and an occasional Volvo for the few who had children. Seldom did Charlotte see more than one child per family. The forty-year-old first-time mothers who chose their career over children until the very last moment were the norm. Looking like grandparents, they wheeled their toddlers to the oasis of the Public Gardens in their starched white shirts and khaki caps.

Charlotte snickered at their bourgeois lives and dismissed them as upper-class toilers with little appeal. They were all charlatans whose law degrees and German automobiles were only props used to convince themselves they were among the elite. Attorneys with no expertise other than cramming for the Bar exam miraculously considered themselves authorities on art, music, and literature without having done one creative thing in their sorry lives. This amused the young socialite to no end; they were nothing but spruced-up middle class fools who decided they were extraordinary because of their address and income. She really believed, silently amongst mixed company, that the middle class was the scourge of America. A bunch of mindless consumers who pollute and tarnish at every turn, serfs as her grandfather used to call them. She smiled when she thought of this. She felt a wave of guilt and sorrow for the old man she owed so much to, she really did love him in her own way.

The hot sun pierced the large front window and warmed her tanned skin. Her thoughts quickly shifted as she caught a glimpse of herself in a full-length mirror near the window. She never allowed her tan to exceed a slight glow, a healthy hint of exposure. Her long fingers traced the outline of her colorful sundress. She admired her tight curves and squeezed her tight buttocks together to further feed her ego. Her finely toned muscles rippled over her freckled shoulders. Her hair was normally a light brown, but the sun added streaks of blond. Her blue eyes were striking against her toasted skin and bleached hair. Summer was her best season; she knew this and planned extensively to look her best during the brief, but scorching New England summers.

Her focus briefly shifted to her upcoming sojourn to Europe. Her friends from Brown had planned the trip at the last minute and it was unthinkable that they would go without their spiritual leader. The entire group gleefully anticipated the planned debauchery; reviving their carefree coed days when they thought they were the center of the universe, a less complicated time when they actually believed they were the enlightened torchbearers of America's intellectual class. The misguided arrogance soon gave way to a softer form of elitism that allowed them to coexist with real world souls, born of necessity rather than maturation.

With all these superficial thoughts occupying her mind she forgot about her ailing grandfather, he was a distant thorn that sometimes pricked her into sadness. She was annoyed when her recent preparations were interrupted by his deteriorating health. His timing could not have been worse. She looked away from the mirror and back down to the contemptible world below. She tapped on the glass when she recognized the awkward figure of her cousin gazing up at her. Wilton Saunders was the son of Charlotte's aunt, her mother's sister and daughter of Sheldon Harrison.

Charlotte sauntered to the elaborate alarm panel and buzzed him in. She was very close to her cousin. He was the breath of fresh air she sometimes felt lost without, a strange dependency she didn't understand. She loved his chubby face; his mischievous eyes were cunning and sometimes frightening. She liked the fact his father had a strained relationship with Sheldon Harrison. She liked gossip and scandal; confrontation between family members in such an exclusive family was a badge of honor.

Sheldon found Wilton's father dull and unsuitable to marry his daughter, it was a feud that was both endless and overt. He called him fat and stupid, dismissing the poor sap like a witless child. He often called him Bilbo Baggins, the short and portly Hobbit from the JRR. Tolkien's fantasy novels. His embittered daughter never forgave him for the constant badgering and Wilton's relationship with his famous grandfather suffered. Sheldon tried to love his grandson like the others, who were generally spoiled and ungrateful, but he couldn't get past his father. He could not look at the slightly overweight boy and see anything but his slovenly father. Charlotte often brought her younger cousin with her to the family estate; he felt awkward and spent much of the time brooding in a corner, wishing he could be alone with his exciting cousin Charlotte.

Wilton stood five foot seven inches tall and was as ungraceful as his cousin was graceful. He wasn't fat, but his soft, often-blushing cheeks gave him a portly appearance. He lacked the boyish charm that is sometimes associated with a person with similar facial characteristics. He did have the classic blue eyes of his famous grandfather, but not much else. He was a recent sociology graduate from Northeastern University with no real prospects or goals. In many ways he was like Charlotte, unfocused and accustomed to a life free of real world pressure and constraint.

Charlotte hugged her cousin as he entered her home, she loved to watch his cheeks blossom from the contact. He stepped back and shyly examined his cousin in her summer dress; she was the most beautiful woman he had ever had physical contact with.

"My love, what an impromptu visit." She excitedly grabbed his soft hands. Charlotte flopped down on the couch and played with her hair, never taking her eyes off him. Wilton squirmed and felt silly for the discomfort. She always flirted with her cousin, figuring he needed a woman's affection sometimes or he would explode. She knew of his failures with women intimately.

"Are you still going to Europe?" He finally broke free of his trance and tried to compose himself. Her expression changed from a warm and consoling cousin to a cold stranger.

"Of course I'm still going." She coiled in her seat and waited for him to push her.

"I just didn't think you would go with Granddad in such…"

"He'll make it until I get back!" She retorted hotly.

"I saw him yesterday and he didn't look like he'll make it to the end of the week."

"I know…I know he's very sick…but he's been sick for months. He's a fighter, I think he'll make until I come home." Her bitterness slowly gave way to sadness; she knew she shouldn't be going.

"He was much better the last time I saw him. It was hard to see him like that, so helpless and weak. It's like looking at a talking skeleton, it's really frightening." Wilton looked disturbed as he thought about his visit. Sheldon had barely acknowledged him; nothing had changed even at the end of his life.

Charlotte did not respond, she was gazing out the window from her seat on the couch. She was angry with her cousin for bringing her down. She knew in a few moments she would be over it and love him like a teddy bear again.

"He coughed and he couldn't stop, I thought he was going to die."

"Don't say that." Charlotte snapped and wondered why her cousin was trying to ruin her trip. She wondered about his motivation.

"I'm just being realistic. We have to prepare…" He was annoyed by her obvious avoidance of the topic. They owed everything they had to their grandfather.

"Stop talking like a fucking priest. I know what the situation is." Charlotte jumped from the couch and walked in front of him. She watched his eyes follow her ass, she laughed inwardly at how quickly he forgot his stricken grandfather. She really enjoyed teasing him; he was so easy to distract. Charlotte did not let him off the hook this time.

"What are you looking at?" She stood in front of him.

"Nothing." He blushed and kept his head down.

"I think I know."

"Stop changing the subject. I don't think you should leave the country." His retort was forced; he was mortified by her boldness. She really understood his mind and that scared him.

"It's none of your concern, Wilton."

"I just think you're being silly about the whole thing."

"Don't talk to me like that! Who do you think you are?" She fired off a round of expletives as she searched for something in the kitchen.

Wilton stood and felt he should leave. Of course he didn't, something stopped him from the justifiable exit. Charlotte noticed his discomfort and was sickened by his weakness. She could do whatever she wanted with him.

"Please don't be mad, Wilton. Everything will work out. Just don't be so judgmental." With her sweet smile reappearing, she kissed his cheek. His legs felt numb and his temples bulged from the increased blood flow.

"You know you can't stay mad at me." She pecked his other cheek.

"Okay, but make sure I see you before you leave."

"Sure." She knew she would have to call him or he would mope around until she got back.

Chapter 4
The Meeting

Drew Engle spent a sleepless night thinking about his meeting with Sheldon Harrison. He felt the spine-tingling fear of death creep into his consciousness. He tried to stop the morbid thoughts but they kept circulating through his young mind. It is common to feel a sense of weakness and mortality after visiting a terminally ill patient.

Drew wiped the sweat from his brow and sat up. Through inky darkness he could make out the shape of his sleeping roommate. He was also a summer intern, but was nothing like Drew. His affluent family owned a house on the other side of the Vineyard. Drew was astonished by his ability to rest so fitfully with so much activity surrounding the health of Harrison. The only reason they were theoretically interning for Sheldon Harrison was to learn from the master. It didn't seem to bother the curly-haired Harvard student whose family connections would surely make up for the loss. He got what he needed after the first night at Harrison's compound, he could now say he studied under the late Sheldon Harrison. It was all he really wanted anyway, elitist bragging rights.

Disgusted and full of contempt, Drew felt the sudden urge to take a walk. He quickly followed a graveled pathway that led directly to the raging ocean. The sea was rough and the mist thick, Mother Nature seemed to understand the imminent death of Sheldon Harrison, mirroring the ferocity of the disease. He stared out into the forbidding blackness of the ocean, the mist soaking his face and cooling his overheated face. He crouched down and picked up a smooth rock and threw it into the ocean. It skipped briefly before disappearing in the rough waters. It was a sad reminder of the smallness of an individual life. The stone was every person that every lived on earth and the ocean was our solar system.

After a few minutes of dour contemplation Drew's gaze shifted to the main house where he couldn't help but notice the light in Harrison's bedroom still burned brightly. He wouldn't let anyone dim the lights for a moment. It was after two in the morning. He figured the old man was having a rough night and his nurse was attending to his ever-increasing needs. His hunch was correct. Sleep for Harrison was nearly impossible, he could feel death coming and feared closing his eyes, afraid the dark would bring death. His favorite music played continuously; when it stopped he would lash out at the unlucky soul nearest the disc player.

Drew tired of his private vigil and retired to his room. He lay awake and thought about his meeting with Sheldon Harrison scheduled for the next day. What could he want? Why such a strange request? Was he suffering from some form of cancer-induced dementia? He would have to wait, he could wait, but could Harrison? He rolled over and was almost asleep when he heard someone enter the room.

"Drew?" Carlton Smithfield nudged the intern.

"Yeah…" Drew fumbled for the light.

"Forget the light…get dressed and come with me." Smithfield's voice was tense and forced. He left the room and waited impatiently for Drew to dress. The guesthouse assigned to some of the summer interns was a short walk to the main house.

"Come, we have to go see Sheldon. He's not going to make the appointment tomorrow. He wants to see you now." Smithfield felt strange saying this, why was Sheldon so desperate to see this specific intern?

"Jesus…this is unreal," Drew said as he fumbled with his shirt. They hustled in silence up the mist-covered path, the crushed stone echoing under their feet. Both looked up when they could see the shining light of Harrison's window. Engle shook with fear as he prepared himself for what he had believed would be the worst moment of his short life.

"How long does he have?" Engle finally broke the silence as they neared the main entrance.

"He is near the end…a few hours maybe." Smithfield's jaw tightened and he felt sick. His hair was disheveled and his clothes in tatters, he had been all night with his dying mentor.

"Is he awake?" Engle felt silly after the utterance, it was obvious he was awake if he asked for him.

"He's been up all night. He can't really breathe; he's just gasping for air all the time. His oxygen mask helps a little. He's in so much pain, but if he takes any more painkillers he'll slip into a coma. All he does is cry and moan. It's pathetic." Sheldon was angry at the world, furious with the medical community for not finding a cure or even a humane treatment.

Drew felt his legs weaken and he thought about turning back. His shirt was soaked with anxiety; he bumped into Smithfield who was also perspiring and trembling.

"Prepare yourself, Drew, he's worse than yesterday." Smithfield made his final warning before plunging through the darkened entranceway and into the house of horrors. Drew barely noticed the shadowy figures of the other mourners; they were huddled in small groups or sleeping at odd angles on anything that could bear human weight. As they approached the bedroom door, the distress was more tangible. Drew heard soft whispers and felt an occasional, questioning glance in his direction. A few openly gawked at him, wondering why this person they had never seen before was being hurried towards Harrison's door in the middle of the night. Only his escort tempered their look of scorn, Smithfield was held in very high esteem.

The smell of disinfectant was overwhelming; this glamorous home had been turned into a working hospital. Drew also caught a whiff of feces, probably recently removed from Harrison's room. The hastily constructed sitting area outside the room was filled with his close relatives. They smiled sadly when he passed, feeling sorry for the young man summoned by the deranged Harrison.

Drew stopped at the opened door, unable to walk the last two steps into the room. Smithfield held the door impatiently and watched the young man struggle to compose himself. The chamber of death overwhelmed him; it was a feeling he would never experience again. One glance at the twisting figure nearly made Drew run from the house. As sick as he was during his first visit the day before, one could still detect a spark of life. No such spark existed in the sedentary figure, his body so ravaged by rampant disease it was a miracle that he was still able to speak.

"Go ahead, Drew." Smithfield gently pulled him into the room and pushed him towards Harrison's bed.

"Okay." Drew barely responded. He approached the bed and was startled when Harrison turned to look at him. His eyes were bulging with fear; pleading for help he knew would never come. His skeletal face was covered with sweat, beading from every pore of his wax like skin, embalmed before his death. He coughed before he could say a word, throwing up fluid and blood in an alarming stream. Drew jumped and started to back out of the room. Smithfield kept him from leaving by applying slight pressure to his elbow. The night nurse quickly cleaned him, she seemed compassionate and dedicated, but it was obvious the severity of his illness was taking its toll on her. Smithfield leaned over the bed and tried to comfort his longtime friend who was already trying to say something. At the sound of the coughing, Harrison's doctor entered the room and tried to talk to his patient. His concerned gaze was met with a wrathful glare. Harrison gestured angrily for Dr. Abrams to leave. The embarrassed physician was annoyed by the dismissal and stubbornly refused to budge.

"I'm not leaving, Sheldon, I need to check you…" He brushed aside his patient's repeated waving and stepped closer.

"Doctor you're agitating him." Smithfield intervened.

"Excuse me, Carlton, if I'm not mistaken he is in my care not yours!"

"Listen to me…"

"No, he's my patient and I will…"

"Get out!" Carlton slammed his fist on a medical tray.

"What? You can't get involved. I'll call the police!"

"Get out, he's trying to tell you he doesn't need you anymore. He wants you to leave so get the fuck out before I call security and they'll throw you out." Smithfield never liked the pompous physician whose desire to treat the rich and famous usurped all other ambitions.

"Try it and you'll find yourself in court."

"This isn't a hospital and I don't give a shit if you sue me. This is his home and he wants you out. Now, Dr. Abrams, please excuse us." Smithfield took a menacing step forward and the clearly intimidated doctor acquiesced.

"Okay. You can have five minutes." Doctor Abrams stormed out of the room, muttering to himself and feeling emasculated. He pleaded his case to the family, but nobody had the nerve to enter the room and confront Smithfield. They were afraid of his temper and they believed he was probably justified in kicking the unpopular doctor from the room.

After the pouting physician left the room Sheldon searched for Drew. His bloodshot eyes rested upon the overwhelmed young man. He suddenly felt guilty for exposing such an innocent youth to the horrors of his disease. He would have given anything to switch places with him. He wanted to be Drew so bad it ached more than the cancer, if only for a moment. The cancer would not be denied its moment in the sun. Harrison strained and finally whispered something to Smithfield. He then turned to Drew and called for him.

"I don't know…" Drew stammered.

"Come here, please." Smithfield said

Drew slowly moved to the side of the bed and gasped aloud at the heaving skeleton that peered at him. The desperate eyes unnerved him. A strong smell of urine and sweat overwhelmed him. He felt unsteady on his feet; he flushed and felt faint. Smithfield steadied him.

"Drew..." Harrison whispered.

"Yes...Mr. Harrison I'm here."

"I'm not..." He stopped speaking and coughed uncontrollably until his body mercifully vomited the blockage. He begged for someone to kill him. After the nurse cleaned him he again gestured for Drew to come closer.

"Drew, I'm not who you think I am...I'm not who the world thinks I am." He grimaced as another wave of pain stunned his already overloaded system. He clenched his morphine plunger and pumped away, refraining enough to keep him conscious.

"I am not a great man...I am not a great writer..."

"What are you talking about?" Carlton pushed Drew aside.

"NO!" He grabbed for Drew.

"I don't understand, Mr. Harrison." Drew shuffled his feet nervously and tried to shake-off the otherworldly feeling of the moment.

"I am not who you think I am. I'm nothing. Try and find him."

"Sir, I don't understand."

Smithfield touched him on the arm and motioned for him to leave. It was apparent that his mentor's final request was not a lucid one. Harrison noticed the move and struggled to grab the boy. It was a feeble attempt, but Smithfield understood what he wanted.

"Okay...Shelly he's not leaving."

"Drew...get me that box." Harrison said clearly, with renewed energy.

"The briefcase?" Drew pointed to a black briefcase in the corner.

"Yes...get it."

Drew followed the order without delay. He returned to the side of the bed with the combination lock briefcase firmly clasped in his sweaty palms. Smithfield looked on curiously; it was an odd request.

"The combination," he coughed and spit angrily, "...is one, five, and nine."

Drew dutifully snapped the metal knobs until they were all lined up correctly.

"Open it!" Harrison blurted in between renewed coughing fits.

Drew felt the eyes of the dying man upon him; he avoided his gaze and opened the case. The case creaked open and he found a brown envelope tucked neatly inside. There was a sheet of paper near the envelope. He looked up and Harrison nodded for him to open it. Drew unfolded the letter and awkwardly tried to hand it to Harrison who immediately shook his head.

"What is it?" Smithfield stepped closer.

"It's an address for a bank in Portugal."

"What?"

"It just says the name of a bank in Sintra, Portugal."

"Sheldon, can you tell us what this means?" Carlton asked with a quizzical look.

"No…he has to go," Harrison said in the most forceful voice he could manage.

"What's in the small envelope?" Carlton asked.

"A key. A key with a number on it," Drew blurted.

"It's a safety deposit key," Smithfield said with a slightly bemused look. Even with death so near Sheldon Harrison was complex and unpredictable.

"Why?"

"Sheldon, why?" Smithfield tried to clear up the confusion.

"Go to Lisbon!" He growled impatiently.

"Okay Shelly I understand." Smithfield's tone sent the old man into a fury.

"Don't patronize me, Carlton!"

"Sorry…we're just confused."

"I don't want you to go! Him." He pointed emphatically at Drew.

"Just him…we understand."

"Inside…inside."

He motioned for Drew to check inside the envelope again.

"There's some cash in here."

"What do you want him to do with the money?" Smithfield searched for an answer to the perplexing turn of events.

"Lisbon…" He uttered faintly.

"I understand."

"Help me…please help." The literary giant clasped his hands together and begged for someone to stop the inevitable conclusion. He was frightened beyond reason with the thought of dying. His wavering faith and intermittent dabbling in a trendy new age philosophy did little to quell the overwhelming fear that shook his body more than the disease. He wanted to live, to live for the few moments each day that he felt normal. With the passing of time those precious moments of respite diminished to once a week, but that was enough for him; he would suffer for a few seconds of life. His eyes grew large and full of tears. He could feel death coming. He lunged forward trying to escape the grave, Smithfield instinctively stepped back before regaining his composure and clasping his friend's hand.

Drew bumped into a table before hiding in the corner. It was too much for a young man unaccustomed to the stark reality of life, sheltered by his well-meaning parents. He saw the hurried doctor storm into the room and pump Harrison with a dose of morphine. His body went limp and he muttered a few harsh words before slipping into a coma. They all knew he would never awake from the drug-induced sleep. The flustered physician said he was still in pain. Drew didn't understand how that could be, but he seemed certain about it. He wondered if he knew he would never wake up. Was he crying for his mother? Was he in a dream-like state where the sickening pain of the ravenous disease is still present but you're helplessly lost in another world?

"Let's go, Drew." Smithfield nudged him from the crowded room.

Drew was eager to leave the stifling smell of death that seemed to fill every nook of the once posh master bedroom.

They walked side by side to the water's edge without discussing what had just happened. Drew broke the awkward silence.

"Why does he want me to go to Portugal?"

"I don't have a clue, Drew. That man is something…" His voiced trailed off as he gazed out to sea.

"When should I go?"

"Whenever you can. If you can, is a better way to put it."

"Should I wait until…" Drew stopped himself from saying the words.

"It's okay, Drew, I know he won't last the week."

"I just think I should go to the funeral."

"Wait until he's dead." Smithfield immediately regretted his harsh tone. The pressure of the long illness was affecting every facet of his life.

"I'm sorry," Drew mumbled.

"I know you are."

"He gave me five thousand dollars…is that enough?"

"Plenty for one person I would think."

"Yeah. But why only me?"

"Who the fuck knows, that bastard is famous for his enigmatic behavior. He has done other things like this before, choreographed and well-thought-out puzzles, I suppose this is his swan song."

"I don't even have a passport…"

"How can God allow such suffering?" Smithfield sighed, ignoring Drew's minor logistical concern. He was visibly upset and made no attempt to hide it.

"I don't know."

"I do, Drew."

"You do?"

"Yes, there is no God." With these parting words Carlton Smithfield left the overwhelmed intern alone with his scattered thoughts. With these parting words, they ended their highly unusual meeting. He empathized with the middle-aged writer, it was only a matter of hours before his most important person in his life became a memory.

Chapter 5

One More Day

Sheldon Harrison outlasted all expectations and saw the dawn of a new day. Through the haze of morphine nothingness, Harrison opened his eyes and glanced out the window for the last time. He marveled at the white caps of high tide and the graceful flight of a seagull searching for its morning breakfast. He thanked God for one last glimpse of the only world he had ever known. With a gentle sigh, he felt the pain slowly ease. He didn't fight the wonderful feeling of relief that came with his last breath.

The loss of a literary icon of Sheldon's stature sent ripples across the country. The national media referred to him as the American Tolstoy and recounted his exploits in glowing terms. The collective praise from the four corners of the globe made one wonder if William Shakespeare had just died. The President of the United States gave a tear-filled press conference, recalling his days at Princeton when he first read the works of the master. He claimed Sheldon Harrison was his only companion during his confused undergraduate days, he held up a battered copy of his first novel for the press to see. It was a dramatic moment and probably won him a few more votes.

Sympathetic citizens congregated outside his home, leaving flowers, cards, and copies of his novels against the enormous front gate. They were quickly ushered off the island, the permanent residents barely tolerated the summer rental crowd but they certainly would not stand for the disheveled group of mourners.

The donations to the American Cancer Society tripled in the days following his death. The word of his terrible suffering quickly spread among the populace and they cried aloud for their fallen icon. They cried for their own family members who suffered a similar fate.

Sheldon Harrison was a towering figure among America's pantheon of talented 20th Century writers. The odd part of his exalted position was his meager body of work relative to his contemporaries. He had published only six novels and all were during a ten-year period starting in the 1950s. The first four novels were considered among the finest novels in American History. Many claimed he must have made a deal with the devil, a crossroads moment. "Divine inspiration" was a phrase uttered many times when any of the first four novels were discussed. His last two were embarrassingly bland and so ordinary they were quickly relegated to the discount bookshelf. The critics, who praised him vociferously in years past, were disappointed by the effort and said so. Their criticism, sometimes muted because of his stature and influence, was at times, cutting and unapologetic. Harrison did not take it well; he publicly resigned and claimed he would never publish again. He kept his word and he never published another piece of fiction.

The most scathing reviews came from one well-respected critic from the *Boston Globe*. Myron Wiseman told readers to avoid the last two novels if they wanted to remember Sheldon Harrison as the genius they all loved. The reader could feel Wiseman's pain, almost a reluctance to rip the venerated writer, but he felt cheated by the last two novels. Eventually it became a crusade for him; he attacked so often it was difficult for him to interact normally with others in his profession. He was obsessed with the obvious slip in Harrison's work. Harrison tried to ignore the attacks by Wiseman, but behind the scenes the specter of the critic haunted his every move. The mere mention of his name infuriated the thin-skinned Harrison to the point of violence.

Wiseman was not unscathed during this period. He received many threats and on more than a few occasions overzealous Harrison supporters physically assaulted the diminutive writer. Eventually he shifted his focus, but would periodically revisit the topic of the last two novels, but never with the same frequency or vigor.

In some circles, he is remembered as the bright and quirky critic who boldly took on a literary giant and didn't lose. His persistent questions and tough reviews would forever link him with Sheldon Harrison. No credible biography would be complete without the name Myron Wiseman cropping up with alarming frequency.

Harrison's royalties from the "golden four" as the press affectionately dubbed them made him a very wealthy man. He was a guest of honor at many universities around the world, getting a handsome paycheck for his lofty speeches about the dire state of American fiction. He treated fellow writers with disdain and mocked any new writer that he did not mentor. His death only heightened his stature among his legions of followers. Their darling was dead.

Chapter 6

Bad News Travels Fast

Charlotte Emerson awoke with the sound of her telephone ringing. She ripped the cordless phone from its perch, annoyed by the unwelcome disturbance.

"What!" She snarled and looked at her clock. It was 6:30 AM on a Saturday morning.

"Charlotte?" The weak voice of her mother startled her.

"Mom. What is it?"

"Honey…"

"What's the matter?"

"Your grandfather is dead." Her voice cracked.

"Oh shit," she whispered.

"What?"

"Nothing, I can't believe it. My God I can't…"

"I know…I knew this day was coming but…" Mrs. Emerson broke down.

"Jesus this sucks."

"What?"

"Nothing. This is awful. I don't…I don't know what to say."

"I know…I know, Charlotte," she sobbed.

"When is the funeral?"

"I don't know. He just died." Her aching mother sniffled and tried to clear her throat.

"How did it happen? I mean what happened?"

"He was dying you know!" Mrs. Emerson was perplexed and agitated by the question.

"Of course...I just wanted to..." Charlotte searched for a proper question.

"Did he die peacefully?" Her mother tried to help.

"Yes. Did he?"

"I think so...I really don't know how anyone can die peacefully."

"I just can't believe it."

"I'll call you later, you know, with all the details. I have so many people to call."

"I understand. Call me later. I love you Mom."

Charlotte flopped onto her wide leather sofa and tried to force herself to cry. She tugged at her long silk nightshirt and thought about the man whose impact on her day-to-day life was immeasurable. She was saddened by the news, but not devastated. Her life would be altered and she would miss him, but her status would go unchanged, if not enhanced by his dramatic passing. Her friends were still alive and her exalted position as the granddaughter of the great Sheldon Harrison was firmly cemented. She had hardly visited her sick grandfather during the last year and was unrepentant; his contribution to her life had long been completed.

Harrison often tried, in recent months, to get his granddaughter to come to his Martha's Vineyard estate, but she always made an excuse and promised to call soon. When she did grace him with a visit, she counted the hours until she could depart from what she referred to as a one-horse island with marginal restaurants and old money perverts. Charlotte had an innate sense of her grandfather's displeasure with her. She always made amends with him before he was forced to choose another as his favorite. A position she took very seriously.

As the disconcerting thoughts of her own failings as a granddaughter threatened to ruin her day, she forced herself to think about how the bad news would impact her life in the short term. She thought about her upcoming trip and how this awful news would affect her plans. She paced her luxury townhouse, calculating and recalculating how she could swing the funeral and the trip without insulting grandfather's memory.

The big trip was only a week away. She swore out loud at the injustice of it all. The national media would over-dramatize the event and most likely cause further delays. The remaining Harrison clan was prone to melodrama and would relish the spotlight. They led such dull lives this would be the high point of their year, a moment to shine and bask in the glow of mass adulation and sympathy. Their celebrity friends would console them, overtly shunning the cameras and media attention, but secretly enjoying the good publicity of attending such a prestigious funeral.

After a long day of answering consoling phone calls, Charlotte entertained a large group of her friends as she anxiously awaited the final funeral arrangements. Her highly anticipated excursion to Europe was in jeopardy and she was sick about it. The problem was not with her schedule; it was her friends from college who had real jobs and somewhat rigid vacation schedules.

Charlotte was an assistant editor for a large New York publisher with an office in Boston. It was Sheldon's publisher; thus her status in the firm was assured and her schedule imminently flexible. She deluded herself into thinking it was her brilliance and editing savvy that allowed her such a coveted position years before the normal progression in that field.

The room filled as her friends dropped by to offer their condolences. As the night progressed, thoughts of Sheldon Harrison faded and the mood changed from somber reflection to raucous laughter and demonstrative storytelling. It was a typical gathering prior to a night out. The only difference was the decision to honor Sheldon Harrison by skipping the bars. Charlotte laughed and drank with her friends as if it were an ordinary night, easily suppressing any feelings of guilt and rather enjoying the attention. Her reverie was interrupted by the buzz of her doorbell. She figured it was a late guest, perhaps Corey Davis. She had decided to seduce him when they were in Paris. She ran to her intercom system and listened for his deep, distinctive voice. The static on the line made it difficult for her to recognize the voice, although she knew it wasn't him. She hit the buzzer and re-joined her party. She was annoyed then slightly embarrassed when Carlton Smithfield presented himself at the door.

"Hello, Charlotte," he said brusquely, a dour expression crossing his face.

"Hi Carlton." She moved aside and let him in.

"Having a party?" Carlton asked stiffly.

"No…just some friends," she stammered and avoided his serious gaze. She resented him for making her feel awkward and selfish.

"Never mind. I came by as a favor to your mother. She asked me to stop in and check on you. She wanted me to comfort you." The last remark was taken for what it was, a shot across the bow.

"I'm doing much better since my friends arrived." She answered back defiantly. Her friends recognized Smithfield and edged closer to the duel. His fiery temper was legendary. They also noticed a young man with Smithfield; he was obviously trying to make himself as inconspicuous as possible.

"I see you've made quite a recovery." The veins in Smithfield's tired neck bulged with anger. He felt like throttling the whole group.

"I guess I'm being mature about it."

"Charlotte Emerson, this is Drew Engle." Smithfield jerked his thumb angrily towards Drew.

"Hello." She had barely noticed him when they walked in. He smiled pleasantly and nodded hello. Her first impression was not favorable. He looked dull and very average. From his simple dress and unsure body movements, she knew he was someone she would never socialize with.

"Drew was one of your grandfather's interns this summer."

"Oh." She didn't care if he jumped from the window at that moment. She doubted whether she would even look at his battered body, perhaps she would dial 911. She was wasting her valuable time even acknowledging his existence.

"He was with your grandfather at the end."

Charlotte colored with anger at the jab.

"Is that right?" She eyed the interloper condescendingly.

"Yes that's right. He saw it all, Charlotte."

"I'm glad it's over. The suffering."

"Yes it is," Smithfield responded coldly.

"So, Drew, I hope my grandfather didn't have you cutting his shrubs like the other interns. Did he make you take his dogs for a walk?"

"No, I didn't do any of that." Drew was painfully aware of all the eyes upon him. He was intimidated by the mocking glares of the group led by Charlotte Emerson.

"He did mostly research and a little bit of writing. Your grandfather thought very highly of him." This was a knife in Charlotte's heart. It was common knowledge that Charlotte's paltry writing skills did not match her intellect; she lacked the creativity of even a mediocre novelist. Her bid to become the only other writer in the family died many years before.

"I must say, Charlotte, you are remarkably composed after such a tragedy, tell me how do you do it?" He wasn't holding back, the room went silent and Charlotte flushed noticeably. Smithfield's loyalty to Charlotte ended the moment her grandfather took his last breath.

"I don't fall into fits of despair for things I cannot control." She had regained her composure and was ready to counter her adversary.

"I see." He stared into her cold eyes for a few seconds before heading for the door.

"So soon." She tried to be nonchalant, but her voice cracked slightly. It would be truly embarrassing for a well-respected and popular novelist like Carlton Smithfield to walk out on her.

"What's left to say, Charlotte? I'll have your mother call with the arrangements. I think I'll save her a trip."

"What do you mean?"

"She had planned to drive up from the island tomorrow to see you. I'll tell her the visit is unnecessary. Have a safe trip."

"Well I'm not sure I'm going," she stammered. She was surprised he knew of her impending journey.

"Maybe you'll cross paths with Drew."

"Why? Are you going to Europe?" She looked at Drew skeptically and reasoned he must be part of a school-sponsored exchange program or something.

"He's going at the behest of your grandfather."

Drew glanced around nervously; he could see intrigue in the eyes of her friends.

"Why?"

"Drew was asked by Sheldon to go to Sintra, Portugal and retrieve something from a safety deposit box."

"What?" She felt a bead of perspiration on her upper lip and she sipped her wine to help with the sudden dryness.

"We don't know. It's a mystery. But your grandfather saw something in Drew that he didn't see in anybody else. He's the only one he entrusted to make the trip. He leaves after the funeral."

"What could it be? I mean to entrust a stranger for such a thing. It doesn't make any sense."

"Good question. We'll all know soon enough. Have a nice night all." With this parting shot, the duo exited the townhouse.

Charlotte was mystified by the whole affair. Her anger with Carlton paled in comparison with the curiosity about her grandfather's strange last request and the unremarkable person asked to carry it out.

Chapter 7

The Engle's

THE DAY AFTER HARRISON's death, Drew Engle cleared out his room and returned to his home in Burlington, Massachusetts. His parents were glad his summer internship was ending early; they didn't like Sheldon Harrison. They had met the sick author a few days before Drew was selected for the summer internship program. They felt he was crabby and aloof.

Joe Engle, Drew's fifty-year-old master carpenter father felt Harrison looked down upon his son because of his lack of refinement and stature. He was surprised when his son was chosen out of the dozens of well-connected applicants.

Mr. Engle was tall and strong with dark hair sprinkled with streaks of gray. He was lean with blue eyes that blazed to life in the summer. He turned heads among his female customers. It was his eyes that attracted them, honest and serious, overwhelming for the easily influenced. The seriousness came from a lifetime of struggle.

His long journey to middle class prosperity began many years before in the dark recesses of his broom-closet-sized room in Charlestown, a working class appendage of Boston. Huddling in his room, he listened to his alcoholic father unmercifully beat his crying mother. The raging fights would last for hours, his frightened mother barely uttering a word as the man she once loved rattled off every expletive young Joe Engle had ever heard. His only brother, Patrick, returned from the jungles of Vietnam a shell of himself. The depressed and deeply disillusioned young man soon became the target of his father's raving binges. He called him a coward and a bum for losing the war. A deadly mixture of easily obtainable drugs mixed with severe depression was the eventual undoing of "Patty" Engle. He died of a drug overdose soon after his return.

Joe Engle did not immediately learn from his father's errors; he, too, became a heavy drinker during his apprentice days. He found his father tolerable when they drank together; he ignored the abuse of his mother and settled into a rut of drinking his problems away.

Engle's alcoholism was fueled by the sight of his sometimes-charming father at the end of the bar. Through the fog of intoxication he seethed with emotion, reliving in vivid detail the pain the popular man afflicted upon his hapless family.

One particular afternoon at a local bar called the Gin Mill, Engle had a moment of clarity. He watched his inebriated father cuddling with some bar slut, confident his new buddy for a son would not betray his trust and tell his mother. In a rush of self-loathing and guilt he thought about the man he was protecting, the vile creature that ruined his life. He thought about his birdfeeder.

As a curious and industrious child, Engle was an accomplished woodworker by the age of twelve. He made colorful birdfeeders for the neighbors, selling them for the cost of the lumber and never for profit. It was on a clear, chilly day in November when he finally finished a very ambitious feeder for his grandfather. His drunken father stormed into his room and berated him for wasting so much time on it. He wantonly tossed the feeder from the sagging third floor apartment porch and laughed as it crashed on the concrete patio below. Joe escaped his father's firm grip and rushed down three flights of stairs only to collapse in tears when he reached the splintered remains. His fingers were numb from the cold, tears streamed down his red cheeks. His mother gently pried him away from the ruins and brought him into the dilapidated house they called home. This kind of heartless destruction continued until Joe learned to hide all of his prized creations.

This was the man he was protecting, shielding from the sorry eyes of his downtrodden mother. That marked the last time he drank with his father and one of the last times he saw him. His father tried in vain for decades to repair the breech, Joe never allowed him to see his children. The old man died of liver failure, alone and nearly homeless.

Joe quit drinking and eventually became the type of father he had always yearned for. He worked hard and was devoted to his children to a fault. He had little patience for anyone who tried to influence or harm his children.

It was his keen interest in history that helped foster young Drew's remarkable reading ability. Joe built a custom mahogany bookshelf and turned a dreary office into a first-class library. After a long day of pounding nails and fighting with surly contractors, he would retire to his library for a moment's peace. His wife often found him asleep on his chair, an open book or magazine strewn across the floor. Many of those blissful evenings Drew would be close to his father's side, reading from the collection or just gazing up at the ceiling and dreaming of the places he just read about. His father's interest in the great battles of Napoleon filtered down to his son. He wished he could visit the battlefields his father colorfully described, but they seemed exotic and beyond his reach.

It was in the spiritual center of this home that Drew learned to think for himself when other children only ingested what their bored teachers thought suitable. As Drew moved through the Massachusetts school system, he found himself at odds with his instructors who were often agitated by his informed opinions and sometimes superior summations. They didn't like the son of a carpenter questioning what they had learned as graduate students twenty years before.

Drew's mother, Sharon Engle was an angelic figure that kept it all together. Sharon, at forty-nine years old had retained her charming good looks that had made her husband quiver and stammer during their courtship. She came from a volatile ethnic background of Europe's most dynamic peoples. Her mother was a Spanish beauty and her father Sicilian Italian. Her brown eyes, black hair, and olive complexion accented her blemish-free skin perfectly; few had to guess her general ethnicity.

Her childhood was dramatically different from her husband's checkered upbringing. Her home in Malden, Massachusetts overflowed with love and family unity. She had four sisters who were all daddy's favorite, her strong-willed mother kept her overly lenient husband from allowing his girls to run their three-story home. She was the youngest and also the most studious. She received a partial scholarship to Tufts University, but only finished two years before transferring to the more economical Northeastern University. She commuted to school, forfeiting the decadent lifestyle of a typical college student of the times, unimpressed by the frivolity of casual drug use.

She worked as a social worker for a few years before meeting her husband at the home of a friend who was renovating his turn of the century home in Cambridge. She was immediately attracted to his lean body and his strong blue eyes. He was different from the college guys she dated; most of them were weak and complained a lot. He was more like her darling father. To the mild consternation of some of her college friends they married a year after their first date. It was only after they had married, did she acknowledge his drinking problem. She endured the pain of the disease until he found the will to change his life. They moved to the suburbs and started their real life together. He never had another drink the moment he stepped into the large colonial style home he built in Burlington. Sharon quit her low-paying job to concentrate on raising her three children.

She was a devout Catholic and it made for a comedic Sunday morning. Her husband viewed organized religion with contempt. His alcoholic and abusive father was an outstanding Catholic on Sundays and holidays. His unholy escapades the night before services meant little if he begged for forgiveness the next day. All the bargirls he slept with on Saturday night only showed he was human and God was great. In the end, Sharon's protestations were in vain, Joe Engle never voluntarily attended church.

Drew found his way home a day before Sheldon Harrison's much anticipated funeral. He smiled at the slumped figure of his father leaning over his workbench, deftly putting the finishing touches on a three-story birdfeeder. His strong, crooked fingers trembled slightly as he effortlessly glued each piece with the care of a surgeon, careful to limit the residue of the adhesive.

He stood and smiled broadly at his son. It was comforting for him to be in a place that had given him so much pleasure as a youth. Joe would grumble when Drew played with his tools, but he really didn't care what his son did to them.

"It's too bad about Mr. Harrison." Joe wiped the glue from his hands and sat on a stool near his bench.

"It was horrible." Drew fingered a plastic model P-51 Mustang before slumping on a worn-out couch.

"Your mother said he was very sick," Joe probed his son to see if he wanted to talk about it.

"Did she tell you I might be going to Portugal?"

"She mentioned it," he replied evenly.

Drew retold much of what his father already knew, but his excited son filled in some of the gaps.

"I don't like it, Drew." He was alarmed and suspicious by the whole affair.

"I know it sounds weird, but I think I'm gonna go. Hey, I get a free trip out of it at the very least. And how often does one of the most famous writers in American history ask an unknown college kid for anything. I don't want to…"

"Did he give you any money?" Joe interrupted his son.

"Yes…"

"How much?"

"Five thousand."

"What!"

"I know."

"Jesus, Drew, will it cost that much?"

"Whatever I don't use I can give it to charity."

"Are you nuts? Whatever is left over you can use it for your education." His exasperated tone amused his son.

"We'll see, Dad."

"When are you leaving?" Mr. Engle opened the door leading to the garage and his son followed. He opened the garage door to get some fresh air. He chuckled at his neighbor's attire, a pair of faded Bermuda shorts and black socks.

"I don't know yet. I think next week."

"Be careful of these people."

"Dad, they're no different than us. Trust me."

"Drew, they will chew you up and spit you out before dinner. They're not like us. They don't know what it's like to struggle for anything, to work for anything."

"Neither do I. Come on Dad, you think the son of such a tough guy is going to be pushed around by the likes of those pampered wimps."

"No bullshit, Drew. Watch yourself."

"Sure." Drew rolled his eyes and left to prepare for his trip.

"Fucking intellectuals." Joe Engle mumbled aloud.

Chapter 8

Back Bay Boston: The Same Day

Charlotte Emerson pushed her bra up and marveled at her shapely breasts. She played with the string of her lingerie and imagined herself with Corey Davis. Her master plan of seduction had been severely compromised by her grandfather's untimely death. She was disappointed by the bourgeois way he died. She heartlessly reasoned he should have died thirty years before either by his own hand or in a tragic accident. At the end he wore a diaper and could not feed himself; this was not how she wanted to remember him. The absurd rationale helped her overcome the feelings of guilt she was experiencing.

Charlotte's voyeuristic side emerged as she pranced in front of her large window. She hoped her hot neighbor across the street would come to his window and look at her longingly. Her body felt warm and she was dangerously close to full arousal. Her sexual haze faded with the sound of her doorbell.

"Who is it?" Charlotte asked hurriedly.

"Wilton."

"Okay." Her feelings were mixed as she let her cousin in. She loved him dearly but it was clearly an inopportune time. Wilton Saunders entered with a rush. His chubby face was flushed and he acted like he had something important to discuss with his cousin.

"What's the matter with you?"

She didn't bother throwing on a robe.

"Did you hear what Sheldon did?" His hurried tone and general excitement intrigued Charlotte. She had seldom seen him so worked up.

"What?" She leaped onto the couch and gave him her undivided attention.

"He gave some flunky intern money and a key to a safety deposit box in Portugal." He was disappointed by her modest reaction.

"That's it. I already know, Wilton." She felt deflated, she was hoping for some new gossip.

"How do you know? Who told you?" He was perplexed.

"Carlton Smithfield came by the other night with the newest member of our family," she remarked sarcastically.

"The intern? What's his story? Why him?" Wilton sat on the couch next to Charlotte. She smiled at his interest; he was the only one who thought he wasn't a major league gossip. He was Charlotte's main source of family news.

"Just some nobody. Nothing really special, just a lucky bastard who happened to be around a delusional old man on his deathbed." Charlotte tossed her hair back and opened her arms to reveal her cleavage. She thought it odd that her breasts didn't transfix him.

"You don't think there is anything to this, do you?"

"No, what could it be?"

"Who knows, a guy like Grandfather could have many skeletons in his closet."

"Hmmm." She twirled her hair and thought about the situation. The safety deposit box was an interesting aspect. What could be hidden in a box so far from home? Why did he want a stranger to retrieve the contents? Why only on his deathbed did he reveal its existence?

"We should talk to this kid."

"When?" She liked the idea.

"I suppose he'll be at the funeral tomorrow."

"You think? Maybe."

"When do you leave for Europe?" His face clouded over and he avoided eye contact with Charlotte.

"I think we're leaving a day or two after the funeral. I was supposed to be leaving tomorrow you know."

"Why are you so obsessed with this trip?" Wilton stood up hastily and made his way to her stainless steel refrigerator. He stopped before opening the door; gnashing his teeth together he tried to control the sudden anger.

"Why do you care?" Charlotte smiled at his obvious discomfort.

"I don't care…I don't!" Wilton said emphatically without facing her. His reddened face would have revealed too much.

"You do care because you keep asking me about it." A hint of anger had slipped into her voice. His frequent questions were becoming somewhat of an annoyance.

"No reason. I just worry about you sometimes." He grabbed bottled water from the refrigerator. She noticed his hands were shaking slightly. This angered her.

"You know why I want to go to Europe. Don't be coy."

"No... I don't." Wilton took a long, uneasy drink from his bottle.

"I want to seduce Corey. I want him to fuck me like a dog. Is that what you want to hear? Can you handle me being so honest?"

"You're disgusting." He laughed nervously and walked away.

Charlotte smiled and playfully chased him around the luxury townhouse. She grabbed at his rather bulbous ass and jumped on his back. He pretended to sag under the weight of his light cousin. He felt her hard breasts on his back and taut legs around his waist. She pressed her body even closer and felt him squirm, but she didn't stop her grinding motion. Charlotte could feel his heart pounding; his breathing was labored from the ecstasy and agony. She jumped off his back and punched him on the shoulder.

"Don't be so jealous. It's very unbecoming and weak." With this parting shot she left the room. He lingered a moment then decided to leave when he heard her shower. He couldn't move, he felt angry with her for doing this to him. Without thinking he started down the long hallway to Charlotte's lavish bathroom. The door was slightly ajar and he could see her circular glass shower. He caught a glimpse of her naked midsection and was sickened by the depravity of his own actions. He shifted to see her entire body, hunkering down at the edge of the doorway careful not to reveal himself until he fully understood her intentions. He almost burst with excitement when she started to shave her well-toned legs.

To Wilton Saunders the dizzying scene felt like a dream. His hand was on the doorknob before he could stop it. He sighed inwardly and prepared to make his final move. He stopped. It was something in her suddenly serious expression that made him reconsider. It was as if she could sense his presence and wanted him to stop before it went too far. Wilton sadly returned to the kitchen and fought the urge to return. Was it too late? Did she see me? What will she think of me? With these troubling questions nearly crippling the sad young man, he forced himself out of the house of his greatest temptation; alone and regretful, he made his way home.

Chapter 9
The Burial

T HE NEXT DAY SHELDON William Harrison was buried with all the pomp and ceremony expected for a national celebrity. The President of the United States sent a private letter of condolences. Along with other popular national political figures were a slew of actors, musicians, painters, and writers who were directly affected by Sheldon Harrison's work. Thousands of ordinary citizens came out to view the spectacle; jamming the narrow sidewalk of the church, they mourned silently for their fallen idol. It was the closest any of them had come to genius. They might stumble with Joyce, scratch their head at Joseph Conrad, but they could understand and appreciate the simple beauty of Sheldon Harrison. Many felt intellectually challenged, but not mocked by the wordsmith. He was accessible to the masses unlike any author since Hemingway.

Many eulogized the fallen titan inside the small church, retelling old stories and working the crowd into a frenzy of emotion. The family soon tired of the endless praise from those who barely knew Sheldon, mostly celebrities who liked the role of the grieving friend. The hollow display of sorrow was transparent in some, others, mostly the actors, performed admirably as if they were born to play the part.

Carlton Smithfield stood with family, shielding when he could and speaking on their behalf when asked. They loved, respected, and feared him. His volatile temper and brutal honesty are what scared them. Drew Engle shadowed Smithfield during the long ceremony. He avoided the curious looks from Harrison's family. The presence of Smithfield as his obvious protector kept them at bay. Drew was fortunate enough to witness his patented bluntness after a particularly overblown, long-winded speech by an actor of high acclaim.

"A bit over the top, Craig." Smithfield said with a deadpanned expression of contempt.

"What?" The handsome young actor was stunned by the comment. He thought it was his best performance of the year.

"You heard me…your speech was that of a best friend. You met him only a few times."

"Carlton, I met him more than that."

"Mr. Smithfield, if you please. I don't really know you either. Your habit of over-familiarity is annoying." With the parting jab, Carlton abruptly ended the strange attack. He turned his back on the red-faced actor and pretended he was alone.

Drew admired his guts for confronting the presumptuous movie star when he could have easily ignored his performance. Sheldon Harrison loved this about Smithfield and would intentionally invite dinner guests he knew would set him off. If Sheldon did not care for the guest he would let Carlton crucify them. It was an amusement for the puppet master.

Drew found himself alone outside the overflowing church. A large group of local police with a contingent of state troopers barred the pulsating crowd from the church grounds. The mourners at the front of the general public viewing area were only yards away from Drew. He felt their eyes upon him, they were trying to figure out who he was and why he was allowed inside the line. A few people asked him how he knew the deceased and when he told them he was his summer intern they snickered and acted superior.

He felt depressed and leaned against the railing of the crowded church steps. Charlotte Emerson emerged from the church and slowly made her way to the bottom. She wore a grim expression and appeared to be genuinely upset. Drew tried to avoid her roving eyes, although he was certain she wouldn't remember him from their brief encounter. The bored, indifferent expression she wore at their first meeting told him all he needed to know about how she viewed him.

A slightly overweight male followed Charlotte closely. She spotted the lonesome intern and relished his awkward, jittery appearance. She didn't think he should be there, an interloper with little to offer. Her enjoyment quickly faded and she began to resent him with every step she took. Was he acting shy or aloof? She was infuriated at the thought that he might be intentionally avoiding her gaze for reasons beyond intimidation and embarrassment. By the time she reached the bottom step she was sufficiently angered to make a detour for Drew. He stood straight and prepared for the attack. He marveled at her impeccable dress and her long legs.

"So…" She cursed herself for forgetting his name. "Did you spend all the money yet?"

"No," Drew answered simply.

"No, that's it?" She was surprised by his curt reply.

"No, I haven't gone to Portugal yet."

"I'm sure there is nothing in that safety deposit box. It's all a big waste of time."

"Maybe…but we won't know until I check it out." He was riled from his stupor by her condescending tone.

"You're one lucky little intern. Just close enough to my grandfather's deathbed to collect the jackpot." She smiled brightly, but there was not goodwill or sweetness in her suspicious eyes.

"Whatever I have left after the trip I'm donating it to charity. A charity of your family's choice."

"Oh how gracious of you. All of the hundred dollars left over from your European orgy," she mocked.

The crowd behind the yellow police tape changed their mind about Drew. They had recognized the niece of the literary icon and figured he must be more important than a lowly intern. They moved closer to see if they could pick up any of the tense conversation.

"I'm only staying long enough to do what your grandfather wanted." Drew felt beads of perspiration on his forehead. He swore at himself for sweating; he knew it was a sign of weakness that someone like Charlotte Emerson would pounce upon.

"You are. Well I hope you discover something of importance on your trip. Maybe I'll see you over there. I'm leaving for Europe tomorrow."

"Are you going to Portugal?"

"No."

"Then how would I see you?" Drew asked with a hint of victory. She was startled by his aggressive attitude.

"One never knows how travel plans can change. The preservation of this family's good name will be protected at all costs." She regained her composure and waited for his reply. He made none. The standoff ended when her cousin Wilton gently pulled her away from the unseemly conflict. Wilton and Drew momentarily locked eyes. Drew lost his breath, the maniacal look of contempt made him shudder in fear. How could a man have such an immediate dislike for somebody he did not know? Drew was unaccustomed to such vagaries of life, naïve to the illogical ideas of the human animal.

"Drew." Carlton Smithfield approached from Charlotte's blind side. He nodded hello to her but didn't stop when Wilton made an attempt to shake his hand. Wilton was furious by the slight, but skulked off instead of confronting the man he never liked. Charlotte smirked and followed her sensitive cousin.

"Hi, Carlton." Drew smiled broadly at the interruption.

"Why are you hiding down here?" It was a silly question. It was typical for the Harrison clan to ignore all outsiders until their station in society was evaluated.

"Where else?"

"I guess…Jesus this crowd is fit for a funeral."

"It's almost over."

"So what did his wonderful granddaughter have to say?"

"She made a couple of remarks about the money for Portugal."

"She's something isn't she?"

"Yes she is." Drew was reluctant to criticize her behavior. He was unsure how Carlton truly felt about her. On the surface there was animosity, but inner feelings are hard to detect.

"When are you leaving?"

"In a few days."

"So soon." Smithfield's gaze caught a young boy in the crowd. He was packed tightly in the front row of the growing crowd of sweating adults. The heat was obviously bothering him, and he looked faint. He was being pressed from all sides, his tiny red cheeks swollen from the sun and the careless elbows of the adults. His mother kept one hand on his shoulder but seemed oblivious to his predicament.

"Will you look at this?" Smithfield pointed to the child. "He looks like he's going to suffocate."

Drew nodded in agreement.

"Christ these morons will do anything to see a fucking celebrity. It makes me sick sometimes."

"Hey…hey…let him breathe." Drew stepped forward and singled out the child.

"What?" The mother perked up and smiled at the attention.

"I said let the kid breathe!" Drew said sharply. Smithfield gave him a curious look and made a mental note not to underestimate him. His boldness was expertly masked by his shy and unassuming countenance.

"What?" The dizzy mother asked again. She was so overwhelmed by the whole spectacle she simply couldn't understand Drew.

"The Kid!" Smithfield gestured angrily.

"Oh." She looked down at her child.

"Do you have any water for him?" Drew asked impatiently.

"Yes." The embarrassed mother reached into her bag and gently gave the boy a drink. She wiped his face and slowly made her way through the crowd to a cooler location.

Charlotte's conversation with a boring politician was interrupted by Drew's exchange with the woman. She watched his sincere effort to help the young boy with mixed emotions. How could this meek or at least unremarkable intern show such flashes of self-confidence? It didn't bother him that he raised his voice in front of strangers and that his actions drew disapproving looks from the Harrison family. He only cared that a child was being crushed by a group of silly adults not acting responsibly. His boyish looks and apparent lack of common sense annoyed her. She hated him for his decency. She watched him closely. He paused his conversation with Carlton and caught her gaze. After a few intense seconds she blushed and looked away. She closed her eyes tightly, screaming inside for giving him the momentary flash of satisfaction. He felt no such glee, only a strange feeling in the pit of his stomach when they locked eyes. He had stopped talking, Carlton continued on with the conversation without noticing his subtle shift in attention.

"Who is that guy with Charlotte?" Drew blurted.

"Who?" Smithfield casually turned.

"Him. Next to her."

"Wilton Saunders. Sheldon's bloated grandson."

"Oh." Drew looked at his feet and wished this day would end.

"He's a real putz," Smithfield said with his usual frankness.

"Really." This brought a smile to Drew's face. Carlton reminded him of his father.

"He's a real smart kid but he has problems. He tags along with Charlotte a lot. He doesn't work much, mostly lives off a trust fund. There was a time that we thought he would be the only other writer in the family. He showed promise when he was very young."

"What happened?"

"I read his work."

"Really bad."

"Atrocious. It was hard to believe he came from the same gene pool as Sheldon Harrison. Not an original idea or a stitch of talent."

Drew laughed inwardly.

"On the surface, he seems unassuming and harmless but I don't think he is. He's the most condescending member of the Harrison clan. His humble appearance is an act he has perfected."

"He doesn't seem shy about his dislike for me. He doesn't even give me the courtesy of pretending to be decent." Drew pushed his hands into his suit pocket and fiddled with his breath mints.

"I can't even talk to the kid anymore. His voice makes me sick. He has some weird kind of crush on Charlotte."

"That's strange." Drew shuffled his feet nervously.

"I'm not sure about it, but I have a gut feeling. I observe people better than I interact with them."

At that instant a short man parted the crowd and stepped in front of Carlton Smithfield.

"Carlton…how are you?" The graying, paunchy man took Smithfield's hand and shook it vigorously.

"Myron?"

"It's been a long time, Carlton," Myron Wiseman said with restrained enthusiasm.

"What are you doing here?" He was surprised Sheldon Harrison's number one critic had the nerve to attend his funeral.

"I asked myself that question this morning."

"What was the answer?" Smithfield was uneasy; his relationship with Wiseman was complicated and sometimes volatile. They stared at each other as if they were alone; the rumble of conversation around them went unheard.

"I think it's good to make amends with a worthy adversary at the end of his life. I still stand by what I said and did, but I wanted to pay my respects to a man that wrote four great novels."

"You still have a hard-on for his later work don't you? Some things never change. Do they, Myron?" Smithfield smiled.

"Let's not get into it, not today anyway."

Smithfield's tumultuous relationship with the literary critic began after he finished his first novel. With the help of Sheldon Harrison, his first novel was a great success and Wiseman's review was more than he could have hoped. Wiseman loved Smithfield's edgy style and his praise helped launch his career. It was during the same period that he was writing scathing reviews of Harrison's fifth novel. The split between Wiseman and Smithfield began when Wiseman made the accusation, indirectly of course, that he had a ghostwriter for his first four novels. The debate continued for years until Myron finally realized his obsession was causing him to lose credibility in the literary world. Harrison weathered the minor storm and prospered while Wiseman faded into obscurity.

Smithfield was in the room when one of Harrison's cronies sucker-punched the defenseless Wiseman in the face. The altercation did not stop him, but it was the beginning of the end of his crusade for the truth.

"How did he go? I heard on the news he was very ill." Wiseman shuffled his feet and tugged at his fat tie.

"I tell you Myron I never saw anybody suffer like that. It was very bad for him at the end."

"Yes…that's the impression I got." His dour expression reflected genuine sadness.

"Myron Wiseman I would like to you to meet Drew Engle. He was one of Shelly's summer interns."

"Like you, Carlton!" Myron excitedly shook Drew's hand.

"Nice to meet you sir." Drew nodded politely.

"Myron was a critic back in the day as you kids say. His one-man war is legendary."

"You know, Carlton, I was a big supporter of Sheldon's early work. His first four novels are of rare brilliance. He was a God to me, a God who betrayed me."

"Don't be so dramatic, Myron." Smithfield smiled at his fire for great literature, his passion untouched by the passing of time.

"It was a crushing blow to me to read the drivel." He was flushed and sweat poured down his wrinkled face.

"Myron fought Sheldon through the newspaper. He had a column that everybody in the business read religiously."

"He's just throwing an old man a bone." Wiseman shifted nervously and looked uncomfortable. He did not handle praise graciously, ignoring his place in history as one of the literary world's most colorful and influential figures.

"You were always very kind to me. More generous than I deserved," Smithfield said sincerely.

"Bullcrap! Whatever I said you earned. You're the one being too modest in front of your young friend. Drew, have you read any of Carlton's books?"

"Yes, but not everything yet." Drew colored slightly. He had read Smithfield's most notable works in college, but not much on his own.

"You should read it all." Wiseman bristled, but softened when he noticed Drew's discomfort.

"Drew has been asked to perform a special task for Shelly."

"What do you mean?"

Carlton recounted Harrison's last day and the odd request. Wiseman was mesmerized by the story, shaking off the lethargy of old age, his mind racing through hundreds of possible explanations.

"Very strange." Wiseman rubbed his bald head and pushed up his sagging glasses.

"It is, isn't it?" Smithfield stared at him.

"Don't you think it is a strange request, Drew?" Wiseman asked.

"I'm as puzzled as you are. I don't know why..."

"He leaves in a couple of days." Smithfield saved Drew. He could see the young man was struggling with his words.

"Well, keep me informed about this will you, Drew."

"Always the newspaper man, right, Myron." Smithfield gently patted his back; afraid even a modest push would knock him down. As the conversation ended he noticed many sharp glances in his direction. It was clear that some members of the Harrison clan still viewed Myron Wiseman as enemy number one. The whole affair was only a small blemish on the illustrious career of Sheldon Harrison, yet he was still regarded as a scoundrel whose only interest was shocking his readers. He avoided family members and spoke to a few colleagues who acted like he had small pox. They liked him and admired his guts, but didn't want the wrath of the Harrison clan thrust upon them.

The thinly veiled hostility didn't bother him, he was there to show respect for a worthy opponent, not to satisfy the vanity of his extended family, many of whom barely knew him. He suspected most of the animosity came from the family members who were horrified by any bad publicity that could affect the earning power of the Harrison machine.

Two hours later, Sheldon Harrison's skeletal body was forever entombed in a grandiose mausoleum in the most coveted section of an exclusive cemetery. Even in death the rich must have the best. Drew was relieved he was not invited to the entrance of the tomb. Only close family and friends were present when the giant door clanked shut, abruptly ending 20th Century American Fiction. Alas, all the new world masters were dead.

Drew used his free time wisely. He stopped at a local bookstore and picked up a few guidebooks for Portugal. He spent the night huddled in his childhood bedroom cramming for the trip, his tired fingers flipping through colorful pages of the exotic European country. His knowledge of the seafaring nation grew by the minute. He found the sections for Sintra, a small mountain town an hour from Lisbon. He planned the logistics with meticulous care. After a long night, he felt confident he could fulfill Harrison's last wish, he was prepared to begin the most distressing and exciting Chapter of his short life.

Chapter 10

Boston: Six Hours After the Funeral

"Can you believe the nerve of that intern showing up at the funeral?" Wilton Saunders stuck his head into his well-stocked refrigerator and grabbed a diet soda. He was talking to an exhausted Charlotte Emerson, who lay sprawled on his couch, aimlessly gazing out the window. His high-rise building on Tremont Street overlooked Boston Common; the spectacular view was the most impressive part of the rather bland, basic two-bedroom townhouse. Charlotte watched the twinkle of lights across the park on Beacon Hill. She couldn't see the street below from her position on the couch, but she imagined it was swamped with vile tourists. She loathed the city in the summer and fall.

"No," she responded in a bored tone to his question about Drew. She felt she had devoted enough time to him already.

"Why are you so intent on going to Europe? You can go any other time?"

"I want to fuck Corey Davis. I told you the other day. Is that what you want to hear? I want him to take me in every position as we sip wine on the Champs Elysees."

"You're disgusting," he chuckled, it was a weak effort to laugh off her tactless, hurtful response.

"Wilton, did I ever tell you that I hate tourists?"

Charlotte was not alone on the couch; her younger cousin Samantha Harrison sat quietly drinking a soda. Samantha was surprised by the lack of emotion her cousins were showing; she was deeply saddened by the death of her grandfather. She was not as close to her grandfather as her more sophisticated cousins, but he was a large figure in her life.

"I'm fully aware of almost all of your likes and dislikes," he snapped, annoyed with her for changing the subject.

"Settle down," Charlotte retorted.

"What about the nerve of that turd Myron Wiseman showing his face at the funeral."

"Oh what the fuck do you care, Wilton. It was thirty years ago, we weren't even born." She leaned back and stared at his chubby face. He looked like he wanted to strike her.

"Fuck off." He knew she cared about what he was saying; her feigned disinterest was a typical ploy to make it seem like she wasn't a raging gossip.

"Charlotte, please. You were pretty pissed off when you talked to the now famous intern." He said intern like it was a bad word.

"You really hate him, don't you? You're a liberal, you're supposed to love everybody." She often poked fun at his staunch liberalism. She was a lifelong Democrat, but found some of his lofty ideals childish.

"I don't hate him, I just…" He couldn't find the right words to describe his feelings.

"He's just an interloper that got lucky. He's a lottery winner, but I suspect he'll find nothing at the end of the rainbow," Charlotte helped him finish his thought. She was alluding to Drew's trip to Portugal.

"I think you're right," he beamed, "Samantha, what did you think of him?" Wilton was fond of his innocent and sometimes naïve cousin. She was short and stout with a frumpish appearance that was not wholly displeasing, but she was certainly not attractive, yet she was rarely without a boyfriend.

"I didn't think much of him. He looked like a regular guy," she answered Wilton's query with a half smile.

"Of course, to you everybody looks and acts the same," Wilton said with a sly grin.

"Wilton, give her a break. What chance did she have growing up in the suburbs?" Charlotte rolled up a tissue and playfully tossed it at her flustered cousin.

"She knows I'm just kidding."

"I'm used to you guys making fun of me," she said with a forced laugh.

"I think he'll find something that granddad hid from all of us," Charlotte said soberly.

"What?" Wilton looked confused.

"I know what I said, but I changed my mind."

"You're unbelievable." Wilton sighed deeply.

"What makes you think he'll find anything important?" Samantha asked.

"No more questions…I'm too tired for anymore questions." Charlotte blurted, looking dismal and eager for an escape.

"Don't do that, you know how much I hate it when you're moody." Wilton was perturbed by her unpredictable behavior.

"I have to pack, I don't know why I'm wasting my time with you two." She rose from the sofa and abruptly left the townhouse.

"What's her problem?" Samantha asked.

"Who knows, she's been acting weird all day." Wilton was still staring at the door.

"Really."

"Yeah…Samantha I'm really tired too…" He stopped himself, but it was too late.

"So you want me to leave?" Her cheeks blossomed and she awkwardly prepared to leave.

"I didn't mean you had to leave." Wilton tried to repair the damage. He was frightened to death that his cousin would think badly of him. He wrongly thought his family regarded him as a jovial and accommodating person, a quirky individual everybody wanted to be around. He was deluded into thinking that his close association with Charlotte, the so-called rebel of the family, elevated him over his rather bland cousins.

"It's always the same with you, isn't it!" Samantha's face burned with anger.

Wilton was stunned by the outburst. Samantha was non-confrontational by nature, particularly amongst her family.

"Samantha, what are you talking about?" He smiled and tried to disarm her.

"Wilton please! Every time she leaves the room you deflate like a balloon and want everybody to leave. As soon as the princess left the room it was time for me to go. It happens all the time, Wilton. You have no use for me unless she's here. I'm fucking sick of it."

"Samantha, what the hell are you babbling about?" Beads of unflattering sweat streaked Wilton's wrinkled face. He hated her.

"Don't act like I'm crazy."

"Samantha, enough of this. I'm in no mood." His displeasure with her sudden revolt boiled to the surface.

"Why aren't you in the mood? Is it because she's going to Europe and you can't deal with it?" They stared at each other; both shocked by what was said. It was the first time a family member alluded to the possibility of an inappropriate relationship.

"I'm going to bed. You should get some rest too. It's been a long day for all of us," he said after a long, simmering pause.

"Okay," she prepared to leave the townhouse.

He watched her awkward movements and smiled. She was crawling back into her shell. He loved her deeply but he also thought she was boring and very bourgeois. Charlotte viewed her acceptance into their circle as an unnecessary act of charity.

"I'll call you tomorrow." Wilton did not offer to see her out.

"Bye, Wilton."

"Goodnight, Sammy." He turned his back on her, gazing out the window into the inky dark, his thoughts already shifting to Charlotte. He collapsed on a large reading chair near the window; exhausted from the rollercoaster of emotions that battered what he believed was a sensitive and unique soul.

Chapter 11
Lisbon, Portugal

"Jesus Christ. When will this plane land?" Drew mumbled to himself as the lumbering Airbus gently touched down at Portela airport four miles from downtown Lisbon. The Air Portugal plane taxied for five minutes before stopping a mile from the terminal. Friendly flight attendants hustled the tired passengers off the messy aircraft and to a bus waiting a safe distance from the plane. The airport was not fitted with American style point of entry gates. The passengers were ferried via the odd-looking bus that was actually part elevator, to the main terminus. Drew was amused when they reached their gate and the entire cabin of the bus rose like an elevator and deposited them near the baggage carousel. Upon claiming his two small bags, he decided to take a taxi to the center of Lisbon.

The drive was short, only a few miles to the commercial and financial heart of the ancient city. His first impression out of the yellowed window of the otherwise tidy taxi was not favorable. It appeared to be a city on the mend, dilapidated buildings along the route made him think of the urban decay of many American cities. The influx of money since Portugal became a member of the European Union was helping to revitalize the jewel of a city. There seemed to be thick layer of soot or grime on many of the buildings. It didn't take Drew long to realize the auto emissions were to blame. Automobiles all around the taxi were belching noxious fumes from their unfiltered talepipes. The open window inside the hot taxi exposed him to the fumes. Drew watched plumes of smoke and felt sick. His virgin lungs ached and he felt the onset of a bad headache. The driver seemed immune to the stench; his body acclimated to the harsh effects.

The English-speaking driver turned and exclaimed, "Hotel Fenix!" The hotel was located on the perimeter of the largest rotary Drew had ever seen. The Fenix was an understated, 1970s era, hotel with a commanding view of the Praca Margques de Pombra, an impressive monument at the top of the Avenida Da Liberdade, a tree-lined avenue reminiscent of its cousin the Champ De Elysees in Paris. From Drew's vantage point outside the hotel, he could see the edge of the Avenida Da Liberdade walking distance to his right. A bustling subway stop was conveniently located in the center of the rotary. On Drew's left the Parque Eduard VII, a magnificent park, was beckoning him to stroll its majestic paths. It was wonderful place to take a nap or have lunch, but at night it was a dangerous place for a tourist to wander.

The polite doorman at the Hotel Fenix greeted Drew with a smile and helped carry his bags into the modest lobby of the respectable hotel. It was a two-star hotel that would be a three-star in many other European cities.

Drew lumbered to the front desk and practically begged the clerk for his room; the pleasant but firm manager told him bluntly that his room would not be ready for another two hours. The head clerk stowed his bags in a secure room and told him to come back at 2:00. He suggested Drew explore his wonderful city, inferring a good walk would help with the symptoms of jet lag. He was suffering from the time change and the long, sleepless overnight flight.

The roar of traffic rudely replaced the silence of the main lobby as Drew exited the hotel. The rotary was a main hub for many of Lisbon's major arteries; to the neophyte traveler it was a bewildering swirl of traffic entering and exiting from every direction. He squinted at the sun and suddenly felt hot; he tugged at his collar and tried to read his map of Lisbon. The temperate climate of Portugal was similar to California. His hands trembled as he tried to follow the map from his hotel; he hadn't eaten since leaving Logan International Airport the night before. The Hotel Fenix had a very good restaurant, but it didn't open until 5:00. He was tired, hungry, hot, and above all starting to feel homesick. He hoped it was the lack of adequate sleep and sustenance that was driving his feelings of regret.

Drew decided to follow the Avenida Da Liberdade in search of a restaurant or a bar. He loved the tree-lined avenue with its upscale boutiques and small fashionable salons. He was amused by the endless succession of currency exchange outlets all claiming the best rates. They had the daily rates in clear view for all the tourists making their way down the long Avenida Da Liberdade to Rossio Square at the end. Drew soon tired of his stroll and stopped at a small sandwich shop. Instead of making the food to order, they displayed their succulent sandwiches in a glass case for immediate consumption. This made Drew uneasy. He was accustomed to America's refrigeration obsession, but he noticed many other tourists including a fellow countrymen scoffing down attractive sandwiches. The tiny café had a few small plastic tables and a long counter with many different types of sandwiches and desserts neatly arranged for clear viewing. The unique atmosphere of shy tourists mixed with annoyed, sometimes-condescending locals was amusing and common in Europe.

Drew waited patiently for his turn, nervously fingering the strange bills, silently hoping he could figure out the conversion before he was called upon. The person working the counter was an attractive young woman who smiled at his obvious discomfort. Like most young locals, she spoke English and happily helped him through the transaction. He bought a Coke and a large sandwich before sitting down at one of the vacant plastic tables. He drank the Coke first; he needed the caffeine more than the food. He watched the girl effortlessly working the line, coaching and grinning knowingly at the befuddled tourists. The few locals kept to themselves. He greedily ate his sandwich, marveling at the quality of the bread and the cured meats inside. The young woman nodded at him as she gathered up a tray from the next table. She wore a white butcher's style jacket to keep her clothes clean. Drew noticed her slim body and very tight jeans. She was slender, but did not have the overly athletic or diet-induced figure of an American woman. She was a product of a quality over quantity European diet. Her active lifestyle and the absence of giant supermarkets peddling an endless array of cheap processed food, all contributed to her shapely, natural appearance.

Drew, somewhat rejuvenated by the meal, made his way back to the Hotel Fenix. The head desk clerk was more accommodating the second time around and Drew entered a simple but nice room ten minutes later. His first day in Europe was far less glamorous than he expected. The tiresome logistics of intercontinental travel left Drew weary and yearning for the familiar.

He slept for six hours before dragging himself from the comfortable bed to the small but highly acclaimed restaurant below the main lobby. He was seated at a small table near the door. A starched and stiff waiter addressed him with marked formality usually reserved for expensive restaurants in America. In many countries in Europe the age-old profession of server was still a respected trade. It was a serious art, with a clear distinction between the Maitre'D who took the order and the waiter who served the food. The bus boy watched beverage levels and cleared the table. They wore different colored jackets to separate each occupation.

Drew found the hierarchy amusing and a bit intimidating. The small

Portuguese staff spoke multiple languages with ease and confidence. They treated Drew carefully, aware of his obvious discomfort and unsophisticated ordering technique. To them, Drew was another young American traveler whose lack of social graces and posture made them wonder about America's alleged superiority. He quickly ate a mediocre Portuguese pasta dish that was simply on the menu for travelers who were unfamiliar with the local cuisine or unwillingly to try something new. Drew watched the confident couple next to him and felt foolish. Their plates were teaming with a Portuguese staple, codfish. The wafting smell of roasted potatoes, chicken, and onions cooked in oil overwhelmed his senses. Drew would have settled for the fresh bread, local cheese, and salad that rounded out his neighbor's delectable meal. The happy couple touched glasses and finished off a bottle of Portuguese white wine, before ordering a bottle of red to end their evening. Drew quietly retired to his room without a customary cup of coffee or dessert, understanding little of Portugal's charm that would soon overwhelm him.

The next morning was blissful compared to the hassles of the previous night. He stared at the traffic below, his soundproof window helped keep the obnoxious horn blasts to a tolerable level. The citizens of Lisbon were going about their business unaware that he was watching them with the curiosity of an explorer. The madness of the colossal rotary made him laugh out loud. They were as crazy as the notorious Boston drivers.

He ate breakfast in his room, enjoying cornflakes, a buttered roll, juice, and hot coffee. It was simple and nourishing. After finishing the strong coffee, he sat on the edge of the bed and felt much better about his coming journey. The fatigue and loneliness that had plagued his first day in Lisbon was gone, replaced by a renewed sense of confidence and purpose.

After a second cup of coffee he shaved his two-day stubble and dressed. He wore a simple white button-down shirt with long sleeves that could be rolled up and fastened into a short-sleeve shirt. It was well-worn with double pockets on the front. His baggy shorts with large pockets and hardy loafers rounded out his attire. He packed a small backpack with a map, camera, two bottles of water, peanut butter crackers, and the manila envelope from Sheldon Harrison. He left his suitcase on the dresser; he planned to return to the Fenix after his short excursion to Sintra.

With a smile and a nod to the pleasant doorman, Drew set out for the train station that would take him to the mountainous town of Sintra. He knew from talking to the clerk in the lobby that the best way to the train station was to cross underneath the rotary and ride the subway to the train station. Drew was not intimidated by the thought of taking public transportation in a foreign country. He was used to riding America's oldest and sometimes inefficient subway system. He figured that if he could survive the Green Line trolley cars from Back Bay to Boston University he could handle anything. He was right; the short ride on the crowded subway was short and uneventful.

Drew wandered around the bustling train station, amazed at the controlled chaos all around him. It was the obvious mode of transportation many Europeans selected either to visit Lisbon or pass through to the Algarve, Portugal's trendy seaside resort area. It was much cleaner and attractive than most train stations he had seen in America. There was a mix of students, families, and commuters, all hustling for a train or waiting patiently. The students seemed to have no place to go, sitting casually on their tattered bags smoking cigarettes. Sometimes one group would merge with another, flirting and comparing notes on their travels. It was a kind of freedom American children did not experience. They could spend an entire summer hopping from one student hostel to the next, visiting the Louvre and the Sistine Chapel in consecutive days. Drew felt a pang of jealousy as he observed their carefree attitude and worldly discussions. How could America's youth compete with them? They were sophisticated and unafraid to travel alone long distances.

As the crowds parted and his view cleared, he noticed a seedy side of Lisbon's main terminus. There were many men milling about; they looked like they were homeless or at least destitute. His view of European life was naïve; he didn't expect a capital city as aesthetically pleasing as Lisbon to harbor so many without means. He had not seen much of the beauty of Lisbon and its environs, but he glimpsed enough of it in the preceding hours to know it was there.

The train stations in Europe are magnets for petty thieves and hustlers. They prey upon tourists, who seem to lose all sense of reality and self-preservation when they don their vacation garb. Drew was aware of the mild danger and watched his personal belongings closely. He watched a short and scruffy-looking local slither among the throngs of unsuspecting tourists. He studied his expressionless face as he surveyed a group of Japanese tourists. Drew's train arrived before he witnessed any crime.

The door of the train clanked shut and he felt relieved. The cool air inside the commuter style car felt good and he settled in for a short ride to his final destination. He looked out the cracked window and was disappointed by the scenery. The railroad tracks were flanked by grotesque urban planning style apartment buildings. It was a depressing sight. As Lisbon vanished in the distance, the stops became more pleasurable for Drew. The picturesque little towns that hugged the railway stations were quaint and inviting. Any disappointment he might have been feeling evaporated the moment the rumbling train entered Sintra. Drew anxiously stuffed his return ticket in his bag and hustled from the train.

Sintra was the last stop on the hour-long trek from Lisbon and the most awe-inspiring. Drew caught a glimpse of the Castelo dos Mauros on a lush mountain peak high above the town. The Castelo dos Mauros, (Moorish Castle), was an 8th Century mountain top citadel. Its military importance was obvious with its clear view of the valley and its approaches, leaving an attacking army with little chance of concealment. The steep climb to the commanding heights of the castle could be disastrous for an invading army short on spirit and commitment. Only the truly fanatical could take the redoubt. Christian Crusaders in 1147 possessed such religious zeal, recapturing the Castelo dos Mauros from the tenacious Moors. He felt like he had stepped into a storybook world of his imaginative youth. The tiny town was in the shadow of looming palaces and ruined castles. The densely foliated mountains were really large hills by American standards, comparable to the Blue Hills near Boston.

Drew exited the train station and smiled knowingly, the area was lined with small bars and gift shops. The ancient town was prepared for the thousands of tourists that came from Lisbon and points beyond. Sintra was a national treasure and it was treated as such. He detected more Americans than in Lisbon; they were assuredly up from the chic Algarve region. He mingled with other befuddled tourists as they tried to find the best way to the treasures above them.

Drew sat on a bench near the station and let the mid-morning sun warm him. He retrieved Harrison's letter from his backpack and reread his final instructions. He was to go to the Bank of Portugal a few blocks from the train station and open the safety deposit box with the key provided. He glanced at his map and set off.

With each step Drew felt a heaviness slowing his eager gait, for the first time since he began the journey from Boston, he was struck by a familiar sense of unease. He tried to rationalize his trepidation, but he was unable to quell the overall grim feeling that had similarly vexed him in the prior weeks. It had returned with renewed intensity. It reminded him, with impolite vigor, that he was not on holiday and the time and distance had only temporarily relieved him of the pounding sense of doom. He tried to convince himself that the information he was to obtain would be of dubious value, an unimportant footnote in the long annals of the author's great life.

Drew, suffering from a sudden anxiety attack, nervously navigated through the crowded street, stumbling on the uneven cobblestones and bumping into irritated tourists. He swore at himself for being so weak, he stuck his chin out and forced his way to the Bank of Portugal.

Chapter 12

Bank of Portugal

The Bank of Portugal was like everything else in Sintra, small and tidy. Drew hesitated at the shiny glass door; he saw movement inside and entered without further delay. A smiling customer service representative greeted him.

"Hello…I don't speak Portuguese, I'm sorry," Drew blurted, he felt stupid for not cramming more on the airplane.

"That's okay I speak English sir. My name is Marie Almeida. How can I help you?"

"That's great, Marie." Drew felt at ease.

"How can we help you?"

"I need to retrieve something from this safety deposit box." He let her see the numbered key.

"We require two keys for a withdrawal or inspection." She was puzzled by the request. It was very rare that an American possessed a safety deposit box in such a small town like Sintra.

"I was told this was all I needed." Drew felt flush and sheepishly searched for another key he did not possess. It was a vain attempt to cover his embarrassment.

"Excuse me for a moment. I will discuss this with my manager." She smiled and gracefully entered a side door away from the bank tellers. Drew sighed and the uneasiness returned. He watched a group of excited tourists at the currency exchange window. He envied their freedom; they were moments away from visiting the fairytale castles high above the town center. Drew felt silly for fretting over a task that would be over in a few minutes and like them, would be free to explore at a leisurely pace. If the journey ended at that moment without any spectacular revelation he would still have a good story for his grandchildren.

"Sir." Marie Almeida returned with haste in her step. "This is a special account. The bank manager will help you. We are also waiting for a third party. He is an American lawyer who lives nearby." Her jovial smile was replaced by a serious expression; she was a professional handling something quite out of the ordinary.

"Alright. Okay." Drew clasped his hands together.

After a few moments of awkward silence, a rather rotund middle-aged man emerged from the same door as his assistant. Drew noticed his glistening forehead from ten feet away.

"Hello, Sir. My name is Joseph Silva. I am the branch manager." Drew was impressed with his English and firm handshake. He politely beckoned him to sit down.

"I'm sure my assistant Marie, has informed you of the third party."

"Yes, she mentioned it."

"Yes, we were instructed to contact Andrew Garrity when the holder of the second key arrived."

Drew tightened his grip on the small unremarkable key, "I really don't understand this whole thing. I'm really confused." He sighed and wished he could hand it to the pleasant banker. The older man eyed the young American until Drew noticed and made firm eye contact. Mr. Silva also found the matter strange and a bit alarming. He remembered the day one year before when the safety deposit box was opened and the instructions drawn up. He was told to wait for a second key.

In an attempt to ease the tension, Mr. Silva engaged Drew in a conversation about his frequent trips to Walt Disney World. He was addicted to the charms of the happiest place on Earth. His assistant, Marie Almeida, could not help but smile at her affable manager. Mr. Silva knew Drew was not enjoying the conversation and listened only out of politeness. The banker thought of his own children reacting to such a boring middle-aged man. They thought their father was long-winded and somewhat stodgy. He found the youth of his country sullen and uncommunicative. He blamed all the high-tech gadgets like video games and CD players for their lack of social skills his generation was forced to learn.

"So where are you from? I'm sorry what is your name?"

"My name is Drew Engle. I'm from Boston."

"Boston…" Mr. Silva stopped and watched Andrew Garrity stroll into the bank.

Garrity's athletic build and confident manner immediately made an impact on Engle. His radiant, auburn hair was carefully parted to one side.

Drew noticed it was still wet and wondered if they had interrupted him. He wore a white cotton shirt, beige shorts, and leather loafers with no socks. His arms were heavily freckled and taut from exercise. He smiled broadly as he approached the group, his straight white teeth gleaming. Mr. Silva rose quickly to greet his charismatic friend.

"Drew Engle, this is Attorney Andrew Garrity." Mr. Silva formally introduced Garrity. He seemed eager to please the American.

"Hello, Mr. Engle. Very pleased to make your acquaintance." He looked Drew in the eyes and shook his hand. He never lifted his gaze; he wanted to see inside the young man. His deep blue eyes were so luminous and clear Drew thought they might be contact lenses.

"Mr. Garrity, what is all this about?" Drew sat down and waited for his response. Garrity paused before speaking.

"Okay, Mr. Engle we have an unorthodox arrangement we must discuss before you're allowed access to the safety deposit box."

"I was unaware of any such conditions." Drew straightened and looked around suspiciously.

"There are conditions, Mr. Engle," Garrity answered with a hint of firmness in his voice.

"What are they?" Drew noticed Mr. Silva squirming in his seat; he was unaccustomed to such cryptic and extraordinary meetings.

"Please…bear with me. I would like to talk to you and briefly explain the legal documents you must sign. Will you take a short walk with me?" His gregarious smile and appealing offer made the decision an easy one.

"Mr. Silva, my friend, we will return before you leave for the day. Although with such a lovely wife as yours at home I think I would leave early." He winked at the blushing banker. It was safe to assume Mr. Silva would not leave the bank until they returned.

The strange duo walked side by side down a cobbled street. Garrity, using subtle movement, edged Drew in the direction of his desire.

"Wonderful place isn't it? Have you been up to the Moorish Castle?"

"No, I just arrived from Lisbon. I went straight to the bank."

"Good…I like that. No nonsense." He patted the younger man on the shoulder and pointed to an outdoor café.

"Want some lunch? Drew, right? My treat of course."

"Sure."

Drew thought the accommodations were sparse compared to what he was accustomed to back home. The furniture was plastic lawn furniture neatly arranged on the clean sidewalk.

"What do you want, Drew?" Garrity started for the counter inside.

"Whatever you get is fine."

"Okay." Garrity walked to the side of the large line and nodded his head to an older man working the counter. The man nodded and pulled two hulking sandwiches from the glass display case. Garrity slipped him some money and winked a thank you.

"These are the best in Sintra." He handed Drew his sandwich and an orange soda made in Portugal. Garrity wasted little time devouring the meal; he seemed to enjoy life on all levels. A simple meal with a new friend under the watchful eye of the ancient edifices high above filled the American attorney with immeasurable joy.

"I bet you're wondering what I'm doing here?" He astutely read Drew's mind.

"Yes I was, Mr. Garrity."

"Call me Andrew."

"Okay."

"Drew, let me ask you this? Would you leave all of this beauty and serenity if you had the means to stay?"

"I don't know. I just arrived. It seems beautiful."

"If you don't say yes without hesitation then your answer would be no. My answer was a resounding yes!" He laughed and took a drink.

"When did you come here?"

"Two years ago. Unfortunately it's the same old tired story."

"What's the story?" Drew liked the sound of his voice. It was reassuring, something like the way his father spoke to him.

"Simple. I was just another overly aggressive lawyer from Manhattan. You know the type, work from seven in the morning until ten at night. I was an attorney who cared little about my clients. The only thing that mattered was billable hours. I came here two years ago on a family vacation. We were staying at a beautiful resort in the Algarve when my wife decided that we needed a little culture. You know, for dinner party conversations with our friends. So we arrived in this beautiful town like the brash and arrogant Americans we were. We bothered everybody and contributed nothing. A month after we returned to New York I filed for divorce and moved here. Just packed up and left. My wife didn't see things as I did. She didn't feel the attachment to the place like I did. It wasn't the only reason we split up, but I guess it was the opening I was looking for. I have two children who spend the summers with me. They just left last week. They love it here and I think it has made the separation easier." When he spoke of his children his voice filled with emotion. His strong and confident exterior suddenly seemed less impenetrable. The loss of his children was the only part of his escape he regretted. His bitter ex-wife received a hefty settlement and a substantial yearly income.

"It must be tough to be away from your kids."

"So, my boy, enough about my mid-life crisis," he pushed his half-eaten sandwich aside, "let me shed some light on the mystery at hand. One year ago, Sheldon Harrison had me draft some documents pertaining to the safety deposit box and the key you now possess. Before you ask, I do not know what is inside and will not know until you reveal it. Sheldon was a friend of mine for many years. When I found out he was ill I insisted he visit me. I felt Sintra could lift the spirits of even the most downtrodden. Before he left he asked me to handle the affair we are discussing today. He said he would give the second key away and that person would have the legal rights to the contents. He did not divulge who or when that person would get the key."

"What are the documents?" Drew felt a strange sense of calm.

"The documents you have to sign prohibit you from revealing the contents of the safety deposit box for six months. The period of nondisclosure starts the moment you open the box and retrieve the contents."

"Why?"

"I don't know that either," Garrity answered honestly.

"This is weird. I really didn't know Mr. Harrison. I was a summer intern."

"As was I, many moons ago." Garrity leaned back in his chair and examined Drew. He was trying to get a clear picture of this special young man.

"Why me? Carlton Smithfield was with me. Why didn't he ask Carlton?"

"Again, Drew, I don't know the answer. I can tell you one thing. This whole thing is in character with Sheldon Harrison. He was my friend, but I always felt I could only get so close to him. He let you into his world, but only on his terms."

"Six months? Why six months?"

"Drew, I wish I knew." Garrity sighed and tapped his fingers on the table.

"When do I sign the papers?" Drew's nervousness about signing legal documents was obvious to Garrity.

"Don't worry about it, Drew. The language of the documents is straightforward with a limited amount of legal bullshit. It simply states that you will under no circumstances reveal the contents of the box for six months. That's it."

"Why do I have to sign anything when I have the key? I should be able to just open it and take what I want without signing anything."

"In order for the bank to give you permission to open the safe I have to sign something that says it's okay. It was all part of Sheldon's plan."

"I see. Okay, how soon can I get this done?"

"After I sign the consent form and present it to the Bank of Portugal, you can finally remove the contents."

"He thought of everything."

"Not really, it's a pretty basic document, just not typical."

"Is it binding?"

"Yes it is."

"In America?"

"Yes."

Garrity smiled in a paternal way, he could feel Drew's anxiety from across the table. After, he finished his drink and motioned for Drew to follow him.

"There is a small issue I didn't mention."

Drew raised an eyebrow and assumed the catch was at hand.

"Sheldon made it very clear where he wanted the contents of the safety deposit box to be examined."

"Where?"

"Up there," Garrity stopped and pointed at the Moorish Castle.

"The Moorish Castle?"

"Yes."

"Why?"

"I don't know."

"This gets better by the minute." Drew sighed and dodged the feverish tourists.

"The Moorish Castle was built by the invading Moors in the 8th Century. The Christian Crusaders took it back for good in the 11th Century. That was it for the Muslims."

"I know, I read the guide book." Drew smiled mischievously.

"Drew, I just want to let you know," Garrity turned to Drew, "you are under no legal or moral obligation, none at all, to follow the wishes of Sheldon Harrison. Leave it alone if you are not sure about it."

"I know that…let's just get it over with." Drew shuffled his feet nervously and waited for Garrity's response.

"Okay, Drew. I feel the same way." Garrity suddenly wanted the whole affair concluded. Something about the arrangement and the cryptic instructions disturbed him.

The walk back to the Bank of Portugal was much different from their leisurely stroll to lunch. The silence was unnerving for young Engle; his upbeat host was now sullen and distracted. Garrity's serious demeanor and hurried step made for an uncomfortable precursor to the main event. Drew's bravado exhibited at lunch vanished as he contemplated the ramifications of the task ahead. He was a scared kid caught up in something that could alter his life. He did not ask for it, but he would not cower from the obligation.

They entered the Bank of Portugal with the rush of the determined. Drew noticed Mr. Silva and Marie Almeida whispering off to the side of the tellers. They stopped upon the abrupt arrival of the Americans. Marie smiled sweetly and asked them if they had enjoyed their lunch. Drew nodded yes; the attractive young woman intimidated him. He hadn't really noticed her subtle beauty and intelligent eyes when they first met. Drew looked for a wedding ring on her slender fingers. His searching gaze remained there too long; she caught his eye and flushed knowingly.

"Mr. Silva, shall we get down to business?" Garrity handed the diminutive banker a second key for the safety deposit box. After retrieving Drew's key he excused himself to retrieve the guard key held by the bank. During his brief absence, Marie Almeida and Garrity made small talk. It was apparent they knew each other well; their banter was casual, bordering on intimate.

"Mr. Garrity, I need you for a moment." Mr. Silva politely interrupted upon his hurried return.

"Okay, be back in a minute Drew."

The young banker and the nervous American silently waited for their elders to return. Ms. Almeida finally engaged Drew.

"So, Drew, are you staying in Sintra?"

"I don't know. I have a hotel room in Lisbon."

"I live in Lisbon also."

"Do you travel back and forth every day?"

"No I have a small room in Sintra. I stay in town three or four nights a week." She smiled and wondered why this young American was so important to the great Sheldon Harrison.

"Were you born in Lisbon?"

"No, I am from the Azores."

"Most of the Portuguese I know back home are from the Azores."

She smiled and told him of all her relatives in the Boston area. The Azores, a small island chain nine hundred miles from mainland Portugal deposited tens of thousands of immigrants to Fall River, New Bedford, and Cambridge, Massachusetts.

"Are you a student, Drew?"

"Yes, at Boston University."

"I went to the Sorbonne in Paris."

"Wow." He hesitated, unsure how to broach the subject of her ending up in Sintra. Seldom do Sorbonne graduates end up in Sintra, an old world village of considerable charm and beauty, yet far from the cosmopolitan life of Lisbon.

"You are wondering how I ended up in Sintra?" She was delighted by his expressive body language, finding it easy to read his mind.

"I was."

"I want to be an executive with the Bank of Portugal and it's mandatory to spend time at a small branch to learn. We do things at this bank that the officers in Lisbon would laugh at. But the top officials want you to have the experience before moving up."

"That's refreshing."

"I will be here for another year."

"Your English is remarkable." He was thoroughly impressed with her flawless command of his language. The pronunciation and range of her vocabulary was a testament to Portugal's bilingual education.

"We are taught English at a very young age. I also took intensive English mastery courses at the Sorbonne. I spent a semester in England and a summer in America."

Drew was about to respond when Garrity and Mr. Silva returned. He swallowed hard and thought the manila envelope Garrity held was the contents of Harrison's safety deposit box. He had momentarily forgotten the steps Garrity had outlined at lunch. He regained his senses and focused on Garrity who gingerly opened the sealed envelope and removed a legal document. He handed it to Drew and waited patiently.

The brief and clear document was exactly how Garrity described. He let Drew read the document and then filled in Drew's full name. Mr. Silva notarized the document and was a legal witness. Drew reread the succinct directions and legal obligations three times before signing and handing it to Garrity. The tension was broken, they all felt a sense of relief that the deed was done. The last wish of Sheldon Harrison had weighed heavily upon the mind of Garrity.

"Okay." Drew exhaled and signed the appropriate spot.

"Great," Garrity scooped up the papers, "I am now authorized and obligated to give you this key. The key you brought was just a key to let us know you were the right…" he searched for the right word, "courier, for the lack of a better term. It was installed as safeguard to prevent an unwitting bank employee from giving the contents away without the proper legal authorization."

Joseph Silva bristled at the mild slight; his employees would never be so careless. He was insulted by the lack of confidence in his staff, but could understand the cautious approach. Marie smiled knowingly, appreciative of his unfailing loyalty to her and her coworkers. He was a good man who cared about his job more than any other bank executive she had encountered during her service with the Bank of Portugal. Silva was a sophisticated gentleman raised in Lisbon.

"That was Sheldon Harrison's paranoia at work. It is not an indictment of this Bank." Garrity smiled at his friend and patted him on the hand.

"That's it I guess." Drew tried to smile.

"Here you go, Drew." Garrity retrieved a small key from the crisp manila envelope. He ceremoniously handed the key to Drew, beaming with the satisfaction that his client's wishes were followed to the letter.

"All for this." Drew stared at the unremarkable key in his sweating palm. Mr. Silva and Marie Almeida were transfixed by the moment, staring at Drew as he nervously caressed the literal key to the mystery.

"There is no time constraint, Drew. You don't have to get it today." Garrity had noticed the look of bewilderment on the young man's face.

"No…no I would like to get it today." He stood up and waited for Mr. Silva to escort him to the safety deposit vault. Silva was surprised by quick response and jumped from his seat.

"This way please, Mr. Engle."

The myriad of security devices was impressive; Drew simply followed the experienced banker through the maze of steel doors until they reached the appropriate vault. The short walk from the office to the vault calmed his nerves; he was ready for the truth.

"Please, excuse me." Mr. Silva closed the titanium mesh door behind them as they entered the vault housing hundreds of safety deposit boxes.

"The box is on this side," Mr. Silva pointed to the left wall, "please follow the numbers."

"Okay," Drew cleared his throat, "thank you." He followed the long row until he reached 98, the number on the key. He carefully placed the key into the lock and felt a hard click as the bolts retracted. With care he opened the moderately heavy door and pulled out a voluminous tray. A similar manila envelope to the one Garrity retrieved from his box sat at the bottom of the tray. Drew felt the package as if it contained a bomb. It was soft and felt like it was filled with papers. He shut the box, put the envelope under his arm and joined Mr. Silva near the door.

"That's it? Are you sure that was the only article?" Mr. Silva said with ease, it was his standard line for anybody who emptied a box. He stared at the package for a moment too long; his curiosity had pushed aside his impeccable discretion.

"That's it," Drew mumbled and followed the stiff banker back to his office. He handed Mr. Silva the key and signed a paper ending access to the box.

"Did you find what you came for?" Garrity rose to his feet and held his hand out for Drew to shake. He obliged Garrity and headed for the front door.

"I will help you get a taxi." Marie grabbed his free arm and led him through the busy bank.

"I want to go to the top." Drew mumbled.

"Okay."

With grace and pity Marie escorted the weary young man to a nearby taxi stand. She leaned inside the taxi and quietly directed the driver in Portuguese. The driver smiled and winked at Ms. Almeida. She turned away in disgust. Drew figured he had responded in an ungentlemanly way.

"Drew, why don't you see me before you leave. Are you staying the night?" Marie asked him from the curb.

"I don't know. I didn't think about it." He climbed into the back of the oddly out-of- place Mercedes Benz cab and immediately felt hot.

"I am working late tonight. Come and see me if you are staying in Sintra." She waved goodbye.

Drew watched listlessly as the figure of Marie Almeida grew small. They followed a twisting cobblestone road to the top of the Sintra Mountains. The sometimes-treacherous road only allowed for one vehicle to pass at certain hairpinned turns. Drew shifted uneasily as the calm driver stopped the taxi as they approached a particularly frightening bend in the road. He beeped the horn and impatiently waited for a response. After only a few seconds of silence, he hit the accelerator and they careened around the corner, the engine screaming, gears grinding horribly. The experienced driver stopped at every corner and repeated the safety procedure; his often-used horn wailing for mercy.

On the short trek up the relatively forgiving mountain, Drew caught a glimpse of the countryside above and below the peaks of Sintra. The lush vegetation on all sides cut the sun out at various points. Drew wiped his brow and tried to keep the precious package free of his body fluids. The gruff driver swore at a passing vehicle that came within inches of sending the converted luxury car down the green slopes to the town center below. The culprits were most assuredly tourists with little experience descending the steep mountain. Many signs with names like Palacio de Pena and Palacio Nacional flashed past as they followed clearly marked signs for the Castelo dos Mouros. The driver quickly downshifted, straining the high-performance engine. He lacked appreciation for its superb engineering.

Drew felt queasy as they neared the drop-off point. Automobiles could not go beyond the designated assembly area that was within walking distance of both the Palacio De Pena and the Castelo dos Mouros. Drew tried to pay the driver but he tore away before he could hand him the money. He reasoned Marie had told him the bank would pay for the ride.

The drop-off point was congested with tour buses and taxis. The momentary respite gave Drew a moment to gather his thoughts before resuming his strange odyssey. He laughed at the excited faces of the tourists who were moments away from the castles and palaces they had read about in their tour books. Their eagerness drove them up the narrow but easily scaled pathways that led to the treasures. Drew felt the coolness of the shaded path, admiring the rich vegetation that made him think of a tropical forest. He noticed others around him spoke softly; their reverence for the unknown impressed him.

As he approached the environs of the Castelo dos Mouros he understood why the English Poet Lord Byron referred to Sintra as the glorious Eden. It was in fact the Eden of Drew's youth, the physical representation of his daydreaming mind. A thin breeze seeped through the overlapping undergrowth, protecting and shading the visitors.

"Beautiful," Drew whispered aloud. The dull sound of a distant flute caught his ear. He approached the ruins of the Moorish Castle and saw the musician. The flutist glanced at Drew and nodded, his expert fingers never wavering as inspiration turned to application. His soulful playing added to the surreal atmosphere that even the most experienced European traveler would have to concede was unique.

The inside of the Moorish Castle was nothing more than exterior walls in varying stages of disrepair. It was not a well-preserved edifice like the much newer Pena Palace on an adjacent peak.

The ruins of the once proud castle were strewn across two mountaintops, the center of the enormous defensive redoubt had no roof or distinguishable rooms. Drew climbed to the top of a sturdy wall and was shaken by the panoramic view. The true height of the mountain revealed itself for the first time. The drop to the valley below was intimidating. His astonished gaze fell upon the blue expanse in the distance. The Atlantic Ocean lay before his exalted eyes. The unforgiving ocean of his terrified ancestors now separated him from his world. He wondered what his family was doing. He steadied himself atop a watchtower that was strategically positioned on the massive walls. He marveled at the red-roofed homes below, they appeared to be clinging protectively to the steep slopes of the once critical military installation.

Impatient tourists trying to push past him interrupted his blissful moment of discovery. Their unbridled eagerness to explore the castle nearly sent Drew tumbling to his death. He wisely headed for the next tower. The walls of the fort snaked from one peak to another. It was an impressive model of engineering over difficult terrain. During his walk to the highest peak he opened the large manila envelope from Harrison. There were two separate articles neatly arranged inside. He grabbed a simple sheet of copy paper with writing on it.

> *To Whom It May Concern:*
> *Please read this on the highest turret on the Moorish Castle wall. It is not necessary, but I implore you to read my confession as directed.*
> *Thank You.*
Sheldon Harrison.

Chapter 13

The Hidden Tolstoy: Sheldon Harrison's Confession

Drew scaled the wall with renewed vigor, passing many slower tourists who were wearing down and turning back. Twenty minutes after he descended and then ascended the spine of the wall he stopped at the uppermost turret. The dominant view was awe-inspiring and somewhat unnerving. It was a grueling climb, the only relief coming from the stiff breeze. Large villas dotted the hillsides below and on distant slopes, obviously the homes of the wealthy.

"Finally," Drew mumbled to himself and nodded to another exhausted traveler who left when he arrived. The imposing and elegant Pena Palace was clearly visible, commanding respect from its higher perch, mocking the older ruins for its brutish appearance.

A long bench inside the perimeter of the turret became Drew's temporary refuge. He sat heavily on the uneven bench, drank a bottle of water and prepared himself. He slowly opened the second envelope. He extracted the document and read the handwritten title page.

The Hidden Tolstoy: Sheldon Harrison's Confession

By Sheldon Harrison

Drew was impressed by the gorgeous handwriting. It was legible and elegant, clearly from the hand of someone who wrote many letters. He took a deep breath before settling in for the most important half hour of his life.

"This letter is for the person I have chosen to be my confessional mouthpiece. My name is Sheldon Harrison. I am the author of 'A Troubled Life,' 'A Life Without Beatrice,' 'The Rolling Willow,' and 'My Burden,' etc.... Please excuse any grammatical and/or spelling errors in this confession. I am very ill. I have cancer of the lungs and will not see another winter. I am hindered by streaks of pain that accompany my every breath. My chest aches along with my heart. I may ramble at times, please do not lose patience before reading the entire document. I will not reveal the reason for this letter until the end. I beg of you not to skip ahead until you have read my story.

"My full name is Sheldon William Harrison. I was born in Brookline, Massachusetts at the end of the Roaring Twenties and came of age during The Great Depression. My father was an influential judge and a respected society man. My world would change forever, like so many others, after the Japanese attacked the fleet at Pearl Harbor. I was a good student who attended excellent private schools until my acceptance to Harvard University. It was a very special time for my family, a dream come true for the youngest of three to attend the most prestigious University in America. My freshman year was interrupted by America's involvement in the most devastating conflict in human history. Nothing would ever be the same.

"My participation in the Second World War was not immediate. I dodged the draft for a year and half under a special education deferment that allowed many of us to stay in college while others fought and died in the Jungles of Guadalcanal, the deserts of North Africa, over the skies of Germany and the shores of Italy. Our nice little ride ended with the invasion of Normandy. The Army needed bodies so desperately all programs were cancelled and I was sent to Officers Candidate School. I became a ninety-day wonder, a derogatory reference to the hurried training we received. I was not prepared for the savage bloodletting that covered all of Europe and most of Asia.

"I shipped out as a replacement 2nd Lieutenant, arriving at the still ravaged Normandy coastline near the end of 1944. I joined the 99th Division in a desolate stretch of snow-covered mountains in Belgium. The 99th Division was an untested infantry division relegated to what the Army Brass believed to be a quiet section of The Ardennes Forest. The Ardennes is a thickly wooded mountainous region that was considered too difficult for the German Army to attack. It was considered a safe place to acclimate troops. It was the invasion route of the Germans during the First World War and again during the opening weeks of the Battle for France in the Second World

War. So it should not have been a surprise that the Germans would again trudge through the mountain roads to the Allies' doorstep.

"I reached my unit on December14th, 1944. I was an inexperienced soldier, pampered perhaps, a complete failure when it came to leading men. That is what they were: twenty-year-old men who were farmers and mechanics back home, far below my level of education and possessing no cultural awareness. Yet they were the ones pounding the Germans into the ground so I could enjoy the life of freedom and opportunity my family took for granted. They were a strange breed of warriors who looked at me with disgust and maybe some pity. Army officers assigned to a front line combat division in Europe did not last long.

"I will not bore you with tedious details of Army life, a life I was ill-equipped to endure. The deplorable condition of the countless towns and villages we passed through in France and Belgium was humbling. So many young Americans sacrificed to hammer the beleaguered Germany Army to the Deutschland. So many civilians obliterated by the incessant shelling of both armies.

"My first encounter with my platoon was brief and forgettable. I never learned any of their names. I made only one lifelong contact. I contributed nothing to America's liberation of Western Europe. I would never lead them; a few might not have known I had replaced their beloved Lieutenant who was killed a day before by a random German shell. It was a rare occurrence in this section of the front where the 99th was stationed, probably a German gunner ranging his weapon before the secret offensive. I could never replace him; I was a ninety-day wonder with limited training and no desire to fight for his country. I knew the moment I crawled into my frozen command bunker on December 15th 1944 I would not last forty-eight hours in combat.

"It was during my second day in the rather sturdy log-covered foxhole that I met Private First Class Sandy Wilson. He was a scared draftee from my home state of Massachusetts. He came from a tough Boston neighborhood called Jamaica Plain, but he didn't fit the mold of the typical urban miscreant of the time. His shy looks; pale skin and bookish appearance made him an unlikely looking combat soldier. He was simply a product of a country fighting a multi-theater war where manpower was at a premium. They were shipping untrained recruits to fill the losses all across Europe. These unfortunate souls, like myself, were dropped into already-formed units and were treated as fodder. We were friendless outsiders everybody stayed clear of. If you lived long enough to become a veteran, you would, in turn, practice the same form of heartless scorn. Ostracized and ignored, many replacements were alone and unknown at the hour of their death. In a kill zone of such savage barbarity where random death was commonplace and on some level accepted, the replacement soldier felt like the loneliest non-person on earth. Nobody cared about us.

"My body aches from this infernal disease! The effects are quite remarkable. The surging pain can leave you breathless and wishing for death. Periods of functional pain and dulled senses can leave you with the childish hope for better days. I am off on a tangent, please forgive me.

"I spent little time learning my new job or preparing to lead men into battle. I was prepared to leave my unit at first chance, to use the connections I had to get transferred to a safer post in England or at least France. Huddled in my command bunker I let the veteran non-commissioned officers run the show. Their contempt was obvious; they knew I would not last. As I brooded and tried to keep warm, my turbulent, sometimes ultimately fruitful relationship with PFC Sandy Wilson began. I will try to recreate some of the dialogue.

'Sir...have you been on the line long?'

'No...I came in on the same truck as you.' I was astonished he had not recognized me. We had sat near each other on the bumpy ride.

'Oh yes sir. You're from Massachusetts.' He spoke without the typical Boston accent that would have marked him as undereducated.

'Yes I am, Private.' I was uninterested until I saw his intelligent brown eyes peaking out from underneath his steel helmet.

'I am too. From Jamaica Plain.'

'Tough place.'

'No, sir, not my street.'

'What are you doing here?'

'I was drafted, sir. I have no skills or college education. They wanted me to work for Stars and Stripes because of my writing skills.'

The look on my face must have told him everything. He blushed and nervously fingered his too heavy M-1 Garand Rifle. A brutal implement of war I was frightened to fire.

'You write?' I asked incredulously, I was a budding writer with the education, the credentials, and connections to make a hard run as THE Boston writer of the post-war era. This is what I foolishly believed, nobody who read my work showed that much confidence or encouragement.

'No, not really. I just like to write stories to stave off the boredom. When I was young I was sickly, I spent a lot of time in bed. It was my only amusement.'

'Interesting.'

'Not really, sir.'

'How old are you?'

'Eighteen, sir.'

"I asked him many questions that short day in Belgium. We discussed our favorite contemporary writers and the merits of writers from Shakespeare to Tolstoy. His knowledge was vast, his opinions thoughtful, bordering on brilliant. I was intimidated and depressed by this unlikely savant. What took me years of education and forced study this unremarkable Private First Class knew intuitively, without the help of tutors and professors. I was enthralled by our conversation, the beauty of art and literature brought to windswept, snow-covered woods of wartime Belgium gave us a momentary respite from the reality of our situation. The others in our frozen hole looked at us with condescension and animosity. We were untested and new, we should have been learning how to stay alive, not talking about the Russian writers we considered the most influential.

"Wilson's sheepish mannerisms disguised a deep intellect, albeit unrefined and sometimes hidden behind a veil of insecurity. He was what I was not, a potentially serious player in post-war American literature. I, of course, did not find this out until much later.

"Our discussion ended only when exhaustion took over, we promised to continue the next day. He was the new radio operator so we would be close together at all times. The previous radio operator left earlier in the day with a severe case of frostbite, to Sandy's delight he traded in his heavy Garand rifle for the much lighter M-1 Carbine.

"We spent the night huddled around a concealed fire bemoaning our misfortune. I did most of the complaining, he would silently listen to my incessant moaning and smile knowingly. I noticed the glares of the others in our command post; they knew I was going to lead them to their death if given the chance. I was not fit to lead men and they knew it. They must have been nauseated by my pompous recollections and smarmy misinterpretations of the literary greats. Sandy Wilson was careful not to indulge me too much, he must have realized I was either going to be killed or transferred the moment the front became active. He wanted to make sure he had allies left that would teach him how to survive. I was a pleasant divergent, but I would not help him get home.

"Sergeant Charles 'Chuck' Connors was the top noncommissioned officer in the platoon and second in command. He was a veteran from the 24th Infantry Division. He landed three days after the invasion of Normandy. He fought tenacious German resistance in the horrific killing fields of Normandy. The German Army with frightening expertise used the high hedgerows that divided the farms, to stall the budding American juggernaut to a crawl.

"Shortly after recovering from a nasty head wound from an exploding mortar round, he was transferred to the inexperienced 99th Division. You can imagine what he thought of me. He barely listened when I spoke and I had the sneaking suspicion he never followed the few orders I gave him.

"Chuck Connors was a tough Irish kid from New York who was the sort of soldier that we were lucky to have on our side. I was with him only briefly, but from what I could surmise he was the type of American soldier that was winning the war. Tough and resourceful; two qualities I was completely devoid of.

"During the night of December 16th, German forces participating in Hitler's last attempt at victory attacked us. The Ardennes Offensive (Battle of the Bulge) came right through our section of the line. We were overwhelmed and pummeled by German forces attacking us like ghosts; their lily-white uniforms briefly illuminated by the devastating artillery fire that made me cower in my hole. I cried and begged for it to stop. My pitiful pleas thankfully went unheard; the din of the constant shelling blocked my ramblings.

'Sir, we need to move!' Sergeant Connors finally screamed in my ear.

'Okay, Sergeant.' It was the bravest thing I said that day.

"We moved a few hundred yards down the nearest road with the stragglers from my platoon along with others from similarly displaced units. We retreated on the icy roads all night until we were overtaken and captured by German infantry supporting a nearby Armored Division. I was frightened beyond words as the rough-looking German Waffen SS Troopers stripped us of our weapons, all of our gear, wallets, and wristwatches. I was cold and startled by the contempt the Germans displayed. We were treated like useless cowards, surrendering was not part of the creed of the average SS soldier. The opening push of The Battle of the Bulge had netted many thousands of American prisoners. We were a tiny group of disheveled soldiers impeding their progress. Soon they tired of tormenting us so they decided to murder us. We were marched to a small snow-covered field that was dotted with blasted earth from errant mortar shells. I was scared and could not hide the fact I was not ready to die. I tried in vain to talk to the SS Officer who was leading the group of would-be assassins. They did not appear hesitant or reluctant. They must have come from the Eastern Front where mass slaughters were common. He laughed at my pathetic German and shoved me hard in the shoulder. Sergeant Connors shot me a glance that said I will kill you if they don't. He understood enough German to understand I was pleading for my life. He was disgusted and defiant. He glared at his German captors who roughly forced him to the open field. The deep snow slowed the death march. Later the world would hear of many similar acts of atrocity by the advancing German Army.

'Keep it together, Lieutenant,' Sergeant Connors snarled at me.

'Okay…yes, Sergeant.' I managed a meek reply. I was only seconds away *from dropping to my knees and begging for my life. There seemed to be about fifteen or twenty of us trudging through the deep snowdrifts of the Belgium countryside. The large German Lieutenant tired of the walk and decided to kill us right there. We were far enough from the road that our bodies might not be found until the spring thaw and if all went well, discovered by German soldiers. He shouted for us to stop.*

'Shit... run,' Sergeant Connors screamed and pulled PFC Sandy Wilson with him. I followed the veteran who headed for the closest wooded area. The mad dash was on. The proud soldiers of United States Army bolted like frightened dogs in every direction, stumbling about as a hail of gunfire erupted. The cacophony was deafening. Bullets of all sizes zipped passed our heads. I will never forget the chaos. We were lucky for the moment. They fired everything they had in our direction and then concentrated on the stragglers who were struggling in the snow. I glanced back and saw many dead only meters from where they started. I did not look back again until I reached the edge of the woods; life was ahead in those tall pine trees. The German fire grew in intensity as they turned their attention back to us. They wanted to eliminate all survivors who may be witnesses down the road. With every hard step we took the German fire was less accurate, but the volume did not subside. As we approached the tree line, I felt a wave of inspiration: keep running and you will live. To my horror, a careful glance backwards revealed the worst scenario. They were pursuing us!

'Move it, Lieutenant!' Sergeant Connors screamed at me all the time pushing PFC Sandy Wilson ahead. We hit the tree line and the branches exploded from the intense small arms fire directed at us. We were covered with snow and broken branches.

'Oh God they got me!' I heard Private Wilson scream and fall against a tree. He was hit in the leg, a massive wound from a German Mauser.

'Lieutenant! Help me,' Sergeant Connors yelled for me. Without a moment of hesitation, Sergeant Connors tossed Private Wilson onto his burly shoulders and crashed through thick woods. I didn't look back I kept running, thinking nothing of my men.

'Lieutenant, slow down I need help!' I heard the Sergeant's desperate plea. He must have been stumbling under the weight of Private Wilson. The shots from the Germans seemed closer, they were not giving up the chase. They knew what they had done.

'Lieutenant, you fucking coward! Stop!' The exasperated Sergeant screamed again. This time I slowed and looked over my shoulder. He was moving like a cornered beast, shifting the weight to gain just a little more speed. The dozen or so German Soldiers who started the pursuit were down to a three. The others must have tired of the deep snow and cold. I traversed

a frozen stream and thought I was going to make it. The embankment was steep but I climbed with the gusto of somebody who was given a second chance. I would not waste it; I planned to immediately use my connections to rid myself of the burdensome existence as a cowardly combat soldier. I found a tree to hide; its massive branches shielding me from the Germans. Their submachine guns wailed away. I watched the Sergeant dive down to the frozen streambed. Private Wilson careened wildly, grimacing in pain; his deep red blood stained the white snow. With the guile of a warrior, Sergeant Connors turned to face the enemy. The first German Soldier to reach the top of the embankment was running too fast, he lost his footing and fired his weapon wildly in the air. He was carrying a bolt action Mauser rifle and could not chamber a fresh round before he crashed into Sergeant Connors who was waiting like a vulture. I started to run again but could not keep my eyes off of the confrontation a safe distance below me. Sergeant Connors used the rifle of the stunned SS murderer to bludgeon him to death with three quick blows. Connors rushed up the slippery embankment and rested the rifle on the frozen ground and searched for the others. He found them quickly; they were nearly on top of him when he fired two times, killing the unlucky German pursuers. He immediately threw down the empty rifle, collected Private Wilson and hustled away from the scene.

"I ran until my lungs felt like they were going to burst, streaks of hot pain shot through my totally exhausted legs. I kept moving, shoving snow-covered branches out of my path. I was scratched and bruised by the unrelenting winter foliage that tried to deliver me to the executioners. I took a short breather against another ancient tree, gasping and searching for any sign of the Germans. I didn't care about my fellow Americans, they were dead or lost and I didn't care.

"I slowed my pace and tried to figure out where I was. My terrible sense of direction and the little time I spent paying attention to my instructors made a bad situation intolerable. I was only saved by the resilient warrior Sergeant Connors who emerged from a thick clump of small trees near where I rested. He had followed my footsteps and I didn't hear him approach. He still carried a now delirious Private Sandy Wilson who was conscious, but looked pale from loss of blood.

'Where the fuck have you been?' He glared at me like a wild animal. I stammered but could say nothing intelligible.

'Let's go,' he said with disgust in his voice. I was not ashamed though; my life was the only thing that mattered. I would get over my cowardice; I never claimed to be anything else.

"We traveled a mile or so before we started to see signs that Americans were ahead. Tragically, before we could be identified we heard the now-

familiar sound of mortars being fired. We stopped and listened for the shells we thought would pass over us. The talented American gunner was on target that frigid afternoon. The ground erupted and I thought it was the end. My ears were ringing and I tasted the foul shell residue. I looked around and saw the torn carcass of Sergeant Connors, his intestines strewn all over PFC Wilson who was moaning loudly. I screamed as loud as I could that we were Americans. A few excruciating minutes later we were surrounded by a gang of confused GIs; they felt terrible for the friendly fire incident. They bemoaned the luck of war and helped Private Wilson. I said nothing.

"The disastrous day ended with a warm meal and relatively cozy dugout in the midst of our rescuers. Private Wilson was transferred to a surgical station where he gave a full account of the German atrocities and the unbelievable escape. High-ranking intelligence officers recorded every word and planned to visit the site as soon as the American Army regained its balance. He accurately recounted the dash to the woods and the wound that crippled him. It was at this crucial juncture of the harrowing tale that Private Sandy Wilson made a dramatic, life-altering error. He remembered every moment of the chase, the trek through the snow, the shootout and finally the heroism of 2nd Lieutenant Sheldon Harrison. Through the haze of his massive leg wound he mixed up the pivotal characters in his salvation. The officers were accustomed to American acts of bravery but were still impressed by the selfless act.

"I was ten miles away pulling every string to get off the line. I was fortunate enough to have a connection that would prove invaluable. One of my father's former law clerks was a rear area ordinance officer who immediately used his influence to get me transferred. Years after the war, I did go to one of my unit's annual reunions. I'm embarrassed to say I was treated like a celebrity war hero that I was not. I didn't know a single soul, but rather enjoyed the lavish praise, never for a moment thinking of dispelling the falsehood.

"My place as THE post-war American novelist has many privileges, including the inflation of common acts too absurd proportions. The bravery of Sergeant Connors wrongly attributed to me, was staggeringly inflated and I loved it.

"I was lucky enough that I did not have to fill out an after-action report. A military oversight allowed me the out of never having to sign a false report. I simply did not refute the report or the citation I received a few weeks later. My Silver Star commendation recounts my alleged exploits in glowing terms.

"I was discharged from the Army in the autumn of 1945. I returned to Cambridge, Massachusetts and resumed my studies. I was a decorated combat veteran admired by my classmates at Harvard, many had served, but few found themselves carrying a rifle in search of the enemy.

"Shortly after completing my studies at Harvard I embarked on a writing career. I was a highly educated young man with the desire and perceived skill to be the next Sinclair Lewis, my favorite writer at the time. There was only one problem with my dream; I was a writer with no creativity, little passion and zero inspiration. My rigorous and overly structured classical education killed any originality I might have possessed. I was like a technically proficient pianist who could play Bach to perfection without truly understanding brilliance of the work. I learned quickly I lacked the talent needed to write a novel of substance.

"In 1949, I started teaching low-level English and Creative Writing courses at Harvard. I was hard on my students. I envied their talent and sabotaged their budding careers. I manipulated and persuaded many naïve undergraduates to enter fields I did not consider a threat. I glamorized journalism and nonfiction, stunting the growth of many aspiring novelists. They were promising young people who looked to me for guidance, I perverted that trust and sent them away out of selfish envy!

"By 1950 or so, my position in the English Literature Department was tenuous at best. My unfounded, sometimes overpowering arrogance, perplexed my fellow faculty members. I was unpopular and depressed by the terrible time I was having with my first novel. During that summer of discontent, I was reunited with PFC Sandy Wilson.

"The once jovial Wilson arrived at my office a desperate shell of himself. He was still limping from the leg wound that sent him home. The Army doctors were never able to set the fractured leg correctly. He avoided eye contact as he softly told me of his life after the war. It was a tragic tale of misfortune and missed opportunity. He attended the University of Massachusetts on the GI bill, but dropped out after his freshman year. He was unable to perform any sort of manual labor due to his severe disability. The government did send him a small check every month for his war-related injuries.

"It was obvious to me that he suffered deep mental scarring from his short stint on the battlefield and the painful rehabilitation in a Veterans Hospital. So many young soldiers died from their awful wounds; he stopped looking beyond his bed. The terrible disfigurements and tearful reunions with horrified families were too much for him to witness. He went into a protective shell for months, not talking and seldom acting like he would recover.

"After a half hour of this I asked him about his accommodations, he quietly said he had none. He had used the last few dollars he had to ride the train from the Veterans Shelter he was staying at. I felt a strange obligation to the boy; I wanted to help him somehow. I noticed he was carrying under his arm a notebook with an elastic band neatly binding it shut. It looked like a sketchbook; he clutched it tightly, concealing it from my prying eyes, but the serpent was too close for him to recognize. I asked him what it was and he mumbled something unintelligible. After pressing the issue he reluctantly confessed that it was his journal. It was really a collection of his stories. It was the only source of pleasure he had in his sad life, a release valve for the anger and resentment he had bottled up inside.

"I then asked him if he needed a place to stay, it was a half-hearted offer I hoped he would not accept. I felt sorry for him but my position would not allow me to associate with him other than as a mentor at arm's length. He was a complex person who I had no desire to know intimately.

"I was slightly interested in his work, a morbid curiosity really. I was looking for an ego boost for my stalled writing endeavors. His inferior attempt would bolster my sagging confidence. We agreed to meet the next day for lunch, my treat of course. It was at this meeting in a local café in Harvard Square, that I convinced Wilson to let me see his black journal. I had talked him into giving me the last thing that meant anything to him. I had done nothing to warrant such confidence.

"The most horrible night of my life followed. I held 'A Troubled Life' in my hands and wept like a foolish child."

Drew lifted his head and absently stared at a woman standing three feet in front of him. Her lips were moving and she was smiling nervously.

"Can you please take my picture?" She held out her camera. Drew looked at the expensive camera and said nothing. She asked again and looked at her bewildered family for support. He grabbed the camera and abruptly snapped the photo. They begrudgingly thanked him and left him alone.

Drew did not immediately return to Sheldon Harrison's stunning confession. He held the document in his hands feeling the weight of the revelation on his fingertips. His hands were shaking; he was reading a confession of enormous significance, on the verge of the greatest literary deception since Shakespeare.

"I don't want this," he mumbled to himself, "I don't want to be defined by this moment." Drew desperately wanted his life back.

The stiff breeze from the Atlantic Ocean chilled him. He pulled on a sweatshirt from his backpack and sipped his water before returning to the document of immense importance.

"The sun had set on my literary career the instant I realized this uneducated kid from a poor working class background had a primal gift for storytelling that I could only dream of. His keen insight and complex characters sent me spiraling into the depths of depression. I bitterly blamed my lifestyle for my inadequacies. My pampered upbringing and rigid education were the reasons I was no more than a wordy hack. What a fool. I am no longer delusional. I am convinced now that regardless of my surroundings and experiences, originality would have remained elusive.

"You may want to take a deep breath after the bombshell I just delivered. The story is quite simple after this. I will try not to leave any crucial details out, but I will keep it as brief and concise as possible.

"I tried to convince him to publish or at least attempt to get 'A Troubled Life' published, but to my surprise he demurred. It was too personal for him; I did not understand his reluctance and pushed him. He agreed to let me edit and correct the mistake-riddled novel; it was time-consuming but it turned out very well. He was typical of many artists; he didn't have the patience to edit his own work. I made a deal to do the heavy edits and shaping of the story for free, but would publish it under my name!

"My absurd rationale for this travesty was that I did all the real work and deserved the credit for the finished product. He agreed verbally and I took advantage of his grateful attitude towards me. He figured without my 'daring rescue' he would have been rotting in a pine box in a graveyard in France or Luxemburg, long forgotten by his family. It was a despicable act of deception on my part.

"I did not stop with a verbal agreement I made him sign what he believed was a legal document that he could never discuss our arrangement. I would give him a small percentage of the royalties if the book ever sold. He signed without hesitation. The document was not official or truly binding, but the specter of a long court battle would dissuade any thoughts of revolt. His debt of gratitude towards me for saving his life made it unlikely he would ever divulge any information. If only he had the presence of mind to consult an attorney he would have been free of my grasp! Free to enjoy the true fruits of his genius.

"I am sure after reading the above you must think I am a monster. I am for sure, but if it were not for my heavy-handed approach the world would not have four novels of the highest quality. With my connections and gift for editing I published a masterpiece in 1951. I don't have to explain the stir 'A Troubled Life' caused. The critics thought it was brilliant and the sales were outstanding. I was living comfortably before the publication of the novel, but the sudden success made me a wealthy man.

"Sandy Wilson said virtually nothing of the success of his novel. He sealed himself in a world of writing and silent contemplation. I gave him enough money to work and live in modest-sized apartment in Cambridge.

I was smart enough to keep him close by and made sure I visited him frequently. I helped tend to his Spartan needs. We were friends on a strange level, sometimes forgetting our sordid arrangement and having long coffee-supported conversations until dawn. It was at those times, that I felt the most guilt.

"Life at Harvard changed dramatically with the publication of 'ATL'; my class size grew exponentially with my newfound fame and credibility. Shortly thereafter, I bought a large Victorian home on a side street off of Kirkland Street near Harvard. After a few months, I tired of the short ride to Sandy's apartment so I set him up in the tiny, detached, guesthouse. I thought it was prudent to keep him under my watchful eye. Always keep your friends close and your enemies closer is what they say. He was not my enemy in the common sense, but a silent partner that could turn into an adversary.

"The complete solitude of the detached guesthouse helped him greatly. He wrote prolifically, seldom leaving his quarters other than to buy a few groceries. His hygiene was questionable and his general appearance can only be described as disheveled. I spent many nights sifting through the piles of work, editing and correcting until I was bleary eyed. At the end of the first year 'A Life Without Beatrice' was completed. I won my first Pulitzer's for 'A Life Without Beatrice' along with a hefty royalty check that I did not split evenly. I took care of Wilson financially, and this seemed satisfactory to him, although I am sure he knew I was raping him with kid gloves.

"As my popularity grew, my need for Harvard diminished significantly; I resigned shortly after winning the Pulitzer. They wanted me to stay, offering me far more than I deserved, but I didn't need the daily grind, it was an impediment to my burgeoning social life.

"Sandy Wilson's third novel was a turbulent, slightly unorthodox war novel titled 'The Rolling Willow.' It was raw, in the vein of Norman Mailer's 'Naked and The Dead.' It took Sandy two years to complete and three months of editing before it was ready for public consumption. Again, critical and commercial success followed, I was inundated with requests for interviews and speaking engagements. It was a stunning rise to the top of the literary world, an all-consuming ride with endless potential for two young men with many years of fruitful collaboration left.

"The last Sandy Wilson novel 'My Burden' was published in 1962. It was many years between 'The Rolling Willow' and 'My Burden.' Five or six years I think. I hounded him night and day, even threatening to cut off his royalty payments. He took his time, as if he knew it was his swan song. When the novel was finally finished he refused to give it a title, I referred to it as the Black Book, a name that mirrored his dour mood. We agreed upon 'My Burden' after an exhaustive fight that nearly brought us to blows. He was far more emotional and combative than ever before. He was sullen and seldom left the guesthouse. 'My Burden' was an exploration into the dynamics of friendship and ultimately the fracturing of a long-time relationship because of a deceitful act. It hit a little too close to home for me, but it was a superb, massive novel.

"The publication of 'My Burden' was a great relief to me. It was the novel that cemented my position as a literary icon. I reaped the financial rewards, buying a huge beachfront parcel of land on Martha's Vineyard. After the completion of the estate I currently reside at, I began the long practice of taking in college students for summer internships.

"It was during this period, that I reluctantly started answering the calls from Hollywood. Many studios were anxious to make any of the four novels into major motion pictures. I picked a studio I felt would honor the integrity of the work. I was adamant that either I would write the screenplay or at least pick the screenwriter. I thought about asking Sandy, but he was against any kind of adaptations. I did not consult him; I simply started to write the screenplay for 'My Burden.' The progress was slow and I soon realized I was incapable of delivering a script worthy of the novel. So I turned to one of my young interns, a nineteen-year-old student who was staying with me. Carlton Smithfield wrote a shockingly good screenplay that the studio loved. I credited him as the co-writer, but he was really the force behind the great movie. We shared the Academy Award for best screenplay. Carlton was the most loyal and able protégé I ever had. I like to think I helped him get started in the business, a business that he would soon dominate.

"My troubles began shortly after bringing home the Oscar and winning a second Pulitzer Prize. The wealth of material that spurned Sandy Wilson to the top of his profession suddenly dried up. He stopped caring about his work and I confronted him about it. This is how the conversation went more or less. My memory is slipping due to this infernal disease and the draconian treatment that will not save me.

'What's the problem, Sandy?' I was standing in the cluttered guesthouse, in my new suit, afraid to touch anything.

'I have no problem, Sheldon. I simply have nothing else to say.' He was building a model airplane, his intelligent eyes never leaving the delicate plane he was constructing.

'I don't understand. Where are all your notes? I saw you working on something a few months ago?'

'There.' He nonchalantly pointed to a pile of ashes in the small fireplace.

'You burned them!' I was furious, so much time and energy discarded in an apparent moment of weakness.

'I burned them, Sheldon.' He looked at me with tears of anger and regret in his eyes. I knew he didn't want to do it but he couldn't help himself. The burden of churning out one masterpiece after another had finally broken his will to continue. He was done, torched like the thousands of pages of notes smoldering in the fireplace.

'You haven't just burned all of your work, you've burned us. We are dead.' I stumbled from his room, disconsolate and hoping for a miracle. Four novels and a student's screenplay may not be enough to cement myself as a literary master. I lamented my bad luck, but did not fall into total despair. I had a wild idea on the ferry to the Vineyard, I would write my next novel without the help of Sandy. I assumed anything I published would garner the same response as the others; the press usually overlooks flaws of established writers.

"The experiment was quite humiliating. I was painfully aware of my own limitations, humbled by the thing I yearned to do most. The fifth novel was a disaster, a ridiculous attempt at originality. It was during this period that we truly grew apart. I might see him once a month to give him his 'cash' allowance. He also was on my payroll as a caretaker. He drove a secondhand car. He asked me for an increase only one time, I quickly agreed and he never asked again.

"My fifth novel, 'Magic Man,' was published in 1966. The critics hated it and sales were off. Shortly after the release, critic extraordinaire Myron Wiseman started snooping around, writing scathing reviews that bordered on personal assassination. He was a smart little sucker who could smell deception through the well-orchestrated rues. Myron was my most ardent supporter during the glory days. He crucified me on 'Magic Man'; I was so depressed I hardly left the house for a month after I read his review. It probably did not seem overly harsh to Wiseman, but he did not know the circumstances in which 'Magic Man' was created.

"After my month-long self-imposed exile, I broke out of my shell and visited Sandy. The conversation went something like this.

'Did you read "Magic Man"?

'Yes.' His response was curt. I remember he was hunched over a very worn copy of 'Henry V.' His knowledge and grasp of Shakespeare was as good as mine or maybe better, and that bothered me. It was hard enough to accept my limitations as a writer, but his appreciation and understanding of Shakespeare was on a higher level. Dare I say as a peer!"

'So, what did you think? I asked with a brave smile.

'Not bad.' He lifted his aging face and tried to lie. He still had some feelings for me, although very little at this point.

'You fucking liar! You hate it.' I walked around the messy room and examined his things. I touched his model of Alan Shephard's Mercury Capsule. I was even jealous of his craftsmanship. He was rabid about the space program. I considered the whole effort to beat the Russians to the moon bourgeois entertainment, nationalism at its worst.

'Did you read Wiseman's review?' I watched for a reaction, there was none. It was obvious he had not read a thing about the monstrosity called 'Magic Man.'

'No.'

'He killed me. He even made an off-handed remark to a mutual acquaintance that it must have been an imposter who wrote it. The Sheldon Harrison of "A Troubled Life" would never have published such drivel.'

"I noticed a faint, almost imperceptible smile cross his face. I wanted to beat the guarded smugness out of him, physically assault him until he swore he would never be so vindictive. I stormed out without saying goodbye; I was disgusted by his ungrateful smirk. Can you believe how irrational I was?"

"I left his cluttered guesthouse in a terrible state; depressed and wishing I could just write an average novel. A novel that some people would like, even enjoy just a Chapter or two. I recovered and was determined to make my final novel the best ever. I worked day and night, even renting a stone castle in Ireland for inspiration. Under a star-filled sky with the cool North Sea wind lapping at my face, I completed what I thought was a great work of fiction.

"After all these years, I can look back and see how flawed my approach was. The reviews for 'William and Mary,' a disastrously boring and trite love story was only slightly better than 'Magic Man.' Myron Wiseman attacked it with such ferocity I believed at the time it had become a personal thing with him. The backlash against him was cutting; he would never fully recover from the crusade. I was the literary darling of the time, a powerhouse who was always available for an interview. I was a living icon.

"After the debacle of 'William and Mary,' I made a very public retirement. I blamed the critics for my early exit, claiming they couldn't possibly understand what I was trying to achieve. I never believed my own rhetoric, but I made a case against the press with the conviction of a man that was wronged by the feeble-minded. They were incapable of understanding my deliberate deviation of style and tone.

"The sales of 'William and Mary' were flat. It was soon on the discount shelves all across America. I was depressed by the whole fiasco. Then a peculiar thing happened, my popularity actually increased with the strange ending to my astounding career. You probably are aware of this; I have lived the life of a king off of the labors of Sandy Wilson. To understand the whole story I must backtrack and focus on our personal lives. Let me introduce the reader to my lovely wife, Emily Shea.

"Emily Shea was a night school student of mine a few years before my meteoric rise to the top of the literary world. I was in love with her from the moment I saw her freckled-covered face staring at me from the back of the lecture hall. She had auburn hair and striking blue eyes. Her pale skin and rosy cheeks were sprinkled with brown freckles, a perfect highlight to her aura of natural beauty. She carried herself with a sort of working class arrogance I did not know existed. She was born and raised in a very tough, tight-knit Irish community of South Boston. She was a full-time student at Northeastern University taking night classes at Harvard to see what all the hype was about. She was smart and breezed through what I thought was a challenging creative writing course.

"After the semester, I learned she had signed up for a trip to Paris sponsored by the school. I was and still am confused how she ended up on the trip; she was not a full-time student, thus unable to partake in school-sponsored trips. Even after we were married for many years I never found out how she managed to fool the organizers. I went along only because I found out she was part of the group. I tried to get close to her during the trip to the city of lights and romance. She did not respond to my subtle advances, unmoved by a moonlight cruise on the Seine River. She thought I was a pompous fool who understood nothing of the real world she came from.

"I bumped into her on campus a year or so after 'A Troubled Life' was published and her demeanor had changed. She was older and maybe a bit wiser. I could give her things she would never have otherwise. Wealth and stability were something she coveted on an unconscious level. As I write this painful confession, we are still married. I am sad to say not happily. We have lived separate lives for decades. She remains an attractive and vibrant woman. It is likely she will find a companion who can give what I could not. The thought of her with another man pains me more than the cancer. That, of course, is an exaggeration, the embellished words of a failed novelist! When the pain starts, nothing else matters, the suffering is private and lonely. I am afraid her recovery will be swift and complete. I know she has had many lovers, but with my departure she may settle into a more permanent relationship.

"We had a large and lavish wedding ceremony. We honeymooned in Europe. It was a period of blissful escapism. It was real; her touch, her affection, our lovemaking was tangible and honest. It was the only part of my life that was not a lie. The whirlwind social life we enjoyed after marriage was both pleasant and gratifying for me. I loved the perks of being one of the most sought-after novelists in America. Emily became a very good hostess, although she never really liked the "overbearing" social elite that frequented our dinner parties. She thought they were a bunch of smug ass kissers who never endured a day of hardship. She used to make fun of their soft hands. My hands were soft, but my service in the war made up for my delicate nature.

"On occasion, I would step back and watch her from across the room. I can picture her now in her favorite red dress, feigning interest and acting gracious, but clearly bored to tears by the stale conversation and the predictable topics. I would salivate when she wore that red dress, yearning for the dinner guests to leave. It was tight and revealing. She was radiant and highly desirable to all the males in the room. I often wonder why she ever married me. I was a fraud and not handsome by any standards, yet she appeared to love me.

"Our three children were born in a five-year period starting eleven months after our wedding. We were happy and busy until Sandy Wilson visited our home after the publication of the disastrous sixth novel. He was clearly out of sorts that day; my impression is he wanted to come clean about the whole mess. I didn't push the issue. He was holding all the cards, but he didn't quite realize it. This is how I remember the brief conversation.

'What is wrong with you?' I asked as he crossed my home office and sat heavily on my leather sofa.

'I'm sick of all of this.' He rubbed his swollen, pleading eyes.

'It's over now anyway.' I was nervous he would crack and reveal the truth.

'It is?'

'Yes…I'll never write again. So it's over. You don't have to feel pressured anymore. The whole charade is over.' I sat on the edge of the desk and tried to act like a commander.

'Good I'm glad,' he mumbled. I noticed his hands were trembling and he never made eye contact. The confidence he possessed during the height of his writing career had evaporated. I suddenly realized his reluctance to give me anything new was not exclusively out of anger or resentment, it was simply writer's block. It could see it in his eyes, he had given up and it was killing him. I suddenly felt all-powerful, not that I wasn't before, but in fact he was fallible. The mighty fall the hardest.

'What are you going to do?' I asked him with false concern.

'I don't know.'

'I will still pay you as long as I can.' I reassured him. Oh what a thoughtful guy.

'I appreciate it.' I thought I detected a bit of irony in his response.

'Well, you know, you're always welcome in my home.'

'Hello Sandy.' My lovely wife entered the room and cordially addressed Sandy. He changed upon hearing her voice. I knew they were occasional acquaintances, but I did not understand how close their friendship had become over the years. They met many times for lunch at our Cambridge home. She asked me many times what he did for me. I circled the wagons and told her he was a wartime buddy who looked after things for me. She realized quickly he was the man I 'saved' during the War. She never pushed the issue, but I sensed she believed there was more to the relationship than I let on.

'Hello Emily... I haven't seen you around lately.' He addressed her in a familiar tone that annoyed me.

'I'm sorry for neglecting our lunch dates.' She smiled politely and with affection.

'Oh I get by.' He shuffled his feet. It was an awkward demonstration of his meager interpersonal skills. As far as I know, my wife was the only person he had a somewhat normal relationship with.

'Are you watching the launch?' She was referring to the launch of Apollo 8 the next day.

'Yes...but my television is so bad I hope I can tell it's a rocket.'

'Nonsense you come here for breakfast tomorrow and we'll watch it together.'

'I don't think...'

'I'll see you tomorrow, Sandy.' She turned and left the room, ignoring his halfhearted protests. They shared a passion for the U.S space program and from what I could gather, had watched other launches together.

"The next morning we all ate a fabulous breakfast at our Cambridge home while we watched Walter Cronkite discuss the upcoming mission. Emily and Sandy were enraptured by his technical description of the massive Saturn V booster that had never been fired with men aboard. They sat, side-by-side on my absurdly expensive Oriental rug, like two high school kids unaware that they were flirting until someone told them. I tried to participate in the conversation, but I was so ignorant on the subject it was foolish to continue. They were openly scornful of my lack of interest, shaking their collective heads and probably wishing I would leave the room.

'Yes...yes go! GO!' My usually reserved wife jumped to her feet and cheered the rising Saturn V and the brave crew of Apollo 8. To possess such bravery must be an intoxicating thing.

'My God, so beautiful,' Sandy whispered softly.

'Grand!' I blurted awkwardly.

'Move,' she ordered as I stupidly moved in front of the television, 'Go baby!'

'Life will never be the same,' Sandy mumbled.

"It was at this moment that I finally understood the nature of their relationship. I could see it in his long gazes and sometimes-agitated behavior when in her presence. I wasn't sure about her feelings for him, or maybe I was too afraid to admit what I feared. After a few moments of jubilation, Emily rushed out of the room to change her clothes. We had a luncheon date at the Ritz Carlton with my publisher. She didn't want to go but I stressed the importance of the engagement, she reluctantly acquiesced. I took the time alone to confront Sandy about what I believed was a breach of friendship bordering on infidelity.

'She is not for the taking,' I blurted awkwardly.

He stiffened and contemptuously stood up; staring at me with such hatred, I was momentarily unnerved.

'What!' I bellowed awkwardly after few moments of silence. He was skinny and weak, but his wrathful gaze was intimidating.

'I've had enough of all of this,' Sandy stated acidly.

'So leave!'

'I will.'

My mind was racing; I wanted him to leave forever, but in the back of my mind I was afraid of the ramifications of such a split.

'Emily showed me something today.'

'Yes…my wife… what did she show you?' I was angry and combative.

'I can be happy. Life is not just a series of hours and days until the end. I have wasted enough time in your shadow. I will always be grateful for what you did for me…Life does not have to be superficial distraction until death.'

'You are so fucking stupid!'

'What?' He was stunned by my vulgar attack. I don't think he ever heard me curse or raise my voice in such a way.

'It's all a fucking lie. You're so fucking gullible it's laughable.'

'Why do you treat me like this?'

'I don't know…I wish I knew.' I was at a loss for words.

'I am tired of it all, Sheldon. I can't go on anymore.'

'What do you want to hear Sandy, that I'm bad person? Is that what you want me to say? Well it's the fucking truth!'

'I don't know what I want from you.' He shrugged his shoulders, defeated by the finality of the brief conversation.

'Neither do I, Sandy. My whole life is a damn lie.' I turned my back and heard him leave the family room.

"The next time I saw Sandy was at a charity event at my Cambridge home two weeks later. The event was open to the press and many of the top local critics and columnists were invited. A few, I should say one, Myron Wiseman, came with an agenda. Sandy stumbled upon the event; strangely he did not immediately leave as he normally did.

"As I made the rounds, I deliberately avoided the skulking Wiseman who was pacing my every step. It was at the worst possible instant that he decided to confront me. I had just begun a very tense conversation with Sandy, who had emerged from the corner, mocking my every movement.

'Sheldon, can I have a word?' Wiseman asked me in the most condescending way. He had no respect for me anymore. His once reverent tone was lost among the ashes of the last two novels.

'How did you get in?' I asked condescendingly.

'I came in with the dogs.' He laughed and sipped his gin and tonic.

'I'm not surprised. What can I do for you?' I looked around, pretending to be disinterested.

'I would like to schedule an interview and clear up all this mess.'

'What mess, Mr. Wiseman?'

'I gather you're aware of my reviews.'

'I am.'

'I just don't understand your latest work. I'm confounded by the style, the tone is so different.'

I watched his intelligent eyes flicker as the question rolled off his forked tongue. I wanted to lunge at him and stomp him to death, but as you can garner from this confession, I am a coward.

'What is there to understand, Mr. Wiseman? Personal preference should not shroud objectivism.'

'Don't lecture me about objectivism, Sheldon. All I am looking for is an hour of your time to put this all to rest.'

'There is nothing to put to rest.' I was obstinate and growing impatient.

'If there is no issue, then what's the harm in an hour?'

'Actually I told you and the rest of press that I'm retired and cannot be bothered by the incessant requests for my time.' I think I raised my voice at this time. I noticed Sandy was shuffling nervously and was looking for an escape.

'That is a bunch of bull, Sheldon. You did a fluff piece three weeks ago.'

'I have made myself clear, Myron.'

'This reclusive, obstinate attitude only started after "Magic Man" was published. You were quite available when the reviews were glowing.'

'Wiseman, get to the point! I'm sick of you already.'

'I don't want to fight with you, Sheldon.' He must have noticed the sidelong glances of the other guests.

'Go away, Sir!' Wilson suddenly demanded. I was as surprised as Wiseman was by Sandy's outburst.

'I'm sorry, who are you?' Myron faced him with dignity and courage. In the blink of an eye he was on the ground staring up at the converging guests. He held his bleeding mouth and said nothing. Wilson had sucker punched him with deadly accuracy.

'What the hell did you do that for?' I screamed and dragged Sandy away from the fray. Wiseman slowly got to his feet and the pain was obvious, but Myron was not your typical literary critic.

"You see, the diminutive critic escaped Nazi Germany in 1936 with his family. He was a German Jew who would have died in the gas chambers had his father not seen the writing on the wall. He became an American Citizen and joined the U.S Army during the Second World War. He wanted to be part of the grand crusade to rid the world of Nazism. He was a language specialist who fought his way from France to the heartland of Germany. He witnessed first-hand Hitler's death camps and was forever scarred by the images.

"He was not the type to take a punch without a fight. He lunged at Sandy, striking me in the process. Order was quickly restored and I hustled Sandy out of the house.

"Sandy and I seldom spoke after the bizarre incident. My wife asked me why he was avoiding her. She asked me if I had anything to do with this sudden, inexplicable change. Of course, I lied and the matter was dropped.

"He no longer held me in high esteem, instead looked upon my very existence as an affront to all that was good in the world. I was an ordinary man with no special talent living as a genius of few equals. I was guilt-ridden, disillusioned and desperate for an end to the whole matter. I received such a conclusion shortly thereafter.

"Seven months after the 'charity brawl' as it was so rudely dubbed, I met Sandy Wilson for the last time. It was a humid, rainy July night when he showed up, unannounced, at the door of my Martha's Vineyard home. Three days earlier, Neil Armstrong landed on the moon and we had an extravagant party to mark the occasion. I imagined Sandy in his apartment, cheering loudly as the pictures from the moon were beamed down to his black and white television. I noticed my lovely wife was truly excited during the event, but was somewhat subdued compared to other historic events we had watched together. I could not help but wonder if she was thinking of him. Anyway back to the events at hand. This is how I remember our parting conversation.

'Sheldon I need to talk to you.'

'Come in.' I beckoned him politely. He was wet and looked like he had walked from the ferry. He stood by the open door and refused to enter.

'I'm very ill and the doctor says I only have six months to live.'

'What!' I was stunned by the disclosure.

'I have six months to live. I won't see you again.'

'Why? I don't understand.'

'You understand. Don't try to find me. I have moved and will not bother you again.'

'Don't be crazy, what will you do?' I felt this strange feeling arise from the depths of my corrupted mind. I was relieved he was dying!

'This is not up for debate.' He shuffled his soaking feet and would not look at me.

'What's wrong with you?' I really didn't care. Cancer, heart disease, whatever, as long as it killed him in six months it was okay with me.

'Does it matter, Sheldon? There is no hope.'

'I'm sorry. Really, I am truly sorry, Sandy.'

'No you're not. Please forget about me, I don't want to be in your thoughts.'

'You're acting crazy, Sandy,' I muttered. 'It does not have to be this way.'

'Goodbye, Sheldon.' He disappeared into the night, gone from my life forever. What a stroke of good fortune!

"My jubilant mood did not last long. As I said earlier, keep your friends close and your enemies closer. I was haunted for years by the ghost of Sandy Wilson. I checked the obituaries every day for three years and with increasing distress, never saw his name. Out of sheer exhaustion, I stopped searching for him and accepted my role as the elder statesmen of American Literature. I don't know if Sandy Wilson is still alive, I hope he is and you can find him. I doubt you will, I suspect he has long expired.

"My family has prospered greatly from my fraud. They are part of the upper crust of American intellectual society and they do not belong there. Their privileged lifestyle sits atop a rotting foundation of my grand deception. They are complacent and comfortable in their exalted roles as blood relations to an icon. They possess a peculiar sense of entitlement foreign to even the most wealthy and influential. It is astonishing how many doors are opened solely because of their lineage.

"This confession is something I should have done long before the hour of my death. I could not for obvious reasons. Please allow my family six months to grieve before informing the world of my deceit. I composed this document in my own hand to ward off any claims of treachery.

"Good luck, chosen one, you will need it."

Sheldon Harrison.

Drew sighed deeply and rubbed his tired eyes, neatly tucking the confession back into its manila envelope. The temptation to toss it from the heights of the Moorish Castle was great, but that sort of cowardly act was for Sheldon Harrison, not Drew Engle.

Chapter 14
The City of Lights: Paris, France

THE THRUSTING AND SWEATING bodies undulated to the heavily altered Bee Gee's hit "Staying Alive." The disco anthem roared; the pulse of the heavy bass pushed the crowded club to a fever pitch. The multilevel dance floor shook from the throbbing beat and the uncontrolled passion of the dancers whose inhibitions were checked at the door.

The ultra chic club was located on a side street near the Arc De Triomphe. The local Parisians avoided the expensive club because of its noxious mix of international jetsetters and curious Americans. It was the sort of place the Parisians loathed, a loud disco specifically catering to the social elite of inferior countries.

Charlotte Emerson lost herself in the flashing lights and the deep bass of the song. As the song reached its climatic end, she was nearly overcome with exhaustion. She was clinging to the son of a Saudi Prince who was mesmerized by her inspired dancing and hard body. He was a veteran of the international club scene, often flying to New York and London on the same weekend. He traveled with an entourage of twelve, six friends and six slaves who arranged the whimsical trips from one capital city to the next.

The fierceness of Charlotte's athletic dancing excited him, he thought about fucking her after the club closed. Her tanned, muscular legs would look nice wrapped around his naturally brown skin. He was disappointed when the music stopped and Charlotte rejoined her friends at a large table overlooking the surging dance floor. The oil prince followed her and tapped her on the shoulder.

"What!" Charlotte angrily turned, her irritation obvious.

"I just wanted to talk." His English was good but with a strong accent.

"What is it? You want me to do what? Do you think we're together because we shared a moment on the dance floor? Get real, go hit on some Euro slut." She mocked him gleefully, glancing at her amused friends who believed they were witnessing a rebuff of legendary proportions. He mumbled something that was lost by the instrumental dance favorite "Sandstorm."

"What did you say, oil boy?"

"I called you a bitch!" He glared defiantly.

"I'm not impressed because your daddy let some Englishman dig a hole in the ground. Should we all bow down to the son of a Prince from a culturally backward country? Go back to your desert kingdom. Go live off the labors of the lower class a little more."

"Cunt!"

"Your silly little caste system puts you at the head of the food chain, but you're nothing to me." She was glowing, enjoying the unprovoked verbal confrontation.

"You are insane." The Saudi man backed away from the group.

"What did you say? Go back to your prearranged wife. Why do you want a girl that doesn't cover her fucking face?"

"You're drunk," he yelled back.

"Go back to your kingdom, oil boy!"

"Jesus, Charlotte take it easy." Corey Davis urged her to stop.

"What?" She turned sharply, annoyed by the intervention.

"You don't need to be such a bitch," Davis said confidently. He knew she was chasing him and this gave him the upper hand. He really didn't care about the Saudi man; it was a power move to show her who was in charge of their little European romance.

"Don't call me a bitch." She was angered by his flip remark.

"Cool down," he retorted with less vigor. He didn't want the game to end or to lose the advantage. It was too late, in just seconds it was over.

"No, I hate these guys. They are such wannabes."

"So are we." Corey kept pushing.

"Shut up, we're Americans." She was raving, her thoughts mixed and her fury uncontrolled.

"So!" Corey jumped on this.

"It means we have Carte Blanche everywhere we go."

"It does?"

"Yes, Corey, it does!" She was so angry her hands shook and her face quivered.

"You're so special you can party when your grandfather dies."

"What are you talking about?" Charlotte was stunned by the attack. She blushed and for the first time, seemed to lose her confidence.

"I'm talking about you partying with us when your grandfather just died."

Many of her entourage felt as Corey did, it was too soon to forget a man like Sheldon Harrison.

"What do you know?"

"I know you're just like me, a spoiled bitch."

"What!" She was astonished by the turn of events. She would have loved to kill the Saudi man for causing all the trouble. They had enjoyed such a wonderful first day in Paris, climbing the Bell Tower at Notre Dame and taking a wine cruise on the Seine. The group as a whole was deflated by the argument and regretted the decision not to cancel the trip.

"Let's get out of here," someone blurted.

"Yeah let's go," Charlotte's college roommate chimed in.

"This is a drag," another added.

Almost in unison, the dispirited group stood up and left the vibrant club, searching for a quieter place that matched the sudden mood change. Outside Corey tried to talk to her; she pushed him away and walked alone back to her Hotel, George V. She hurried to her spacious room and fell upon the bed in total distress. Her three-month courtship of Corey Davis had dissolved in minutes; the spark of romance so brilliant and beautiful on the eve of the European trek had faded before she unpacked. She twisted and turned, the emotions of her grandfather's death and the recent events at the club prevented her from sleeping. She was on the verge of tears when the sound of her cell phone ringing stopped the inevitable flow.

"Hello?"

"Charlotte, it's me," her cousin Wilton said tentatively, unsure he had reached his cousin. Her voice sounded disjointed and unfamiliar.

"Wilton baby!" She sat up and was relieved it was Wilton and not Corey trying in vain to make amends.

"What's happening in Paris?" His tone was strange and tentative, perhaps feeling she was not alone.

"It sucks!" She roared with laughter.

"Why?" He relaxed.

"Oh please Wilton…you don't want to know."

"Oh come on I need some good gossip." He was thrilled by her despondency.

Through fits of sometimes-forced laughter she recounted the blowup at the club.

"So you're alone then?" He could barely contain the joy in his voice. She would be home soon and without the companionship of the obnoxious Corey Davis.

"Yes, alone in the most romantic city in the world." She sighed.

"So."

"So I'm done with Corey."

"You never started."

"We were started in my mind," she responded with a hint of sadness.

"You'll survive. You always do." He was annoyed by her weakness.

"I'm tired my love. I have to get some sleep." His usefulness had passed.

"Did you know that guy Drew Engle went to Portugal?" He wanted to keep her on the phone and he thought the touchy subject would invigorate her.

"So, I expected nothing less from the little freeloader."

"What's sort of strange is that he went alone."

"So he's a loser with no friends. Where's the story, Wilton?"

"I don't know. I just find the whole thing very weird. What is he going to find out? How will it impact us?"

"You worry too much, cousin. How could it impact us?"

"Who the fuck knows?" He lied, he had spent many hours contemplating Engle's journey.

"Where in Portugal is he?" She had pushed the specifics of his trip to the deep recesses of her shallow mind.

"He's in Sintra. He should have arrived yesterday or the day before, I don't know. He started out in Lisbon and was taking a train to Sintra."

"How do you know that?" She was amazed at her cousin's ability to ferret out information so quickly.

"I spoke with the A-Hole. He told me."

"Carlton?"

"Who else?"

"Interesting," she said more to herself than to her cousin. Her body reacted with a sudden surge of energy. She fumbled through her bag and retrieved a thick train schedule for Western Europe. She half listened to Wilton as he espoused his many theories about Drew's trip. Charlotte's slender fingers traced the many lines of the complicated grid, stopping her manicured nail on Lisbon and then Sintra.

"I have a wild idea." She interrupted his nonsensical ravings.

"What?" He was surprised by her alert response.

"I'm going to make a surprise visit to Mr. Engle."

"What!"

"I need to get away from Corey anyway."

"You just got there."

"So. I'm sick of them. Anyway it's been awhile since I saw Andrew Garrity."

"You don't even know this guy." There was alarm in his voice. He was never comfortable when Charlotte shirked conventionality.

"Don't worry, sweetheart, I won't seduce him. You know you're the only guy for me." Her sexy voice was back. She could sense an immediate change in him.

Wilton's stomach churned, his body shook with anticipation. He waited for her next words, sweating and praying for deliverance. He fumbled with his boxer shorts, they were loose and his hand free.

"Wilton, are you still there?" Her voice was back to normal, the seductive tone disappearing without reason or mercy.

"Yes, sorry." His disappointment could not be disguised.

"I'll call you in a couple of days."

"Bye." He tore off his boxer shorts and ranted, tearing the books from his bookshelf and searing his flesh against a lightbulb. He stalked about the darkened room and swore at the world. In one final fit of anger he threw himself onto the bed and pounded it with such ferocity the springs screamed out in protest.

Chapter 15

The Encounter

Drew staggered down the mountain, unable to find his driver who undoubtedly departed after an hour. He didn't care; he needed time to digest Sheldon Harrison's confession. The setting sun cast shadows on the uneven cobblestone roadway that weaved its way down to the center of Sintra. As he descended, he realized the safest way to avoid the careening motor traffic was to take an alternate route down. He consulted his map and located a more scenic route. He passed small stone homes with tame chickens in the doorway and stray cats fluttering about. It was truly a place of solitude and reflection. Many of the stone homes Drew passed were in various stages of disrepair, but it did not change the impression of old world charm and beauty. These were simple folk who had lived for generations under the prying eyes of the Moorish Castle and The Pena Palace. They were accustomed to throngs of nosey tourists who seldom understood they were trouncing around in someone's backyard. Drew saw a few people who smiled politely and went about their business. To be raised in such a place was too foreign for Drew to comprehend.

The slow walk down did not ease the new burden that weighed upon him like a thousand stone houses. The intriguing scenery slowly receded, replaced by the reality of his discovery. His knees felt weak and he tasted vomit in his mouth as he reached the Polacio Nacional de Vila. He watched with detached interest, a funeral procession passing the road he had to cross. A majestic-looking horse pulled the hearse and the coffin was visible to all. The sight sent a chill down Drew's spine, an omen of what was to come. He hustled away from the growing crowd around the slow moving horse; its hooves clattering loudly on the cobblestones.

Twenty minutes later he was near the Bank of Portugal and searching for his new acquaintances. He peered through the glass door and saw Marie Almeida working at her desk. The bank was closed and it looked like she was the only one left. She was in deep concentration and Drew decided to leave her alone. It was something about the way she tossed her hair and appeared to sigh deeply that kept him rooted to the spot. He should have been thinking about the last train to Lisbon.

Drew banged softly on the door to get her attention. She lifted her gaze and smiled at him, his sheepish grin was charming.

"Hello, Drew." She opened the locked door and let him in.

"You're still working?" He blushed from the awkward and predictable greeting. He felt ashamed for what he knew and could not tell her. For some reason he felt she should know. She escorted him to a sofa for bank customers. He rested on the comfortable furniture and felt some of the anxiety slip away. Her confident smile and positive disposition made him somewhat at ease.

"So, my weary American, what have you discovered?" She smiled brightly and innocently, unaware of the magnitude of her harmless question.

"You know I can't discuss it."

"Oh yes all that paperwork says so." She poked him in the leg.

"Yeah all that paperwork." He sighed and rubbed his eyes.

"You look very tired."

"Oh shit! What time is the last train to Lisbon?" He looked at his watch and cursed himself for being so distracted. He had not planned to stay in Sintra.

"It left five minutes ago." She glanced at her expensive watch.

"Didn't you say you lived in Lisbon?"

"I do, sometimes. I have an apartment in Lisbon and a small one in Sintra. I spend so many late nights here, the bank helps pay for it. I was taking taxi rides home three nights a week and that was much more than what they pay for my small flat." She smiled coyly; she must have lobbied for it.

"Where are you staying in Lisbon?"

"Hotel Fenix."

"Nice, I've had dinner there many times. Do you want to stay at my flat tonight?" Her invitation on the surface seemed like an innocent proposition, but there was a tiny, barely perceptible glimmer in her eyes.

"No, no thanks, Marie."

"I insist! This is August, do you think you can find a hotel room?" She followed with a dramatic speech detailing the sound reasoning for staying the night. He was tired, drained to the point of collapse.

"Why, Marie? I don't understand your concern."

"You don't have to understand." She was excited and did not bother answering the foolish question. She shut off her computer, set multiple alarms, and escorted Drew to the door.

Their leisurely pace was complemented by a marvelous sunset. They could not actually see the sun dip below the horizon but the deep shadows and glowing skyline was unlike anything Drew had experienced before. The warm breeze down the main avenue was a gift from the colder hills above. The hulking Moorish Castle was barely visible, its skeletal shell hidden from the peering eyes of a stranger who had walked its walls only hours before.

"Did you see the Pena Palace?" Marie used the English phrase for the Palacio de Pena.

"I saw it when I was on the walls of the Moorish Castle."

"I hate the Moorish Castle." She shivered at the thought of it at night.

"Why?" He was amused by her unexpected reaction.

"When I was child, I was taught about the horrible Moors in their castle. The place has always given me nightmares. I know the truth now, but it's hard to shake the images of youth."

"Childhood myths I guess."

"Yes, I guess. But the Pena Palace is my favorite."

"I wish I could have seen it."

"We can."

"It must be closed."

"I know somebody who works there, let's go." She grabbed her cell phone and made a hurried call to a friend at the Pena Palace.

"We're in." She smiled and led him to a nearby taxi stand. They would be dropped off at the same point Drew had made his trek to the Moorish Castle.

The steep grade approaching the secluded Pena Palace easily exhausted the weak and elderly, Drew and Marie found it only mildly taxing. The few tourists they encountered were leaving the Palace, their satisfied expressions and animated discussions made a favorable impression on Drew.

The steep incline ended at the gates of the sprawling castle built by Don Fernando II, the husband of Queen Maria II. The romantically inspired structure was a mix of Moorish, Gothic, Manueline, and Bavarian influence. It was Don Fernando's Disneyland, his attempt at a physical representation of his romantic ideas and feelings.

Drew knew little of the background of the Palace but was impressed by the thousands of colored tiles that covered the outer walls and its storybook beauty that always attracted Americans. The lengthening shadows would have obscured most of the tile work if not for the newly installed lights that kept the tourist attraction illuminated at dusk. His heavy mood soon slipped away, a smile creased his worn face.

"I told you." Marie smiled at his positive expression.

"Fantastic," he mumbled, his tired eyes roaming over the massive walls. He was physically and mentally exhausted from a day like none other. The confession was never far from his mind, seeping into his thoughts at each tortured turn.

"Let's go." She grabbed his arm and they were off. They ducked into a side door and she talked briefly to a friendly security guard who knew they were coming.

The Pena Palace was darkened as they moved from one ornate room to the next. The former home of the Portuguese monarchy was now a museum to show off the absurd splendor of the chosen. The opulence was mind-numbing considering the relative poverty of the average Portuguese at the time it was constructed.

Marie glided from one gilded room to the next, pointing to frescoed ceilings and explaining the relevance of the inspirational artistry. The after-hours lighting mimicked the illumination of candlelight, adding to the surreal atmosphere of the Palace and its great rooms of leisure. Drew let the weight of the world slip from his shoulders and imagined himself as a besieged monarch waiting for the enemy to scale the treacherous hill and kill him. The darkened, hulking walls the only protection from the angry populace pooling at the foot of the mountain, screaming for blood and justice. It was a pleasant diversion. He studied a simple desk for correspondence; he liked it for its simplicity amongst such overwhelming craftsmanship. They entered the gargantuan kitchen designed to feed the entire royal family and guests at a moment's notice. Drew thought of his mother and how she would like the uncluttered aspect of the royal kitchen.

Marie saved the best for last. They emerged from the protective walls to an outside patio that overlooked the heavily wooded valley and the distant Atlantic Ocean. The rolling hills below were a few moments away from total darkness as day faded to night. He could see the darkened shape of the Moorish Castle, watching his every move, aware of the secret revealed upon its turreted walls.

"I can't believe this place." Drew leaned over the perfectly sculpted railing and gazed at the treetops far below. He imagined Sheldon Harrison contemplating suicide from such a perch. He could feel Harrison in the hills of Sintra, he should have died amongst the ruins dating back to the Crusades, among the natural beauty of a place where pain and suffering seemed so inappropriate.

"It's so peaceful on this side." Marie sighed. She smiled and wondered why she was inclined to such bold behavior. He was a virtual stranger under tremendous stress, yet she felt a peculiar obligation to ease his burden.

Marie frequently had lunch at the Pena Palace with her friend, yet never tired of the commanding view and lush wilderness on the steep slopes. Her senses, sometimes dulled by Lisbon's crowded and dirty streets, were rejuvenated each time the train dropped her off at Sintra's humble station.

"I don't know much about you, Marie." Drew felt obligated to make small talk as they quietly absorbed the infectious night air.

"You don't need to know anything," she snapped; her serious expression illuminated by a halogen lamp near the doorway.

"Okay." Drew looked away and felt embarrassed.

"You're so easy," she laughed and tucked her hand through his arm, "I like to fool with people." She beamed; she enjoyed being an attractive young woman at the height of her flirtatious powers.

"I'm easy." He smiled awkwardly and said nothing.

"What did you want to know, Drew?"

"Anything I guess."

"I was born on a small island in the Azores."

"I know somebody from the Azores."

"There are many immigrants from the Azores in America. I lived there until I was eighteen. I left when I went to the Sorbonne."

Drew was impressed, what he knew of the Sorbonne made him feel intimidated by her education.

"I have many relatives in Massachusetts." She smiled and made him think of home.

"Where did you study in America?"

"Columbia."

"Impressive." He felt parochial and unimpressive. It was his first trip out of North America.

"Yes, I worked very hard."

"Where is your family?" They walked towards the exit arm in arm.

"In the Azores. One of my brothers moved to America when I was at university. My mother and father are schoolteachers on St. Michel. They are close to retirement age. They have a small house and enjoy the slow pace I did not want. It's an old world island set in its ways, change and excitement are not common occurrences."

"Is that why your brother left?"

"No, he's gay and the Azores is not the most accepting society for such a lifestyle. Plus how was he going to find a mate in such a small place. He lives in San Francisco and is very happy. Enough about me, what are you going to do with that?" She pointed to the manila envelope tucked under his arm. He winced as if someone had punched him in the gut. She noticed the protective reaction and made a mental note to tread lightly when discussing the mysterious package.

"I have to wait six months and that's all I can say about it." His posture was defensive; she could feel his muscular arm tighten instinctively. Marie also felt his extreme fatigue; she was amazed at his endurance after two draining days in a strange country.

"Let's go." She pushed him passed the front gate and down the dark path.

"Where…I need to find a place to stay," he mumbled.

"You are staying with me," she said authoritatively.

"I am?"

"Yes, and I won't take no for an answer."

Marie Almeida's weekday home was a no-frills one-bedroom flat halfway down the mountain. The amenities, by American standards, were sparse and seriously dated. The front door was pink and peeling badly. The brass doorknocker was askew, waiting for the budget-conscious landlord to fix it. Marie casually tossed her bag and keys on a new kitchen table. The walls were similar to the front door, uneven and pitted with poorly patched holes, flaking paint visible on all walls. The living room was the largest room and it was quite small. The main selling point of the tired flat was the view of the town below. The view was not as dramatic or picturesque as from the Pena Palace or the Moorish Castle, but was impressive compared to the modest monthly rental fee.

"I'm going to change, I'll meet you on the balcony."

He stepped onto the balcony and imagined the sleeping valley below. Twinkling headlights and occasional light from another home gave him an idea of the geography below. He leaned against the rotting doorframe and took a deep breath. He sagged, his head felt heavy from the events of the day. The slightly thinner air invaded his lungs, adding to the sudden lethargy. He found a small chair on the balcony and sat down with a heavy sigh, already tired of the unwanted burden.

Marie returned moments later wearing casual pants and a loose fitting blouse. Her flowing hair down and unbound, she held two glasses and a bottle of wine.

"Wine?" She sat on a black chair that did not match his.

"Sure."

"Great!" She expertly poured the Portuguese wine and savored the first taste of her only vice. A low moan escaped her perfect lips; the stress of the day eradicated; she was free to enjoy the warm breeze across her young face. Her hair fluttered and she closed her eyes before speaking again.

"What are your plans?" Marie asked softly.

"To go home I guess. My job is finished."

"Yes…you are done." She seemed disappointed by his answer.

"Why? Should I stay here and romance you?" He flirted amicably.

She noticed his thin smile under the dim balcony light. His self-confidence, sometimes shielded by layers of shyness, broke through with a resounding thud.

"Sure." She looked away, surprisingly embarrassed by his boldness. Her hands trembled and she found it difficult to respond.

"Relax, sometimes I say things for the shock value."

"That's good to know." She was disheartened; did he say that to everybody? Was she nothing special? She cursed herself for being so immature.

"I'm totally exhausted, I don't think I should impose on you anymore. I really should call a taxi and head back to Lisbon."

"You are not! You are staying here with me."

"I really can't…I need to get back." His mind was awash with conflicting thoughts.

"You just got here."

"I know." He yawned and rubbed his eyes vigorously.

She grabbed his arm, "Don't worry I am not going to seduce you. I have a boyfriend in Lisbon."

"I didn't think you were." Drew sat upright, suddenly alert by the revelation.

"Please stay and get a fresh start tomorrow. I like having company. It can be very lonely during the week in Sintra." Her pleasant tone convinced him to stay.

Soon after the debate ended, Marie transformed her couch into a rather comfortable looking bed. After a moment's indecision about how to say goodnight she left him on his new bed.

Drew stripped down to his boxer shorts and lay upon the clean sheets, his gaze shifting to the paint-spackled ceiling. Without warning the cooling breeze died down, he ripped his shirt off and wiped the sweat from his forehead. He wished she had a small air conditioner. It was an unheard of luxury in such a flat.

A few steps away Marie was resting comfortably in her double bed, her mind on the stranger in her living room. Why did she insist he stay? What was her motivation? It could be dangerous, physically and emotionally to act in such an irresponsible way. What would her fiancée say to such an arrangement? The ease she felt in his presence only added to her misgivings about her guest.

Marie Almeida prided herself for being a person always on the edge of conventionality and her irreverent attitude was something she wore as a badge of honor. Some would argue the very acknowledgement of such a personality trait might be, in fact, a planned behavior pattern to garner a certain response from others. Her early life in the ultra Catholic Azores helped forge her rebellious attitude. It didn't take many indiscretions to earn a reputation as an individual with strange thoughts and desires. Her adventures at the Sorbonne transformed her from a country girl to a cosmopolitan woman who felt more at home on the bustling streets of Paris than with her family back home. Her conservative family traveled to Paris many times, each time returning more horrified at her appearance and actions than the previous visit.

The underlying pulse of the city infected her and she became a person of the streets. Not, of course, a homeless person, but someone who spent most of her free time in cafés with the artists and students. She had affairs with a few of her fellow Sorbonne classmates, nothing to remember or regret, except one. Her somewhat liberal lifestyle during her undergraduate years in Paris scarred her relationship with her parents for many years. They were pleased by her career choice and her recent drive for success, but they would never forget the frightful images of her during the Sorbonne years. The second-hand clothes she insisted on wearing horrified them. Her friends were arrogant and superior, belittling them with their mocking glances and sly remarks. The Almeida's were everything her friends opposed; orderly, religious, hardworking, and polite.

Marie felt the sudden change in the temperature and turned on an ancient fan she had found in the closet when she moved in. It was black and heavy with no safety measures to keep your hands safe, it harkened back to a time of little litigation and more personal responsibility. The whirling fan helped circulate the hot air and she started to doze off. Then she thought of her guest. She swore at herself for being so rude. She pictured him bathed in a pool of his own sweat, cursing himself for not taking a cab back to Lisbon.

Drew was hot and uncomfortable, but it wasn't the only reason he was unable to sleep. Sheldon Harrison's monumental confession and the ramifications of the eventual disclosure were at the forefront. He was however, not despairing over his decision to sleep amongst the steaming hills of Sintra. He was close to the source of Harrison's inspiration; he was forever connected with the sleepy Portuguese town.

"Drew? Drew, are you sleeping?" Marie whispered from her bedroom doorway, her voice sailing across the stuffy apartment.

"No."

"It's too hot out here. How can you stand it?" She whispered.

"It's okay." He sat up and could see her silhouette through the inky darkness.

"No, come in my room. I have a small fan. We can share."

"That's okay."

"Come please." She crossed the room pulled him from the sofa bed and escorted him to her room.

The neatly arranged bed had clean sheets and the fresh aroma of Marie's body wash. She led him safely to the bed and the oscillating fan.

"Are you sure about this?" He hesitated before joining her. He felt the artificial circulation of air and knew he was not leaving.

"Yes."

Silence reigned during the first few minutes of the awkward arrangement. The only sound came from the humming fan and an occasional car on the road nearby. He glanced carefully at her body. A slim beam of light from the porch light illuminated her slim figure.

"Are you okay with this?" She asked.

"Sure." He swallowed hard, staring intently at her protruding nipples, itching for release from the flimsy fabric of her nightshirt.

"It's not bothering me, so don't worry." She turned and looked at him.

"It's fine really." He tried to think of something else, but his young mind was fixated on the sexiest woman he had ever shared a bed with. He could smell her hair, her deodorant, her perfume, her soap, absorbing it all, relishing every moment he knew could not last.

"What are you thinking about?" She nudged him with her naked elbow.

"I can't say."

"I know."

"Then why did you ask me?" He laughed and nudged her back.

"Is it keeping you awake?"

"Yes." He answered somberly.

"Sheldon Harrison was a very important man. We studied his novels in high school and at the Sorbonne."

"Unfortunately I know how important he was." His anguished tone was revealing.

"What's wrong?" She sat up and leaned on her elbow, her supple breasts touching his paralyzed arm. He shuddered, his body immobile by the casual contact.

"I can't tell you anything, Marie. It's part of the agreement. I can't talk about it."

"Yes, but it keeps you awake."

"It's only the beginning, Marie," he said painfully.

"I can help you." She pushed closer to him, her left nipple touched his wrist bone.

"You can't. I'm alone in this."

He flinched as her sweet tasting lips parted his, probing and darting, seeking a sensual home. She pressed her body on top of his, rubbing his shoulders and neck with the affection of a long time-lover. The actual kiss only lasted the briefest of moments, but to Drew it was an eternity, a blissful black hole of sexual delirium. It felt so right, so remarkably right, he fought the urge to make a permanent bond. He almost cried in desperation, he knew he would never be so close to her again. He wanted to leave his mark with her, to make love so she would never forget him. She would remember his passionate embrace, his quivering lips, and their loving climax.

She was aggressive and passionate but ultimately not willing to go further than the hot embrace. She slowly eased her mouth from his, kissing his forehead and cheek before laying back down. He settled down, his mind free of the somber details of the reality of his discovery.

The strong smell of fresh brewed coffee assaulted Drew's nostrils, stirring him from his deep sleep. The heat that had slipped away in the early morning hours returned with a vengeance. The hard-working fan was fighting a battle it could never win.

He felt sticky and in desperate need of a shower. He yearned to brush his teeth more than anything else. Marie entered the bedroom wearing a work skirt and a black bra. She was ironing a crème colored blouse when she heard him stir.

"Do you want to take a shower?" She smiled at his disheveled appearance.

"Please."

"I thought so." She tossed him a clean towel and a new toothbrush.

"Thank you."

Drew stared aimlessly into the bathroom mirror and was startled by his appearance. He had two-day stubble and deep circles under his eyes. He stripped down and fought with the foreign shower nozzle until a steady stream of warm water swept the grime away. He used her sweet smelling soap without trepidation; his trust in her grew by the hour. It did occur to him as he lathered his tired body that he really didn't know her. They were virtual strangers thrown together by the most unlikely of scenarios. The crude shower rejuvenated his mind and body.

"Drew?" There was a tiny knock on the rickety door.

"Yeah?" He watched her small hands slowing push open the half closed door. The steam from his shower escaped into the living room in a great rush. Drew quickly wrapped the towel around his lower extremities. She laughed inwardly at his modesty.

"I just wanted to say goodbye. I don't like to be late. Stop by the bank on your way to the station, please."

"Thank you for everything, Marie." His awkwardness faded and he stood erect, his wet hair dripping on the crudely tiled floor.

"It was my pleasure, Drew." She leaned over and kissed his wet lips. It wasn't a seductive kiss but an innocent mark of affection.

"I made coffee. Please take anything you like." She shut the door and was gone.

Drew finished dressing and capped off an agreeable morning with a cup of tasty coffee on the balcony. Small pockets of haze fought the otherwise bright morning sun. He found a note and a clean shirt on the sofa. He thought about the owner of the white shirt, but it really didn't matter, he would send it back to her from Lisbon. The soft cotton felt nice against his skin. He inhaled the warm breeze of the European paradise. It was easy to understand how Harrison fell in love with the lush cliffs and temperate climate; it was the only truth serum he ever knew. Drew grabbed the only reference book he brought with him, *Frommer's Portugal* travel guide, and tried to identify what he was seeing and smelling. He easily picked out the lemon groves and eucalyptus trees described, but he struggled to find the pink and purple bougainvillea. He made a mental note to look for them on his way down. The handy book told him the sweet aroma that cleared his nostrils of Lisbon's urban potpourri, was the yellow mimosa plant. At home he seldom had the time or energy to examine and appreciate his surroundings with such preciseness; it was a welcome change of pace.

Drew enjoyed the ten-minute walk to the bustling train station below. The station was overflowing with tourists arriving from Lisbon. Their hurried pace and excited glances amused Drew, he felt like a veteran of Sintra's charms. He grabbed a train schedule and escaped the crowd without incident. He checked the departure time for the next train and then decided he had enough time to visit Marie at the bank.

He found her embroiled in a dispute with an irate customer. He left her alone and headed for the café he had gone to with Andrew Garrity. He sat at the same table and ordered some kind of Danish. The owner recognized him as a friend of Garrity's and gave him preferential treatment.

"So, Drew, you really liked this place I see?" Andrew Garrity patted Drew on the shoulder.

'Mr. Garrity, how are you?" Drew stood and shook his hand.

"I thought I might find you here. I just spoke with Marie and she said she saw you heading in this direction. I had some more bank business, two days of work, I don't think I can handle it," he laughed and ordered a coffee.

"I'm glad you decided to stay the night." He paused and hoped Drew had some good gossip. Drew's expression disappointed Garrity, he knew immediately nothing juicy had occurred between the young bank executive and the American student.

"Yes…it was late and Marie insisted. I'm glad I did, it's a whole different experience waking up to such beauty. I can't say enough about her hospitality."

"Good, I'm glad to hear that." Garrity leaned back and let the sun warm his face.

"You never get sick of it?"

"Sintra?"

"Yeah."

"Never. I want to die right here."

"It is beautiful."

"So my boy what was in the package?"

"You know I can't tell you." Drew smirked knowingly.

"I was just testing you. Remember six months, and then the world can hear what you already know. Then everybody will know the last words of the great Sheldon Harrison. My friend, the greatest American writer of my lifetime." Garrity acted casual, but he was very curious about the package.

"What are your plans?" Garrity tried to think of something besides the package.

"I'm not sure. I guess I'll fly home as soon as I get back to Lisbon. I have an open-ended ticket."

"Did he give you any money for the trip?"

"Yes." Drew was cagey about the details.

"Do you have any left?"

"Yes, of course."

"Then spend it in Sintra, don't go home with a penny of it. Sheldon would want it that way."

"It's very tempting but I really need to go home."

"Well I still have time to convince you."

"Do you know Marie's boyfriend?" Drew blurted, unsure why he needed to know.

"Yes, I've met him a few times. He's a joke. He doesn't deserve her, no way. He comes from a very wealthy family in Lisbon. He is the most arrogant son of a bitch I have ever met. She will never marry him." Garrity was disgusted by the thought and didn't try to hide it.

"Why not?"

"A flower like Marie will never settle for a man like that. Her chemical makeup will prevent her from being with him." His lips quivered with the strong words.

"I think she said they were engaged already."

"Bullshit! She won't marry him." His voice was strained and the veins in his neck bulged in protest. The very thought of a permanent bond between the two was unthinkable.

"I'm not really sure if that is what she said. I think she alluded to marriage. At some point that's the impression I got."

"I don't believe it. Hold on Drew. Jesus…I must be seeing things." Garrity stood up and gazed down the street.

"What?" Drew turned in the direction he was staring.

"Wait," Garrity ordered, and then fumbled with his prescription sunglasses.

"What is it?"

"Well, look what the cat dragged in." Garrity left the table and waved vigorously.

"Charlotte!" Garrity cupped his hands and yelled across the street.

"Who?" Drew stood up and saw the figure of a resolute woman briskly approaching the table. She looked familiar but he wasn't sure.

"Andrew! I thought I would find you here." Charlotte Emerson did not have to feign excitement; she was genuinely happy to see her old acquaintance. She was wearing beige shorts and a white shirt that was stylish and practical. Her streaked blond hair was neatly arranged in a bun atop her head. She was a stunning example of what a moderately attractive woman could achieve with designer clothing, a deep tan, and hours in the gym. Her blue eyes, the only part of her appearance that was not chiseled or enhanced in some way, were breathtaking upon first glance.

"Charlotte Emerson, this is Drew Engle." Garrity proudly introduced them.

"We've met." Drew's sagging shoulders told Garrity all he needed to know of the nature of their relationship.

"Yes, we are acquainted. Drew's little adventure has caused quite a stir in our gossip-starved family. You know the way they can be, Andrew." She used a familiar tone when addressing Garrity.

"Sit!" Garrity gave up his seat and pulled one from another table.

"Always the gentleman," she remarked before collapsing with a sigh.

"What are you doing in Sintra? Why didn't you phone me? I didn't even know you were in Europe."

"It was last-minute thing. I was in Paris for a few days but decided to take a chance and come to Sintra. I wanted to see how our friend was coming along." Her eyes lit up. The challenge of getting him to divulge all he knew was intoxicating.

"Oh really." Garrity seemed slightly miffed by her admission.

"So, Drew, what is all this cloak and dagger nonsense? What skeletons did my grandfather lay upon your humble feet?"

"I can't tell you what he gave me," Drew said firmly.

"He can't reveal the contents of the package for six months. I have all the paperwork if you want to see it." Garrity leaned back and waited for her response.

"Wow," she stared with a shocked expression, "it must be something important for such secretive measures."

"Perhaps. Likely, I would think," Garrity said without looking at Drew. He did not want to put undo pressure on the young man.

"What a strange man." She tapped her manicured nails on the plastic table.

"He was a good man." Garrity was turned off by her cavalier attitude.

"It's just such a strange way for him to tell us something. Why couldn't he give it to a family member, we deserve to know first. Don't you think?"

"He can't talk about it, Charlotte." Garrity cut her off.

"I understand, Andrew…"

"Why are you alone?"

"My travel companions are still in Paris. I left without telling them." She was proud of her unannounced flight. Garrity smiled at her reference to "travel companions." She could have said friends, but she always chose her words carefully, crafting her language to give the impression of intellectual aloofness.

"Why did you leave them?" Drew asked brusquely. His open contempt angered and enthralled Charlotte. It was a challenge to figure out his complex, sometimes contradictory personality.

"I came to see you cart off a few million dollars from my grandfather's estate. Maybe I wanted to see you win the lottery. Perhaps, Drew, I wanted to witness your lecherous behavior firsthand." Her scathing attack was met with a raised eyebrow from Garrity and a menacing glare from Drew.

"I didn't ask for this."

"I didn't mean to infer you did. Why are you so defensive? Do you have something to share with us?"

"Charlotte." Garrity warned.

"Why are you really here? What did I ever do to you? Did I infringe on your exclusive right to your grandfather? From what I gathered his death was nothing but an inconvenience to you."

"You're ignorant, "she lashed out, "you're nothing but an insignificant fly on the wall!" Who was he to give her lecture on the proper way to mourn the loss of a family member? His insolence was intolerable.

"Charlotte, calm down." Garrity had little patience for such bickering.

"Andrew, can we go someplace? I'm tired of all this." She rose to her feet and walked away from the table. Her luscious figure stirred both men.

"Well, I see you two are fast friends." Garrity patted Drew on the shoulder and sensed that he was hurt by the childish attack.

"Yeah she really hates me."

"Oh come on, she's volatile by nature. She's okay behind that nasty façade."

"I'm not sure about that."

"I'll be back in a few minutes, excuse me please." Garrity bowed politely and followed Charlotte around the corner.

Garrity kept her in view as he navigated through the midday foot traffic, amazed at her agility and speed. He finally grabbed her arm near the Bank of Portugal.

"Hey, not so fast, Charlotte."

"Andrew…I'm sorry about that. I hate being so rude." She tried to look sheepish and repentant, but the effort was transparent.

"Sure you do," he smirked. "Let's cut the bullshit."

"What?"

"What do you have against him? He seems pretty harmless; this whole thing was dumped on his lap. From what I can see."

"I don't know for sure," she gently moved him out of traffic, "there is something about him that just brings out the worst in me, I become defensive and quite nasty. I'm not like that."

He smiled incredulously, marveling at her delusional mind. Was it possible she was unaware of her virulent intolerance and ingrained superiority? Andrew often wondered if there was a real person behind the unflappable, supremely confident exterior that both intrigued and disgusted him.

"Why are you here, Charlotte? I know it isn't to see me." His sly smile was not lost on her.

"How do you know?" She touched his arm seductively. Strolling down the busy street under the hot Portuguese sun Drew Engle vanished from their thoughts.

Chapter 16

"Drew, why the sad face?" Marie Almeida sat on Garrity's vacated chair.

"No reason." He tried to brighten up, but the altercation with Charlotte was still eating at him.

"Put the umbrella up! The sun," she exclaimed and did it for him.

"Thanks." He felt better in the shade.

"What's wrong?" She touched his hand and looked concerned.

Drew briefly explained the bitter encounter with Charlotte.

"She is not a very understanding person I guess." Marie was not surprised by it. She recalled meeting Charlotte Emerson at a party hosted by Garrity. She was pleasant but aloof, not a particularly interesting or engaging conversationalist. She expected more from the granddaughter of the great Sheldon Harrison.

"I don't understand her attitude, I didn't ask for this." He was weary and depressed; Charlotte's presence seemed to resurrect old insecurities. "I think I'm going home today."

"Lisbon?" She asked.

"No, America."

"I don't think you can make it today. Why so soon?"

"You know I've been fighting the Charlotte Emerson's of the world my whole life."

"What do you mean?" She affectionately rubbed his arm.

"I was the only one of Sheldon's interns that had a real job. I was framing houses with my dad the day before I started the internship. I busted my ass during the summer, six days a week. It might be hard for you to understand what I mean."

"I understand, keep going."

"My mother went to college but never really worked and my father barely graduated high school. This set them apart from many of my friend's parents."

"What do you mean?" She knew what he meant, but she wanted him to keep talking, she was enraptured by his sincerity.

"For example, when I was young I always had the feeling that my parents were treated differently. There was a subtle condescension that kept them from socializing outside a game or whatever I was involved with. It wasn't as if anybody said anything, it was more like a silent wall of superiority that I'm sure they could sense. My mother was thought of as a flake, was immune to the opinions of the pseudo intellectual suburban class, but it bothered my father. I think he had an inferiority complex. He tried too hard to ingratiate himself with the other parents; I think it was partially for my well-being so I could in turn make friends easier. It didn't help, I always chose my friends carefully. I was unimpressed by the occupations of their parents."

"I also come from a humble background and can sympathize with you. The caste system is stronger in this country than in America. The cultural gulf between the rich and the poor is definitely wider. It can be frustrating and sometimes impossible to overcome." She sadly thought of all the times she was ashamed to admit to her friends that her family was simple folk from the Azores. Her reluctance had vanished with time; in her current career nobody cared where you came from as long as you produced. It was a refreshing departure from her academic career where almost all her schoolmates were from affluent, politically connected families of great influence. Even her close friends at the Sorbonne, who on the surface appeared to be impoverished artists languishing on the Left Bank, secretly received monthly stipends from their amused parents. Of course not all her classmates fell into this category, but ironically she avoided the companionship of those from similar backgrounds. She found them boring and quite pedestrian. She hated herself for the obvious contradiction.

"I don't want to complain. It's just the way things are," he said with a nervous sigh.

Marie kept talking about her chaotic life and the trials of being a woman in a male dominated field. He should have been home preparing for another rigorous semester at Boston University not thousands of miles away at a café on the ancient shoulders of the Sintra Mountains.

"Hello, Andrew." She smiled at Garrity as he approached. Her face clouded over as she recognized Charlotte Emerson in tow.

"Marie Almeida this is Sheldon Harrison's niece Charlotte Emerson. You may have met before."

"Hello." Marie's simple reply was unfriendly.

"Nice to see you." Charlotte stiffened at Marie's snare and tone. It was obvious Drew had told her about their contentious relationship and the hostile engagement that had just occurred.

"Why did you come to Sintra?" Marie asked boldly, making no attempt to hide her allegiance.

"Do you work for the tourist bureau?" Charlotte responded with equal venom. The familiar-looking woman did not intimidate her.

"I do not. Just curious about what brings you to our humble little town." Marie's hands began to tremble and her face burned.

"I applaud your English, but be careful you don't shed your entire identity. I knew Drew was here on a mission of my grandfather's doing so I decided to check up on him. Andrew has told me of the gag order and I'm very disappointed that he cannot speak of his discovery."

"Would you like to join us for dinner at my home tonight?" Garrity interjected quickly, he believed the conversation was only seconds away from an open exchange of insults.

"No, Andrew, I believe Drew is leaving today," Marie said quickly.

"You are?" Garrity was surprised by the announcement.

"I think so. I have to start school soon and this trip has really put me way behind. I need to go home and work a few weeks to make up for the loss of the internship."

"I guess my grandfather's death was very inconvenient for you," Charlotte pounced.

"I didn't mean it like that." Drew fumbled with the package between his legs; it made him look awkward and ill at ease.

"This is nonsense, Drew," Garrity intervened, "a few days in the sun in this glorious town will do you wonders. You won't regret the decision." He was a marvelous salesman with his confident words and radiant smile.

"All my things are in Lisbon."

"So take the train back, get a few things, and be back for dinner."

"Okay, maybe."

"Don't give me that maybe crap. I'll see you tonight. Meet Marie at the bank at six and she'll take you to my house. I insist."

"We will be there." Marie grabbed Drew's hand and led him away from the table.

"Nice to meet you." Charlotte called out, a small amount of sincerity slipping into her voice.

"Yes." Marie's curt response was predictable.

"Are you staying with me, Charlotte?" Garrity stared at her until she responded.

"Of course, my love, who else?" She tried to act excited, but she was hot and uncomfortable. She regretted leaving the most exciting city in the world for the small town with much charm but little else. She undoubtedly appreciated the beauty of Sintra but it was less than a year since her last visit and nothing had changed. She felt some relief in knowing she was staying at Garrity's hillside home.

"Can we go now? I want to relax."

"Sure…of course." Garrity responded quickly to her request. He flagged down a familiar taxi and in a cloud of dust was whisked away.

The well-dressed driver was pleased to have Garrity in his humble taxi. He knew Garrity to be a generous tipper and a pleasant conversationalist. His fellow drivers also thought highly of him. They thought he was a courteous gentleman who treated them with respect seldom exhibited by the tourists from Lisbon. Garrity's amiable personality should not be mistaken for weakness, he was ferocious when he believed he was being cheated or overcharged for a ride. The veteran drivers knew of his fierce temper and avoided confrontation. The last incident occurred a year before with a rookie taxi driver who insisted his bloated fare was legitimate. Garrity knew the fare was bullshit and was not intimidated by the surly young driver from the streets of Lisbon. He wrongly thought the mild-mannered American would simply accept his declaration. The young man learned a valuable lesson outside Garrity's villa. The refined American lawyer pummeled the stunned driver until he begged for mercy. The authorities laughed at his subsequent complaint against Garrity, they were convinced of the driver's dubious calculations and dismissed him outright. Later, Garrity made peace with the embarrassed driver and out of the ashes of violence a friendship grew.

Charlotte leaned on the strong shoulder of Garrity and dozed off as the car bounced over cobblestone streets and dodged unwary pedestrians. She was glad for the ten-minute respite.

Chapter 17

Gin and Tonic

Drew felt a sense of relief as the worn commuter train pulled into Lisbon. The intoxicating mountains that had swept Garrity from his unrewarding life in New York City and inspired Sheldon Harrison's confession had temporarily lost its grip on Engle.

The presence of Charlotte Emerson in Sintra seemed to dim his vision and cloud his judgment. He stumbled into the Hotel Fenix, unsure of his next move, debating and deliberating until the hotel clerk informed him of his messages. Two were from his worried parents and one from Carlton Smithfield wishing him good luck on his journey. He retired to his room for a long nap and a thorough shower.

The short rest seemed to rejuvenate his flagging spirits, thoughts of Charlotte Emerson relegated to the recesses of his mind. He descended to the hotel bar and ordered a gin and tonic. The pleasant bartender had just opened the bar and was glad to see his first customer. He oversaw a large bar along with the many tables and chairs scattered about the room. The décor of the bar was strangely dated. Drew chuckled at the 1970's-era colors and style of everything from the ashtrays to the green plastic chairs. It was inviting, but clearly designed for intimate encounters after dinner when discretion ruled.

Drew was a light drinker turned heavy by the rigors of college. He rubbed his freshly shaved face and let the smooth gin ease the tension of the day. He thought about his future, the strain of being the bearer of such unwanted news. Nobody, from scholars to rabid followers wanted the monstrous figure of Sheldon Harrison harmed in such a way.

"What if I just throw the thing in the ocean? There is nothing in the legal papers that says I can't do that. I can't destroy it! But why should I forever be linked with such a horrible man? He was such a deceptive and manipulative person. Why such an elaborate plan? His arrogance is appalling. Did he think he was doing me a favor by entrusting me with the most extraordinary confession in American literary history! He has burdened me with the truth his cowardice prevented him from revealing. He waited until what he believed was his last coherent moment to tell the world of his life of lies."

"More?" The bartender started to make another gin and tonic.

"No, thank you." Drew smiled awkwardly and paid the bill. He wandered to the front desk and asked the smiling clerk about the hotel safe.

One hour later, Sheldon Harrison's confession was in the care of the staff at the Hotel Fenix. The Rosetta Stone tucked away in the bowels of a bomb-proof safe. Like the author's cold, hard fingers touching the inside of his gilded coffin, the manila folder containing his deepest secrets creased against the steel walls of its tomb.

The subway ride to Praca Dom Pedro IV Square or Rossio was short and uneventful for Drew. The lack of air-conditioning in the cars left him hot and slightly annoyed. He entered the square and was surprised by the bustling crowd that seemed to come from every direction. It was by no means an extraordinary square by European standards, however to the unaccustomed eye of a novice traveler it was nirvana. The Teatro Nacional Dona Maria II, the national opera house, anchored one end of the square in direct line with famous Portuguese heroes bronzed for eternity. Hundreds of wizened pigeons huddled about the monuments looking for a quick meal, they were a disruptive part of the landscape for some; others felt they were a beloved part of Lisbon's fabric. Drew noticed large groups of Africans milling about the square; debating in their native tongue about topics Drew felt ignorant about. Some were disheveled, but they were hardly the majority. Most were dressed with careful dignity and spoke with great animation about issues that affected their lives as the new underclass of Lisbon. Portugal was struggling to shed its imperialistic past; the presence of unemployed Africans on the streets of Lisbon brought the issue to the forefront of current politics.

After a short walk around the square, Drew was surprised to see the imposing Castle of St. George looming above in the Alfama district of the city. He followed his map and exited the square opposite the opera house. The maze of tiny streets that led him through Alfama, the oldest part of the city, was both charming and depressing. It had survived the devastating, cataclysmic earthquake of 1755 that destroyed most of Lisbon. The impoverished dwellings that lined the near vertical climb to St. George's Castle were tame by American standards, but not exactly storybook Europe. The old world charm of the winding streets and hidden alleyways made up for the dilapidated conditions of the buildings. Drew imagined age-old rivalries and treacherous plots hatched in the shuttered back rooms of the red roofed hovels.

His reward for the steep climb through the residential heart of the city was a view that can only be described as breathtaking. The entire city of Lisbon was at his feet as he stood upon the ramparts of the ancient walls of the Castle of St. George. The turbulent Tagus River below was deep blue and very wide as it headed for the salt waters of the Atlantic Ocean. He slowly walked along the massive interior, admiring the view of the hundreds of red roofed homes and buildings scattered across the city. Many of the homes were only a stones throw from the hulking outer walls, hugging it for protection.

The interior of the Castle St. George was shaded by small trees and neatly planted vegetation; it afforded a nice spot for reflection. The tumultuous journey that began the moment he stepped into Sheldon Harrison's convoluted world seemed without end. Drew enjoyed the cooling breeze upon his sweating face. They would attack him, his credibility; maybe his family would be pressured into saying something that could hurt him. It could not end without devastation on all sides. They would attack to preserve Harrison's place in the literary pantheon of American writers. Above all, they would attack to preserve their way of life.

Chapter 18

Dinner

"What are you doing?" Charlotte Emerson yelled to her host Andrew Garrity. She was casually clipping her fingernails and daydreaming about her adventures to come.

"Nothing." Garrity reentered the top deck of his multilevel villa. He tried to squeeze past her, placing a sweating glass of water on the sun-baked table. She stopped him with her legs, trapping him in a seductive embrace. He stopped and gave her a sly grin.

"Come on, Charlotte, not again."

"Yes again." She rose to her feet and pulled him by the waistband of his shorts. She could smell alcohol on his breath. He tried to free himself from her groping hands.

"Charlotte..."

"What?" She coyly slipped her hand down his shorts and massaged his growing excitement. He managed to free himself from her clutches and step back.

"Charlotte, what we did before was a mistake." Garrity tried to conceal his raging hard-on.

"It doesn't look like a mistake to me." She pointed to his erection.

Garrity swore at himself for not wearing any underwear that morning. He was a bachelor who always ran out of socks and underwear.

"What we did was wrong. You were only twenty years old. Jesus, my kids are almost twenty."

"It didn't seem to bother you at the time."

"It did bother me, it was the beginning of the end of my marriage. You were just an impressionable kid who had an affair with somebody who should have known better."

"It wasn't wrong," she protested, slightly taken back by Garrity's view of their affair, "it was beautiful and you know it."

"It was wrong." Her indignant body language made him nervous. She was a volatile person who could be vengeful and cruel.

"Don't be so sure you seduced me, Andrew. I wore that string bikini in front of you for a reason. Didn't you notice that we always ended up going to the beach together? How I always flirted with you? You were just an unwitting pawn in my master plan to sleep with you." She smiled and did not alter her gaze. Her bold confidence unnerved him.

"I see." Garrity had always regretted their passionate affair. He leaned over the railing.

"Don't be ashamed, Andrew. You were the best I've ever had." She stood behind him and rubbed his crotch again.

"Charlotte, they'll be here soon." He reluctantly pushed her hand away.

"Oh come on…you know you used to think about me when you slept with your wife. Fantasizing about our lovemaking."

"Knock it off, Charlotte!"

She stopped and looked away from him, dismayed by his reproach. She felt an overwhelming sense of sadness, depressing thoughts seeped into her mind.

"You know I want to but we…" Garrity never finished his weak explanation. She grabbed the back of his head and kissed him deeply.

Garrity was unprepared for the passion of the kiss; his knees felt weak and he knew there was no turning back. He wanted her more than the first time at Sheldon's home on the Vineyard. She rubbed his legs and drove her ferocious tongue deeper. She felt his arousal and loved the power.

"Let's go." He took her hand and led her to his spacious bedroom. The late afternoon sunlight flooded the open beamed bedroom from skylights high above. Three ceiling fans moved the warm air; Garrity rarely used the air-conditioning system.

He gently pushed her onto his large bed. The thought of uncomplicated intercourse fueled their desire. They explored each other's salty bodies, caressing and kissing until Garrity couldn't stand the suspense any longer. The slow start evaporated as the older man made her cry out in a fit of uncontrolled pleasure. Sweat poured from their heaving bodies, they clutched and clawed each other. His powerful strokes kept her from catching her breath, body fluids sloshing in an amalgamation of lust and joy. It was as she remembered, intense and completely satisfying.

A few miles away, Drew arrived on the commuter train from Lisbon.

"My Knight from Lisboa!" Marie kissed his clean cheek and tucked her arm under his, escorting him away from the station.

"How are you?" He glanced at her sleeveless white dress that clung to her heavenly body. Graceful. A simple elegance that made her stand out in the crowd. Her topaz shoulders contrasted with the white dress perfectly. She was a picture of casual beauty, a fitting partner for any occasion.

Marie examined him closely and was pleased with his dress. He seemed more relaxed and comfortable; she figured his day away from Sintra did him well. She noted the absence of Harrison's document.

"We need to go quickly." She ushered him to a nearby taxi stand and they were off.

The ride was only ten minutes; it felt like an eternity for Engle. The jolting, twisting ride made him ill; motion sickness he had not felt since his days in the backseat of his parents' two-door car. They didn't talk much during the ride; they were strangely comfortable with each other, like a longtime couple perhaps.

Drew leaped from the taxi the moment the somewhat amused driver stopped rolling in front of Garrity's sheltered villa. Garrity allowed the natural vegetation that surrounded the home to grow freely, adding a thick layer of privacy and conserving the beauty of the hillside.

"Hello, folks." Garrity bellowed from the doorway. He was dressed in a white cotton shirt with pockets over each breast and sleeves rolled up to the elbow.

"Please come in." He gestured for them to follow him. The inside was typically decorated, nice colors, African art on the wall, and leather furniture that gave the impression of an English safari club. It was straight out of a Bombay Company catalog. He could be excused for his lack of originality; he was a single male with no previous decorating experience. The African art was authentic and expensive; he collected them on his frequent trips to the continent. The rest of the living space was clear of clutter and neatly arranged to give the appearance of a larger room. The high ceilings were a nice touch to what was in essence a smallish home expanded to accommodate Garrity's lust for openness. The kitchen was quaint with a Mediterranean feel leading to gold-trimmed glass doors that opened to the large deck. He led his party outside soon after they entered.

"Hello," Charlotte leaned back in her chair and smiled brightly, beaming from her recent orgasm. She motioned for them to sit at the large glass table. Her afternoon sexual encounter had transformed her into an unlikely hostess.

"Can I get you a drink?" Garrity headed for the bar inside.

"Yes, wine please," Marie, answered politely.

"Yes, wine thank you." Drew felt strange asking for wine; it was not the drink of choice for his age group. He felt like a gangly college kid amongst refined adults, their experience and sophistication intimidated him.

Charlotte's sexual bliss soon evaporated at the sight of Marie Almeida leaning effortlessly against the railing of the balcony, her dress fluttering in the stiff breeze. Charlotte bristled at the sight of her natural beauty and sultry demeanor. Drew noticed the glare and wondered what was behind the venomous look. She seemed to shudder with rage.

"So, Drew, do you like Sintra? It's a long way from Boston, isn't it?" Charlotte forced a smile.

"It's beautiful."

Garrity emerged with two glasses of wine.

"Wonderful!" Marie exclaimed and affectionately patted his arm.

Drew noticed the subtle expression of attraction between Garrity and Marie Almeida as they interacted. Garrity watched her slight hand clasp the glass, his interested eyes hoping for a private moment with the ravishing banker.

"Charlotte, what do you do for a living?" Marie forced herself to be somewhat pleasant.

"I'm an editor," Charlotte answered rather blandly.

"That sounds interesting."

"Yes, I can see how you would think so."

"Why would you say that?"

"Because any profession is interesting when you're a banker," Charlotte said in a mocking tone.

Marie's face burned, she fought the nearly overpowering desire to slap her haughty face.

With narrowed eyes and deep resentment, Drew thrust himself in the middle of the burgeoning conflict, "Charlotte, is there anybody you don't offend?"

"It's not an insult," she bristled "just an observation."

"Come on, Charlotte, will you ever let up." Garrity was not amused with her attitude.

"Why are you like this?" Drew exclaimed, putting down his drink and glaring.

"What are you talking about? What is it you don't understand, lottery boy?" Charlotte said with breeziness reserved for the truly confident.

"Fuck off." Drew stood and prepared to leave.

"Hey, Drew, calm down." Garrity placed a firm hand on his shoulder.

"Fly away, lottery boy." Charlotte made an angry gesture with her hand, as if she were swatting a pesky fly.

"Live it up while you can," Drew snapped, his contorted face and bulging veins impressed Marie. She was enthralled by his feisty attitude.

"What?" The deliberately vague warning perplexed Charlotte.

"Nothing," he retorted quickly, remembering his oath. He marched inside to settle himself; regaining his composure was critical at this first moment of weakness.

"Good, Drew, go inside for a few minutes." Garrity encouraged him.

Charlotte felt uneasy. It was his tone that warned of something she could not foresee or prepare for. She sat straight and tried to act casual but her hands were shaking and her mouth felt dry. She wondered what he knew, what was in that safety deposit box that made him so cocky?

"Charlotte? Charlotte!" Garrity nudged her back into reality.

"What?"

"Want another glass?"

"Yes."

"Andrew, can I use your phone? I left my cell at home." Marie held up her pink beeper to see the number of the caller. The bank insisted she carry both devices.

"Of course, use the one in my office," he opened the door for her, "Drew, come back and join us."

"In a minute, Mr. Garrity," Drew answered with little enthusiasm and did not come out.

Marie returned, gathered her things and prepared to leave. "I'm sorry Andrew but I need to leave for a short time."

"Why?"

"Mr. Silva broke the computers again. I will try and come back if I can."

Drew heard the exchange and was ready to leave. Garrity, with all his charm, convinced him to stay without his beautiful chaperone. Drew's reluctance annoyed Garrity, who felt he was being less than an agreeable guest.

"But you must excuse me for a moment also. I need to go to the market." Garrity hastily followed Marie back into the house to call a cab for both of them. He needed to go to the store before they closed. He had used his last two condoms earlier and wanted to be prepared for the night of debauchery that was surely to come.

"This gets better by the minute," Drew said aloud and shrugged his shoulders in defeat.

Charlotte took the news harder than Drew; she rolled her blue eyes and took a stiff belt from her freshened drink. Garrity promised to return within the hour, she knew this was unlikely for he loved to gossip with the local storeowner. He told her they often closed the store together, adjourning to the back room for a drink of his homemade wine.

"Drew, please come out and play." Charlotte snickered, amused by her own sense of humor. It was enough of a positive enticement for him to step back onto the deck.

"Why do you detest me? What is so bad about me?" She asked with only a hint of sincerity.

"Would you please stop with this crap? I barely know you. We don't need to talk. Why don't we…"

"Let's go for walk. Come on let's go."

"Where?" He looked at her suspiciously. The sloping yard was covered with heavy underbrush that extended as far as he could see. It didn't appear to be a yard one would take a casual stroll.

"There is a path on the side of the house. We don't have to walk through all of that."

"Okay."

"Good, Drew, let's get to know each other."

Drew followed her shapely figure down a wrought iron spiral staircase that emptied onto a small patio and the partially hidden trail. The seldom-used path was overgrown but clear enough for them to walk single file. Drew figured the previous owner cleared the way and maintained it over the years. Garrity didn't seem like the type who cared for such things, dirty hands and manual labor did not fit his personality. It ended abruptly in a natural grotto that was enhanced artfully by the person who cut the path.

"Wow that comes up fast." Drew peered down at the jagged rocks twenty feet below.

"Yes it does."

The view was especially exhilarating for the two Americans. She watched his face; his blissful, involuntary sighs triggered a change in her that was swift and contradictory. He was not the vile, threatening stranger she had traded barbs with only minutes before. He was a simple student bewildered by a strange twist of fate, a soft and sensitive person she had hurtfully discounted at first sight.

The effect of the mountainside grotto on the two combatants was remarkable. For a moment they were just another young couple romantically influenced by the charms of nature. The late evening sun vanished behind a thick bank of clouds that chilled the air.

"You have goosebumps." Drew noticed her arms were dimpled.

"I know," she said through clenched teeth.

"Stay close." Drew pulled her close and rubbed her shoulders. She felt nice against him, smooth to the touch. He glanced at her body and wished she wasn't so awful. She leaned her head against his shoulder and felt content.

"It's so beautiful here. America is such a dirty place with such dirty people."

"What do you mean?" Drew asked.

"I hate America, not literally, but just the whole idea of it all."

"Hmmm." He was confused.

"Our cities are so ugly and drab. We have no style or grace. We're a bunch of gluttons compared to other countries." Her commentary was only half serious.

"Really."

"We are quitters."

"How so?"

"Our ancestors quit their homeland instead of staying and fixing the problems." She laughed at his knitted brow. He was getting annoyed with her again.

"You're such an elitist snob."

"I'm a Liberal." Her voice was steady; she was ready to take him on.

"That's the worst combination."

"What is?"

"An elitist Liberal."

"How so?"

"I don't want to get into it with you."

"Are you afraid you will hate me again?"

"No, I never stopped."

"Then why is it the worst, an elitist Liberal?"

"Because you live in an ivory tower, dispensing your wisdom from gated communities."

"So."

"So you live in communities where there is no crime or poverty. You think you help people by throwing money at the problem then you go back to your big house with the SUV in the driveway."

"I don't have an SUV." She laughed at him.

"You pander to the groups that cry the most."

"You're partially right, but you don't understand what it's like for us."

"I don't?"

"There is a small group, a secret sort of group of the best and brightest, the most enlightened, evolved if you will."

"Elitist."

"You say it like you actually understand what it means." She was truly amused by the conversation.

"Don't treat me like a child." He retracted his warming arm.

"Did you see the movie with Tom Cruise, Stanley Kubrick's last film? Do you remember the scene where he is sneaking around the secret party?"

"Yeah."

"It's like that in one sense. America is made up of foolish consumers with less formal education than in most Western European countries. We have large groups of people who still believe they should follow the Bible to enlightenment. Can you imagine such ignorance? Do you really believe all men are created equal?"

"Go on." He knew she really didn't care what his opinion was, it was simply less taxing to let her proceed.

"Why are some people physicists and others are barely literate garbagemen. They're from the same country, in some instances educated at the same public schools. It's genealogy, Drew. My grandfather's superior genes put his descendants in the one percent that matters. We're not equal; in fact, we're the most maligned."

"How do you figure?" Drew was growing weary of the conversation.

"We live in a country that is continuously diluted by immigration. The bar will never rise as long as we are a haven for the destitute."

"Wow." Drew was astonished by her views. She was not angry or bitter, but soberly reciting what she believed all people of her stature believed, the verbalization of a dogma felt by many who are too ashamed or afraid to admit it.

"Don't misunderstand me please, Drew. I'm not against people coming to America who are oppressed or poverty-stricken; I'm simply pointing out the dire effects of an open-door policy. The results are poorly educated adults and overcrowded prisons. We are no longer seeing the immigrants of established countries with rich histories. The well of immigrants from countries with vast records of human achievements or artistic brilliance has dried up. The majority of the new Americans are from Third World countries with horrific human rights records and no appreciable impact on the world other than unwavering reproduction. Many are illiterate and come from zealously Catholic countries, yet they trample the commandments with laughable regularity. We're the only country on earth that absorbs so many useless citizens."

"Do you want to stop immigration and set up a caste system?"

"No, that can't work. How can we in good conscience turn our back on those people?"

"You don't make any sense!" He was exasperated by her seemingly convoluted logic.

"For example, just before the trip, I went to the Registry of Motor Vehicles, the downtown office to renew my license. What I saw made me sick."

"The lines?" Drew snapped sarcastically.

"No, Drew, it was the individuals in the line. It looked like a tax collection office in a corrupt Third World country. Anyway it was a haunting example of human underachievement. English rarely used, a woman with five disheveled children who were loud and obnoxious to everyone. Of course, they should have been in school; it was the middle of the week and not a holiday. Arguments broke out over trivial clerical errors that made the atmosphere almost unbearable! It was comical; they had a State Trooper behind the counter to protect the help. It was a glaring confirmation of America's permanent underclass. I thought about the tremendous gulf between the people I engage with on a daily basis, writers, painters… the best of the Boston's intellectual community, yet I had to listen to an illiterate woman berate a slovenly clerk because he asked to see her old license. She had no documentation that I could see, yet she wanted a new license anyway. The State Trooper finally intervened and she was removed. But her little demonstration fueled the anger of all the other people in line. It was like I had jumped into a spaceship and ventured to another universe. I was in two completely different worlds in the same day. I had started the day reviewing a manuscript so brilliant I cried with envy and then ended it in the ashtray of urban decay."

"Nice line." Drew understood her rant about the gap between her social circle and the struggling immigrant population. He liked to blame the Charlotte Emerson's of the world rather than the newcomers.

"I consider myself a very liberal thinker, but our collective worth should not be diminished by burger flippers at McDonald's."

"You're the most cynical, arrogant person I have ever met. You are so two-faced; I bet you work at a soup kitchen at Christmas but sneer at the people you're feeding."

"Don't be so dramatic, it's understandably hard for you…I don't expect you to…" Charlotte stopped herself.

"To understand!" Drew finished her thought.

"Don't take it the wrong way."

"I'm one of them to you. That's why you keep saying I won the lottery."

"Now that I know you, I've changed my thinking."

"You haven't changed anything!" It sounded harsher than he meant.

Tears moistened her eyes. "You think I'm a monster."

"You're not a monster, Charlotte. You just have a strange way of looking at things."

"Thanks, Drew. I would like to stay here forever. To die on this hill would be okay, not so frightening anyway."

"Morbid. Why don't you? I mean live here, not die."

"That's not possible. My life is in Boston. I'll never leave like Andrew did. Frankly speaking, I think he's a coward for dropping out."

"That doesn't surprise me that you think like that. I think we should go back."

"Why? Are you afraid you might like me?"

"That's not possible."

"Nice one." She smiled and gave him a playful push.

Chapter 19

Fall River, Massachusetts

With a commanding view of the churning Taunton River and the distant Dartmouth shoreline, Fall River's Christian Charities Nursing Home evoked monastic tranquility. The ornate building perched high atop the city's affluent Highland Avenue section was once the object of local pride and religious reverence. In recent years, it had degenerated into a place of sorrow and death only braved by the most dedicated family members. Hidden behind a veil of perceived benevolence, society's most vulnerable endured the ceaseless mental anguish of the abandoned. Suffering and hopeless, some almost welcomed the inevitable physical abuse that occurred at the decrepit facility, pathetically yearning for any acknowledgement of their existence.

Hunched over under the flickering bank of fluorescent lights an old man stared aimlessly at the cracked linoleum floor of the nursing home, the smell of industrial disinfectant burning his sensitive nostrils. His tired body ached for sleep, but he fought the urge to rest. The harshness of his surroundings prevented him from ever sleeping soundly these days, fearing comfort in such a place. He seldom went to bed at a reasonable hour. From the antiquated hospital beds to the foul odor known to many as "hospital smell," it was hard to forget your own personal decay amongst so many props of the infirmed.

He lifted his head at the sound of a passing nurse, his wrinkled face and gray hair hinting at his age, but it was his brown eyes that seem to confirm his seasoned and woeful existence. The eyes were sad and clear, like a person of sound mind who knew his predicament and simply could not alter the inevitable conclusion. The drip of the nearby sink vexed him, it had been leaking for months and nobody bothered to fix it. He sighed and cupped his mouth to stifle the frustrated screams of terror. Each night, at the same sadistically predictable hour, like an internal clock of despair, he was reminded of the suffocating loneliness that pervaded every part of his being. He breathed deeply and slowly regained his composure.

He was clutching a worn newspaper clipping in his twisted hand. It was dated two weeks before but looked decades old. It had been folded and unfolded hundreds of times since the original printing. Each time the sleep-deprived old man scanned Sheldon Harrison's obituary he was wracked with spasms of bitterness that spread through his body, altering his mood for hours at a time.

> *Sheldon W. Harrison, the world-renowned writer...the most important American writer in one hundred years...most influential and well-written novels of all time...every school in America has his novels on their mandatory reading list...the novels were all written in a very short time. His fame, money, and place along side Hawthorne, Thoreau, Steinbeck, and Hemingway could not save him from his most challenging obstacle of all, lung cancer.*

"Sandy...Sandy!" a tired voice from the next bed whispered.

"Yeah...Eddie what is it?" Sandy Wilson folded the obituary and tucked it inside a magazine.

"I shit myself again...Jesus Christ. I couldn't hold it," the distraught man sobbed, his tearful convulsions visible in the darkened corner of the poorly lit room.

"Eddie, I'm sorry but you know I can't help you. I can't lift you..."

"Please...maybe I can clean myself. I don't want to ask him. I can't! Not again, Sandy."

"He's the only one who can help you. You can't stay like that."

"But he makes me feel like a baby. I still have my dignity."

"His sins will be paid for at another time by someone more capable of dealing with such vermin as Frank Burns," Wilson grunted and twisted in his uncomfortable chair.

"I don't want the humiliation, not tonight."

"What's so different about today?"

"You know who Jim Lovell is?" Eddie sagged over the edge of his bed, "Jim Lovell...you know..."

"Sure Eddie I know, the astronaut."

"He mentioned me in his book. I worked with the crews quite a bit, especially on Apollo 8. The nurses couldn't believe it. I could tell they looked at me a little differently. Maybe they thought I was important or something. Not just some slab of meat in this rotten place."

"Take it easy, Eddie. You know what the Doctor said." Sandy tried to calm his agitated roommate.

"Fuck him! He's a moron. I used to work with the best minds in the country, not some C student from a medical school in the Bahamas."

"Alright... just calm down will you," Sandy said with a hint of unintentional harshness.

He looked at his soiled "cellmate" and felt outraged. The man who was begging to be cleaned was Edward Dufresne, a former NASA engineer who helped America reach the moon. Thirty years after NASA reached for the stars, this brilliant engineer couldn't persuade the detested Certified Nursing Assistant, Frank Burns, to clean him without ridicule and humiliation. At the aged facility, the Certified Nursing Assistants were charged with the most menial of tasks, hanging on the bottom rung of the nursing hierarchy, they had the unenviable job of cleaning, dressing, feeding each patient, basically handling all of their substantial daily needs. They were poorly compensated and oftentimes under-appreciated by both patients and staffers. A few were glaringly deficient in their ability to deal with the most human of responsibilities, the sensitive cleaning of the ailing and incontinent. Frank Burns was in a category all his own.

Sandy Wilson pulled himself out of his chair and used his cane to shuffle to the yellowed window. Freedom was only millimeters away in the inky darkness, just on the other side of the cheap glass. The windows didn't open anymore, painted shut decades earlier by poor immigrants using toxic products, unknowingly sealing a generation of their friends and relatives in a communal coffin.

Sandy turned and watched the once proud man cry like an infant, shifting his skeletal frame to adjust the discomfort in his pants. The stench of fresh feces made its way across the pitifully cramped room. He tried his best to block the offensive odor, but it was useless. Frank Burns, the loathsome assistant nurse, eventually came into the room and roughly cleaned the sputtering engineer; cursing loudly he made sure Sandy knew about the incident.

"Sandy, did you shit too?" He glared in Wilson's direction after he was done.

"No, Mr. Burns, I did not." Wilson turned and responded curtly.

"Don't give me an attitude, old man. Do you think you're special because you didn't use your wheelchair today?"

"Leave me alone you insignificant waste of a life."

"You know you were supposed to be in bed hours ago. It's 11:30, dummy.

You old fucks are usually looking for breakfast at this time," he chuckled cruelly.

"I was just sitting here, what's the difference to you? The bed is three feet away. Does that distance warrant such treatment? Is it worthy of such insults? You're nothing but an ignorant fool."

"Shut up, smart ass, and get to bed! I don't want to come in here again. I'm sick of your fucking mouth. You think you're so much better than all these driveling fools. Don't you? You're not!"

"It feels good to yell at an old man, doesn't it? You feel powerful; it's probably the only sense of worth you get in your pathetic life. You're a poor excuse for a man." Sandy grinned and waited for the predictable response. The irate caregiver was tall and intimidating, wiry but strong, his menacing gaze was often enough to frighten people into compliance. His arms were covered with cheap tattoos of clichéd tough guy symbols, poorly done and old, they looked like a random splash of green paint. His stringy hair was greasy and long, it matched his acne-scarred face and Hitler-like mustache. He had beady green eyes and a long nose that looked like it had been broken a few times.

"You piece of shit, if you won't go to bed, I'll make you go," he snarled as he grabbed Sandy's feeble arm and yanked him from the wooden chair. The old man didn't protest audibly, but struggled fiercely. The futile resistance annoyed Frank Burns, so he punched him in the ribs three times. Sandy collapsed near the bed. Burns stared at him with a reluctant hint of admiration.

"Now be a good boy and stay that way until morning. That's how all you old fucks should sleep, like babies." He smiled vindictively and started for the light switch.

"Frank! What's happening here? Why is Sandy on the floor and where are you going?" Donna Winters, a Licensed Practical Nurse, stepped into the room and gave Burns a ferocious look of disapproval.

"This piece of work tried to hit me with his cane and he fell on the floor. I was on my way to get you. I won't deal with this kind of abuse. I'll go to the Director." He stood his ground.

"I'm reporting this." Nurse Winters tried to act brave, but she was clearly afraid of him. She knew of his violent past.

"Go ahead…you think I care about that. Fire me and see if you can get anybody else to clean shitty diapers for what they pay me. I'm not gonna let somebody hit me with a cane. Maybe I should have let the old loon hit me, and then I can go out on Compensation." She knew he was right, they had a hard enough time getting the few RNs they had at the facility, but low-level caregivers was another story.

"You're really out of line."

He stepped in front of the diminutive nurse and stared into her fluttering brown eyes. She tried to go around him to reach Sandy, but he temporarily barred her way. Finally he flashed his yellow teeth and let her pass. He reeked of cigarettes and body odor. She wondered how his girlfriend slept in the same bed with him; it was inconceivable that any woman would agree to consensual sex with such a vile human being.

"Idiot," Nurse Winters muttered and helped Wilson to his feet.

"Thank you." Sandy looked at her with profound gratitude. He didn't sit on his bed when he reached his feet but instinctively returned to the chair by the window. His drooping shoulders and listless gaze saddened her; he didn't belong in the awful facility. The quiet man was defiant and intelligent, but his chief nemesis was wearing him down.

Sandy rubbed his side and wondered how he had ended up in such a miserable place, a place where antidepressants were handed out like candy. He was terrified by the prospect of his final days, in the care of others and drowning in the stench of filthy diapers. The deterioration of his mind and body started the moment he arrived in the facility one year before. He was hobbled by a bad leg and vision problems bordering on blindness. He felt the familiar churning of his insides, the crushing pain made him shiver; he needed to evacuate his bowels. The overwhelming sense of isolation and worthlessness often caused the illness. He would have preferred death to having an accident. He prayed for morning.

The sun did rise, filtered through tattered windows, but it was still there, vibrant and warm on Sandy Wilson's relieved cheek. His stomach cramps had passed without incident, the day might be just awful instead of unbearable. A new Nursing Assistant came to Sandy's bed and wheeled him to a small breakfast area for those who didn't like to eat all three meals in their room. As usual, he sat alone and ate a bowl of oatmeal in silence. He looked around at the other patients and felt sick. Mood-altering medications kept most in a near catatonic state. After a cup of foul-tasting coffee, he asked to be wheeled back to his room. His roommate Eddie offered little companionship; he was farther down death's highway and only lucid when he talked about his days with NASA.

"Sandy, are you sure you wouldn't like something to help you relax? I can ask your Doctor." Nurse Donna Winters said with a tired smile upon entering the room. His savior from the night before was one of the few nurses who actually cared about the inmates. She was on her second double shift that week.

"No, Donna, why would I?" He asked before wheeling himself to the window.

"Well, to help you get a little sleep."

"Why do I need sleep? I just had eight hours of sleep. Isn't eight hours enough for you?"

"Well...yes I guess it is, when I can get it these days. But I'm much younger."

"You're also more active than I am, what the hell do I do all day? I can't move because of this goddamn leg. Forget it, Donna, give the pills to Mrs. Jones."

"You know she already had her pill at this time of day."

"Maybe a second one would take care of her pain. I'm sure if she knew what was going on she would ask for the whole bottle."

"Don't be fresh."

"Sorry."

"Hey Sandy...did you like Sheldon Harrison?"

"Why do you ask?" His defensive tone caught her off guard.

"Because this *TIME* magazine has been on your night table for weeks. I noticed it just after he died. It looks like a collector's issue; you should keep it inside the drawer. People in this place tend to have sticky fingers."

"Sure."

"So did you like him?"

"Yes...I suppose at one time I did like him."

"Me too. It's really sad, isn't it? In college I minored in American Literature. I loved reading his books, such a brilliant writer. I feel like our country has lost a national icon."

"I guess so, Donna. I'm not much of a literary historian."

"And I am? Yeah I just moonlight as a nurse, I like all the abuse. My real job is at Harvard...you know...nursing keeps it real," she laughed and made a choking gesture.

"You are such a comedian." He liked her jocular personality.

"Sandy, can I ask you something?"

"Shoot."

"Where did you come from? I know you're not from Fall River. Do you have any family?"

"Is that all?" Sandy asked sarcastically.

"Oh yeah how did you hurt your leg? That scar is really nasty."

"That one is easy. A German soldier, who was really annoyed that he didn't execute me, instead gave me a going away present. I was shot in the leg with a German Mauser."

"You were in World War II?"

"Not really, one day in combat is all I lasted. Sent home with a useless leg and a lifetime of wonderful images." He rubbed his eyes and thought about that winter day in Belgium, he feared it would be his last thought.

"I'm really interested...tell me more."

"I don't really like to talk about it. You know. I've never really talked to anybody about it...at least in the last thirty years anyway. The death and destruction...it never leaves you. An incomprehensible thing, really, war." He wore a pained expression, it was obvious to Donna he was not comfortable talking about his experiences.

"What about family?"

"I was an only child. My parents died many years ago. I never kept in touch with my cousins and I've never been married."

"How about a girlfriend? Sandy, have you ever been in love?" She knew she was pushing her luck with the last question, but she figured she had nothing to lose. She thought it was charming that he blushed ever so slightly, a hint of embarrassment that could only mean one thing.

"Donna, you're a real card. You know that?" He tried to cover his discomfort with a forced smile.

"So. Spill your beans, Mister."

"Well, I don't know. I do know I had girlfriends over the years, not too many though."

"There is never too many for you men." She gave him a good-natured look of disapproval.

"In love...hmmmm...I'm not sure about love."

"There's your answer right there. If you had been, you wouldn't hesitate."

"You think so?"

"Yes I do. Us woman, we know those kinds of things; we are experts in the art of love. We've been studying it our whole lives."

He grew somber and retrospective, rubbing the gray stubble on his sagging chin; he dove straight into the black hole in his heart.

"Is it love when you have a spiritual connection with someone that's as intimate as physical contact, in fact better than any sex you could imagine? Is it love when you watch her push her hair behind her ears and believing her exposed cheek is the most exquisite thing you've ever seen? Is it love when you think you would have been better off if the German soldier had better aim so you wouldn't have to see her cross the room on the arm of another?"

"Yes...I would call that love," she whispered, stunned by the words of the usually reserved Wilson.

"Don't listen to me, I'm an old fool." He turned his face and wished they had never started the uncomfortable discord.

"What was her name, Sandy?"

"Nobody, Donna. Just somebody I liked to watch television with, an occasional companion who remained just that."

"I'm sure there is more to it than that."

"Perhaps for me there was. Please forget it, will you. I can't talk about it right now."

"Alright."

"Sorry for being like this."

"I know you are, Sandy. Well what did you do for a living?"

"A little of this and a little of that, I guess. Never really had a profession. I worked at the Air and Space Museum in Washington shortly after it opened. I was there for a few years before they fired me."

"Why?"

"I refused to take a large V.I.P group assigned to me."

"Why did you refuse?"

"There was somebody in the group I didn't want to see."

"Who?"

"Let's leave it alone," he said politely, but firm in his desire not to answer the question.

"Okay what about your last job?"

"I bagged groceries a few years ago."

"You worked into your seventies!"

"Of course…what else would I do? Retire to my Vineyard estate?"

"Go on, funny guy. What was the best job you ever had?"

"I taught English."

"Where?"

"In a school."

"No kidding."

"In Thailand."

"Are you kidding?"

"No. Why would I lie? I was there at the end of the Khmer Rouge reign in Cambodia. I helped teach English to many of the refugees who sought asylum in Thailand. That was the most rewarding experience of my life. The utter hopelessness, the wrenching stories of death and torture were more than I could take at times."

"Fascinating. I would love to talk to you all day."

"You are too kind, Donna. Why do you bother with such a pathetic old man?"

"I like you, you have a spark underneath all that self-loathing. I know you really don't believe what you say about yourself. You know you're special but hide behind all these walls to protect yourself. I think you have been wounded too many times and are reluctant to let people into your life that really care. I suspect you were a rather engaging gentleman in a different time and place."

"Perhaps I was, Donna, but I'm afraid the spark you speak of is long since extinguished."

"Why are you so sad, Sandy? Tell me."

"It's not sadness as much as soul-aching depression," he said with a wry, but serious smile.

"Why? Why is the great Sandy Wilson so sad?" She smiled and winked at him.

"I want you to reverse our positions. If you can, fast forward fifty years and think about it."

"I don't want to, Sandy." Donna Winters did not like the topic of mortality and thought it might be time to leave.

"Exactly, too distasteful to think about. I don't wish this upon you, Donna, but sadly it's more likely than not you will end up in an institution similar to this, probably nicer but a clearinghouse of the unwanted nonetheless. It's a truly inhuman way to end a life. My life hasn't been what I had hoped, obviously, nor could it be thought of as a fulfilled life, but it wasn't all bad. I had some good moments that I cherish. I don't think I deserve this, nobody does."

"I agree," she admitted, her downcast eyes revealing her distress.

"Then you must understand my predicament? Why I'm like this," Sandy said in a pleading voice.

"I guess I do, Sandy. I know you don't feel like you belong here, but you should learn to accept things as they are, it's easier that way. Really. We're not all bad here. So please try and make the best of what little we can offer you. I suspect we'll be closed down soon anyway, the State is blind for only so long. Try and find a friend, Sandy. Please for me. Anyway, my dear, I must be off, I have other patients you know. I'm not all yours," she joked and gave him a sincere, comforting hug.

"Thank you, Donna." He pressed his face against the window and gazed down the steep hill until his eyes rested on the river below. The river was wide and swift, vibrant and alive, everything he wasn't.

Chapter 20
Boston University, Three Weeks Later

Chad Curtin eyed the rigid, serious posture of his new roommate with disgust, annoyed by the enigmatic loner's voracious appetite for learning. Drew immediately recognized Curtin's feelings, but did nothing to bridge the gap. He was too engrossed in his schoolwork to worry about his lazy, shallow opinions.

Curtin's family history was typical at the high-priced university; his parents were both professionals who worked in Manhattan, lived in Connecticut, and summered in the Hamptons. College for Chad and his group of friends was a place to party and make lifelong contacts. The actual education part of it meant very little, the diploma and the establishment of a network of important people was the primary goal.

"Hello," a loud tap was heard at the door and a female voice inquired, "Drew?"

"Come in." Chad answered irritably.

"Hello." Charlotte Emerson opened the door and made her way to Drew's desk.

"Charlotte!" He was surprised by the unannounced visit.

"How are you?" Her confident voice got the attention of Curtin. He watched her closely, looking for the fatal flaw that she was surely to possess if she was associating with Drew Engle.

"Good, what are you doing here?"

"Visiting."

"This is my roommate, Chad Curtin," he said dryly, introducing his roommate as a formality, not a courtesy.

"Hello." Her smile and sleek figure aroused him. Curtin understood immediately that she was of similar background and upbringing as his own. His perplexed expression annoyed Drew.

"Hi." Curtin leaned back in his chair and tried to act cool. His unskilled attempt to seem aloof and uninterested was obvious. It was clear from his sparkling eyes he was enthralled by her.

"Sit down?" Drew cleared a spot on his bed.

"Sure, you don't mind excusing us for a moment do you, Chad?" Her forceful expression made him leap to his feet and sheepishly leave the dorm room.

"Why did you ask him to leave?" Drew thought the request was odd.

"No real reason. I just didn't want him bothering us." She stood up and paced the room, touching a book before flipping through his notebook. She examined his meager personal items.

"How have you been?"

"It's only been five weeks, Drew." Charlotte mocked.

"I know…how did you find me?"

"They have a thing called a Student Directory, Drew. Dummy."

"Sure. Why do you have to be so nasty? Is it in your blood?"

"I wanted to see you. I'm not sure why, I just felt like I should come over. I know we can't discuss what you know…"

"I can't." His emphatic denial seemed to depress Charlotte. The secret was eating her up, she thought of nothing else than the possible revelation entrusted to a lowly college student. She had hoped her outward charms would be enough to sway him, but he held firm.

"Do you want to come over for dinner? Believe it or not I can cook."

"Beats the food around here."

"Don't act so excited." She smiled knowingly; his deliberate lack of enthusiasm was obvious.

Fifteen minutes later, they arrived at a rather dreary underground parking garage near Charlotte's townhouse. The outer door of the cold garage led directly to the sidewalk, a convenient place for the homeless to congregate. Drew held his breath as the foul smell of urine attacked him.

"Jesus."

"What, Drew, you don't like the homeless. You don't like the foul odor of bodily fluids from your people?" She gave him a slight nudge.

"Shut up. I just don't like the smell of urine every ten feet." He was disgusted by the sticky sensation on his shoes.

"Some people are simply better off dead," she remarked casually. Her building was a long walk from the underground garage where she parked her SAAB. There were other garages closer, but she didn't trust them with her car. Her garage was where the wealthy parked their vehicles.

"That's nice." Drew inhaled the cool autumn air, purging the stench of human waste from his nostrils.

"Hey, pal, do have any extra change?" A shabbily dressed homeless man cut them off.

"No…sorry," Drew responded stiffly.

"Yes you do, Drew. Why is your first instinct to say no? Isn't that queer?"

"I don't have any spare change." He stopped and angrily looked at her.

"Yes you do. Everybody does." She pulled out a ten dollar bill from her pocket and stuffed it in the battered coffee cup of the somewhat stunned homeless man.

"Thank you, miss, God bless you," he muttered.

"Okay." She smiled weakly and stepped around him, afraid to breathe the same air as her ailing beneficiary.

"What was that about? I told you I didn't have any change." Drew pulled his pockets inside out to show her. He had a twenty-dollar bill along with his license and no change.

"So." She grabbed his hands and strolled on like nothing happened.

"You're fucking deranged," he snarled, but did not remove his arm; her gentle touch sent a shiver up his arm.

"Drew, sometimes you have to help those that are less fortunate than yourself."

"Than you maybe."

"You have the money you stole from my grandfather."

"What the hell, Charlotte?" Drew roughly pulled his arm away, his patience running short.

"You go to Boston University, you must have money."

"I don't. I have school loans, that's what I have." He clenched his teeth and maintained a defiant stance.

"Don't give me that. We're not so different, my friend."

"I'm going back to school." Drew turned towards the subway stop.

"Drew."

"What!"

"Come with me."

"What?"

"Come with me!"

"No."

"Yes."

"No…I'm not." He felt a restrained smile creasing his face.

"You want to. Stop letting your middle class sensibilities cloud your destiny."

"Go away, Charlotte."

"Stop fighting me." She grabbed his arm and escorted him to a small elevator inside the front entrance of her building. It was obviously added many years after the building was built, a luxury seldom found in similar structures in the area.

"It's like a coffin in here," Drew remarked as the decorative elevator lurched to a stop outside the front door of her townhouse.

"It's better than walking." She fumbled for her keys, her confidence waning on the threshold of her home. Drew noted the slight loss of control and wondered why. He was the unwilling guest lured up with no clue of her intentions.

Charlotte turned out to be a feeble cook; a bland chicken and rice dish from her gourmet cookbook did not fill Drew with hope for dessert. They did not talk much during the food preparation or the dinner. She was distracted by the task at hand, unsure of her abilities. Drew took the opportunity to examine her closely.

She was indeed beautiful, but not in the traditional sense, her attractiveness was a blend of her sun streaked brown hair, sparkling blue eyes, and hard body. Charlotte had many suitors who wanted to sleep with her for various reasons, ranging from deep, unrequited love to pure sexual conquest of the granddaughter of a living legend. She never had any steady boyfriends, yet she was not as promiscuous as she sometimes insinuated. She was, of course, a modern woman who had many sexual partners, but she was not considered an easy conquest. Charlotte held herself in such high esteem, she felt tarnished if a person she deemed unworthy entered her.

"So, why did you do all of this?" Drew sat back and admired her contemporary dining area attached to a magnificent kitchen that overlooked the Charles River. Her townhouse, high above the bustling streets of the Back Bay, was luxurious and insanely convenient to the best of Boston. It was one place Drew would have lived voluntarily; he hated the urban sprawl of the metropolitan city, but he loved Beacon Street.

"What?" She was playing with her food.

"Why did you do all this? Why the effort to be civil. It doesn't seem like you." He smiled, hoping to break her obvious discomfort.

"What did my grandfather tell you?" She blurted.

"Is that why you invited me over?" He grimaced.

"Please…try and understand."

"I do understand. You know I can't, so why do you bother? Do you think I like this fucking burden? I don't, Charlotte!" He stood and walked to the door.

"No! No, Drew." She pressed her hand against the door and gently clasped his hand. He felt a nervous excitement in his stomach; it was her touch that seemed to overwhelm his senses. They stood only inches apart, her piercing, questioning, deliberating eyes trying to understand her new adversary. He felt weak under her spell, he could smell her soap, her moisturizing cream, her shampoo, all of it clear and vibrant, swaying his aversion to her tactics.

"I think you're interesting." Charlotte's manicured hand gracefully caressed his stubble-covered cheek.

"Charlotte…"

"Shhh…" She pressed her finger against his lips and smiled broadly, her charm becoming irresistible.

"You protest too much. I'm sorry for asking you."

"It's okay," he mumbled, his palms were sweaty and his breathing forced. She was back in complete control, his resistance crumbling with the depth of her eyes.

With the care of a tender seducer, Charlotte pressed her hand into his heaving chest and pushed him across the room. He collapsed onto the sofa with a surprised grunt. His protests went unheeded; she leaned over and kissed his lips, her tongue darting inside his suddenly receptive mouth. She straddled him, her hips grinding against his crotch. Her aggressive kissing encouraged him to roll up her shirt. He felt her shiver from his touch, moaning softly before pushing him away.

"No Drew." She smiled seductively.

"What?" Drew panted.

"We can't…it's not the right time." She stood up and playfully walked to the bathroom.

"Jesus…" Drew said to himself, his arousal diminishing by the second. He wasn't surprised by her behavior; it was consistent with her maddening mood swings. He felt lost. It was unclear whether she liked or hated him; her approach, he sadly noted, would be the same in either case.

"Sorry about that. I got carried away for a moment. It was nothing," she glided back into the room.

"Is that it?" Drew prepared to leave; he was tired of the games; saddened by the way she made him feel.

"Listen, I let it go too far. I'm a tier one girl and you're a tier three guy. That's not a good combination."

"So you have categories for people?" He shook with anger; his face was red with embarrassment. He didn't understand exactly what she meant, but the insult was obvious, just the degree was in question.

"Yes. Nothing personal. Just a way to keep the minions in their place." Her nasty smile revealed how much she regretted their kiss.

"Tell me why I'm a tier two guy?" He opened the front door, holding his breath on the threshold of freedom.

"I said tier three my little egotist, maybe a tier two though. I don't have the energy to explain it all, but you're in that category for many reasons. You're cute, but not nearly good looking enough to leap-frog out of your predestined path."

"Screw you."

"Don't you want to hear it?"

"No! Don't bother me again."

"Don't take it so personally," she hollered as the door slammed in her face. She was taken aback by the abruptness of his departure. She had again underestimated his fortitude.

Collapsing on her absurdly expensive sofa she wondered why she had acted like such a raging bitch. What was it about him that brought out the worst in her? There was something in his character that threatened her deep sense of entitlement.

"Forget him, he had his fifteen seconds of fame just associating with the Harrison family. He has nothing to reveal, nothing more than an indiscreet affair by grandfather or a last-minute apology to a long-lost friend. He's insignificant!" She said this loudly, hoping he could hear her as he waited for the elevator. A second later, she was on her feet rushing out the front door.

"Drew, stop!"

"What! This fucking elevator is so slow. You think with all your money you would have the fastest elevator in the city."

"I want you to take a ride with me tomorrow. I have something to show you. It might make up for my outrageous behavior."

"Forget it." The elevator opened with a clang.

"Please, I'll pick you up at ten. I won't take no for an answer." She closed the door before he could say no again; he was left to ponder the strange invitation. He nearly cried out in frustration, he was wracked with feelings of guilt for he knew he would be with her again.

Chapter 21

The Antman

"How can you take the day off without calling in?" Drew asked after a long silence. The road flashed by in a blur, Charlotte's black SAAB chewing up the miles with each second. They were heading for the western part of the state, but their destination was still unknown to Drew.

"I didn't feel like working today. When I don't feel like working, I don't." She adjusted her sunglasses and passed a slow driver on the left.

"Because you're irreplaceable or the granddaughter of Sheldon Harrison?" Drew was disgusted by her arrogance.

"No!" She turned and glared at him, searching for a plausible explanation as to why she was given special privileges.

"Where are we going anyway? We've been driving forever."

"Does it matter?"

"Yes."

"To see the Antman."

"Who?"

"The Antman! Open your ears. I don't like to repeat myself."

"Come on."

"Trust me."

"I don't"

"You will."

They were surrounded on all sides by the bucolic mountain range called the Berkshires near the New York border. Drew knew very little about the Berkshires other than its reputation as a haven for a large artistic community sprinkled across the many towns that made up the region. The unfamiliar, but stunningly beautiful and peaceful terrain angered him. He felt like a child who discovers a wonderful toy he is too old to play with. He wondered why his parents never visited the area. Soon after, they exited the highway with a screech.

"Where are we going? Slow down. You're a maniac."

"To see the Antman. I told you already."

"I wouldn't have come if I knew you were taking me way out here."

"I know."

"Who is the Antman?"

"What you are about to see might be a little hard to understand. Have you ever heard of the artist Hiro?"

"Yes, of course." Drew was half listening to her. He was transfixed by the changing colors of autumn. The Berkshires is an exquisite place to view the ebb and flow of the changing New England season.

"He was the real deal in the late '60s through the mid '80s, a superlative conceptual artist, peerless in this country. He is of Japanese descent, I think he came to America when he was in his twenties. He was also considered irreverent. No, not irreverent. More like an enigmatic introvert with no common sense. He is a tragic figure really. When his wife died about ten years ago, it had a profound effect on his work. Her death is what pushed him over the edge, it turned him into a hermit. I know what you are thinking, another hermit artist, what a cliché. Right?"

"What does he have to do with us?" Drew raised his eyebrow and hoped his intuition was wrong.

"We're going to see him, he lives a few miles from here." She swerved off the main road and onto a dirt path that was overgrown, but clearly driven on.

"You just said he's a recluse!"

"He is, but I can view him when I want."

"View him?" Drew was puzzled by the adventure. He regretted going on the foolish trip, hours wasted for nothing.

"Hiro has a caretaker. He knows me. His name is Bruce and he's a very scary guy. Big and burly, looks like a white trash lumberjack, but he's everything to Hiro. Literally."

"View him? What does that mean?" Drew repeated.

"You will see." Her voice sounded tense.

Drew sighed and watched closely as a dilapidated trailer came into view. Behind the trailer, Drew could see a large stone and wood cabin with a strange sort of structure attached to the main house. It looked like an anthill.

"Jesus, what kind of place is this," Drew mumbled to himself.

Heavily wooded and barely accessible, the escape route was frighteningly singular.

"Hello! What do you want?" A huge man with a long black beard and deep black eyes stormed out of the trailer, eyeing the SAAB with devilish venom. Drew sat silently as Bruce circled to the car and tried to see inside the tinted glass.

"Hi Bruce." Charlotte emerged from the car and smiled.

"Oh...hi Charlotte." His harsh tone softened, but he didn't appear to be excited about her unannounced visit.

"How is he?" She shut her door and motioned for Drew to come out.

"Same. Who's this?" He arched his back and glowered at Drew.

"This is my friend, Drew Engle."

"I never said you could bring visitors I don't know."

"He was a friend of my grandfather."

"Sure he was," his incredulous glare was unnerving, "so go look at him." He stomped away in disgust, his suspicious eyes steeling glances at Drew.

"Come on." Charlotte nervously motioned him forward.

"Where are we going?"

"To see the artist."

"Aren't we going inside the house?" Drew had started for the front door.

"We won't find him in there." She grabbed his hand and circled the house until they came to the large structure resembling an anthill. Drew touched the strange walls. They were packed with mud and twigs obviously to simulate the look and feel of a natural object. His mind burned with curiosity. He saw a wooden ladder that appeared to ascend to the top of the dome-like structure.

"What's up there?"

"Hiro."

"I don't get it, Charlotte, is this a joke?"

"Be patient and you will be rewarded with something you can tell your grandchildren about." She apprehensively started to climb the ladder. Drew followed her, perplexed but curious by what lay ahead.

Charlotte brushed herself off when she reached a small platform halfway up. She motioned for him to follow her up another, smaller ladder that led directly to the top. Drew found Charlotte peering down through a glass window at her feet. She turned and whispered to him, "don't look too long, he might freak out."

"Who?"

"Hiro! Jesus, who else?"

"My God," he whispered to himself, dumbfounded by the spectacle unfolding in front of him.

The room, ten feet below the rooftop viewing area, was a disgusting tomb of a man who had clearly gone insane. Drew froze, he felt physically ill when he saw the skeletal figure of a man just over five feet tall rushing from wall to wall dressed only in some sort of undergarment that resembled a diaper. He was an Asian male in his sixties with long hair and terrifyingly long fingernails. His bedding consisted of wood chips and piles of shredded newspapers. Drew noticed feces in the corner and what appeared to be a bowl of urine. He was living like a caged animal, pacing back and forth with the unbridled determination of the clinically insane. There was a stairwell leading from the room. It was obvious he chose this sickening lifestyle, a sad case of an artist whose brilliant mind was destroyed by severe mental distortion.

"My God," Drew repeated.

"His wife is buried over there." She pointed to an identical window a few feet away. Drew looked down and saw a casket covered with dusty flowers and curling pictures. The room looked like it had not been opened in years; there was a window between the two rooms for Hiro to see his beloved wife. He stopped his pacing and looked into the room and banged the glass angrily, his yellowed nails scratching the hard glass until his fingers bled. He streaked the glass with his blood and then tasted it. The glass was smeared with blood and feces from days past.

"How can you come here? He needs help. Charlotte he's sick. I can't believe I'm watching this."

"He won't go. His wife died and he died with her. He erected this tomb as his last work of art. It took him two years to complete. Bruce was his handyman at the time. He helped him construct it. He's been here ever since. Bruce manages his affairs; all his major works have been sold or are in museums. Bruce sells a few small ones each year to keep this place solvent. He still has many wealthy patrons who come and see him."

"To gawk at him. This has to be a sick joke."

"No Drew! He is not always this bad, in fact sometimes you can talk to him in his house." She looked at him indignantly.

"Why doesn't somebody call the police, he shouldn't be living like an animal."

"He chose it, it's his last great piece of work. He is inside his own creation. I think it's beautiful."

"He's mentally ill, he didn't fucking choose anything!" Drew was ready to leave.

"Hello Hiro." She waved down to the motionless artist who was staring blankly at the couple. Their shadow gave them away. His long black hair was streaked with gray and matted beyond repair. His skinny face was etched with deep ruts of suffering. Hiro's body was covered with hundreds of scars from apparent self-mutilation. He tilted his head to the side and examined Charlotte but did not acknowledge her. His dead, sullen eyes unnerved Drew to the point of revulsion.

"Are you okay?"

"No." He walked to the ladder and started to descend.

"Drew!"

"I'm leaving."

"I wouldn't have brought you if I knew he was this bad. Don't say anything to Bruce…please, he frightens me." She warned as she followed him down to the ground.

Charlotte watched Drew's indignant walk and smiled. She understood his strong feelings, viewing Hiro was never an easy experience, but it was a regular ritual for a select few. It was a way to pay respect to a great artist and to be among the few who had an open invitation. The latter was most likely the motivation for many, not excluding Charlotte Emerson.

"All set Charlotte?" Bruce asked gruffly, but with a hint of respect for the granddaughter of Sheldon Harrison.

"Yes, thank you, Bruce."

"He belongs in an institution." Drew couldn't hide his anger. Charlotte gave him a sharp look, a look that demanded his obedience.

"What?" Bruce's puzzled expression told Drew very few people ever confronted him.

"He needs professional help, Bruce. It's not right what you're doing."

"Don't worry about it. I'm his caretaker and guardian." His ferocious gaze didn't faze Drew.

"He's living in squalor."

"Of his own choosing. He lives in his art. He will die inside the canvas of his work," Bruce pronounced proudly.

"It's crazy."

"Drew's an idealist." Charlotte nudged him to the passenger side of the car, concerned for his immediate well-being.

"Is this the kind of people you bring here, Charlotte?" Bruce screamed and threw his Budweiser long neck against a tree.

"Bruce, he's just shocked by…"

"Fuck you, bitch. You're banned from the property! I'll call the police if I ever see you here again. If I find you, maybe I won't even call the police." He gnashed his yellow teeth together in a fearsome show of anger.

"Let's go." Drew opened his door and waited for Charlotte to get in.

She was hesitant to get in the driver's side; she had to pass uncomfortably close by Hiro's deranged caretaker.

"Don't worry, Charlotte, I won't bite." He hissed. His malicious smile lingered as she passed by him and jumped in the car.

"Don't forget, Charlotte, I don't like trouble."

"Is that a threat?" Charlotte lashed back.

"No, my love, of course not."

"Goodbye, Bruce." She rolled up her window and thrust the car into reverse. Bruce did not move, but steadily watched the shiny SAAB back all the way off the property. He regretted not killing them both, he was not beyond the drastic measure to protect the lucrative deception.

"Thanks, Drew. I can't go back."

"Are you upset that you can't see that horror show again?" He was exasperated.

"Yes," she answered stubbornly. Charlotte was painfully aware of the absurdity of her position, but was too angered to think clearly. She had intended to use the visit to impress Drew, perhaps enough for him to realize he was out of his league socially, culturally, and intellectually. It had backfired, his knowledge of art was minimal, thus the impact of seeing the living legend was far less than she expected. The few visitors she had brought to see him would not have cared if Hiro was hanging from a tree in a birdcage. They were solely interested in the inspirational aura that they believed emanated from the great man; the physical well-being of the artist was only a distraction not a concern, an inconsequential byproduct of true genius.

"You're as sick as him," Drew mumbled and groaned at the thought of the long ride. The sexual tension and unbridled passion that had brought them together the night before was gone.

"Don't say that, Drew." Her response was quiet and uncharacteristically understated as she mulled possible responses to his harsh, justified rebuke.

"Let's just go home, Charlotte."

"Okay." Charlotte's face burned, she had never felt so powerless, so insignificant in the eyes of another.

Chapter 22

Fall River

Sandy Wilson fidgeted nervously in his wheelchair as the images of Sheldon Harrison's funeral flickered on the ancient television set. The History Channel was replaying portions of the funeral as part of a larger series honoring the legend. He saw many familiar faces in the crowd, faces he had not seen in thirty years. Their names tucked away in a dormant part of his once agile mind.

"Are you okay, Sandy?" Nurse Winters asked from across the room. She was helping another patient with his day clothes, which were nothing more than brightly colored pajamas.

"I'm fine, Donna," he responded quickly and coherently, but she caught a quiver in his voice.

"Are you sure?"

"Yes."

"Come on, Wilson, time for a potty run." Frank Burns, the combative nurse's assistant strode into the recreation room and glared at Sandy.

"I don't have to go." He turned his back and stared at the screen.

"It wasn't a question, Mr. Wilson. I'm the sorry bastard that has to clean you up when you poop yourself." He forcefully spun the old man's wheelchair around and pushed him towards the bathroom.

"Donna, stop him," he pleaded for Nurse Winters to intervene.

"Frank, he said he didn't need to go." She stopped what she was doing and stood erect.

"Nurse Winters, if he has an accident what happens?" His voice carried across the recreation room. The other patients turned and watched the scene with fear and disgust. They were also thankful Frank Burns did not single them out for that day's humiliation.

"What does that have to do with anything? And stop yelling!"

"I do! I have to clean him. So you do your job and I'll do my job. Stay out of my goddamn business." He angrily pushed Sandy's ancient wheelchair towards the bathroom. Sandy lurched back and tried to grab his falling magazine, his right hand was crushed in the spoke of the heavy chair.

"Ahhh!" Sandy screamed and clutched his mangled hand.

"Jesus, Sandy, are you alright? Let me see your hand." Nurse Winters rushed to his side and tried to examine the injury.

"He's fine. He's a dummy, but he's fine." Burns tried to mask his instantaneous regret.

"Keep quiet, Frank. His fingers are broken. Get Carl to bring the minivan around. Dale isn't around to do it. He has to go to Charlton ER."

"Fucking guy, I wish he'd fucking die." Burns mumbled to himself and went off to get Carl, the handyman who sometimes doubled as a driver. Burns stomped down the hall, calculating how much grief he would catch for the incident.

"Sandy, we need to get you to the emergency room." She knew his hand was broken.

"I don't need to go." He winced; the searing pain was almost too much to take. He felt lightheaded as streaks of pain shot from his fingers into his wrist.

"What an asshole," Nurse Winters cursed. She gently placed Sandy's hand on his lap and wheeled him to the front door. Sandy lifted his head and looked back at the fading television set. Carlton Smithfield's poignant and heartfelt eulogy sent shivers through his battered body. The deep lines of sorrow etched across the face of Sheldon's most distinguished protégé made Sandy Wilson physically ill. Sheldon did not deserve the respect of such an extraordinary writer as Smithfield.

"It must be wonderful to be loved like that," Wilson said to himself, "to be remembered with such emotion, to be loved unconditionally. It must be nice, yes I would have liked for one person to care whether I lived or died. Just one, I don't need a whole group of family and friends; I just need a single person to take pause when they hear of my death. I guess Nurse Winters will think about me for a second, but she will go home and be with her family and I will be forgotten. Just another patient who died during her long career, there will be hundreds more before she retires and joins the walking dead. Maybe she'll end up in a nursing home, but she'll have visitors. Her children will bring their children to see grandma. They will be afraid of her and wish they didn't have to see the wrinkled old lady who smells funny and lives in a tiny room with other strange people. They will stop on the way home from a soccer game, staying just long enough to rid themselves of the guilt of sending their ailing parent to a rest home."

"Let's go, Mr. Wilson," said Carl the handyman. The surly ex-con hated his job almost as much as Frank Burns. He roughly loaded Sandy into the mini-van and sped towards Charlton Memorial Hospital. Sandy gazed helplessly out the window, mesmerized by the sight of people going about their daily chores. How much he missed simply going to the post office and mailing letters. He missed the smell of unfiltered air; with his good hand he cranked open the window and let the Indian summer breeze tantalize his neglected sense of smell.

"Mr. Wilson, roll up your window. The air conditioner is on," Carl angrily ordered.

"Just a moment, Carl." Sandy closed his eyes and inhaled as deeply as his aged lungs would allow.

"No, I said shut the window. You're letting out all the cold air. Jesus you people must lose your common sense the minute they lock you up in that joint." Carl was so frustrated that he didn't have power windows he slammed the steering wheel and hit the accelerator.

"You lose more than your common sense, Carl."

"What? What did you say?" He felt like striking the old man, no job was worth listening to the constant babble of the infirmed.

"I said you lose more than your common sense!"

"Really, you are mouthy today."

"You lose your dignity, your self-worth is gone. You lose all vestiges of what it is to be a viable human being."

"Morbid. I hate old people." Carl turned up his radio to blurt out the ravings of a dead man.

"You lose your soul, Carl," Sandy whispered and shut the window. Yet another isolation chamber left intact.

Chapter 23

Gloucester

The morning breeze, slightly cooler than Myron Wiseman would have liked, but he was still enjoying one of the last days of autumn on his large deck. With his customary steaming cup of coffee in hand, he gazed upon the glistening Atlantic Ocean and felt a deep appreciation for its natural beauty. The seaside home on Good Harbor Beach in Gloucester, Massachusetts was located on a tiny patch of land at the far end of the sandy beach. He had purchased his modest home decades before, paying a tiny fraction of the current market value.

"There's someone on the phone for you, Myron," said a distinguished-looking woman who handed him a cordless phone.

"Who is it, hon?" Wiseman gave his wife a queer look. They seldom received calls before 10:00 a.m. and never before 9:00 a.m.

"I don't know." She turned and headed for the kitchen, her long bathrobe swooshing on the tile floor.

"Hello?" Wiseman answered gruffly, convinced it was a telemarketer.

"Wiseman?"

"Yes. Who is this please?"

"My name is…"

"What? Say again please." Wiseman stood up and listened intently.

"My name is Sandy Wilson."

"Yes."

"You don't remember me?"

"No, should I?" Myron asked politely.

"I was a friend of Sheldon Harrison years ago. I was the guy who used to talk to you at Sheldon's home, you know, when you came to interview him."

"I'm sorry, I don't remember."

"At his Cambridge home, in the yard, when he wouldn't let you in until all the others were done with him."

"Sandy…" Wiseman rubbed his chin and slowly recalled the introverted handyman that lived in the guesthouse. He was an amiable and bright guy whose conversations he enjoyed as he waited for Harrison.

"I need to talk to you, Mr. Wiseman."

"Sandy, I do remember you. How are you? What can I do for you?" Wiseman expected a pleasant exchange between old acquaintances.

"I need to talk to you." Wilson coughed loudly and Wiseman heard him put change in what he concluded was a pay phone.

"About what, Sandy?"

"I would like to talk to you soon."

"About what?"

"I would rather not talk to you over the phone."

"Okay, where are you? Can you come to my house?"

"No. I'm at the Christian Charities Nursing Home in Fall River."

"That's quite a ride." Wiseman lost some interest when he thought of the distance.

"I know it is, Myron. I'm not well and I need to talk to you."

"Hurry up, dummy." Wiseman heard a harsh voice in the background.

"Who's that?" Wiseman asked with alarm in his voice.

"Nobody. I'm here if you want to talk to me, if not, I understand. It's just very important. You were more right than you knew."

"Sandy. Sandy? Crap." Wiseman turned the phone off.

"Who was that?" His wife asked from their newly renovated kitchen.

"A strange call. It was one of Sheldon Harrison's friends who I used to talk to on occasion. You know from the old days. He was a nice guy, somewhat detached and introverted but harmless enough I think. A very bright guy, I always thought he was Sheldon's secret lover masquerading as a handyman."

"What does he want?" She threw her dishrag on the table and watched her husband aimlessly shuffle about the living room. It was his typical maneuver when he was deep in thought.

"What did he want?" She asked again.

"I'm not sure. He wants me to go see him in a nursing home in Fall River."

"Fall River! That's near Rhode Island for God's sake."

"I know. I've been there before. It's not that far. We went to the Battleship Massachusetts, remember?"

"I remember. Are you going?" She gave him a worried look.

"I don't know."

"I don't think you should."

"Why?" He smiled wryly, his aged face showing his affection for his longtime wife.

"It's a long ride and you don't take care when you drive. You drive like a maniac."

"Oh bullshit. You worry too much, mother." He laughed and plodded off to the shower.

The engine of Wiseman's new Buick Le Sabre purred and seemed to welcome the challenge of the steep hill that led to the gates of the Christian Charities Nursing Home in Fall River.

"Hello I'm here to see Sandy Wilson," Myron said with a smile to the receptionist at the front desk. She looked overworked and underappreciated, her faced etched with the deep scars of endless toil, the decades of minimum wage work crushing her spirit.

"Who?" Her bored tone annoyed Wiseman; he hated any form of mental laziness.

"I said Sandy Wilson and I said it quite clear the first time."

"Sure." She flipped through the copy of her roster and called the duty nurse on his floor.

"Somebody will come and get you. Please sit over there." She pointed to an old orange chair in the corner. Myron flopped down with a great sigh, unsure why he had bothered making such a long journey.

"Hello sir. Are you here to see Sandy Wilson?" The incredulous nurse asked.

"Yes…my name is Myron Wiseman." Myron quickly stood.

"Good. My name is Donna Winters. Sandy hasn't had any visitors since he came here and he doesn't talk about any family." Nurse Winters remarked as they walked down the hallway. Myron, who hated hospitals of any sort, reluctantly followed the pleasant-looking nurse. To his utter dismay they had to cross Alzheimer's ward. The unnerving stretch seemed to last forever for Wiseman, the hollow stares of the indigent unnerved him.

"Please Mister, I need to go. I need to go to work. Please drive me," a desperate woman in a wheelchair begged. She grabbed his sleeve and pulled herself up in the chair. Her pleading eyes disturbed him to the point of flight.

"Sorry, dear, you can't leave," Donna gently placed the woman's hands in her lap.

"Okay, but come back for me. Please come back for me," she screamed, her eyes moist with tears.

"Sure, dear." Myron patted her hand and turned to leave.

"Don't forget me! Please don't forget I'm here!"

"I won't, dear." He felt a lump in his throat as he turned his back on her.

"She has Alzheimer's."

"I figured," Myron mumbled, glad they were moving away from the hellish ward.

"He's been sick lately. Sandy has."

"Really."

"Yes. He broke his hand and he just had some tests done for severe abdominal pain."

"Should you be telling me this? I'm not his family."

"No…I shouldn't have. I thought you were a close friend." Nurse Winters was angry at herself for being so casual about confidential information without checking with the patient.

"It's okay. I'm really an old acquaintance, not so much a friend. He called me yesterday and asked me to come down."

"Really, that is strange. He never uses the phone," Nurse Winters said over her shoulder as she pushed Sandy's door open. He was alone, a temporary precaution until they found out why he was having such severe abdominal pains. Myron knew immediately Sandy was dying, his emaciated body and pale face told the whole story. He must have concealed his condition from the staff for months. Blood tests and X-rays would soon reveal Wiseman's hunch correct.

"Sandy?"

"Myron." He sat up quickly and rubbed his eyes vigorously.

"What happened to your arm?" Wiseman pointed to his thick cast.

"Nothing. Just an accident. It's my hand really."

"You're okay, right Sandy?" Nurse Winters smiled and stood by the door.

"Yes, Donna, please excuse us."

"Sure. Nice to meet you, Myron."

"Yes thank you, Donna." Myron nodded

"Sit, please." Sandy pointed to a chair near a yellowed window overlooking the snaking river below.

"What can I do for you?" Myron settled in, studying the sagging features of the terribly aged man.

"I need to tell you something before they cart me off."

"What do you mean by that?"

"I'm dying, they'll tell me so later today. They'll send me to Charlton Memorial and then it'll be over. A few weeks of morphine-induced delirium and then death, that is all that awaits me." He looked out the yellowed window and already missed the natural world.

"Well I think you should let the…"

"The doctors tell me! No, Myron, I've never been so sure about anything in my life."

"So what is it I can do for you?"

Sandy smiled, "you always did cut through the bullshit. No nonsense Myron Wiseman."

"Always."

"I am the hidden Tolstoy." His suddenly serious expression made Wiseman sit straight, the reason for the summons was at hand.

"I don't understand, Sandy."

"Those articles you wrote, they were very perceptive. Your career suffered for it. The scorn from your colleagues was humorous."

"Not to me." Wiseman bristled.

"You were right."

"What part?"

"You never really said it, but you insinuated it, deep in your last few reviews."

"What?"

"That somebody else wrote the best works of Sheldon Harrison."

"Yes." Wiseman felt his stomach churn, his leg bounced uncontrollably and his mouth felt dry.

"I'm the hidden Tolstoy," Sandy mumbled in pain.

"You are? You mean a ghostwriter? How many? Which novels? Can you prove it?"

"No, well maybe. The first four."

"The best of course," Myron snarled knowingly.

"Yes."

"Why did you wait so long if you're the one? Why not before he died?"

"I don't know. I never wanted the trouble I guess. Something changed a few months back, I just felt like it should be revealed. Sheldon was very careful to leave no trace of our charade."

"It's funny."

"What?" Sandy smiled.

"I just remembered something."

"What?"

"After you and I had a conversation outside in Cambridge I went inside and questioned Harrison about you, what you did for him, etc…He was very evasive and almost belligerent about it, I made a mental note to investigate further in case I ever wrote an unofficial biography. I thought you might be his lover."

"Ha!" Sandy laughed out loud for the first time in years.

"Yes…silly I suppose. You know I always suspected something about his work, but I can't believe he would go to such an extreme. I'm sorry I just can't take your word for it. Trust me, Sandy, nothing would please me more."

"I understand. I don't have any proof and I'm too tired to rehash the whole affair anyway. I just needed to tell someone. Someone who could understand."

"It was good to see you, please feel free to call me anytime." He patted the bed softly and prepared to leave.

"I thank you for the time. Don't forget what I told you. I know you, you will not let it rest."

"I will, I have no proof and he's dead."

"I know you."

"I'm sorry."

"Thank you, Myron."

"You know what is sort of strange though," he halted at the door, "Harrison sent one of his interns to Portugal to retrieve something. He gave him the instructions on his deathbed. Whatever he recovered, he can't divulge for a few more months."

"Really, that is curious. A strange act for such a coward, perhaps he feared his judgment," Sandy Wilson said without bitterness, smiling calmly, he was at peace.

Chapter 24

Lexington Public Library

THE SLOW AND STEADY rain knocked the few remaining leaves still clinging to the ancient trees in the historic town of Lexington, Massachusetts. Perhaps their distant kin had watched in grim silence the opening salvos of the American Revolution, the blood-letting unfolding beneath their somber limbs. In the backyards of some of the older homes, untouched by developers, romantics were transported to a time when America was still a frightening place of dark woods and winters of isolation. The hallowed ground, forever linked with American independence and birth of a fledgling republic, was still inspiring to many, but sadly inconsequential to most. These days, the once quaint town, was overflowing with Volvos and BMWs of the super elite. Homes of gargantuan proportion were erected on tiny parcels of land with alarming regularity. There were large, stately homes untouched by the self-indulgent class, but the more modest homes were ripped from the earth because the children of the beautiful people needed the ultra trendy Great Rooms. The town still retained its charm and history, its erosion clear but not terminal.

Deep in the heart of Lexington's Public Library, Sheldon Harrison's most successful intern and protégé, Carlton Smithfield, stared at the wall of his sanctuary in a desperate attempt to clear his mind. His writing career had slowed and he was entering the phase of his life where it became necessary to live off past royalties. This depressed him, but could not overcome the placid lifestyle he had grown accustomed to. The domestication of Carlton Smithfield had killed the edge that made his early work so provocative.

Carlton loved the smell of the older books and the privacy of the medium-sized library. It was well-funded and accessible, but did not rival other larger institutions like the Boston Public Library. He stretched his hands and sighed, his inability to compose a coherent paragraph since his mentor's death was distressing to the famed writer.

"Hello, Carlton. I thought I would find you here."

"Myron!" Smithfield was surprised by his old friend's appearance.

"How are you? I see you still come to this place for inspiration."

"Not so much inspiration anymore, more like peace and quiet." He smiled and grabbed a chair for Wiseman.

"I understand that. I just took a chance that you would be here."

"What brings you here?" Smithfield pushed aside his books and folded his notebook.

"I don't know, well I do know, but I'm not sure what it is." Wiseman looked confused, Smithfield wondered if he was okay.

"What is it?"

"I got a call from Sandy Wilson."

"You did?" Smithfield's cordial expression changed dramatically.

Wiseman went on to explain the entire episode in detail.

"That is strange," he put down his glasses, "he is obviously suffering from some kind of dementia."

"Maybe."

"What do you mean maybe? There is no maybe, the alternative is he is telling the truth and Sheldon Harrison is the biggest fraud of the Twentieth Century."

"Calm down. I'm not saying I believe him. Did you get anything out of that intern who went to Portugal?"

"No, what does that have to do with this?" He was angry; his mentor was being dismantled upon the word of a lackey of dubious credibility.

"Nothing I guess, why are you so defensive?"

"I'm not, Myron, I'm simply pointing out that the word of some guy who used to live in Sheldon's guest house should not be taken as gospel."

"No doubt...no doubt."

"Then why are you wasting your time?" Carlton asked.

"You're unreasonably angry about this, I don't understand it!"

"You don't understand it!"

"Shhhh." Myron placed his hand on Carlton's arm.

"This is a man that helped me immeasurably, I owe my career to him and you can't understand why I'm offended when somebody makes baseless accusations."

"You're a supremely talented writer, he only kick-started your career, you would have made it without him."

"Bullshit."

"Look, I didn't come here to anger you, I just wanted to get your opinion, to pick your brain about it. I made a mistake. Get back to your reading. I'll talk to you another time."

"Okay, Myron, I'm sorry I snapped at you. I just think it is a bunch of crap." Smithfield stuck out his hand and they departed friends.

"You may be right." Myron smiled and shuffled off, the burden of his conflicting thoughts clearly adding to his labored, hunched-over posture.

Carlton Smithfield's day was ruined by Wiseman's unbelievable story. Myron was simply the messenger, yet he had treated him as if the indictment came from his lips. He reasoned his hostility stemmed from Myron's previous stance against his mentor. He tapped his fingers lightly on the new table and wondered about Drew's trip to Portugal. He looked up and was surprised to see a frizzy-haired young man leaning over and smiling broadly.

"Carlton Smithfield?"

"Yes." Carlton sighed.

"My name is Josh Wilkins and I just wanted to tell you what an honor it is to meet you." Smithfield could tell from his expression that this was a false statement. The genuine reverence that usually accompanies a true devotee of his work was not present.

"Thank you, Josh."

"I'm studying film at Columbia." His frizzy hair and ill-fitting clothes were a costume for his carefree hippie image, a coordinated neglect so common among suburban rebels looking for attention. He was everything the tough-nosed writer fought against. Assuredly a son of privilege, reared in an affluent community where his radical views were tailored so as not to affect a respectable career in an exciting field. He was artistic because he chose to be, he wanted the label. He desperately needed an identity that fit with his jaded and cynical view of his life of leisure. A life he shunned until the tuition bill came due, or another exchange program in Europe caught his fancy.

"So." Carlton leaned back and smirked. He loved torturing people who he did not respect. He knew, of course, he was prejudging him but he was confident his first impression was correct.

"So? I was hoping you had some advice for me." The budding filmmaker confidently sat and readied himself for the life-changing advice he would proudly recount at the Academy Awards.

"Why would I have any advice for you? I don't know anything about movie-making. I've never been in a movie. What makes you think I have anything to offer you?"

"Well I thought because they made a movie out of..."

"You were wrong."

"But you won an Oscar for your screenplay…"

"Josh, you were wrong."

"Sorry?" The confused student noticed the evil glint in Smithfield's eye.

"You should leave. I have nothing to offer you. I'm a novelist, plain and simple."

"Sorry, I didn't expect anything… I just…"

"Are you a rec room rebel?" Carlton asked.

"I don't know what you mean?"

"Recreation room. Did you have one?"

"Yes."

"Then you're a rec room rebel. What does your father do?"

"He's an attorney."

"Shocker."

"What does that mean?"

"Nothing. Have a nice day kid."

"I will."

"And don't use this little encounter as a dinner party anecdote when you're successful. Forget me, I have forgotten you."

"Rude asshole," the student muttered under his breath and stormed away.

Smithfield laughed inwardly, it was probably the most adversity the young man had ever experienced in his whole life. He felt good about it, not everything in life was a forgone conclusion, with pitfalls only for the less fortunate.

Chapter 25

Boston University

"**You have a message.**" Drew's roommate handed him a note scribbled on a piece of paper.

"Thanks." Drew read the barely legible note.

DREW. My grandmother wants to meet you. I will pick you up in the morning. Sorry about the thing last week. Charlotte.

"Shit." Drew crumpled the note in disgust. They had not spoken since debacle with the Antman and insane caretaker.

"Problem?" His roommate asked, without interest. It really didn't matter to him if it was a problem. Drew's life meant nothing to him.

"No."

"Good."

He spent a restless night thinking about Sheldon Harrison's widow, Emily Harrison. What would he say to her? Would she ask him about Sintra? How will Charlotte act after their last meeting? He was startled out of his insomnia by his drunken roommate barging into the room. Two equally inebriated and noisy friends accompanied him.

"Drew!" He bellowed in a confrontational tone.

"What?" Drew responded while turning to face them.

"What the fuck are you doing man?"

"Sleeping. What does it look like I'm doing?"

"On a Friday night! You are such a loser." He whispered the last part under his breath, but loud enough to be heard.

"Hey, I'm trying to sleep."

"Yeah so are we." He laughed and winked at his friends.

"Go someplace else if you want to party." His roommate, Chad, was seated at his desk and his two bleary-eyed cohorts were sitting on Chad's messy bed.

"Come on lighten up, Drew. I'm sick of being quiet because you're in here sleeping or studying. You're such a fucking dud man. I can't believe I got you as a roommate. We're staying here and people are coming over. You better wake up, my man."

"Whatever." Drew turned over and tried to sleep.

"Fuck you, faggot!" One of Chad's friends hollered, his bull neck bulging with emotion. He was drunk and agitated, looking for a release of his pent-up aggression. Chad gave a nervous glance at his friend. He wanted to harass his strange roommate but he didn't want any physical contact.

"What?" Drew rolled over and stared at him.

"Fuck off, you mother fucking faggot! Don't you fucking look at me, you motherfucker." His rage was uncontrollable. Drew noticed his fists were clenched and he was on the edge of the bed. He was a large football player type who had a reputation as a bad drunk who liked to fight.

"What's his problem?" Drew looked at Chad for help.

"Don't look at him!" He tossed a rolled-up piece of paper at Drew's head.

"Real mature." Drew tensed up; he was losing his patience for the intruder.

"Real mature," the agitated guest mimicked mockingly.

"What is your problem?" Drew sat up.

"You're my fucking problem. Every time we come in here, we have to be quiet because you're studying or sleeping. Fuck that! It all stops tonight, you little faggot." Chad's enraged friend walked over to Drew's dresser and grabbed his mail.

"What's this? A financial aid application! Let's see how much help this boy needs." He pretended to read the notice.

"Hey, get the fuck out of there!" Drew sprang to his feet.

"No! Wait…wait a minute. Let's see how much you need…" He held Drew back with his large hand.

"Get the fuck out of here!"

"Stop, so I can read." His strong forearm stopped Drew from cleanly retrieving the application. With his free hand he dropped the letter and swept the top of the dresser clear of all Drew's things. Among the debris was a small model airplane built by his father when he was child. It might have been an embarrassing article for the typical college student to possess, but Drew never allowed such pedestrian hang-ups bother him. It reminded him of home and his happy childhood.

A fight broke out with blinding speed. Drew grabbed his tormentor around the neck and tried to drag him to the floor, but he was a former wrestler and easily shook Drew off, shoving him violently towards his bed.

"Hey!" Chad shouted and tried to break it up.

"Fucking faggot!" The ex-wrestler eagerly pounced on Drew's head. Pummeling him with rights and lefts. Drew managed to use his knees to push him off. It was enough of a break for Chad and his other companion to intervene. They roughly pulled their enraged friend out of the room. He was screaming and ranting until they ushered him from the floor.

Drew sat up, dabbed his bleeding nose and felt his swollen eye. He felt weak and depressed. The attack was not surprising, he had been the victim of similar acts of aggression his entire life. His quiet, quirky nature made him an easy target all the way back to his grammar school days; the incident with the brawny ex-wrestler was just the latest Chapter. He wasn't weak, afraid, or easily intimidated, but simply could not avoid the ire of the insecure; too many found his sometimes-brooding attitude and intellectual maturity infuriating. He thought about his father as he glanced at the mirror and tried to see if he needed stitches. The facial wounds were cosmetic. He scolded himself for his awkward, off-balance attack. His father wouldn't have allowed himself to fall into such a defenseless position. He simply wasn't as tough or street smart, he attributed it to his rather tame childhood devoid of the hardships his father endured.

Drew sat on the edge of his bed and tried to calm down. He couldn't shake the images of the altercation. He dressed quickly, unsure where he was going, but positive he needed to leave the scene of his latest disappointment. He found a small Band-Aid in his desk drawer and covered the small cut over his eye. It was already swollen and turning yellow, it would be a nasty reminder of the incident for at least a week.

He slinked out of his building, unnoticed and hesitant about where he was going. He stood on the sidewalk and looked at the full moon. The cool night air helped clear his mind and ease the throbbing over his eye. As a child, he spent hours gazing at the Earth's cratered satellite, envisioning himself stepping upon the dusty surface and staring at this home planet from tens of thousands of miles away. He dreamed of landing on the dark side of the moon, shrouded in permanent darkness and hidden from human view until recently, its hostile environment excited his young mind. He wondered what it would be like to look out into deep space from the battered landscape of the moon, would he feel small and insignificant? Would the vastness of space scare or inspire him?

Drew smiled at the thought and touched his eye, the tenderness bringing him back to reality. With a moment's hesitation, he hailed a taxi and was off. The short ride was over before he could seriously consider what he was doing.

"Who is it?" Charlotte's tired, slightly annoyed voiced croaked through the intercom system. Drew did not respond immediately.

"Who the hell is it!" Charlotte called out.

"It's Drew." He finally mumbled, his head leaning forlornly against the brick of the sturdy building.

"You think this is funny ringing people's bells at this time of night. Fucking immature asshole!" She didn't hear him and thought it was drunken college students getting their rocks off.

"It's Drew," he responded more clearly this time.

"Drew?"

"Yes."

"Come up."

"What are you doing here? Is something wrong?" Charlotte asked as soon as he emerged from the tiny elevator. She was dressed in a revealing blue nightgown that accented her curves.

"I just wanted to talk to you." He avoided her penetrating blue eyes.

"What happened to your face?" She grabbed his cheek and examined his swollen face.

"Nothing."

"I'm sure." She smiled knowingly. Charlotte found it amusing; an immature college student brawling was, on a very base level, quite charming. She didn't understand the depth of the confrontation and teased him without concern.

"Can we go inside?" He asked.

"Why?" She asked coyly.

"I don't know, forget it." Drew turned and pushed the elevator call button.

"Drew, come on." She grabbed his shirt from behind and pulled him inside.

"Why do you want me to go to your grandmother's?" Drew asked, referring to her message from earlier in the day.

"Because she wants to meet you."

Drew felt a twinge of dismay. Was that all? Was she doing it just to appease her grandmother? A chore she reluctantly performed?

"I also wanted to see you again." She sat on the sofa and tossed her hair playfully. She looked like she was ready for bed, her make up was cleaned off and Drew could smell the freshness of her breath from across the room.

"You did. I'm not a tier one guy remember." He bristled with the recollection.

"So." She smiled but did not back away from her sweeping generalization.

"So. Maybe you aren't a tier one girl."

"I am."

"So you say."

"I am, Drew. Debate is futile." She stood up and grabbed a bottle of wine.

"Arrogance is unbecoming." He sighed and started to think he had made a mistake.

"Don't fret, Drew, I like you all the same. I always have. I didn't want to, I really tried to hate you. It didn't work." She was somber, her smile vanishing in a cloud of honesty.

"I like you sometimes," he whispered. He looked at his hands, unwilling to raise his head and look her in the eyes. It was an awkward moment that seemed to last forever, each party unwilling to make the next move. Charlotte looked at the ceiling and chastised herself for getting involved with a lowly college student. He was in her world because of a bizarre deathbed request by her obviously demented grandfather.

"Only sometimes, Drew?"

"Yeah, only sometimes, Charlotte."

"I like when you say my name." She felt an unexpected shiver of attraction.

"You do?" He managed a weak smile; his face was still throbbing from the fight.

"Are you in pain?" She noticed how he winced when he smiled.

"Yeah it hurts. Do you have any aspirin?"

"Sure, follow me." She led him to her lavish bathroom. She rummaged through a well-stocked medicine closet and found a tube of antibacterial cream. She applied it to his abrasions with nurse-like firmness.

"Who did this to you?" She was angry.

"Some guy." Her concern pleased him.

"I figured that." Charlotte poked him in the ribs and then caressed his face with her free hand. She tilted her head to the side and examined him as if it were their first time together. She noticed his serious and trustworthy brown eyes. They glimmered with life, she felt safe under their gaze, like she could trust him unconditionally. She seldom dated anybody that was not well-off or connected, it helped alleviate her paranoia about the intentions of her lovers.

"What about the aspirin?" He backed away, unsure how he should respond to her gentle touching.

"Yeah…sure." She reached under the sink and grabbed a bottle for him. She watched him remove the lid, take two pills and sigh with relief.

"No water?"

"No."

"Too tough for water?" She smiled and led him back to the living room.

"I guess."

"Let's go to the roof."

"You have access to the roof?"

"I have a deck up there. I had it built when I bought the place."

"How do you get there?" He looked about for a staircase.

"We have to take the elevator." She threw on a heavy robe and warm slippers.

The elevator ride was short, Charlotte's townhouse was on the top floor and nobody else had rights to the roof. Drew was awed by the glittering view from the neatly arranged deck. He felt like he was in the center of the city. To his right, thousands of twinkling lights outlined the massive skyscrapers of the Financial District. Ahead, the rushing Charles River looked formidable, unforgiving in its blackness, yet dutifully separating Boston from Cambridge as it always had. Below, traffic on Berkley Street sped wildly through the last light before disappearing on the infamous Storrow Drive, a white-knuckled surface road running along the river.

The night was clear and cool, a full moon adding to the romantic allure of the moment.

"Colder than I thought." She shivered, just like she had done on the isolated mountaintop in Portugal.

"I'll keep you warm." He pulled her close, invigorated by the beauty of the city he cherished.

"Save me." She smiled and felt his strong arms pull her close. She could smell the masculine soap he used. "I love it up here. I feel like I'm closer to some sort of inner harmony if you believe in that kind of thing. Spiritually I feel at ease."

"I can understand that."

"Are you my inner harmony?" She turned around and clasped her hands around his waist.

"Maybe." His swollen lips touched hers.

The unlikely duo passionately embraced under the dim stars of a full moon. All the anger and frustration that had defined their relationship was released in a moment of unrelenting sexual energy that few experience in a lifetime.

"Let's go inside." She finally broke from the most intense kiss of her life. Her legs trembled and she felt helpless in his arms.

"Okay." He led her to the elevator where they kissed again.

They ripped the door open and raced to the bedroom, Charlotte's robe dropping to the cold hardwood floors, stopping on the threshold of her large bed.

"Stop... please," pleaded Charlotte.

"Do you want me to stop?" Drew's chest heaved and his heart pounded. He knew he was only moments away from making a permanent imprint on her life.

"Drew, I don't know about this." She stared at him for an answer, hoping he would ravage her before she could say no.

"It's right, Charlotte." He kissed her neck and lips. She moaned and answered with equal fervor. They stumbled onto the bed, squirming and caressing each other until Charlotte found his pants. She pulled at his jeans until he was free. Drew lifted her nightgown and tugged at her revealing panties. She laughed aloud, her voice ecstatic for what was about to happen. Her insides churned and then ached as he penetrated her; her stiff nipples pressing against his chest made him pump faster. He wanted to be inside her forever, the warm, forbidden place was his.

The next morning, Drew was jolted awake by the warm sunlight pouring through two large windows in the unfamiliar bedroom. He sat up and looked confused, Charlotte was awake and staring at him. She was propped on one elbow, watching his every move, her breasts exposed and inviting. She smiled, her gleaming white teeth greeting him, straight and perfect from years of visits to the best orthodontist in the city.

"Good morning," she said.

"Hi," he said meekly. He was self-conscious and slightly embarrassed by his out-of-control actions the night before. He vividly recalled her arching thrusts and whispers of encouragement as he went as hard as he could, hurting and loving her at the same time. Suddenly he felt ill, his head became dizzy with fear, hot beads of sweat formed on his forehead. He hadn't used a condom. He chastised himself for being so careless, so ridiculously irresponsible in an age of HIV and AIDS.

"We need to be careful next time." Charlotte seemed to read his mind, but did not appear as alarmed.

"Jesus. I can't believe we weren't more careful." Drew rubbed his face to hide his burning cheeks.

"Don't spoil it, Drew, don't overanalyze the details." Charlotte seemed offended by his remark.

"Sorry."

"Do you want to take a shower here? We can go to my grandmother's after that."

"Sure that would be easier."

Charlotte pulled off the covers and confidently strode to the bathroom. Drew felt the stirrings of an erection. She flaunted her chiseled body, naked and beautiful, she was the most sexually attractive woman Drew had ever slept with. He was overwhelmed by her seductive glances and sexual maturity, swallowed up like so many before in the whirlpool of her unmatched charms.

Charlotte left her conquest idling in her bed, settling for a hot shower in her custom glass circle stall. She intentionally left the door ajar as she lathered her long legs and arms. Drew watched her bend over and gently use the soap on her most private parts, carefully removing the aura of sex. Drew was mesmerized by the woman he had made scream with pleasure.

"Want to join me?" Charlotte hollered above the din of her rushing shower.

"No, I really can't," he answered from just outside the open door. He tried to hide his full erection from her penetrating blue eyes. Her tactful smile had vanished, replaced by the lustful, half-conscious glare of arousal.

"In here now!" She ordered and opened the shower door; the spray of warm water spattered his face. Through the mist of the powerful shower Drew saw the outstretched hand of Charlotte Emerson. He clasped the wetness and let himself be pulled inside. He caressed her face and felt a strange warmth he had not felt the night before. The intimacy of showering with a virtual stranger was an intoxicating and frightening experience. Stripped down to the essence of a man or woman, all cosmetic aids swirling down the gold-plated drain, all flattering clothing resting on hangers many feet away, nary the place for the self-conscious or inhibited.

Exposed, vulnerable, and helpless, they made love under the warm waters of the distant Quabin Reservoir; Drew's concern about protection but a distant memory as the cloud of sexual gratification and burgeoning love again impaired his judgment.

Chapter 26
Emily Shea Harrison

— *Winchester, Massachusetts.*

NESTLED IN THE HEART of one of Boston's most affluent suburbs, Emily Shea Harrison listlessly performed her morning rituals anticipating the arrival of her granddaughter for afternoon tea. Her home, the most sought-after estate in a community brimming with the lavish homes, kept her busy enough to forestall the dour thoughts at the edges of her fragile mind. The once strong and independent wife of the late Sheldon Harrison had grown passive in her golden years. Her station as the matriarch of an American literary family bored her, but she embraced her life of privilege and wealth.

Emily brushed back her gray hair and gazed out her office window into the courtyard below. Her home, modeled after a European castle, was once the rage of the town. She insisted that the unique home go unseen from the street, only adding to her mystique as the enigmatic wife of the great Sheldon Harrison. The heavily wooded acreage around the multilevel home and the long driveway gave the casual visitor the impression of great wealth and stature. In fact it was this very impression Sheldon wanted to convey when he meddled during the design phase. The parlor and her office were decorated with a modern flair, but the rest of the house was rather bland and dated. The old home needed many repairs and upgrades.

In contrast with her aging home, Emily Harrison still retained the beauty that overwhelmed Sheldon some forty odd years before. She adhered to a rigorous exercise regime and watched her diet. Her attractiveness and seemingly positive countenance was a mask for a painful life of regret.

Their relationship was never the perfect love affair Sheldon liked to brag about. The exciting romance of a teacher and his pupil soon cooled to a convenient partnership, a loveless union she found impossible to escape. Their problems were hidden by the success of Harrison's early works, erupting to the surface after his career ended and his legend took hold. She was never comfortable with his position as an American Literary Czar. She found it hard to connect the cold, uncaring man she slept with and the passionate man of letters who made her cry with his words. His insecurity and her lack of reverence caused friction that was never smoothed over.

During the early years of his successful career, Sheldon often tried to rekindle their relationship only to be met with a blank stare and a request for a divorce. She wanted to end the suffocating marriage that shattered her spirit and turned her into a recluse. Recluse may be an exaggeration, but she lost her gregarious personality and became a respectable woman, living out her days staring across the trimmed grass of the courtyard and wondering where her life went.

Shortly after the unofficial separation, Emily had a few years of superficial enjoyment, spending her hefty monthly allotment with the vigor of someone who was accustomed to poverty. She spent half the year traveling through Europe; the summers on the coast of France or winters on the slopes in Switzerland. She was a veteran of many subtle affairs, brief encounters, and summer romances, all discreet and off Sheldon's radar screen. He, of course, had countless indiscreet relationships that only added to his reputation as a hard-charging artist. The impression was incorrect; on the contrary, he was a meek coward who couldn't sexually satisfy any of his partners.

Her period of sexual freedom slowly gave way to her present semi-reclusive state. She suffered from a deep sadness that she could not shake or temper, it was permanent loneliness that drove to the depths of despair. She was seldom alone, family visitors were common, yet she was lonely all the time.

"Soon all the leaves will be gone," she muttered to herself. There were many already on the ground, withering helplessly on the cold ground. The dazzling colors of autumn comforted her; the majestic elm and oak trees that surrounded her compound shed their burdensome leaves in preparation for a long New England winter. It was usually her favorite time of year, but the recent passing of her husband depressed her.

Emily was inundated with requests for interviews and publishers called for the rights to her biography. She politely acknowledged each request, personally replying to every one, but each time declining. It was absurd that they wanted information from her, she felt like she hardly knew him.

With care, she cranked open her office window and inhaled deeply, sucking in the autumn air that hinted at winter. Winters were, in the past, a busy and festive season for Emily Harrison. The Christmas parties, The Nutcracker, The Boston Symphony, Aspen, New York City on New Year's Eve, all the customary rituals of the privileged. Her waning interest in such exclusive events surprised her friends who quietly eliminated her from the tight circle of Massachusetts's elite.

She gazed at herself in the custom full-length mirror in her office. She was wearing a gray silk suit that hugged her fine physique. Her gray hair was stylish and supremely well kept. Her glowing feeling of self-admiration quickly faded with the startling arrival of her ever-intrusive grandson, Wilton Saunders.

"Hi Grandma, are you busy?" Wilton strolled into her office and wondered why his grandmother looked so surprised.

"Oh Wilton, you startled me." She kissed his cheek.

"How are you?" Wilton asked with mock sincerity.

"I'm doing fine, Wilton. Your grandfather and I didn't have the closest relationship in the last few years. In some ways we were virtual strangers." She bowed her head and wished she felt more emotion; she was riddled with feelings of guilt and disloyalty.

"Don't say that!" He was angered by what he thought was callous remark.

"I'm sorry, Wilton, but you getting angry does not change the truth. I won't lie anymore. I did that for too many wasted years." Her disgusted tone hung heavy in the air, she was in charge and would not be bullied into a dramatic show of love and loss that did not exist.

"You were always together…"

"When, Wilton? Birthday parties? Christmas? We did it for the grandchildren. Wilton, we both knew the truth about our relationship."

"Okay!" He walked to the window and shifted his brooding eyes to the big yard he always hated. He recalled the many days when he was forced from the comfort of the television room to play with his boisterous cousins on the lawn. He was terrible at sports and lacked the imagination for the role-playing games typical of children under twelve. His cousins would encourage him, but his snotty attitude alienated many, permanently marring his relationship with his closest relations.

"Wilton is something bothering you?"

"Do you know about the whole intern farce?"

"Yes, I have heard, what's the problem?"

"The jerk went to Portugal on some wild goose chase."

"I know, but at the behest of your grandfather." She examined him closely. His hunched shoulders and tense body motions made her wonder how he achieved the reputation as a jovial, friendly sort. She had seldom witnessed it and believed if he did show a different side to others it was not genuine. He was a solemn kid who always seemed to be thinking of others and not in the positive light that it might suggest. Something lurked behind the personality of Wilton Saunders that disturbed her. Sure she loved him but she did not necessarily trust him and never confided in him. He was, she hated to admit, her least favorite grandchild. When she thought about the reasons why she felt this way, it came down to his personality. Like his famous grandfather, in the right circles, he could be a funny and charming. If you were a plumber in his home fixing a leaky faucet, he was moody and surly, answering questions in hostile monosyllables. His chameleon-like disposition was hard to pick up if you weren't attuned to his family's legacy of such behavior. He was only a child when she first noticed the familiar flaw in his character.

"We call him the lottery winner," Wilton boasted.

"I spoke with Carlton last week and he speaks very highly of young Mr. Engle."

"So he says," Wilton snarled, bristling at the very insinuation that he was human. His loathing had grown exponentially since Drew's return.

"Why would Carlton lie? I find him a very good judge of character."

"I'm telling you he's lying. Do you know who Charlotte has been hanging around with?" Wilton angrily fingered his keys. He avoided the curious look from his grandmother. He was enraged by her obstinate defense of Engle.

"I do. I would hardly describe it as that, Wilton. Isn't that why you're here? Charlotte must have told you he was coming."

"Yes she mentioned she might invite him, but that's not why I'm here."

"Are you sure?" She looked at him quizzically, searching and probing for a reaction.

"I said no, I know she's coming, but I also came for a visit."

"Okay. You know she's a big girl, you don't have to worry about her so much."

"I don't," he protested weakly.

"You do, Wilton." She was building her courage to speak frankly with her confused grandson.

"Enough." He stormed off to the corner of the office, hiding his red face and planning his escape.

"She is your first cousin, Wilton. You can't get any closer than that."

It was only a moment in time, just a miniscule few seconds in his life, yet it was the first time his concealed feelings were detected by a third party.

He felt himself losing control, his indignant anguish reaching a point of no return. He wished it was her who had died, his grandfather was rotting in a gilded casket and this crazy old fool was making accusations about something she couldn't comprehend.

"I don't understand you sometimes," he shot back with false bravado.

"Understand this, Wilton, nothing can come of it. Nothing." She was firm and honest.

"I really think you're sick to think there is anything more than what it is." His irritated tone seemed to confirm his grandmother's suspicions.

"Cut the… the act, Wilton!" She stood and stared at his slumped shoulders and downcast eyes.

"Enough, you're making way too much of this." He tried to lighten the mood by smiling awkwardly.

"They're here." Emily Harrison sighed and pointed to Charlotte's sleek SAAB entering the upper end of the long driveway.

"Good."

"Behave yourself, Wilton. He is my guest, and apparently a friend of Charlotte's, so you better control your emotions." Her admonishment angered him to the point of physical violence. His soft hands trembled and beads of sweat trickled down his flushed cheeks.

Chapter 27

Ten Minutes Earlier

"How are you feeling? Are you nervous?" Charlotte asked.
"About some things, not this though." Drew smiled at Charlotte who was weaving in and out of traffic trying to make up the time they lost in the shower.

"What? What are you nervous about?" She glanced at him and thought about what they had done, how things would never be the same. The hatred may return, in fact it was likely that it would, but the venomous, malicious loathing would not survive their intimacy.

"About you. I'm not ready for this sort of thing. The thing with your grandfather was surreal enough," he chuckled and looked out the window. It was a bright Saturday afternoon with only a hint of winter on the edges of a stiffening breeze.

"What he told you, is it something I should be concerned about?" Charlotte asked.

"I can't tell you Charlotte. Why do you keep asking when you know I can't?" His pained expression made her nervous, for the first time she was truly concerned about what he knew. What did he know? How will it impact me? My God this is bigger than I thought. What could he know!

"Okay…but you must know it's really getting to be a drag. I don't think a hint is divulging anything."

"I can't! I wish I could Charlotte. I signed the fucking paper!"

"What can they do to you? Sue you? Come on, Drew, it's just my grandfather's last act of power. He needed to be in charge, even on his deathbed."

"I can't." He turned away and then smiled.

"What is it? Why are you smiling?"

"No reason." He was staring at a group of young boys huddled off to the side of a football field. They had an array of model rockets tucked under their arms. They appeared to be patiently waiting for the football game to end to launch their carefully constructed rockets. Drew imagined a long day of shrill whistles, wildly cheering parents and a cranky public address system belching out yardage gains. He thought about the huddled group of rocketeers waiting far out of view from their classmates, somewhat self-conscious about what is universally considered the hobby of the super nerd. It was a tragic tale of American youth abandoning the hobbies of their older fathers and grandfathers. Unstructured, immeasurable activities such as rocket-building did not help you get into college or enhance your stature in the community. The typical college recruiter isn't interested in a silly hobby that was impossible to quantify or measure.

The moment the last whistle blew, the sounds of the game would abruptly give way to the purring of eight-cylinder engines as the hurried parents raced their shiny SUVs to the next scheduled event. The brief stillness soon giving way to the high-pitched whistle of the arching rockets crisscrossing the sky. The stomping ground of the conventional was transformed into a launchpad for a group of shy young people who preferred the cerebral to the physical. They knew they did not have long to enjoy the fruits of their labor, an unenlightened town worker would inevitably show up and send them home.

"What are you thinking about? You're so quiet all of a sudden."

"I was just thinking about those kids back there."

"I didn't see them."

"Nobody ever does," he added wistfully, unwilling to divulge his true feelings.

"Drew Engle, you are a strange boy, sometimes anyway." She shook her head and felt sorry for him. He was fighting battles she could not appreciate.

"Here we are." She pulled into the sheltered driveway and up the long path to her grandmother's house.

"Wow." Drew observed quietly.

"Nice, isn't it? I spent a lot of time here when I was young."

"Stunning." He loved the aura, the old world feeling of the very private estate. Every angle, every potential view from the outside world was elegantly concealed with strategically placed trees and shrubs. The natural folds of the land combined with the large lot all helped to conceal the actions of the Harrison's and their guests.

"Don't be nervous." She smiled as she leaned over the top of her car.

"I'm not." He lied; he was somewhat anxious about the impromptu meeting.

"Honey, you're a bad liar." She sighed deeply and rested her chin on her bent hand. Drew looked stunning in the sunlight; her new lover was pure and uncorrupted with a hint of mystery behind those deep brown eyes. He blushed and looked away.

"Adorable!" Charlotte bellowed for all to hear.

"What?" Drew pretended not to understand her.

"You are adorable. Blushing boy." She playfully tossed her keys at him. He missed and they landed on the roof of her sports car.

"Nice throw."

"Clumsy. You know how much that will cost me."

"It's a tiny scratch." Drew circled the car and ended up behind her.

"It will cost you," she repeated.

"How much?" He gently placed his hand on her hips.

"You can make it up to me later," she said with a seductive grin.

"I can't wait." He backed up; he knew it was inappropriate for such action in her grandmother's driveway.

She glanced nervously at Wilton's car. "Oh, shit. My cousin is here."

"So."

"So nothing, I just don't know what he's doing here." She rubbed her stomach uneasily, the thought of him made her stomach churn. It was a feeling she had since she got back from Europe, a feeling of dread in his presence.

"Let's go, she is probably waiting for us," he said.

"Yeah, she must think we're having sex out here," she mocked and headed for the front door.

"How are you, sweetheart?" Emily Harrison embraced her granddaughter and glanced at Drew behind her. She was examining him closely, immediately looking for a clue of his intentions and possibly a hint of his trip to Portugal. She was looking at his comfort level, his mannerisms, anything that would reveal what she desperately wanted to know. It was killing her inside that there was a stranger who possibly possessed damaging information that could do irreparable harm to her family.

"This must be the famed Drew Engle," she said with a wide smile.

"It is." Charlotte blushed. Wilton observed her discomfort and recoiled.

"Hello." Emerging from the corner, Wilton assuredly witnessed their playful banter.

"Wilton, you know Drew."

"Yes." He did not move to shake his hand or properly greet him. His grandmother's wrathful glare had little impact in his defiance. Drew did not flinch at the slight, he knew that Wilton did not like him, barely acknowledging his existence the few times they were in the same room together.

"Sit down." Mrs. Harrison ordered. Her fiery eyes boiling over with anger, Wilton was going to cause trouble, there was little question of that, call it a grandmother's intuition or simply common sense.

"You have a really unique home, Mrs. Harrison."

"Call me Emily, Drew. I never liked being called Mrs."

"Okay." He did not feel comfortable with such informality, but would adhere to the wishes of his host.

"I used to love it," she was referring to her home, "not so much anymore though. It's big and lonely now. Twenty years ago, this place was rarely without one of my grandchildren wrecking my flowerbeds or breaking the sprinkler system. It was nice though. Then everybody is gone, grown up and busy with their own lives."

"I come all the time," Wilton interjected haughtily.

"Yes I know, too much I think." Emily laughed and smiled, but it was obvious she meant what she said. Drew cheered inwardly.

"What happened to your face?" Wilton asked.

"Excuse me, please?" Drew was looking at Emily and did not hear him clearly.

"What happened to your face?" Wilton accented each word as if talking to a child.

"I was in a fight last night," Drew responded honestly. He figured there was no use trying to cover it up.

"Why? What did you do?"

"Does it matter?" Drew bristled.

"Are you okay?" Emily Harrison tried to divert his attention.

"Yes, it was really a small altercation with someone at school."

"At Boston University?"

"Yes."

"I should think things of that sort should not happen at such a prestigious school."

"Grandma, things have changed since your day," Charlotte poked fun.

"I suppose they have and it wasn't that long ago, wise guy. You should have reported it to somebody."

"Why do you presume he didn't start it?" Wilton interjected.

"I didn't."

"Wilton, what's up with you?" Charlotte gave him a scolding look.

"Nothing, I'm just making small talk. I was just commenting on why she is presupposing he didn't instigate it, that's all."

"You've had an attitude since we walked in. What's the problem?" Her direct questioning sent Wilton spinning; he did not expect to be called out so quickly.

"I don't have a problem."

"Sure you do, let's hear it, Wilton!" Charlotte's aggressiveness did not surprise him; he chided himself for not being prepared.

"Enough." Emily grabbed Charlotte's hand and led her away from her cousin. Drew looked him over closely; he was twitching with anger and avoided eye contact.

"You know it's the first Saturday of the month," Emily said.

"What does that mean?" Charlotte asked.

"Carlton's due any minute."

"Why didn't you tell me?" Charlotte gave her an angry look.

"Why? You don't get along with him anymore?"

"We're fine, he just irritates me. Drew gets along with him."

"I really don't know him that well, but we're, I guess you can say, new friends," Drew interjected politely.

"Pffff." Wilton guffawed.

"What is so funny?" Drew turned and looked at him irritably, he was losing his patience.

"Nothing," Wilton snapped and walked away.

"If you have something to say, say it. Don't dance around it." Drew followed him to the corner. His movements were menacing and aggressive.

"Hey, what's this?" Wilton protested to his unsympathetic relations.

"Never mind them, talk to me. If you have a problem with me I want to hear it. I didn't ask to come here. I was invited."

"Drew, it's alright." Emily touched his arm in a calming way.

"You have some nerve talking to me like this in my grandmother's house. You don't have any class. Goddamn nerve of you!"

"What is it? What is your problem?" Drew raised his voice and clenched his fists. It was the moment of truth, the moment when all the pressure of his discovery came to a boiling point.

"You're a goddamn interloper. My grandfather was sick and medicated and you took advantage of him. We don't know what you said to him; maybe he thought you were somebody else, we don't know. You're a suck-up trying to attach yourself to the family to get your fifteen minutes of fame. We don't want you; we don't want to be a tale for your grandchildren. Privacy is something we cherish, you can't understand our world because you are not part of it no matter how many times you've slept with my cousin."

"Wilton!" Charlotte screamed. She was horrified by his last remark. The first part of his tirade she could understand, she had held the same view only a short time before.

"Get out!" His grandmother angrily pointed to the door.

"What!"

"How dare you speak to one of my guests like that! You're way out of line. Leave please," Emily said firmly.

"Of course, Wilton you have the whole thing wrong." A deep voice from the rear of the room got their attention.

"Carlton." Wilton sputtered and turned red.

"Mr. Smithfield, Wilton. I was in the room when your grandfather gave Drew the key. He only wanted Drew. He didn't ask for it, nor did he want it. It's a burden."

"I didn't say…"

"Yes, you did, I heard the whole thing. You weren't in the room yet so you assume there must have been some treachery involved because none of us were chosen. He wanted Drew and that is it."

"I think I should leave," Drew said softly. His dreary, battered face made Carlton angrier.

"This goddamn character assassination is getting ridiculous," he snarled, eyeing Wilton, but shooting Charlotte a glance of inclusion.

"Well it's good to see you, Carlton." Emily forced a smile, temporarily breaking the tension.

"Good to see you, doll." Carlton managed a heartfelt hug and kiss.

"Let's go for a walk and cool off, all of us." Emily grabbed her sweater and ushered her party through double sliders to the courtyard. They silently followed her down the stairs to the yard below. They paired off to discuss the incident. In the lead were Carlton Smithfield and Emily Harrison.

"So, my dear friend, how have you been?" She tucked her arm under his and held him tightly. He was one of her oldest and dearest friends.

"I didn't want to add to the problems in there, but it isn't fair. Drew is taking the heat for something he had no control over. He's a good kid, he's not the type who cares about Wharholian fame. Just the opposite really."

"Nice word."

"You like?"

"I like the word and I liked Andy," she said wistfully.

"I only met him once. No opinion of him really."

"I was very fond of him. A brilliant and sweet man."

"What a day," Carlton exclaimed loudly, marveling at the blue sky and fluttering leaves. The trees on the sprawling estate were shedding their beautifully colored leaves, gearing up for a long winter of wilting branches and frozen trunks.

"What have you? What news?" Emily pushed. She had a sixth sense when something was bothering him.

"A bit of strange news." They shuffled along, out of earshot of the others. Drew was the last in line with Charlotte and Wilton in the middle. They were engaged in a heated argument.

"What is it?"

"Do you remember Sandy Wilson?"

"Of course!" She almost stopped him. The name was a jolt from the past.

Carlton calmly recounted the tale without interruption. The bizarre meeting between Myron Wiseman and Sandy Wilson transfixed Emily. She accelerated her pace, deliberately putting distance between them and her grandchildren. She didn't want them to hear the conversation; it was primal instinct to protect them until she could figure out the validity of the story.

"Does Myron believe him?"

"I'm not sure. Perhaps."

She was stunned; she expected an emphatic no to her question. She respected Myron Wiseman and secretly agreed with his assessment of her husband's latter work.

"Jesus Christ. This can't be true, Carlton."

"It isn't true. He's dying and even Myron admitted he may not have been of sound mind."

"He's dying?" She held him tight.

"Well Myron thinks so, but I don't think it was confirmed."

"He was such a quirky guy, he was a war buddy of Sheldon's."

"Was he the guy he saved?"

"Yes."

"Oh what a tangled web we weave."

"Indeed. I spent a lot of time with him. Very smart and amiable, it's hard for me to imagine him making this up. I was very fond of him. Maybe he was on painkillers or something."

"Maybe…but my impression is he was fairly lucid on the phone and in person."

"Weird, isn't it?" Emily looked up at her companion.

"Yes, then you add in the whole thing with Drew," Carlton whispered.

"It makes you wonder, doesn't it?"

"Sure."

"What the hell did he give to him?" Emily glanced back at Drew, briefly making eye contact. She smiled and looked away.

"He can't talk about it. Do you think it has anything to do with what Sandy alleges?" Carlton asked.

"I don't know. But is it coincidental that he is saying this after he died? Maybe he felt like he owed him something for supposedly saving his life."

"I just think he's a crazy old man. What do you mean 'supposedly'?"

"Nothing, really nothing." She looked away.

"Okay." His disappointment was palpable.

"Sheldon said something strange to me many years ago when he went for surgery for his leaky heart valve. He really thought he was going to die, surgery on your heart was a risky proposition in those days."

"What did he say?"

"Not much, I just remember him talking crazy. He said that what happened in the War was not as it seemed and he was no hero."

"Interesting. Any other explanation?"

"No, but I think he was frightened to death and was just trying to let me know he wasn't a brave soldier so I would comfort him. It could have been his way of getting sympathy or something. He was truly a strange man with motives I could never understand. I do know their relationship was strained at times with moments of outright hostility. It's funny though."

"What is?"

"I just remembered how much Sandy liked to talk about literature and the position of American writers of the time. He had a large library in the guesthouse. I never really knew what he did for Sheldon; he didn't seem to have a real job."

"It could be Sheldon felt like he needed to take care of him after what they went through together." Carlton's reasoning was halfhearted.

"No, you knew Sheldon better than that. He didn't possess that kind of a heart."

"I know Drew can't tell us much about what he knows, but we can confront him directly, you know, to judge his reaction."

"That doesn't sound right. I don't like putting that kind of pressure on him."

"I know, I know. But we won't let him tell us, we'll just judge the reaction and decide if there is any connection." Carlton didn't like it either but he felt they had no other choice.

"Later." She looked back again.

"Okay later."

"I don't understand why you are acting like such an ass?" Charlotte walked with her disgruntled cousin, following her grandmother and Carlton who were engrossed in inaudible conversation just described.

"I don't understand you! For weeks, you did nothing but badmouth him. Why this dramatic change? All of a sudden he's your Prince Charming. What happened to change your mind? I can only imagine." His cutting words infuriated her.

"Lower your fucking voice! Things change, Wilton. He isn't what we thought, well maybe he is, but it doesn't matter because I like him."

"Great. How long will that last? Two weeks and then you'll be on the phone with me saying how right I was and what a leech he is."

"You're so cynical. Why does it bother you? Really. Why Wilton?"

"It doesn't bother me."

"Liar! You almost caused a fight after two minutes together."

"Charlotte! Watch out!" Drew exclaimed.

"Will you shut up for one minute? I'm talking to my cousin," Wilton lashed out.

"Oh shit, I just stepped in dog crap." Charlotte examined her soiled shoe.

"Oh." Wilton looked at Drew with a sheepish, but defiant grin.

"What did you say?" Drew moved quickly, challenging Wilton.

"Okay, Drew, let's go around the other way." Carlton Smithfield grabbed him and dragged him away from the altercation.

"Don't be so bold unless you know who you're dealing with," Wilton boasted loudly. It was amusing; everyone knew he would not have said it unless Carlton had intervened.

"You should learn some manners," Drew said over his shoulder.

"You should learn when you're not wanted," Wilton responded.

"Wilton, be quiet and go home!" Emily Harrison spun him around and held his arm tightly. He yanked his arm free and glared at her with such ferocity she stepped back, afraid for what he might do next.

"Fine." He stormed away. When he reached his car he felt weak, his uncontrolled display of anger put him in a bad light. He looked like a jealous fool who could not restrain himself. In one fell swoop, his secret obsession was revealed. He was no longer Charlotte's happy, slightly paunchy cousin who was both her friend and confidant. In ten minutes of futile, ill-conceived aggression, he was transformed into a fat, embittered young man with no discernible prospects or quantifiable accomplishments. Charlotte's unwavering friendship made him think he was something other than the family disappointment. She tried to shield him from the rest of the Harrison clan. It was a wasted effort for most figured out early on that his jovial personality was just a mask; a mean-spirited boy corrupt in spirit lurked behind the artificial barrier.

Wilton sped off like a crazed man, the dust from his luxury vehicle momentarily obscuring the scorching eyes of his grandmother who seemed to have a window into his soul. He watched her from his rearview mirror, her look of anger and disappointment made him curse and pound his steering wheel. He fought the demons that churned inside his fuming mind.

"Drew, I'm sorry about Wilton's behavior. That is not what I expected from him, although it isn't totally unexpected either. I'm ashamed that a guest in my home was treated like that." Emily Harrison placed an affectionate hand on Draw's knee. They were all seated in the large living room below her office and overlooking the elevated courtyard. It was roomy and comfortable but not nearly as large as the Great Rooms that were currently in fashion. Emily often chided the owners of the monstrous homes being built by the dozen. She believed it was a grotesque perversion of what she considered the obligation of the wealthy to conceal their accomplishments. A home should be a subtle hint of one's economic station and not a frivolous display for all to see. She held a particularly scathing view of the dot.com millionaires who made their fortunes before the predicable market correction left many so-called geniuses out of work. It was a hot button topic and Charlotte enjoyed teasing her about it.

"Don't worry. This entire fiasco has been an eye-opening experience," Drew responded gravely.

"How so?" Emily prodded.

"Your world is very different from my world. I was very fortunate to get the internship but I would never have taken it if I knew it would cause such turmoil in your family."

"We thrive on turmoil, Drew," she paused. "We wouldn't know what to do if somebody wasn't overreacting about something or another. You could call us a family of drama kings and queens. We don't like peace and harmony; it's foreign to us. Sheldon's position set us on a path of dysfunction and privilege."

"That isn't true!" Charlotte looked mad with the assertion that she was out of touch with reality.

"Yes it is, Charlotte. You are too close to the situation to understand the depth of this family's sense of entitlement."

Carlton stretched his legs and laughed inwardly. He knew Charlotte would never understand what her grandmother meant.

"Let's not talk about it anymore. How are your new neighbors?" Charlotte changed the subject.

"Who?"
"Across the road."
"Oh them," Emily said with disgust.
"Why what's wrong?" Charlotte beamed.
"Dot.com people."
"Oh now I know why the sour face." Carlton burst out laughing.
"You keep quiet. You know how I feel about them."
"I know, that's why I'm laughing."
"What's wrong with them?" Drew asked cautiously.
"My grandmother thinks they are the worst source of new wealth."
"Don't say it like that! You make me sound like such an arrogant snob. I just don't like overnight success stories." Emily could not help but smile; she knew it was an absurd position.

"Go on," Carlton urged.

"It sounds so arrogant, but it just bothers me to no end that these dot.com brats are one generation removed from Somerville or Medford yet they act like there is no learning curve. They think by writing a check they can join the country club without putting their name on the waiting list. That is not a literal example but you get my point. They assume class and dignity are in direct proportion to the amount of money you have in your bank account. The bigger the better!" Emily stated with animation, her face reddening as she thought of her loathsome neighbors.

"Their monstrous SUVs, their mini-vans, their soccer games! What a world. They wear their wealth on their sleeves. It's infuriating! The blondes! I have never seen so many blondes on the East Coast than in this town. Blondes in SUVs driving their spoiled children to one activity after another, they can barely see over the hood of their Range Rovers. The pharmacy must have a run on dye." They all laughed except Drew. This sort of talk was new to him.

"These little porcelain dolls and their yoga classes, little doting princesses wasting their Ivy League educations to become housewives for their portly husbands. They couldn't possibly be attracted to them, the receding hairline, and the chubby waist, how disgusting! They have to accommodate them so their little six-figure man doesn't go off with some little tart straight out of college. The prospect of divorce is too ghastly to think about."

"Okay now you are going off on a tangent," Carlton interrupted, "it's hard for me to feel sorry for you my dear, look around you. And if I remember correctly, you didn't acquire such refinement until you left your cozy abode in Southie."

"That's different, I never wanted it and you know that, Carlton!"

"Nevertheless, I bet more than a few people felt the same way about you when you were building this house."

"Maybe," Emily conceded.

"You had nothing and then you met Sheldon."

"Yes. But he was a lowly professor then. My lowly professor," she reflected sadly.

"But he did come from money, he was never lowly," Carlton said with a laugh.

She winced, Carlton was narrowing his criticism, making it personal and she hated him for it.

"What is your point?"

"Calm down. Let's talk to your guest."

"Yes, you're right. Dear, would you mind excusing us for a few minutes? We want to talk to Drew alone," Emily said sweetly, smiling at her dumbfounded granddaughter.

"Sure..." Charlotte stammered.

"Just a few minutes."

"Okay." She staggered to the door; it had been many years since she had been dismissed from a room.

"So, Drew, how was your trip to Portugal?" Emily moved a seat closer to him. Carlton stood near the fireplace and pretended to be looking at the family photos.

"Eventful," Drew replied evasively.

"Eventful. Hmmm." She leaned back and paused. The awkward silence lasted too long for Carlton.

"I had an interesting conversation with Myron Wiseman the other day, you remember him right. I introduced you at Sheldon's funeral."

"I remember." Drew felt like he was being probed.

"Well he told me about a strange conversation he had with an old acquaintance of Sheldon's. Sandy Wilson is his name. He's a sick old man in Christian Charities Nursing Home in Fall River."

Drew shifted in his seat and clenched his hands together. His obvious discomfort spurned Smithfield on.

"He claims he is the true author of many of Sheldon's finest novels. He says that Sheldon used him for his own gain, basically saying he was a fraud."

Drew desperately tried to control his fluttering emotions. He could feel their penetrating eyes upon him, searching for validation of Sandy Wilson's seemingly outlandish account. He knew immediately what they were doing; sending Charlotte from the room and then raising the issue to gauge his response was a clever move by two intelligent people.

"It can't be true," Drew replied reflexively.

"We don't think so either," Emily said slowly, glancing at Carlton to continue.

"Does it have anything to do with your visit to Portugal?" Carlton asked.

"I can't discuss it!" Drew snapped, angered by the mere suggestion that he would break his word.

"I know, I know…I shouldn't have asked," Carlton's voice trailed off. Drew's flushed cheeks and darting eyes left him speechless. Was it really true? Could he be privy to the biggest literary deception since William Shakespeare? Carlton suddenly felt weak and old; his youthful vigor gone with the revelation he prayed wasn't true. It didn't seem to affect Emily as dramatically, she seemed satisfied and at peace. Maybe she always suspected something, but this was too much even for the most outlandish conspiracy theorists.

"I can't talk about it." Drew reiterated.

"We understand."

"It's…" Drew stopped himself.

"Drew, stop. We don't want you say anything that will jeopardize your agreement."

"I know what you were trying to do. My reaction is the answer to your question."

"No!" Emily protested vainly, she avoided his eyes, perhaps ashamed by the tactics they employed.

"Drew, don't say another word. It's over, we have made no judgments. Charlotte!" Carlton called out for her in an attempt to break the impasse.

"She must have gone for a walk or something," Drew blurted. He wanted to escape from the room as soon as possible. They knew! Sandy Wilson was alive and in the state! A faint glimmer of hope surfaced, maybe he didn't have to be the one who broke the news. Sandy Wilson could tell the world, he could reveal the confession. With the resolve of someone who suddenly realized what he must do, he rose to his feet and excused himself.

"Where are you going?" Carlton pressed.

"I need to go. I'm very sorry but I need to leave."

"Where? Why?" Emily asked with alarm.

"I'm not sure." He did know, he just felt like he must keep his thoughts and intentions to himself.

He met Charlotte in the hall on his way out.

"Hi. What's up?" She was alarmed by his fast pace and disturbed appearance.

"Can I borrow your car?"

"Now?"

"Yes."

"Why? How am I going to get home?" She was perplexed; his strange, furtive glances worried her.

"I didn't think of that."

"If you need to go, just go. I'll catch a ride with Carlton. But why are you leaving? What happened in there? Did they say something?"

"I just need to do something. To talk with somebody and I just want to do it now."

"Okay, sure." She kissed him lightly on the lips and handed him her keys. She wasn't surprised by the odd turn of events. Their complicated relationship was filled with similar twists and turns bordering on the irrational.

"Thank you. I'll see you tonight."

"I hope so, Drew. I'll be waiting, with my poop-covered shoe," she said with a mischievous smile.

Drew's hasty departure caused a stir at the Harrison home. Emily and Carlton vigorously interrogated Charlotte, eager to know his state of mind and possible destinations. They were alarmed by the abrupt manner in which he concluded their private meeting. They were unaccustomed to such boldness; Drew didn't seem to adhere to any social code or convention. They were careful to keep their questions non-specific, hoping to glean information without alerting Charlotte to what was at stake. Charlotte responded to their questions with questions of her own. They were evasive and mumbled that they didn't know why he walked out. She didn't believe their choppy answers; they were hiding something behind their knit brows and pursed lips. The awkward afternoon gathering ended soon after. Carlton and Charlotte leaving the matriarch alone with her dour thoughts.

Chapter 28

The Road to Truth

Drew gasped and hit the brakes, careening wildly and barely making the fast-approaching exit. He was distracted and failed to recognize the clearly marked signs for the City of Fall River. He managed to make the second exit and headed for the interior of the unfamiliar city. Luck was with Drew this day, after exiting the long two-lane highway; he climbed a steep hill towards the pinnacle of Highland Avenue. Looming in the darkness was the harshly illuminated, hulking structure of Christian Charities Nursing Home.

After a brief conversation with a surly desk clerk, he was told that Sandy Wilson had been transferred to Charlton Memorial Hospital. She told him to follow Highland Avenue to the hospital.

Drew's legs wobbled upon entering the bustling lobby of Charlton Memorial Hospital. He had an active phobia of hospitals. His anxious body movements caught the sympathetic eye of the older woman at the information desk.

"Yes, can I help you?" She asked pleasantly.

"Sandy Wilson's room please."

"Sure, honey." She glanced at his pale, puffy cheeks and nervous eyes.

"Is he here?" He blurted, she was taking too long, and he needed to get away from the steady stream of sick people coming too close to him.

"Wait a minute, honey, the computer's a bit slow today." Her reassuring look did not alleviate the pressure in his chest.

"Sure, thank you," he muttered.

"Oh, here he is. Third floor, room 306."

"Okay." Drew stumbled to the elevator and pressed the button. He was overwhelmed by the moment. He felt a sense of awe. He was going to meet the genius behind Sheldon Harrison's fame. The hidden Tolstoy stashed away for decades was suddenly crying out for recognition. The aging elevator door opened with a clang, startling Drew out of his trance. He kept a low profile as he passed the busy nurse's station and entered the room. Its gloomy interior further depressed him. It was a typical room, no better or worse than many metropolitan hospitals, but it seemed particularly dreary to Drew.

"Hello, sir." Drew stood a few feet from a shadowy figure on the bed closest to the door. The other bed was empty and the lights dim.

"Who is it?" A raspy voice croaked.

"Sir, my name is Drew Engle." He stepped into the light.

"Son, I think you're in the wrong room." Drew knew immediately, as did Myron Wiseman, that Sandy Wilson was dying. His sunken cheeks lifted into a pleasant smile. His complexion was yellow and his eyes were glazed from the morphine pumping in his veins.

"I'm here to see you, Mr. Wilson." Drew blurted, ready to leap out of the window to escape the confines of the death chamber. His loathing for medical paraphernalia stopped him from coming closer to the bed.

"Why? Do I know you?" Sandy sat up with a grimace, wincing and smiling at the same time. His hair was combed and his bony face clean-shaven. He looked angelic, respectful, and honest in what were his final days.

"I came because of Mr. Wiseman. Myron Wiseman…" Drew stumbled, unable to put a coherent sentence together.

"Are you the one who went to Europe? The intern?"

"Yes."

"What can I help you with? I think you know the truth already," Sandy said with a sigh, leaning his head back.

"I'm sorry, I didn't ask how you're feeling." Drew felt silly for not asking about his health.

"They told me yesterday…that I have stomach cancer and probably won't last three weeks. Can you believe that?" Sandy chuckled bitterly.

"I'm sorry."

"That's the breaks, I guess." He softly rubbed his throbbing abdominal wall.

"Are they giving you anything for the pain?"

"Yes. Pretty soon it will be so much I won't be conscious. I'm trapped here. Can't leave, can't walk around, can't see a sunset or sunrise unless I look out that smudged window. I'm trapped in an inescapable box with death my only escape. I have two destinations left, the morgue and the grave. It will be handled by others, I won't have to worry about a thing," he said with a laugh.

"It's terrible, sir." Drew's fear of hospitals and illness made him sweat profusely.

"If I was mobile, I would not have stayed here. I would have stolen a car and driven up to the mountains. I would walk until nature took its course. To die with dignity and become dinner for some other creature trying to survive is preferable to this hell on earth. It would be nice if my last thoughts were of the pine trees high above and the sweet mountain air filling my lungs. If I survived until dark, the night sky would be my company, twinkling stars waiting for me."

"I am sorry," Drew said with genuine sympathy.

"Enough ravings of the infirmed," Sandy said then paused, "You know the truth about Sheldon, don't you? I can see it in your eyes. The reserved reverence for me, please don't. I am nothing special."

"Why don't you tell somebody?" Drew moved a few inches closer.

"I did. I told Myron. He won't do anything because it would mean taking the word of a crazy old man with crazy notions."

"He's suspicious. He told Carlton Smithfield. I left them to see you."

"Really, why? You must have some sort of proof. Did he leave something?"

"I can't say."

"I see, but I can tell by your body language I'm right. That's fine."

"I have a gag order."

"I understand. Why did you come then?"

"To find out if it was true. To see the real genius."

"It is true."

"Jesus," Drew sat on a fake leather chair in the corner and felt nauseous.

"Do you want me to sign something? I will write it down so you can stymie the vultures. The Harrison clan is full of them. They're a ravenous bunch. Except for Emily." He stared wistfully at the wall.

"It would help." Drew felt awful as soon as he made the request.

"Okay." Sandy feebly grabbed a pen and a pad of paper near the unconnected phone. He wrote for a minute and signed the bottom. He carefully put his fingerprints all over the document and placed it in a plastic zip lock bag.

"Does your family know you're ill?" Drew probed after taking the bag from him.

"I don't have anybody. My family is dead or long forgotten. I really don't have any friends anymore. My only conversation from here on in will be with the nurses. They're my only family." He closed his eyes and absorbed the weight of the pathetic admission.

"I'm sorry."

"Don't be, it's my fault. I gave my life away."

"I don't understand."

"I thought life was art, shunning everything normal and not appreciating family or friends. When you reach the end, it's easy to see the errors in this way of thinking. All the knowledge, all the time I spent reading great fiction and ignoring the pleasures of the real world is truly a misguided way to live. I let a precious life slip away. Now I have no interest in reading and I yearn for the mundane. Isn't that ironic?"

"I'm sorry," Drew repeated, unsure how else to respond.

"Well, thank you," he said with genuine appreciation.

"How did you end up with Sheldon?" Sandy asked with renewed vigor.

"It's a long story."

"So give me the abridged version."

Drew leaned back in his chair and laid out the unbelievable sequence of events leading up to their meeting. He left out the contents of Harrison's confession.

"You know, the bastard, saved my life. He told me once that he didn't do it, but I never really believed him. I think he said it to get me out of his life. It wasn't much of a life, maybe it would have been better if he saved someone else that day."

Drew held his tongue, there was much he could say to comfort him, but the gag order prevented him from speaking his mind. Sheldon Harrison, even in death was still in charge, calling the shots from the grave.

"I don't think that is a good way to think of it."

"You're right. I'm ungrateful. Simply stated, I never accomplished a damn thing, never did a damn thing with the life Sheldon gave me."

"I don't believe that." Drew's mind raced. Could he let this sick man die knowing only half the story? Would it make a difference? Would it add to his suffering? It would be a violation of the contract. Didn't he just say Sheldon tried to tell him before?"

"Are you okay?" He observed Drew's downcast eyes and wondered what else he knew.

"Yes, but I can't say anything else, Mr. Wilson."

"I didn't ask you to." Sandy watched the young man shifting nervously in his seat and clutching the arms of his chair.

"I know you didn't, it's just complicated."

"I'm an old man who is dying, whatever you tell me will never leave this room. Like me, it will never leave this hospital," his voice cracked, bitterness evident in his tone.

"I signed an agreement. I can't reveal anything for six months."

"What can they do to you, Drew? You aren't making any money on this. It sounds like a contract without any teeth."

"On principal alone, Mr. Wilson." Drew bristled.

"Commendable." Sandy admired his response; Sheldon always surrounded himself with the best people. Sheldon was not a literary genius, but he was assuredly a savant when it came to evaluating talent and character.

"Thank you." The tension was unbearable for Drew. Why was he protecting such a loathsome man whose deceit and calculated cruelty injured so many? He fought the urge to blurt out what he knew, to end it all at the feet of the unknown Tolstoy. Strange thoughts surfaced as he stared at the yellowed linoleum floor. Should he take a picture of Sandy Wilson? How could he capture the man, he would soon be the most sought-after individual in America? Should he conduct an interview? What should he do? The world was watching his every move, judging his actions, they just didn't know about it yet. Would he be skewered for not revealing what he knew, for letting Wilson die thinking he was indebted to his rapist? Drew felt a sense of desperation for he knew what he had to do, his chest heaved in dreadful anticipation. He avoided eye contact with the pitiful, jaundiced eyes of Sandy Wilson who was patiently waiting for him to continue.

"He didn't save your life, Mr. Wilson."

"What?"

"In his confession he details how you were the writer of the first four, but he also recounts the battle where he supposedly saved your life."

"Jesus," Sandy gasped.

Drew spent the next ten, agonizing minutes revealing all he knew about that fateful day in Belgium. Sandy wiped his perspiring brow, each revelation another unbearable body blow. His hands shook so violently Drew had to help him put the flexible straw into his brown water container.

"My God, my God. The bastard, the bastard, he was telling the truth for once," Sandy whispered to himself.

"I'm sorry." Drew was visibly pained by the emotional torment he had inflicted upon the sick man. He seemed aged and pathetic now, unable to compose himself enough to respond intelligently.

"Please, Drew, I would like to be alone. I'm so tired…so damn tired."

"I understand. I'm sorry for all of this. I didn't want any of it." Drew's exhausted voice bordered on hysterical.

"Don't burden yourself anymore. It has nothing to do with you. Please I'm very tired."

"It's too late. We're both burdened." Drew clasped the hand of the American treasure, a peerless writer in the depths of despair over the betrayal and his loss.

"I know, Drew, we are nothing more than disposable chess pieces in a madman's game."

Chapter 29

Seven Weeks Later

Sandy Wilson, 1925-2000

The United States Army Veteran and survivor of The Battle of the Bulge died Saturday after a brief illness at Charlton Memorial Hospital. Mr. Wilson was a lifelong Massachusetts resident. No services are planned. Donations can be made to the American Cancer Society.

The pathetic announcement of Sandy Wilson's passing made little impact on the average Fall River resident. He was a stranger with no connections to the tightly woven community thus his name was passed over quickly. The sympathetic nurses at Charlton Memorial Hospital had paid for the obituary; it was a fitting conclusion to his lonely existence. They cared for him and cried for him as he stoically fought the ravenous disease. Sheldon Harrison and Sandy Wilson were connected at the end; both men were stripped of their human dignity.

Drew found out about his death after checking the local newspaper's website. After their emotional meeting he checked daily for the inevitable news. It was the climatic moment after seven weeks of anguished solitude for the twenty year old. He had been functioning only by habit, as the nights grew cold and the days shorter.

His depressing visit to Sandy Wilson temporarily ended his relationship with the Harrison clan. The irony of the situation was too much for him to handle. Charlotte left many messages urging him to call her; he erased her anguished pleas with no thought to her feelings or motivation.

Two days after reading the bleak obituary, Drew found solace in resolving a complicated calculus problem. His life had changed since his visit to Sandy Wilson. He was no longer the serious loner so easy to ignore. Wild rumors were circulating on his floor; the root of all the talk was his relationship with Sheldon Harrison. The strangest part of the gossip and innuendo was his sudden popularity with the opposite sex. His murky personality and reasonable good looks made him irresistible to the shallow-minded. He shunned the fabricated attention. Of course, his disinterested attitude and general aloofness only added to his growing reputation. Even his loathsome roommate showed him a newfound respect and courtesy, trying to link himself with the enigmatic star on the rise.

Drew tossed a worn notebook to the side and swiveled his desk chair for a better look outside. The cracked Plexiglas window gave a disappointing view of the sprawling city skyline in the distance. He could feel the ice-cold air swirling around the edges of the poorly insulated window frame. The dreariness of the winter season was mitigated this day by the blazing midday sun and the clear blue sky.

He focused on a small group of dirty gray pigeons on the windowsill. The resolute birds were nestled against the glass, high above the dangers of traffic and humans below. The once proud bird that had roamed freely amongst the untouched meadows and deep woods of pre-European New England had sadly been transformed into flying scavengers, scorned and harassed at every turn. They pressed their bulbous bodies against the long spike strips placed on the paint-flaked sill to keep them off the building. The spikes had wilted against the weight of thousands of pigeons that would not be denied their perch amongst the urban metropolis. Drew admired their simple dignity, surviving, even flourishing in the midst of chaotic human indulgences.

He shifted his focus to his roommate's television in the corner. It appeared to be another boring program about the English nobility and its modern day relevance. Drew smiled at the condescending rationale of the descendants of nobility defending their entitlements. When questioned about the methods that their ancestors used to gain their exalted positions, such as murder, intrigue, and deceit, they were predictably dismissive. Many were offended by the mere suggestion that their bloodlines were not pure and distinctive. A few even went as far as defending the actions of their distant relations as justified, even inevitable. If they performed alleged atrocities, it was because they somehow had to show their individuality, to rise above the mediocre masses to display their superiority and thus assuring their special position in society. Drew shook his head and turned the television off.

"Hello." A soft female voice startled Drew from his trance.

"Hi."

"Why haven't you returned my calls?" A bleary eyed and nervous Charlotte Emerson sat on his bed. He hadn't heard her feeble knock.

"I don't know," Drew answered honestly; his insincere smile infuriated her.

"Don't lie to me! Who do you think you are?" She gazed into his eyes, trying desperately to figure out what had changed him, what event caused him to abruptly cut her off. She was in a vulnerable position; his total alienation of the Harrison family was an uncommon occurrence.

"Why are you so angry?" Drew asked. Her raised voice got his wandering attention.

"I don't like to be ignored. You drop my car off in the garage and leave a message on my machine and that's it! Do you think you can just fuck me and then disappear? That doesn't happen to me, Drew."

"No, I don't, but I can't explain my actions. Not now." Drew sat next to her and found it difficult to respond to her justified outrage.

"You really aren't who I thought you were. I didn't think you could be so cruel." Her downcast eyes and overall disheveled look was a stark contrast to her normally impeccable appearance. Drew was alarmed by the dramatic change, their brief relationship was not important enough to garner such a dramatic reaction. He was not worthy of such distress; she attracted countless suitors who felt privileged to be in her company.

"What's wrong, Charlotte? I didn't figure you to be so emotional about…"

"Nothing is wrong!" Charlotte angrily cut him off. She folded her arms and paced the room defiantly.

"Why are you here then?" He regretted the question immediately.

"Why! How dare you! You really are an asshole." Her fury was unsettling; she was clearly out of control.

"Calm down, Charlotte."

"I need to sit." She flopped onto the bed, the emotional strain of the confrontation made her weary. She was pale and looked ill.

"You look terrible. Are you sick?"

"No."

"What's wrong? Come on tell me." He put his arm around her and tried to lighten the mood with a smile.

"No." She pushed him away and buried her head in her hands.

"What is it?" He was perplexed by her unusual behavior.

"I'm pregnant, Drew." Her barely audible explanation caught Drew off guard.

"What?" Her somber expression told him he had heard right.

"I'm pregnant. Yes, you're the only one it could be. I did the math." She managed a weak smile, her troubled blue eyes clouded with tears.

"Oh." He closed his eyes as if in tremendous pain, unable to comprehend the life-altering words uttered by a woman he barely knew.

"Oh. Is that all you can say?" She stared at him and was annoyed by his silence.

"I don't know... I don't get it," Drew mumbled incoherently.

"What's to know? We had sex and we were obviously careless. This is the kind of thing that happens to young men when they play with fire."

"I know that." His noncommittal, emotionless tone irritated the emotionally sensitive Charlotte.

"Say something! And don't ask if I'm sure. I'm positive." She instinctively rubbed her stomach and closed her eyes, deep anguish shredding her usually self-assured personality. The prospect of being a mother frightened her beyond words.

"Have you thought about what you're going to do?" He walked to the window and smiled at the unsuspecting pigeon that politely gazed back.

"Yes. I have thought about what WE are going to do." She stressed the word "WE" sharply.

"What have you decided?" He turned to face her imploring eyes. It was obvious she had struggled with the decision.

"You have a say, Drew," Charlotte cried out, her emotions released in a torrent of grief and anger.

"I know.... I just don't know what to say. It's been such a strange year."

"Such a strange year? Is that all you can say? You are an immature asshole." She rushed for the door, crying and pulling at the tricky doorknob.

"Charlotte, don't go. Please I'm sorry." Drew came up behind her and gently shut the door. She leaned her head against the cheap door and cried. He hugged her from behind, his head buried in her sweet smelling hair, kissing and whispering softly. He moved her hair to the side and kissed her neck. She stopped crying and turned to face him. Drew was unsure if she was going to respond to his affectionate advances or slap him. He was prepared for both.

"You idiot," she punched him lightly, a tired smirk appeared on her tear-streaked face.

"I know." He moved closer.

"No."

"No what." He parted her reluctant lips with his.

"No, I hate you." She wrapped her arms around his head and passionately kissed him. Charlotte's desire for him outweighed her displeasure with his reaction. The intensity of the embrace was not unexpected; their relationship was defined by such wild swings of emotion, a dangerous love and hate pendulum that produced their current dilemma.

"No…please," she gasped. They fell onto his messy bed, her weak protests giving way to short breaths and deep moaning. The thought of him being the father of her child aroused her deeply, the biological miracle occurring inside of her linked them forever.

Chapter 30

Vengeance

"Wilton! What are you doing?" Charlotte yelled playfully as she barged into her cousin's townhouse. She hoped to catch him watching a porno or performing some other lewd act. She was disappointed to find his sulking figure on the couch watching television. He turned and smiled happily, his narrow shoulders arching in triumph as the light of his existence burned in front of him. Wilton noticed her puffy cheeks and loose-fitting clothes. Her weight gain, albeit small, could be explained as stress-induced from the tumultuous winter. He figured she must be eating her troubles away, languishing in the depths of depression from what he believed was the first snub of her life. He was unaware of her recent contact with the caretaker of the Harrison secret, Drew Engle.

"What has made you so happy?" Wilton asked. She was prancing around his living room, apparently shedding the sullenness that had dogged her since Sintra. Her narcissistic personality, much admired by her cousin, seemed ready to burst through the layers of self-consciousness that had stifled her recently.

"Nothing. Just felt like visiting." She brushed passed a delicate plant near the couch and sat next to him. She looked apprehensive and excited, as if she had something to tell him but couldn't find the right words.

"Liar! You haven't given me the time of day in weeks. What the hell have you been up to? I don't like being ignored." He stopped smiling and frowned disapprovingly. His bloated face and glistening forehead were a perfect manifestation of his disagreeable personality.

"I don't blame you, Wilton, my love." She wrapped her arms around him and sighed deeply. He inhaled as if it were his last breath, intoxicated by the sweet aroma of her soap and light perfume. He inadvertently stroked her silken hair, grimacing at the maddening closeness of their embrace. She pulled away and smiled at his muted, subtle advances that had become commonplace.

"I have some news, Wilton."

"Really. What is it?" He straightened up and wondered if it had something to do with his grandfather and the detestable Drew Engle. The six-month moratorium was approaching and his anxiety increased by the day.

"I'm pregnant," she blushed excitedly and turned away before continuing, "I know it's shocking, but I'm surprised you didn't notice my fat bum." Her cheeriness slowly slipped away as she observed the frightening transformation in her cousin. All of the blood drained from his face as he began to tremble with rage. Not an imperceptible tremor, but a violent shaking that could not be hidden or excused. His eyes narrowed into a frightening glare, a hate-filled gaze that made Charlotte stand straight up and step backwards. Her fear was real, she thought about fleeing but didn't want to provoke him further. It is never wise to run from a frothing dog.

"You're pregnant? Did you just say that? Please tell me I'm fucking deaf and you said something else." He ground his teeth together and clawed at the back of the couch.

"What is wrong with you, Wilton?"

"Nothing. So who is the father?" He gagged on the question.

"I don't think you can handle…"

"Who the fuck is it!"

"Calm down, Wilton. What the hell is wrong with you? You're my fucking cousin not my boyfriend." Her boldness bordered on foolishness.

"Is there in any sense in that little fucking mind of yours?" He stood up and paced the room.

"I'm happy, Wilton. It's not a bad thing."

"Who's the father Charlotte?" He stood with his back to her, slumped over in defeat.

"Does it matter?" She hesitated.

"Who is it?" He whispered through pained lips.

"Drew."

"My God." He spun around, his imploring eyes and pathetic posture annoyed Charlotte.

"It's not a surprise, is it?" Charlotte said boldly, regaining her will to torture him at every turn.

"That nothing! You let him do that to you. Defile you. You're the granddaughter of Sheldon Harrison, for Christ sake."

"Don't say he's a nothing. He's far from a nothing." She smirked cruelly; the brutal sexual innuendo was not lost on him.

"Nice, Charlotte. You really make me sick sometimes. And you're going to be a mother, please, there isn't a more selfish person." He was right; she was not naturally suited for motherhood.

"I don't care what you think, Wilton. I'll do the best I can. It's none of your business how I raise my child."

"What about your job? Your career? Are you going to throw it away for this?"

"This!"

"You know what I mean." He shuffled about the room.

"Wilton, I don't regret what happened."

"You are so immature, Charlotte. Such a disappointment."

"I'm sorry you're so upset. I should have guessed you would act like this. I'm leaving, I have an appointment."

"I think this is a little bit more important than some stupid meeting."

"This isn't a group decision, Wilton. You have no say in this."

"Go then!" He turned his head, tears streaming down his boiling face. She knew he was crying and she felt sorry for him. His pitiful life was disrupted by her carelessness.

"I'll talk to you later." She put her arm on his shoulder.

"Sure."

"Bye."

"Bye."

Wilton cried into his hands before rushing to the balcony to watch for her. He caught a glimpse of her blond hair as she passed below him, walking gingerly but purposely towards her car. The moist air tasted bitter to him, he grabbed the rail for leverage. He wanted to end it all, to soar like the birds buzzing through the trees ringing the Boston Common. He closed his eyes and envisioned the endless silence of death. In death there would be no rejection or judgment, just everlasting peace. She would pay for her deceit! If he were certain she would lose the baby upon hearing of his untimely death, he would have jumped into the abyss. The very thought that Drew was alive and breathing only miles from where he stood was unbearable, an injustice of the highest order.

He cried like a child and collapsed to his knees, his somber head resting on the bare metal of the reinforced railing. Wilton yearned for his journal, to write his feelings down might help relieve the paralyzing grief that seemed unending. He crawled to his desk and grabbed his hefty journal from its special perch, scribbling away the sorrow.

"I can't stand the pain, My Lord, why have you forsaken me! I am insane with rage. Why did you give me the same blood! It pumps through my veins like nothing is wrong. It doesn't know how wrong it is. It keeps us apart. TABOO. I am dead…"

Chapter 31

Five Weeks Later
Isabella Stewart Gardner and The Russian: On the Eve of the Revelation

THE SMELL OF WATERED ferns and damp concrete added to the menagerie of tantalizing scents and sounds of the internationally acclaimed Isabella Stewart Gardner Museum. Walking distance from Boston's prestigious Museum of Fine Arts, the pair made a formidable corner of high culture. The home was built to house the bulging collection of the socialite, Isabelle Stewart Gardner. In a relatively short period, she amassed a staggering collection of work in the four-story edifice. The Venetian influenced interior had a large courtyard in the center with various galleries and a music hall surrounding it. It was an overwhelming experience for the first-time visitor to be thrust into the center of the exquisite building, the rather bland and pedestrian exterior hinting little to the world of beauty inside its hulking walls.

Charlotte was a frequent visitor and respectable patron of her grandfather's favorite museum. It was the centerpiece of his relentless fundraising for the arts. It was a spot of reflection for him, similar to the Moorish Castle in Sintra.

The philanthropic drive that pushed Isabella Gardner to collect over two thousands pieces of art from sculptures to invaluable Rembrandts impressed Charlotte to the point of worship. Each time she walked the hallowed galleries she was transported to the late 19th century. A time when Americans of recent wealth discovered they could purchase many of the world's treasures with impunity, and much to the consternation of superior-thinking Europeans who snobbishly thought taste, breeding, and sophistication could not be bought.

Charlotte imagined herself as a childless heiress wielding her financial power with class and dignity. She would search for beauty across the world, unfettered by the daily grind of modern day existence. She would smile graciously as desperate art dealers sought her audience, the masters only a pen stroke away. Her frustrating thoughts of stunted glory were soon washed away by the reality of her wealthy grandfather's recent demise. The prospect of a similar lifestyle, of course on a smaller scale, was virtually guaranteed upon settlement of his complicated estate.

The momentary feelings of envy disappeared sooner than usual as she circled the courtyard, her buoyant step and ebullient smile an embodiment of her new outlook on life. She was a mother in the making; a selfless carrier of life and this excited her like nothing else. The regular bouts of morning sickness were not as bad as she envisioned. She found herself inadvertently caressing her bulging stomach and marveling at her tight-fitting pants.

Charlotte and Drew were wading through uncharted territory, the probing, plodding relationship full of potential pitfalls as they approached parenthood. They were happy and fully committed on occasion, seldom simultaneously and this led to an uneasy truce of sorts. When he avoided her, it was distressing but not so worrisome that she let it affect her pregnancy. She was only days away from breaking the news to her mother and then of course the rest of the Harrison clan. Charlotte's reluctance to get involved with an unremarkable college student was curtailed by his sudden relevance. His last-minute relationship with her grandfather and their bizarre meeting in Sintra made for a good story to tell her friends. He was the bright young intern who her legendary grandfather took under his wing and sent on an errand entrusted to no one else. Drew held a special place in Sheldon Harrison's biography, provided the document held any relevant information. Even if it were a scandalous item, it would have little influence on his standing in the literary community and could add to his mystique. Once that part was settled in her mind, she thought about the permanency of their relationship, imagining better days with the father of her wonderful child. Her jubilant mood soared upon reaching the stairway up to the galleries. She looked out onto the courtyard and saw the familiar, slouching figure of the Russian.

The Russian was the first participant in a novel new program that allowed certain, high-profile writers to work in the main courtyard. It was simply an extension of the numerous other programs the Gardner Museum had to highlight the works of artists, mostly painters, who they deemed relevant or groundbreaking. It was a purely subjective process of elimination, but overall their selections were made without much dissent or lingering animosity. The Russian was an easy choice. It was truly a monumental coup for the Museum, orchestrated by the well-connected Charlotte Emerson.

The frumpy, disheveled, and unshaven former golden boy of modern Russian fiction gazed about the Venetian style courtyard as if it was his own backyard. Impervious to the sometimes-gawking crowds and ceaseless flow of guests heading up the stairway to the recesses of the upper galleries and music hall. His wavy, thick salt and pepper hair reminded Charlotte of photos of John Steinbeck. Even from a distance his intelligent hazel eyes sparkled, they were windows into his genius and ultimately to his past suffering.

Charlotte leaned against a wall and watched his lean, nicotine-stained fingers gracefully plucking the keys of the ancient Underwood typewriter he would not part with. The loud metallic sound of the keystrokes echoed in the courtyard, turning heads and garnering whispers such as, "he's working" or "I wonder what he's writing about?"

Charlotte pitied the proofreaders that worked closely with the Russian God before she eventually reviewed the manuscript. The stubborn Russian ignored the technological evolution in publishing that made all of their jobs easier, he would likely smash even the most basic computer the moment he got his first error message or lost a bit of data.

Charlotte liked to think about the look of astonishment on the faces of staff at the Gardner Museum when she presented her catch only days after the program was launched. It was similar to the reaction that occurred at her publishing house when she boldly announced that the newly arrived Russian wanted to publish with them. His only request was that Charlotte be his only contact, he trusted her because she was the granddaughter of the great Sheldon Harrison. His legendary hostility towards editors and publishers did not end when he signed on with Charlotte's firm. He ignored their endless pressure, skewering them in the press at every turn. He would laugh at their efforts to calm his temper, often asking them the question they had no answer for. "What are you going to do to me? What can you do to me? What form of humiliation can you put me through that I have not endured? Unless you have a reeducation camp that I never heard about, please allow me to do what none of you can."

The allure and beauty of Gardner Museum went a long way in persuading the notoriously reticent Russian to act like a monkey and perform for the crowds. Some of his peers thought it was demeaning, yet privately they yearned for the coveted second slot and many made inquiries. Charlotte even received calls from harassed publicists asking for help getting their clients next in line.

She smiled at his harsh typing style that sadly abused the frequently serviced antique typewriter. Each time it needed repair, they had to fly in a specialist from a dingy store in New York City. His old leather chair squeaked defiantly, mocking the efforts of the discreet museum staff that lubricated it at night. Originally, he only committed two weeks of his busy schedule to the exhibition, six weeks later he was still going strong, the heady surroundings stoking the embers of his sometime flagging inspiration.

The abrupt fall of the Soviet Union had a negative effect on his work. The ten thousand pound Gorilla of state-sponsored censorship had a strangely liberating affect on many artists, the threat of discovery and subsequent imprisonment gave each line written even greater importance. The Isabella Stewart Gardner Museum was the muse he had longed for since the gray days in his dirty, rat-infested apartment in Moscow.

Charlotte made her way around the courtyard, never taking her eyes off her most envied client. She relished the awed expressions of her co-workers when the Russian told of his unabashed reverence for her grandfather. Sheldon and the Russian were friends of sorts, having met three or four times, but it was their exchange of letters that made them close friends. Both were voracious letter writers and correspondence between two literary giants was predictable. In the last year of Sheldon's life, he wrote less, sometimes apologetic about things said in the past, sometimes accusatory of things the Russian had said in the papers. It was the bizarre series of letters that pushed him to visit Sheldon's Martha's Vineyard home two months before his death. He was horrified by his condition and left after an hour. Sheldon was not appreciative of his charmed life; instead, the sickly man never stopped bemoaning his ill health and constantly cursed at the good-natured medical staff around him. He did not respond to Sheldon's last letter nor did he attend the funeral, cherishing the positive memories and shunning the recent past.

Charlotte stared across the expanse, waiting for him to look up. He sensed her unwavering gaze and lifted his head. He caught her vivid blue eyes and smiled broadly. He stretched his long arms and stood up, grabbing his Camel cigarettes out of his shirt pocket for a smoke outside. No matter the stature of a museum guest, smoking was strictly prohibited.

"Hello, how are you?" He leaned over the rope that separated the closed courtyard and the rest of the gallery. Her infectious smile warmed him, a welcome diversion. He noticed her puffy cheeks and altered physique, she was either pregnant or skipping the gym. He could hardly believe the latter, but he thought the former was as unlikely. She was too smart, too dedicated and above all too selfish for childbearing. The world-weary and permanently jaded Russian thought the last two were admirable qualities. The spirit of Soviet collectivism did not stick with the gruff writer, he believed in self-preservation and individual fulfillment regardless of the casualties.

"Good sir, how are you?" Charlotte asked brightly.

"Terrible." His scowl was forced; it was against his creed to show overt happiness. Sometimes it seemed like he was playing the role of the disgruntled genius. Charlotte suspected a guarded contentment buried deeply beneath layers of pessimism.

"I'm sure. How is it today? Good or bad?"

"Awful." He dropped his head in defeat, he always answered her query the same way.

"Oh come on. How can every day be a bad writing day and yet your work is so brilliant?" She waited for his familiar reaction.

"Please do not say that." He blushed and instinctively cracked his twisted knuckles. His burly hands were battered and broken from years of harsh work as a lowly laborer. The authorities discovered his subversive novels and he was barred from Moscow University where he was a student. Denied a career academia, he survived by breaking his back for twenty years under the watchful eyes of his captors.

"You look tired." His rough hands caressed her cheek. He was more affectionate since her grandfather's death, he wrongly believed she needed the attention and consolation.

"I'm okay. I do have some news though."

"What is it?" His genuine smile bolstered her courage.

"I'm pregnant."

"You're what! I hope I misunderstood you." His thick Russian accent roared to life, emotional inflammation normally caused the relapse. He had worked so hard to shed his obvious heritage.

"You heard me. I'm going to be a mother."

"I didn't even know you had a boyfriend." He frowned disapprovingly. He believed children killed the fires of inspiration and made the gifted rather ordinary. Caring parents were heinously subjected to a lifetime of distraction and worry.

"Well, I really don't," she stumbled, "I'm with the father. We're trying to work through it."

"I see." He looked pained by her sudden discomfort.

"Don't worry, I can handle this. No problem."

"I know. But what kind of guy is this who won't scoop you up without question!" His booming voice echoed in the cavernous environs of the courtyard.

"Shhhhh. What makes you think I want him?"

"You're right. He doesn't deserve you." He angrily gripped his cigarette package, crumpling the short and deadly non-filter cigarettes.

"Stop, you'll ruin them." Charlotte grabbed his rough hands.

"So, I'll buy more. That is what's good about living in a society of fools, they never stop buying my drivel so I can smoke myself to death."

"I don't want to hear that. You're my number one guy, without you I might have to put in a full week of work."

"Or at least a full day!" His boisterous laugh revealed his shamefully yellowed teeth. It ruined his striking smile. He was still handsome and charmed many women of all ages.

"Bite your tongue..." Charlotte stopped suddenly, distracted by something she saw on the other side of the courtyard near the entrance.

"What's wrong?" The burly Russian turned around and didn't see anything out of the ordinary.

"Nothing I...I just thought I saw somebody." She blushed and closed her eyes in anguish.

"What's wrong?" He noticed the sudden beads of sweat forming on her upper lip.

"I need to leave, I'll talk to you before I go." Charlotte kissed his cheek and fled. He called after her, but she only waved and headed towards the tiny restaurant and the gift shop. She walked past a security guard she knew and slipped into the staff-only bathroom. She stood in front of the chipped mirror and gasped for air, appalled at her appearance she waited for the emotional pain to subside.

"Hello, Charlotte, are you okay?" Abigail Johnson asked with concern. The museum's personnel director had emerged from a stall and was startled by Charlotte's ashen face.

"I'm okay. Thanks, Abby. Just a personal matter." She wiped her face with a paper towel, regaining her composure and hoping to cover up her blind fury.

"Fucking bastard," she said through clenched teeth and stormed out of the small bathroom.

The last steps before a major confrontation can feel like an eternity as the injustice is crystallized and the attack is planned. Charlotte turned the corner and headed for the restaurant with a purposeful step.

In the back corner of the compact museum restaurant that was similar to the almost communal eateries of Europe, Marie Almeida, Drew Engle and his parents, Joe and Sharon sat for lunch. Joe, who did not enjoy their semi-annual trek to the museum, looked uncomfortable as he tried not to bump elbows with the other patrons.

"Could I have a glass of water, please?" Mr. Engle asked.

"Sure. One moment." The smart-looking art school student turned waiter nodded to Mr. Engle and stepped into the tiny kitchen clearly visible from their seats. The menu was simple and the food very basic due to limited space.

"Marie, how is your trip so far?" Mrs. Engle faced Marie Almeida. She smiled cordially at the attractive girl whose positive spirit and personal strength distinguished her from many of the young woman she knew. Marie was a glowing young woman whose presence made one feel better for being in her company.

Joe Engle smiled at her polite, articulate responses to his wife's probing questions. He sighed and felt sad for the young woman whom he had just met. It was only a matter of time before her untamed spirit would be crushed by the expectations of a modern woman. Her confident, noncommittal answers regarding her current romantic attachments would not last long. The soul-killing acts performed by most men unconsciously or consciously would certainly occur the moment her self-assured personality eroded with age. Long-established views of what a woman is supposed to be can break even the most stoic, breaking their will to think independently, relegating them to nanny management and SUV service. These flashing thoughts depressed Mr. Engle, who bitterly realized he was guilty of such a crucification of his own wife's spirit. His intentions were good, his boorish acts of selfishness were not deliberate or malicious, but the focal point of their marriage was his happiness and fulfillment. He swore at himself, for at that very moment, he was conducting such an attack. His begrudging, complaint-filled acquiescence to the day's itinerary sapped some of the enjoyment for her, she did not reveal her feelings, but he detected her disappointment. It was once every two years for Christ sake! In college, she was a member of the Museum of Fine Arts and went to the museum on a weekly basis.

Marie was a sparkling example of an uncorrupted and seemingly invincible woman who did not allow a man to dictate the course of her life. It would not last; it was coming, on the horizon, maybe his son was her executioner.

The ever demure and sophisticated Marie Almeida was casually dressed, her blue jeans and off-white turtleneck sweater hugging her tight frame, accentuating the sleek lines of her healthy body. Her simply tossed hair was neatly pulled up in a clip and her make-up was exquisite, but with restraint sometimes lacking in European woman. She drew glances from the male patrons who could not conceal their pleasure at sitting so close to her. Angry pokes from their annoyed girlfriends or wives startled them from their inadvertent trance, soul killing on a different level.

Drew and Marie had kept in contact after their brief encounter in Portugal. A budding friendship developed from their flirtation amongst the hills of Sintra. The wide, cold Atlantic seemed the only impediment to a more serious relationship.

Their conversations of late often ended with a brisk exchange regarding Charlotte Emerson and Marie's low opinion of her. Drew never revealed the full extent of their heated relationship, preferring to skirt the issue or change the subject. Marie understood from the inflection in his voice and slight hesitation when he discussed Charlotte that their involvement was far deeper and exponentially more complicated than he led on.

"Hi," Drew said to someone behind his father's left shoulder. Mr. and Mrs. Engle turned to see a red-faced Charlotte Emerson, flustered and enraged she looked unstable.

"Hello," Charlotte's curt reply startled the Engle's. They were unprepared for a confrontation amidst so much beauty and serenity. Marie was not surprised by the abrupt interruption, she expected nothing less from such a spoiled debutante. She was not intimidated by her scowl; in fact she reveled in Charlotte's bloated appearance.

"What are you doing here? I didn't know..." Drew shifted his gaze and caught his mother's curious expression. She was examining Charlotte closely, her keen eyes narrowing on the unnatural bulge around her waist. Her face clouded over and she sighed inwardly. She knew.

"I'm always here, Drew. You know that. What are you doing here? I'm always here," she repeated herself nervously.

"Honey, would you like to sit down? I'm Sharon and this is my husband Joe."

"No... No thank you. Nice to meet you. I'm Charlotte Emerson."

"This is Marie Almeida," Sharon said pleasantly, glaring at her son for his rudeness.

"I know Marie. We've met before, we have mutual friends in Portugal." She nodded stiffly.

"I'm sorry, Charlotte, sit please." Drew finally regained his composure.

"Charlotte, we've heard so much about you." Joe Engle tried to break the tension, an impossible task at this point.

"You have?" Charlotte smirked and eyed Drew.

"Please sit with us." Drew looked around for the waiter to ask for another chair. It was a ridiculous gesture. The table barely accommodated four people and there was no room on either side for an extra chair.

"No, thank you. There's no room, Drew."

"So how have you been, Charlotte?" Marie sat back and eyed her wearily. It was obvious Charlotte intended to make a scene; many in the restaurant were already listening to the exchange.

"Oh just fantastic. I'm feeling truly liberated. You know why?"

"No I don't, why don't you tell me?" Marie was ready for the engagement.

"Let's go outside for a minute." Drew stood up and tried to escort her out.

"Wait, Drew, I have to answer your friend's question."

"Stop, Charlotte, come on." He gently pushed her arm towards the exit, petrified at what she might reveal.

"I'm liberated because I finally understand where I stand with the father of my child." She instinctively rubbed her stomach, her bravado weakened by the mere mention of her unborn child.

"Shit...ahhhhh." Drew sighed and sat back down. He felt nauseous; this was not how he wanted to break the traumatic news of his impending fatherhood to his conservative father and worrisome mother.

"What?" Joe Engle angrily turned and faced Charlotte.

"Joe." His wife placed her hand on his knee to calm him down. She had been dealing with the revelation internally for a minute longer than her smart but not so perceptive husband.

"Oh. I didn't know." Marie Almeida bowed her head; it was not what she had expected. She felt ashamed for engaging Charlotte so forcefully, the importance of the issue far outweighed their contentious relationship.

"Yeah, OH!" Charlotte fumed.

"Sit down, please." Joe Engle tried to give up his seat.

"No, thank you. Have a nice lunch," she said sadly, abruptly fleeing the now silent restaurant.

"Follow her, Drew," Joe instructed firmly, his dumfounded son seemed incapable of reacting properly, as a man should.

"Okay...I'll be back. I'm sorry about this..." Drew jumped up and followed her.

"Charlotte! Jesus Christ, stop!" Drew stopped her only after she had reached the curb. She was frantically trying to find her car keys, slamming her fist deeper in her bag with real pain inducing force, a childish attempt to punish herself for the sudden lack of dexterity.

"Leave me alone, Drew." Her cold tone and resistant body language highlighted her uncanny ability to recover her icy persona with inhuman speed.

"We're just friends. She was visiting…"

"Listen, you don't owe me an explanation. You don't owe me a fucking thing, Drew. We're not married and you're not my boyfriend. Okay."

"Stop please." He grabbed her arm as she fumbled with the door.

"What!"

"Why are you so angry?"

"I don't know." She bowed her head and tried to block the images of Marie Almeida.

"Come inside."

"No…no. I'll talk to you later." She touched his cold reddened cheek and smiled faintly.

"Charlotte, come on. All this drama, it's so unlike you. You're better than this." He felt strange complimenting her on her inflated self worth.

"It won't be long now."

"What?"

"The world will know your dirty little secret. You will be the most famous nobody that ever lived."

Drew stepped back in disgust, his mind awash with a dour vision of the future. He was thunderstruck by the thought of his child's impressionable young mind being exposed to Charlotte's instinctive, irrational disdain for people not of her class. How would his child escape the chains of unbridled entitlement under the tutelage of such a woman?

Drew reentered the café and avoided the disappointed gaze of his confused parents. They were crushed and excited by the news, the pleasurable vision of their first grandchild playing in their arms faded as they contemplated their young son's predicament. The lunch broke up soon after with Drew begging his parents to leave the discussion for another day.

Outside, a depressed Drew Engle and sullen Marie Almeida walked in silence to the subway station. The awkwardness of the short ride ended with another confrontation.

"I don't understand it, Drew."

"What?"

"The way she treated you, the way she treats everybody."

"How could I get her pregnant, right?"

"I know how. I just don't understand why. With someone who treated you…with so little respect." Marie noticed the veins in his neck bulging from the stress.

"She isn't always like that, Marie."

"One positive, I guess, is she is the granddaughter of Sheldon Harrison."

"What is that supposed to mean?" He glanced nervously at her.

"If you're going to have a child before you are ready, with a woman of dubious character, it may as well be with someone of her stature."

"That's bullshit, Marie." Drew snapped, she was needling him, but for what reason he did not know. Was she jealous? How could she be? She was aware of Drew's borderline infatuation with her and only responded with a flirtatious friendship that neither encouraged nor discouraged.

Drew felt the tug of Charlotte's will upon him as they skirted the bottom of Beacon Hill on the way to the bustling Omni Parker House. Marie held his hand and sighed deeply, she caught the brief scent of the nearby ocean. It reminded her of her beloved Portugal.

"What am I supposed to do now? How can I be a father?" His anguished look brought Marie to tears; she clutched his arm and pressed her face into his shoulder.

"You will make it. Please don't worry." Her words floated away, unheard by the anguished young man whose six-month reprieve ended that very night. Tomorrow the world would know the heir to Hemingway was a fraud, the American Tolstoy was nothing but a well-bred charlatan.

Chapter 32

A Frenchman in America

After their emotional argument and a few Vodka shots at the hotel bar, Marie convinced Drew to accompany her to an exclusive house party in Cambridge. Her former lover and classmate at the Sorbonne, Jean Michael Laurent was hosting the affair. The reunion was the main reason she made the trip and not to see Drew as she insinuated. Jean Michael was a celebrity of sorts at the Sorbonne; he was a distant relative of the titanic French writer, Victor Hugo. It was always a treat when they made the short pilgrimage to Hugo's tomb in the rather bland catacombs of the Pantheon. They treated his final resting spot with reverence usually reserved for religious icons, quietly touching the heavy door for inspiration and wishing they could inhale his dust.

Jean Michael was an eclectic Parisian of wild tastes and vices, a sometimes-snarling poetry teacher with a superior glare that turned most away. He was a supremely confident aristocrat who chose to live like a pauper at the Sorbonne, shunning any help from his well-connected parents. He lived like the rest of the close-knit group of Left Bank tramps. The strange sensation of poverty was empowering to the pampered youth, he relished the soiled cloths and the empty feeling in his stomach. He would sit for hours staring at the dank waters of the Seine, disheveled and aloof until somebody dragged him to a party in some dank apartment nearby. There, he would enter as Jesus upon his Apostles, holding court for his ragged band of disciples as they pondered the meaning of life, debated art, and got high. He was a roguish scholar revered by all who came in contact with him, regularly espousing his progressive theories with ease and considerable confidence. His dominating personality made his friends feel like they were in the center of the universe when he confided in them, leaving them always yearning for his undivided attention.

Marie was a bewildered first-year student in the most exciting city in the world when she fell under his spell. Jean Michael was immediately attracted to the strange, introverted girl from the exotic island he had only read about. She was attractive and innocent, a breath of fresh air amongst the burnt-out continental European girls that dominated his circle.

They were inseparable from the moment they shared a table at a seedy café catering only to students and artists, openly shunning the lucrative tourist trade. They both spoke fluent English; Marie also spoke textbook French, which she used during intimate moments.

The two bombastic years she spent huddled under the distant shadow of Notre Dame with Jean Michael were the most exciting time of her short life. The constant buzz, the exploration of mind and soul in the center of such a city was almost unbearable for the conservative girl from the small Catholic island. Every day felt like the first day of her life, each moment something exciting would be said or done, a fresh idea and novel view introduced to throw them into endless debate. None of the ugliness of the world seeped into the cocoon of their intellectual circle. They were above the fray, a privileged generation of thinkers unable to connect with the day-to-day problems endured by the thousands around them. The bourgeois middle class frumps who could never appreciate how lucky they were to be surrounded on all sides by the genius of others.

The passionate relationship did not last long after Jean Michael finished his studies at the Sorbonne. He went to America to study at Harvard and the magic left the banks of the Seine. It was a deflating experience for Marie to lose her seer, it was strange to be around so many friends and feel so alone. Marie's final year at the Sorbonne was a miserable affair; she abandoned her life as a Left Bank tramp and concentrated on her schoolwork. It was at this time she began to realize there were others at the school and not all of them were bourgeois assholes with no taste. Her new friends were from varied backgrounds and were equally dynamic, but not as exciting as Jean Michael's or his brilliant urchins. She cried each night and wondered what he was thinking, what great idea or theory was he expounding to some lucky girl thousands of miles away.

Jean Michael also suffered from his rash decision to leave the close-knit group that could have carried on their raucous, sometimes depraved existence for a few more years. He was disappointed by his rather tame life in America. He could not duplicate the grand feeling of being on the edge with so many interesting people. His overt superiority was a turn-off to his fellow graduate students at Harvard. Few wanted to sacrifice valuable study time to join his pseudo-intellectual playgroup.

It was a miserable existence for such a mind as Jean Michael's. He stayed at Harvard out of pure defiance and was eventually offered a part-time job teaching creative writing. It was out of the question to return to Paris when all of his worshippers had departed in a similar haze of disillusionment, forced to find work in traditional occupations. How ghastly a thought! Jean Michael found it so painful to think of the Sorbonne days, he had not seen any of the group since the day he boarded the Air France Airbus three years before.

Jean Michael rented an apartment on an impressive street within walking distance from the university. It was an old home of an important physicist suffering from Alzheimer's disease, his family mercilessly destroyed the home by cutting it up into three apartments. Jean Michael had to rely on his caring parents to supplant his meager salary in order to live in such an exclusive part of Cambridge. The thought of his parents actually supporting his career choice and giving him a stipend until he became a full professor left him feeling empty and worthless. He drank heavily and tried to write away his doldrums, this was not a wise choice. The more he wrote, the more he realized it was not his calling, he stumbled around in a fit of despair at his own uselessness. He wasn't special or unique; he was an ordinary European braggart who languished in the vastness and anonymity of America. The party was his last grasp at sanity; he wanted to feel the closeness of like-minded people who looked up to him. An open invitation to America was a sign of weakness he would never have displayed in the old days, but desperate times require desperate measures.

Jean Michael's spirits temporarily rose by the positive response he received regarding the party. The very informal gathering was set and he counted the days until the afternoon when the first plane arrived carrying his guests. It would be a grand occasion, a taste of the life he so hastily discarded for his romantic escape to America.

On the way to the affair, Marie gave Drew the abridged version of her time at the Sorbonne; he looked disturbed by the casual admission of Jean Michael as her lover. She smiled out of the corner of her attractive mouth at his boyish jealousy. He was still very much a child with very adult burdens weighing him down.

"I really don't want to go," he complained.

"You need it. After today and what might happen tomorrow. I think you need a night out…daddy." Marie laughed and pushed him off the curb of the quiet street.

"Nice."

"You did the dirty deed. I didn't sex her up, you did."

"Really, you are too much," he scoffed.

"Grow up please." Her tone had changed; a serious expression crossed her face.

"Go to hell," Drew snarled.

"This is it, I think. Yes!" Marie grabbed his reluctant hand and roughly dragged him up to the second floor apartment.

The simple but large apartment was full of young people engrossed in what appeared to Drew as important conversation. He felt intimidated by their intelligent eyes and serious demeanor. They were internationalists, a brotherhood of intelligent people who ignored the distorting influence of nationalism.

There was a heavy stench of cigarette smoke hanging in the spacious room, a nightmare of carcinogenic poison rolling across the innocent as well as the guilty. All eyes shifted to Marie as she strutted into the room, her farm girl shyness had long since been replaced by the cosmopolitan chic of a fearless woman who demanded respect.

Jean Michael excitedly pushed through the fluttering crowd to embrace his former lover. With tears of joy cutting a path down his chiseled face he let three years of frustration and loneliness froth to the surface in a dramatic display of affection. She held him tightly as the others formed a line to greet their queen. Drew was politely shoved to the side. He envied the closeness of the circle of friends, he was jealous of the way Marie held them and whispered lovingly. Jean Michael's handsome face and penetrating hazel eyes made Drew feel inadequate. In another time and place, Jean Michael could have been a daring general in the Napoleonic Wars. He was a revolutionary without a cause, a leader of men whose natural instinct for greatness was tempered by the rather boring rise of modern day Western Democracy.

Jean Michael and Marie quickly split off from the frenzied group, laughing and teasing each other with a familiarity Drew yearned for. The physical attraction between the two was staggering, Drew half expected them to fall onto the ground and ravage each other on the spot. Twenty minutes later Drew was finally approached.

"Hello. Who are you?"

"Excuse me?" Drew turned towards a short, balding American who was smiling pleasantly. He wore a puzzled expression.

"You're with Marie, right?"

"Yeah."

"So who are you then?" His smile vanished; he seemed perturbed at having to explain such an obvious question.

"My name is Drew. I'm a friend."

"A friend?"

"Yes, and you are?"

"My name is Rory Gallagher."

"Hi."

"Hello."

"So you went to the Sorbonne?" Drew sighed and tried to make conversation.

"Yes. I joined this wild band of characters," Rory said with a manufactured sigh and pointed to the others with his drink, "during Jean Michael's final year."

"You're an American."

"Yes…the only one."

"At the Sorbonne?"

"Of course not! In our group," Rory snapped.

"Sorry."

"Don't be sorry, just be right." He smiled cruelly. Rory enjoyed making people unhappy.

"Alright." Drew turned away, his face burning with anger.

"I'm only joking, don't get so excited. How do you know my dear Marie?" Rory lit a cigarette and blew the smoke in Drew's face.

"Rather rude, don't you think?" Drew waved the foul smelling smoke from his eyes.

"Sure. I'm rude by nature."

"Well don't do it again." Drew locked eyes with the unexpected adversary.

"So sensitive this one is." Rory looked over his shoulder to an eavesdropping Marie Almeida.

"Rory, are you bothering my friend."

"Of course."

"Drew, he's doing it to annoy you. Ignore him."

"If he blows smoke in my face again, I won't ignore him," Drew replied acidly, the muscles in his face tightening for a fight. Marie smiled knowingly as if she had predicted the whole thing. She side-stepped an equally amused Rory Gallagher and sat next to Drew.

"Drew, calm down and meet Jean Michael Laurent," she said his last name for the first time.

"Hello, Drew." Jean Michael clasped his hand and shook it vigorously.

"Hi. Nice to meet you," Drew mumbled.

"So how did you meet?" Jean Michael smiled amicably and appeared genuinely interested.

"I met him in Portugal. He's the last person to see Sheldon Harrison." Marie smiled proudly.

"What!" Jean Michael exclaimed, utterly astonished by the announcement.

"That's not true, Marie."

"Technically not the last person to see him, but he did send Drew to Sintra."

With the eloquence of an experienced narrator Marie recounted Drew's strange odyssey, leaving nothing out and embellishing when appropriate.

The silent expression of awe on Jean Michael's face was a shocking reminder to Drew of his lowly status. The tentacles of entitlement were long and seductive, infecting every part of his life. He thought his brief relationship with Marie was solid; yet the foundation was weak and crumbling before his eyes. He suddenly realized her interest in him was solely based upon his association with Sheldon Harrison. The suspected importance of his mission to Sintra was not lost upon the ever-charming Marie Almeida. She had brought her prize to the party to impress her friends before the rest of the world knew his secret. They were entitled to know him before the mindless minions chewed over every aspect of his life, debating the revelation with their bourgeois theories and overly simplistic opinions. Marie, along with many others, instinctively believed the contents of the manila folder were something of great importance.

Drew suddenly hated her smile, her luscious lips were now repulsive to him, moving like a serpent, bending words and accentuating each syllable with the ease of a snake oil salesman. She was eerily comfortable and content as his spokesperson.

Marie noticed his distress and looked apprehensively at his clenched fist and narrowed eyes.

"What's wrong?" She stopped and grabbed his knee. The most interesting part of the story remained, the confrontation at the Gardner Museum would surely leave them asking for more.

"I feel like I'm part of a show and tell. I'm sure they're all thoroughly impressed with your catch," Drew said.

"What?" Her embarrassed smile only added to the unbearable tension in the air.

"I thought we were friends." Drew stood erect, proudly eyeing the other guests.

"We are! What are you talking about, Drew?" She placed her hand on his, imploring him to sit.

"You're no different. You think you're above it all."

"Be clear, what are you saying?" Marie stood up, her notorious temper flaring up.

"You hate Charlotte for what she is, but you're the same, just packaged differently."

"That's not true, Drew."

"Packaged in a nice box of artificial humility. You fight with her because you want to be her."

"This is insane. You have let this thing drive you crazy. Act like the man I know."

"Please calm down, Drew." Jean Michael smiled serenely.

"I have never been calmer in my life. She did the same thing to you." Drew smiled sadly; he noticed a glimmer of recognition in the faces of her friends. They knew intimately what Drew was trying to say.

"Please, Drew, don't bring me in to this," Jean Michael remarked politely.

"You think it was an accident that you met? Think again. It reads like a bad novel, the poor farm girl and the intellectual, oh how romantic. Calculated love."

"Shut up! Please leave. I want you to go, Drew." Marie bowed her head and pointed to the door.

"Sure." Drew stepped passed Rory Gallagher who was smirking condescendingly.

"What are you smiling about?" Drew asked.

"Nothing. Why don't you do what Marie asked?"

"You don't understand RORY, I don't have to be polite anymore," Drew said calmly, his body only inches from the suddenly shaking Rory Gallagher.

"What is the point?" Rory looked terrified.

"Yeah, what is the point?" Marie stepped in front of Drew.

"Be careful who you taunt." Drew looked around with disgust, his eyes challenging and his body language aggressive.

"How poetic," Rory mocked tentatively.

Drew flinched as if he was going to strike him, Rory jumped back, spilling his drink and thoroughly embarrassing himself. Jean Michael laughed inside; he never really liked Rory and sympathized with Drew. Jean Michael understood the isolated, almost delicate world they lived in. They pretended to be from the streets of Paris, intellectual vagabonds living from meal to meal, in reality most had wealthy families that could save them at a moment's notice.

"Asshole!" Rory screamed.

"Drew, go home," Marie's somber voice trembled with emotion.

"Sure." Drew found the door and quietly departed. The stunned silence soon erupted in a burst of laughter and glee, what a great show! Their reaction surely would have been different if he wasn't linked to Sheldon Harrison, their derision and superiority was checked only by the potentially momentous secret he possessed.

Marie did not share in the reverie; she followed Drew to the first floor porch.

"What is wrong with you? What was that bullshit? Who do you think I am? How could I be like you say, Drew, you know me better than that," she sobbed, tears streaming down her face.

"What can I say, Marie?" He felt sad, but convinced of his position.

"That is all you can say after you embarrassed me in front of my friends!"

"There it is! Always just below the surface. That's all you care about. How you will look in front of my friends."

"No!"

"Yes! You want to be able to call me tomorrow when I'm flooded with requests. You want a direct line to the killer of Sheldon Harrison. You've made it this far and it would be a shame to be cut off at the finish line."

"You're a cruel bastard." Marie raised her voice and stopped crying.

"I've said too much." Drew looked up when he heard his name called from above. Jean Michael was standing on his second floor porch.

"What?" Drew snapped.

"You're right, you know," Jean Michael said whimsically.

"I know," Drew answered defiantly, not really sure what he was right about. Marie looked hurt by Jean Michael's words.

"She is using you. She uses everybody to some degree. I know she used me to make up for her own insecurities. Her weakness is absurd."

Marie shook her head in disbelief.

"But I think you should feel special that such an extraordinary person invites you into her circle. We don't deserve the light of Marie Almeida. Feel privileged to be used by her. It does not last forever and the darkness is worse than you can imagine."

Chapter 33

In the Den of the Beast

The last person Charlotte Emerson wanted to see after her hellish afternoon at the Gardner Museum was her brooding cousin. Wilton was waiting inside her townhouse, he had used her spare key and he knew the alarm code. He seldom would act so bold, but on occasion she would find him nervously awaiting her arrival, looking guilty and ashamed.

"I'm in no mood for any crap, Wilton." She threw her heavy bag on a chair and flopped onto the couch. She gently rubbed her stomach with one hand and kneaded her pounding headache with the other. This unconscious move to soothe her unborn child made Wilton snort in disgust.

"What's wrong?" Wilton asked.

"Nothing, Wilton. What are you doing here? I didn't want company." His furtive glances annoyed Charlotte. Wilton sensed her disgust and it enraged him. The rage he felt when she told him of her pregnancy paled in comparison with the white hot, delusional anger that gripped him now. It literally shook him to the core, nearly extinguishing a lifetime of worship. He thought of ways to punish her, to inflict as much pain as he felt, to export the suffering.

"I'm sorry for being such a bitch, Wilton, it's been one of those fucking days from hell," Charlotte finally blurted, aware of his unnerving glare.

"It's okay," he answered coldly.

"I had a fight with Drew..." She went on to describe the entire ordeal, sniffling with emotion at certain points. Wilton lashed out, relentlessly ripping Drew until she told him to stop. She tried to defend the father of her child, a bond had been fostered upon conception and nothing her demented cousin could do or say would alter that. She bit her lip, for her defense of Drew was an embarrassing weakness; an intolerable attachment the old Charlotte Emerson surely would have scoffed upon.

"Enough, Wilton. I have a headache. I'm going to bed. I've talked enough about this."

"Why are you acting like this?" He stood up with such force she felt he would physically assault her if she did not handle him with caution.

"Please, Wilton. I feel like shit. I'll call you tomorrow." She managed a weak smile to placate him. It didn't work. His march towards madness was briefly interrupted with the sound of Charlotte's buzzer. She felt relieved as she pressed the button and asked who it was.

"It's me," Drew said. His voice sent a chill through her.

"Okay." She buzzed him up and felt sick.

"What does he want?" Wilton felt his legs giving way; the root of all his torment was so near. He sat on a kitchen stool and raked his hands through his thinning hair.

"Wilton, I don't want any trouble. This is none of your business." She wagged her finger in his face; suddenly emboldened by the arrival of her Knight in somewhat tarnished armor.

"Sure…whatever."

"I'm serious. You should leave now anyway."

"Just like that, Charlotte. Dismissed like a schoolboy."

"Or schoolgirl," she mumbled under her breath, "yes, please leave. I need to talk to him privately."

"No."

"What do you mean no! Fucking leave." Charlotte pushed his flabby shoulder

"Don't touch me." He stared with a blank expression.

"Isn't that what you always wanted, you fucking pervert!" She lashed out.

Drew entered the open door and was surprised to see Wilton Saunders. From their tense demeanor, it was obvious they had been fighting.

"Hi. What's up?"

"Hello. Nothing," she answered. Drew was unconvinced by her nonchalance.

"What do you want?" Wilton asked angrily, but avoided Drew's surprised expression.

"What?" Drew stepped forward.

"Why are you here?" Wilton brushed aside Charlotte's protests.

"None of your business, Wilton."

"It is my business! She's my cousin…and you barely know her."

"I don't want to argue with you. I came to talk to Charlotte. Can you please give us some privacy?"

"Come on, Drew, let's go to the roof." She motioned for Drew to follow her.

"No, don't, Charlotte!" Wilton grabbed her tiny wrists.

"Let go, you idiot!" She ripped her arm free, aghast at his behavior.

"Wilton! Don't lose your head," Drew warned and moved closer.

"Oh here comes the hero to save his knocked-up queen!" Wilton's mocking tone was filled with shaky confidence.

"Let's go Charlotte." Drew gently touched her elbow.

"No!" Wilton lunged for her arm again.

Drew knew he had to act quickly and end the tug of war before it got out of hand. He didn't think Wilton wanted to fight; yet something was driving him to this insane behavior.

"Enough, Wilton!" Drew deflected his outstretched arm.

"Fuck off!" Wilton screamed in defiance, but stopped the aggressive move. His thin lips quivered, a bloodthirsty grin crossed his face. He retreated to a corner of the large room.

Sometimes a small gesture, a momentary lapse in judgment can have ramifications far beyond what they seem at the time. Wilton fuming in the corner and somewhat cowed by Drew's firm stand, heard Drew utter something softly to Charlotte.

"What did you say?" Wilton turned on a dime to face Drew.

"Nothing, Wilton." He didn't want to inflame the situation any further.

"Say it, you fucking coward!"

"I told her not to worry about it, guys like you are big talkers but always back down," Drew said calmly, his fist clenched for the attack he knew was coming. Charlotte also knew the outcome and hustled Drew out of her home to the roof. Wilton slumped over the kitchen sink and vomited, a symphony of voices in his head buckling his knees. The walls of his self-delusion collapsed amidst the cacophony of his past tormentors. He heard their shrill taunts; they called him a wimp and a worthless member of the lucky sperm club. The earsplitting volume of insults rushing across his brain made him cry out in pain, as if struck by a car he slid to the floor.

Wilton Saunders had reached the end, the lifetime of lies and perceived superiority had crumbled at the feet of the woman who meant everything to him. His protector, his best friend, his fantasized lover would never look at him the same way. The harmless flirting, the tantalizing innuendo; the small hope of a future together was lost that sad evening. Wiping the bile from his lips he felt the steadying resolve of a condemned man. It was all out in the open; Drew Engle's innocuous statement had crystallized his position with frightening clarity.

The cloudless night sky invigorated Drew; a false sense of purpose and control instilled a sense of confidence that overtook his normally sound judgment.

"Why did you bring your bag?" Charlotte asked. She led him to a four-person table located near the edge of the roof. It was situated far away from the door to give the best view of the city skyline and a glimpse of the Charles River.

"I want to show you something. You can't tell anybody for a few more hours. I want you to be the first person to read it." He pulled her grandfather's confession from his bag and handed it to her. Charlotte hesitated a second before greedily taking it from him. She ran her fingers along the manila envelope before switching on a small light in the center of the table. She also flipped on a large outdoor heater near her feet. She spared no expense for her rooftop utopia. It was unseasonably warm for March.

"Are you sure? It's before the deadline. Will you get in trouble?"

"No. Who will know?" He smiled sadly and reclined his chair to gaze into the heavens. The unfortunate part of living in a large city is the artificial light obscured the stars. Drew sighed and glanced at Charlotte. She was engrossed in the document that would change her world forever, permanently destroying all of the connections and goodwill she had received since the first grade. All of the overlooked tantrums, the wide open doors of unearned opportunity, the unbridled sense of entitlement that she wore like a family crest were slipping away with each word. She sagged in her chair, the pale light illuminating the look of horror upon her suddenly sallow face. She was a reader of exceptional skill, pouring through the document with blinding speed. Drew marveled at her scanning power, she was accustomed to reading manuscripts when she found the time to actually work.

"My God," she blurted as the papers fluttered in her hands. Drew could see her hands trembling in the poor light, her grief-stricken fingers effortlessly, almost mechanically ripping through the pages.

Ten minutes later she neatly placed the papers back into the folder and looked at Drew with the endless gaze of the disheartened, crushed by reality of her bleak future.

"So." Drew finally broke the silence.

"What's there to say, Drew?" Her icy tone and steely glare surprised him. The helpless expression had slipped away, replaced by the more familiar look of defiance.

"I understand this is hard to take but…"

"Why? Why would it be hard to take?" Charlotte asked calmly.

"Because of what it says? It debunks everything he ever did. It's all a lie. From his Pulitzer Prize to this fucking townhouse, it's all a lie. This view should not be yours!" He sat up, angry and perplexed by her unnatural response.

"Oh Drew, you're so naïve. A little boy really, I hope our child isn't so easily fooled."

"How so, Charlotte?"

"What makes you think anybody will believe this?" She stood up and paced the rooftop patio.

"I met the real author! I met Sandy Wilson. He told me the same fucking story! He confirmed everything Charlotte." Drew was disgusted by her attempt to discredit the document.

"You did? When?" She stopped and stared at him with a curious look of disdain. He was the enemy; maybe he was the deceptive and dangerous interloper Wilton professed.

"Yes, Charlotte, I did. He's dead now. He was very ill when I saw him," Drew said sadly, his voice trailing off. He noticed a flicker in her cold eyes as he spoke of Sandy Wilson's death.

"Interesting," she mumbled, fiercely clutching the confession. He instantly wished he had made a copy of the most important document in Twentieth Century literature. His fear of having the second copy stolen kept him from taking this very basic precaution.

"What is so interesting about it? He was a good man deceived by a rat."

"Don't you dare call him a rat! You haven't earned the right, DREW ENGLE," Charlotte said haughtily. She emphasized his name to make him feel inferior, to bring him back to the reality of his position. Charlotte examined his honest face in the shadowed light of the table lamp. She was peering into the clouded eyes of her assassin.

"Sure, Charlotte," Drew said bitterly, his muffled tone a sign he understood her jab. He moved to the edge of the roof and admired the city that had become his second home, an urban escape from the homogenous landscape of his hometown. He loved the vibe of the city; the exciting pulse started on the ramparts of Beacon Hill and ended on the doorstep of Boston College.

A twinkling streetlight below caught his eye, its wavering beam exposing a young couple kissing passionately. With the suddenness of a car accident, he felt himself falling towards the light, his body flailing and grappling to right itself. The light grew bigger and his heart leaped with the realization that he was hurtling towards the ground. The fall seemed to last many minutes, in reality it was only a matter of seconds. Drew thought about his mother, he screamed for her before reaching the unforgiving pavement. His last rationale thought was of his father and how grief-stricken he would be upon hearing of the death of his son. He heard screaming, a guttural cry for help amidst the low rumble of night traffic. A millisecond before Drew Engle hit the ground, he realized he was the one screaming, hopelessly begging for his life. He felt his left foot hit the ground and shatter. For a cruel moment, as brief as an eye blink, he was filled with elated thoughts of survival. It was all too unbelievable, too terrifying to be actually happening, a badly broken leg might be enough to satisfy the gods. He could feel the pain in his leg! My God, I can feel pain!

The wonderfully flawed human being who called himself Drew Engle lived no longer, fading quickly to the unknown. The physically strong young man had been reduced to a mush of splintered bones and massive hemorrhaging. The millions of memories and experiences of his short life, the very things that made him unique, drained away into the dirty street, his crushed skull freeing the world of his presence.

Chapter 34

A Choice

"My God!" Charlotte screamed in abject horror, her body shook with such severe convulsions Wilton thought she was going to slip off the roof. He tried to comfort her with an impassioned hug.

"Don't fucking touch me! You fucking killed him! My God, you killed him!" She sobbed, her streaming eyes fixed on the shattered body of Drew. She knew he was dead.

"He deserved it," Wilton said coolly. Her inconsolable response annoyed him.

"What! You fucking lunatic! Call 911." She frantically grabbed her cell phone. She broke down before she could tell the anxious operator what had happened. Wilton grabbed the phone and calmly explained where they were and how one of their friends had accidentally fallen off the roof.

"You fucking liar," Charlotte stumbled to the door and tried to open it. Wilton assisted her.

"Charlotte, I don't know what you saw. I startled him and he slipped. He was too close to the edge."

"You fucking murderer," she slurred, "I saw you! I was right there, Wilton…Wilton why? You fucking pushed him off. He didn't see you. You killed him, Wilton! You coward… you fucking coward."

"You sound like a lunatic. How could you really see anyway? It's so dark up here. You don't know what you saw." Wilton was suddenly frantic.

"Get out of my way you fucking murderer!" Charlotte shoved her stammering cousin to the side and headed for the elevator.

"You don't know what you saw, Charlotte! You don't know what you saw!" Wilton screamed in panic.

Charlotte ignored him and descended to the horrific accident below.

"Drew…Drew!" Charlotte fell to the ground and hugged his lifeless body; soaked with his blood she would not leave him. She caressed his wet hair, stroking the blackness until she felt the death wound.

"I love you. I love you. I love you, Drew. You're not alone." She rocked him in her arms and whispered goodbye.

The arriving emergency medical technicians and fireman surrounded her, gently prying her away from the father of her unborn child. She felt a sharp pain in her midsection; she fell to the curb and tried to calm down. With a sudden gasp she rose to her feet and screamed for help. The burning sensation in her womb overwhelmed her senses. She collapsed in a heap, doubled over with pain she knew was the death of her child. Her last vision of the chaotic scene was of her cousin talking quietly to a police officer. The lawman wrote in his notebook and nodded sympathetically. Wilton acted like a friend in distress, ringing his hands and touching his sweating forehead in a mock show of grief. His sweating palms making an imprint on the manila folder of his grandfather's confession.

Chapter 35

The Aftermath

Carlton Smithfield woke with a feeling of elation; it would all be over today. Drew Engle would tell the world and it would be over. He gripped the steaming coffee cup just delivered by his young assistant from Harvard named Zachary Snyder. He smiled at his eager face; he was another budding writer with all of the pre-qualifications for a splendid career. Zachary had one fundamental flaw, the inability to conjure up an original thought. He was smart, well-read and savvy enough that he could probably bullshit his way through at least one novel, temporarily escaping his glaring lack of creativity. Eventually his career would end amidst a pile of bad reviews and poor sales. He, of course, would become a creative writing instructor at an Ivy League school, effortlessly recounting his wonderful days as a young intern with the late Carlton Smithfield.

"Did you see this?" Zachary Snyder asked as he passed him the morning paper.

"What the hell!" Carlton snarled. The headline nearly made him spill his coffee.

THE GRANDAUGHTER OF SHELDON HARRISON INVOLVED IN TRAGIC ACCIDENT...

"My God." He didn't feel the cup slip from his hands onto the tile floor. The young man jumped back as the molten spray singed his arm.

"Ouch...are you alright?"

"Shhhhhh!" Carlton waved him off and retired to his study. His insides were on fire; he had never felt such an overwhelming sense of gloom and desperation. He was frantic with grief, crying and muttering to himself as he read the article again to make sure he wasn't delusional. With tears staining the top of his oak desk, he picked up his phone and called information. One minute later he heard the gravely voice of Myron Wiseman.

"Myron!"

"I know I just saw it on the news."

"Can you believe it? God, the poor kid. I can't believe it." Carlton tried to control his raw emotions.

"I can," Myron said softly.

"What?"

"What timing. A few hours before he was able to reveal Sheldon's…"

"What are you saying, Myron!"

"I'm not saying anything…"

"You don't think it was an accident?" Carlton stood up and tried to comprehend what he was clearly insinuating.

"I have no idea, Carlton. I just think it is strange that's all. It's so sad no matter. I really liked that kid."

"He was a good kid," Carlton agreed.

"That fucking family is like a curse," Myron remarked bitterly.

"They are. They bring out the worst in people. Cursed."

"And there are so many of them left."

"Dogged for all eternity by the nitwit offspring of a gigantic fraud," Carlton said, managing a small ironic chuckle.

"So you believe me then?" Myron made no attempt to hide his surprise.

"I do." Carlton winced. He wasn't convinced until that moment that his mentor was a lecherous man hidden behind a veil of success that afforded him a lifestyle he thought he rightly deserved. The fact that he didn't write a single novel worth the paper it was printed on was a mere technicality.

"What are we going to do? Should we call somebody?" There was a long silence as Carlton thought about the almost impossible road of proving their theory. With the death of Sandy Wilson and now this tragedy involving the bearer of the secret, they had little to go on.

"Nothing." Carlton grimaced under the weight of his own words.

"Nothing!"

"You'll be portrayed as the senile old nemesis who waited until Sheldon died to bring this thing up, a doddering old fool with an axe to grind."

"And you?" There was a hint of anger in his voice.

"The ungrateful protégé who could never get out from under the shadow of his master. Bitter and angry fool trying to get his name in the papers again."

"Bullshit! You're just scared," Myron snapped, he was unconcerned with what people thought of him. The fervor of the press did not frighten him.

"Maybe I am," Carlton said wistfully, "maybe some things are just better left alone. Nobody really knows who Shakespeare was, but that doesn't change the relevance of the work."

"I never thought I would live to see the day when Carlton Smithfield would cower before the likes of Charlotte Emerson! What are you afraid of?" Myron was nearly screaming as he reached a level of exasperation he had not felt in years.

"My legacy." With this parting remark, Carlton gently hung up.

Chapter 36

Confession Lost

THE SMOLDERING ASHES BURNED Wilton Saunder's sensitive eyes as he buried an iron rod amongst the ruins of Sheldon Harrison's confession. The flame arched up and then died down in a final gasp of elation; its destruction complete and irreversible. The small steel barrel was blackened with the destroyed words of his repentant grandfather.

In one supremely gratifying act, a moment of sheer jubilance for the disgruntled killer, Wilton emptied the bin full of ashes off his balcony overlooking the Boston Common. The falling embers were re-ignited by the stiff breeze as they cascaded down to the darkened sidewalk, stinging the necks of the pacing homeless. They looked up and muttered about the rich assholes from the heavens.

The storm caused by the untimely death of Drew Engle had not passed, but was fading with each day. Charlotte lost the baby and was recovering from major surgery. She would never have another child; the damage was extensive and permanent. Wilton was not without pity for his cousin, although it would make their eventual decision to adopt easier. A child conceived by first cousins might be too risky a proposition for the selfish and conceded.

In her drug-induced delirium Charlotte spoke of the night on the roof, it raised a few eyebrows among her immediate family. The emotional strain of losing her baby and lover was blamed for her strange, accusatory ravings.

The outpouring of love and support was far more than she deserved, her family rallied to her bedside, encouraging her to fight the nasty infection she contracted during the hurried operation. The police were convinced it was a tragic accident and sought her version of the events only after she had recovered sufficiently. It wasn't necessarily standard procedure but they were not overly concerned by what seemed like a cut and dry accident. Every year in Boston there were cases of college students falling to their deaths from a dorm window or an apartment roof. Wilton was a convincing, somewhat charming witness with no apparent negative connection to the deceased.

Chapter 37

Time Heals All Wounds

Charlotte's mangled body slowly healed, the scars deep and permanent, but not fatal. The long days of debilitating depression lifted, leaving in its wake the haunted nights of cruel imagery; a rubble strewn landscape of sorrow and despair so distressing, surviving unscathed was unlikely. Yet, Charlotte possessed a unique ability to overcome severe emotional strain with cold, calculating effectiveness.

Her pitted road to full recovery coincided with her emerging desire to set the record straight. She refrained from making wild accusation about her cousin Wilton and his part in the tragic events. She was aware enough to realize that her caretakers were not taking her early claims seriously; their sad eyes and quizzical glances hindered her mental recovery. She knew her credibility had to be reestablished and her case dutifully presented before justice was done. Wilton's incarceration for the rest of his natural life was a pleasant thought. She believed this sort of plodding logic kept her from downing a bottle of sleeping pills. How close she actually came to taking her own life is impossible to discern, but likely her strong ego and lack of faith would prevent such a dramatic end.

The Russian appeared at her door two months after the incident, insistent that she get dressed and accompany him to a book release party at the new European Hotel near City Hall Plaza. She felt a sense of obligation to the Russian, a faithful servant who had been at her side for most of the ordeal. He stopped everything to be with her, holding her hand, caressing her forehead and longing to be twenty years old again. The shock of seeing her helpless and reliant on life support was earth-shattering to the overly sensitive Muscovite. He likened it to a beautiful, untouchable Queen caught in a moment of unguarded privacy by her unworthy subjects, perhaps as uncomely as defecating. A vile desecration so painful he wished he was strong enough to save the floundering swan; to resuscitate her ravaged soul, to relieve her from her towering Cross so burdensome and unnatural.

The Russian clasped her hand firmly, guiding Charlotte's unsteady steps from the subterranean parking garage at Center Plaza to the blandness of Court Street. The brutalist modern City Hall sulked in the distance, squat and ugly amongst the bleak wasteland of the uninhabitable plaza.

The steady, calloused hands of the Russian helped Charlotte enter the party with growing confidence. She was mesmerized by the brilliance of the chandelier dangling in the main function hall in the exclusive International Room. The thundering applause made Charlotte feel like she was lighter than the perfumed air, floating on a cloud of good will and genuine encouragement.

The scattered, mingling sea of Boston's Super Elite rose in unison, their exuberance momentarily tempered by the sight of the ghost-like figure clinging to her burly chaperone, dismayed by Charlotte's obvious ill health they edged closer. She shook off the rust of psychological atrophy, the shards of lethargy falling away with each step. She straightened her back and stuck out her chin, she was in her element, soaking up the sympathetic, but respectful looks of her admirers.

In the middle of her triumphant strut amongst the tables of the famously popular and influential guests, a troubling, oppressive thought flashed across her brain. She pushed it away and kept smiling, she tasted bile in her tightening throat. The room suddenly felt hot, the air foul and the concerned faces turned to a blur.

In a millisecond it became crystal clear; she winced momentarily with guilt, cringing at the mere thought of it. She nodded to a novelist of some quality, winked at a celebrated Hollywood star, and touched the elbow of a local rock star. They were all trying to catch her eye, to make that momentary contact with the granddaughter of the great Sheldon Harrison. They couldn't have known the battle raging inside of her.

The pain eased and she regained her composure just in time to relish their lavishly decorated table. The incessant drumbeat of self-loathing gave way to a low rumble of controlled guilt.

In the end it wasn't a hard thing to say, internally of course, an inevitable and fitting admission. Three words.

Thank you, Wilton.

THE END